*For Mary Shelley, mother of monsters*

Praise for
## The Strange Case of the Alchemist's Daughter

WINNER OF THE LOCUS AWARD FOR
BEST FIRST NOVEL

WORLD FANTASY AWARD FINALIST |
NEBULA AWARD FINALIST

"Theodora Goss is a wonder. Her elegance, wit, and powerful voice pull no punches. A brilliant, deeply felt, and nimble book."

—Catherynne M. Valente, Hugo–Award winning author

\* "A tour de force of reclaiming the narrative, executed with impressive wit and insight."

—*Publishers Weekly*, starred review

"A swiftly paced, immaculately plotted mystery full of winning characters you always thought you knew, as well as ones you would never have imagined."

—*NPR Books*

"Goss skillfully balances the revisionist feminist themes with a crackling conspiracy adventure and a colorful portrait of Victorian London."

—*Chicago Tribune*

"They are just as much fun as their fictional fathers, and like *The League of Extraordinary Gentlemen*, their talents play off against one other, anchored by Mary, the most normal of them: prudent, thrifty, genteel, her father's revolver loaded and ready."

—*The Wall Street Journal*

"A delightful romp through Victorian gothic literature, with a decidedly feminist slant."

—*Library Journal*

*The Extraordinary Adventures*
*of the Athena Club*

BOOK III

# THE SINISTER MYSTERY

—— *of the* ——

# MESMERIZING

# GIRL

*Theodora Goss*

SAGA PRESS

LONDON SYDNEY **NEW YORK** TORONTO NEW DELHI

SAGA ✸ PRESS
AN IMPRINT OF SIMON & SCHUSTER, INC.

1230 AVENUE OF THE AMERICAS, NEW YORK, NEW YORK 10020

SAGA PRESS and colophon are trademarks of Simon & Schuster, Inc.

For information about special discounts for bulk purchases, please contact Simon & Schuster Special Sales at 1-866-506-1949 or business@simonandschuster.com.

The Simon & Schuster Speakers Bureau can bring authors to your live event. For more information or to book an event, contact the Simon & Schuster Speakers Bureau at 1-866-248-3049 or visit our website at www.simonspeakers.com.

Interior design by Brad Mead

The text for this book was set in Perpetua.

Manufactured in the United States of America

First Saga Press trade paperback edition June 2020

1  3  5  7  9  10  8  6  4  2

Library of Congress Cataloging-in-Publication Data

Names: Goss, Theodora, author.
Title: The sinister mystery of the mesmerizing girl / Theodora Goss. |
Description: First Edition. | New York : Saga Press, [2019] |
Series: The Extraordinary adventures of the Athena Club ; book 3
Identifiers: LCCN 2018047694 | ISBN 9781534427877 (hardcover) |
ISBN 9781534427891 (ebook)
Subjects: LCSH: Holmes, Sherlock—Fiction. |
Missing persons—Investigation—Fiction. | GSAFD: Mystery fiction.
Classification: LCC PS3607.O8544 S56 2019 | DDC 813/.6—dc23 LC
record available at https://lccn.loc.gov/2018047694

ISBN 978-1-5344-2787-7
ISBN 978-1-5344-2788-4 (pbk)
ISBN 978-1-5344-2789-1 (ebook)

*Finally, they realized they*
*were the monsters.*

MARY: Now you're just trying to upset me.

CATHERINE: Did it work?

MARY: No, not really. I mean, I know perfectly well that we're monsters. Even me. I didn't want to admit that for a long time, but I can't deny it, can I? It's not such a bad thing, after all.

CATHERINE: I told you so.

# CONTENTS

# VOLUME I

## THE MESMERIST

# VOLUME II

## The Mummy

# The Sinister Mystery

## *of the*

# Mesmerizing

# Girl

VOLUME I

*The*

*Mesmerist*

# CHAPTER I

## The Temple of Isis

Princess Ayesha stared down into the lotus pool. The orange fish had hidden itself under one of the floating leaves. The lotus flower rose up, yellow and conical, perfectly still in the hot summer afternoon. A dragonfly landed on it, spreading its iridescent wings. The orange fish was also iridescent, and the water shimmered in the sunlight. It was as though everything here shimmered, nothing was stable, nothing ordinary—like a mirage. Would it all disappear? Would she be left sitting on desert sand? That, she had been told by her nurse, was what happened to travelers who ventured out beyond the verdure on either side of the river, beyond the date palm orchards and barley fields.

"Come, child," said Queen Merope. "The High Priestess is ready to see us."

She looked up at the queen. Her mother was the most beautiful woman she had ever seen—tall, with the long neck of an ibis, and slender hands just beginning to lose the suppleness of youth. Her skin was a burnished brown—she had come from Heliopolis, and was said to be descended from the ancient kings who had ruled Egypt, long before Alexander marched across the world and installed his general, Ptolemy, as its ruler. Ayesha took after her much darker father, who came of an even older lineage. She shaded her face with one hand—the sun was just over her mother's shoulder. She opened her mouth to ask a question.

Her mother looked down at her, eyes rimmed with kohl—it was usually impossible to guess what Queen Merope was thinking. The black wig she wore over her shaved head had small bells sewn to the end of each braided strand, and they chimed softly as she moved. "Yes," she said. "You do have to stay here. No, there is absolutely no use in arguing." The queen held out her hand.

Ayesha shut her mouth, took the hand held out to her, and stood up. She was not quite as tall as her mother, but soon would be. Perhaps, after all, it was for the best? If she was not accepted into the temple, her father would arrange a marriage for her. Did she want to be married? Judging by her brothers, from her mother and her father's other wives, boys were in general a great bore. They were always boasting, or going out to hunt, or getting drunk on honey wine. So perhaps it would be best after all to serve the Goddess here at Philae? Already she liked the temple, with its massive stone walls painted in bright colors and its great stone lions that looked as though they might be friendly, however fierce. And she liked this garden, with its still pools filled with lotus flowers, the small fountains, the tamarind trees.

The priestesses were a little too solemn—none of them seemed to smile, unlike the courtiers and servants of her father's court. The one that had come to fetch them, for example—standing several steps behind her mother. She did not look Egyptian—Assyrian, perhaps? Priestesses came from all over the world to serve at Philae. She stood very still in her white linen robe, with a cloth wound around her head—the priestesses did not wear wigs. No kohl around her eyes, no carmine on her lips, no gold rings in her ears. Being a priestess was a serious business, evidently. Would Ayesha be as solemn when she was a priestess of Isis?

Queen Merope tugged sharply at her hand, and she followed her mother through the sunlit garden, into the cool, shadowed temple complex.

"You must be on your very best behavior," said the Queen in a low voice. "Remember that the High Priestess was once queen of all Egypt. When the old King died and his son ascended the throne—his son by his first wife—she was sent here to serve the Goddess."

"Did they not want her in Alexandria anymore?" asked Ayesha.

The Queen gave her a swift, shrewd glance. "It is a great honor to serve Isis," she said, but her lips curved upward, as though she did not want to smile but could not help herself. *My daughter is a clever one,* she seemed to be thinking. "Anyway, it's best to get out of the way when the sons and daughters of kings quarrel. We are done with that now, I hope, and Egypt is prosperous again—it is bad to have instability on our northern border. Although the Romans—well, this is no place to talk politics. You must show such honor to the High Priestess as you would show to your father's mother. Do you understand?"

"Yes, Mother," said Ayesha, listening with only half her attention. She always respected Nana Amakishakhete, didn't she? It was Netekamani, her youngest brother, who was so disrespectful, pulling on Nana's robe, asking for sesame seed cakes. The temple of Isis was almost as large as her father's palace. She had been told that it was inhabited only by the priestesses—worshipers were allowed in on feast days, but not ordinary days, and the inner sanctum could be entered by the priestesses alone. What was it like? Soon, she would find out.

They passed through a series of bare stone halls, the slap of their sandals echoing back at them. At the entrance to the audience chamber, the priestess who had led them opened a set of painted cypress-wood doors that were twice as tall as she was. The audience chamber was large and shadowed. Sunlight shone in through tall, narrow windows, but did not reach the central dais. To either side of that dais stood priestesses in white linen robes, perfectly still and silent. On the dais itself was a stone chair, as plain as the throne of Egypt on the head of Isis in the carvings on the temple walls. On it sat a woman almost as old as Nana Amakishakhete. She had long white hair that she wore in a single braid down one shoulder. Ayesha could not help staring at it—everyone she knew, even her mother, had short curly hair, although it was generally shaved off. Servants replaced it with colorful head cloths, the fashionable people at court with elaborate wigs, in which gold and glass beads were intertwined. This woman was lighter than even Ayesha's mother—it was clear that she came from the north, where Egyptian blood had mixed with Greek. But she did not look quite Alexandrian—Ayesha had seen envoys from that city and wondered at their strange, pale skin, which reminded her of the slugs that ate gourd leaves in the kitchen gardens. Sitting in her lap was the largest cat Ayesha had ever seen, pure black, which stared at her with unblinking yellow eyes.

The priestess who had led them bowed before the dais, and then moved to one side.

"Thank you, Heduana," said the High Priestess, nodding at the priestess who had led them. "Come forward, child."

Ayesha felt a hand on her right shoulder blade. Her mother propelled her forward until they were standing the correct ceremonial distance away from the dais, then bowed. Had Ayesha ever seen Queen Merope bow? She could not recall. She was almost too awed by the large, silent room and the small, wrinkled woman up on the stone chair to remember what she was supposed to do, but feeling once again the pressure of her mother's hand, she knelt and bowed her head down to the floor until her forehead lay on the stone.

"You do the temple honor, bringing your daughter yourself, Queen of Meroë," said the High Priestess. She had a foreign accent—not Greek, but close to it.

"You do Meroë honor allowing my daughter to come, Priestess of the Goddess with a Thousand Names, Bringer of Light and

Abundance, Who Produces the Fruit of the Land," said Merope. "She is not worthy, but if she should find favor in your eyes, I pray that you will accept her into the temple, to serve the Queen of Heaven."

"Stand, child," said the High Priestess. Ayesha lifted her head up from the stone floor. She was allowed to stand now, right? She looked up sideways at her mother, who gave her an almost imperceptible nod. She stood, awkwardly because she was feeling light-headed. For a moment the temple seemed to shimmer around her, as though it too were a mirage. *Stop that,* she told herself. After all, she was a princess of Meroë. She would not allow herself to be intimidated by this situation or any other.

The High Priestess stood, put the black cat on the stone chair behind her, and descended from her dais. The cat meowed in protest, but then sat like a statue of Bast with its tail curled around its legs. When the High Priestess reached out her left hand, Ayesha almost drew back in surprise and consternation. On that hand the High Priestess had seven fingers! But she had been trained well, by both her mother and Nana Amakishakhete. She did not flinch as the High Priestess lifted her chin, so that her eyes, which had been cast down in a sign of respect, looked directly into the dark eyes of the High Priestess, who considered her with as little emotion as though she were a rather interesting insect.

"Do you truly wish to serve the great Isis, with your heart and mind and spirit? Will you pledge yourself to her, leaving your father and mother, your sisters and brother, your house and your lands, giving up the ordinary life of a woman, to become one of our sisterhood, from now until the hour of your death?"

"Yes, High Priestess," she answered as steadily as she could.

"My name is Tera, and here in this temple, my order is the word of the Goddess. You must obey me as you would her. That is the first of many things you will learn here." The High Priestess withdrew her hand—Ayesha could feel a tingling in her chin where the High

Priestess had rested her seven fingers. She turned to Queen Merope and said, "I accept your daughter into the temple as a novice. She shall go with Heduana to the dormitory where the novices sleep and learn the rituals of our order. If she serves the Goddess well for a year, she shall become a priestess at the Festival of the Inundation. You may bid her farewell. She is a daughter of Isis now, and the priestesses are her family. The tributes you have brought, which I understand are in a wagon outside the temples gates, may be brought in."

Queen Merope bowed once again to the High Priestess, then turned to Ayesha. "Serve the Goddess well, my daughter," she said.

Ayesha wished she could embrace her mother. She would have liked, once again, to inhale her mother's scent—the fragrant oils in her wig, combined with the warm, human smell of her skin. But it would not be dignified in front of all these people.

Queen Merope leaned down and kissed her on the forehead, then turned and walked back out of the room, leaving her daughter behind. Ayesha watched her depart with trepidation. Did she truly want this new life? Was she ready to be a priestess of Isis? She did not know.

> MARY: Why in the world are you starting with
> Ayesha? This is supposed to be a book about *us*.

> CATHERINE: Our readers won't understand what
> happens later if I don't tell them about Ayesha—
> how she became a priestess and her time at
> the temple. Anyway, Egypt is very fashionable
> nowadays. Everyone wants Egyptian furniture,
> clothes, jewelry. Why not a book?

> MARY: But this book isn't about Egypt. It's about—
> well, England. And us, as I said.

CATHERINE: Fine, I'll start with us. But it's not going
to be anywhere near as exciting.

Mary Jekyll stared out the train window. She was so tired of
traveling! Three days ago, she, her friend Justine Frankenstein, and
her sister Diana Hyde had boarded the *Orient Express* in Budapest.
They had disembarked at the Gare de l'Est in Paris, made their way
to the Gare du Nord, and boarded another train from Paris to Calais.
This train was not an express—to Mary, it seemed unbearably slow.
Sometime that afternoon they would arrive in Calais and catch the
ferry across the English Channel. Then yet another train from Dover
to Charing Cross Station in London. And then a cab. And then—
finally, finally—*home*. Sometimes in their travels she had missed the
Jekyll residence at 11 Park Terrace terribly. Now, all the details of
it came back to her: the front hall with its dark wood paneling and
the mirror in which she checked to make sure that her hat was on
straight, the parlor with a portrait of her mother above the mantel,
the library where her father had once planned his experiments, the
kitchen where Mrs. Poole presided, and her own bedroom, her very
own bed, soft and cool. She would sleep in her own bed tonight. . . .

"You look very far away," said Justine with a smile. Diana was
asleep, sprawled on the seat beside Justine, with her head in the
Giantess's lap. At least she was not snoring!

"I was thinking about how happy I'm going to be to get home," said
Mary. "But what about you? Will you miss Europe?" After all, Justine
was not English, although she had lived in England for more than a
century—she had been born in Switzerland. Would she miss being
able to speak French and German when they were back in London?

"I will miss it—a little," said Justine. "Although I am in no
sense a *gourmande*, I will miss the Austrian pastries. But I think I
will miss our friends more." Irene Norton, and her maids Hannah
and Greta, in Vienna. Carmilla Karnstein and Laura Jennings in

Styria. And of course Mary's former governess Mina Murray and Count Dracula in Budapest. Without their help, the Athena Club would never have been able to rescue Lucinda Van Helsing from her father, the despicable Professor Abraham Van Helsing, who had been conducting experiments that turned his daughter into that dreadful thing—a vampire!

LUCINDA: Catherine, if you'll forgive my interrupting, it really is not such a dreadful thing to be a vampire. I have a different diet than you do, that is all.

CATHERINE: Can't you all just go away and let me write this book?

DIANA: Not if you're going to get the details wrong! And you should be nicer to Lucinda. She can't help being a blood-sucking creature of darkness.

CATHERINE: *What* sort of trash have you been reading now?

LUCINDA: Of darkness? But I do not require darkness.

Diana snorted in her sleep. Well, at least she was asleep! On the *Orient Express*, she had pestered Mary endlessly: Why did she have to wear women's clothes? It was so much easier traveling as a boy. Justine was traveling as a boy, or rather man, so why couldn't she? And why couldn't they have taken one of Count Dracula's puppies? There were plenty in the litter. And why couldn't she have some money? Yes, all right, the last time she had stolen some of Mary's francs to gamble with, but she had won more at *Écarté*. Anyway, it was so boring on the train. She would probably die of boredom.

THE TEMPLE OF ISIS

"Because Justine is over six feet tall, and it's too conspicuous for her to travel as a woman," Mary had told her. "You are not over six feet tall—you're not even five feet tall—and we need you to share a cabin with me. And because I don't think Alpha or Omega would appreciate having one of the Count's white wolfdogs in the house, plus Mrs. Poole would have a fit, and then where would we be?" But she had finally given Diana five francs, just to make her stop talking and go away. Diana had come back that evening with fifteen, won from a card game with the porters. Mary, thoroughly ashamed of her sister, had given half of it back in tips.

"I'm going to miss everyone too," she said to Justine. "But it will be lovely to see Mrs. Poole again, and sit in our own parlor, and walk in Regent's Park. If only I weren't so worried about Alice and Mr. Holmes! And Dr. Watson, of course, if he is indeed missing as Mrs. Poole indicated in her telegram. Perhaps he's simply on the case, as Mr. Holmes would say? It would be like him to go after Mr. Holmes and try to rescue him from whatever predicament he's in. I hope Dr. Watson hasn't actually disappeared, despite Mrs. Poole's statement."

"If so, would Mrs. Hudson not know his whereabouts?" asked Justine.

"Not necessarily. You know he and Mr. Holmes are—well, despite how much I like and respect them, they're not always *considerate*. Sometimes they do not let anyone know where they are going, or what they are doing there."

"Perhaps," said Justine, seeming unconvinced. Then she added, "We'll find them, Mary, wherever they are. We are the Athena Club, after all." But she looked worried as well—Mary could see the small frown lines between her eyebrows.

*Well,* thought Mary, *we have reason to be worried, the both of us!* She remembered that afternoon in the basement storage room of the Hungarian Academy of Sciences—had it really only been four days ago? She, Justine, and Beatrice had been going through the files of the Alchemical Society when Catherine had rushed in, breathless, and said, "Telegram from Mrs. Poole!" The telegram had informed them that Alice, Mary's kitchen maid, had been kidnapped. And then Frau Gottleib, who had once served in the Jekyll household as nurse to Mary's mother, but whom they had discovered was actually a spy for the Alchemical Society, had told them that Alice was not who they had thought either. Although Alice herself did not know it, she was Lydia Raymond, daughter of the notorious Mrs. Raymond, who had been involved in the Whitechapel Murders.

> MARY: How in the world do you keep all this
> straight in your head? It's like a giant tangle
> of string. The hardest thing about our trip to
> Budapest was finding out that no one was who
> I thought they were—Nurse Adams, who took
> care of my mother for so long, was actually Eva
> Gottleib, and Mina wasn't just my governess, but
> had been spying on me for the British Society's
> Subcommittee on Bibliographic Citation Format,
> and Helen Raymond wasn't just the director of the
> Society of St. Mary Magdalen, but the result of
> an experiment in biological transmutation by Dr.
> Raymond, who had been the chair of the British
> chapter of the Alchemical Society. . . .

> CATHERINE: I keep notes, of course. Although
> sometimes it's hard to remember things like dates
> and train schedules. You're better at those sorts of
> things than I am.

As soon as they had learned that Alice was missing, Mary and Justine had packed their bags—and Mary had packed for Diana, to make sure she did not sneak a wolfdog into her suitcase! They had left the next day. Catherine and Beatrice had stayed to fulfill their contract with Lorenzo's Circus of Marvels and Delights, which was performing in Budapest to packed houses, but they would leave as soon as their obligations were over. Mary would be glad when they were all back in London! Where were Alice, Mr. Holmes, and Dr. Watson? As soon as she and Justine arrived back at 11 Park Terrace, Mary would try to find out. Mrs. Raymond might be connected in some way—Mary still remembered the formidable director of the Magdalen Society, with her iron-gray hair and cold, hard eyes. Was the mysterious Dr. Raymond connected as well? This was another adventure, coming right on the heels of the last one—adventures seemed to do that. They never gave one enough time to rest. Whatever dangers awaited them in London, they would need the full strength of the Athena Club.

> MARY: Are our readers going to know what the
> Athena Club is?

> CATHERINE: They will if they read the first two
> books! Which they should, and I hope if they are
> reading this volume and have not read the previous
> ones, they will go right out and purchase them.
> Two shillings each, a bargain at the price!

While Mary was staring out the train window at the houses of Calais with their neat gardens, and mentally calculating how many francs she would have to pay for ferry tickets, Justine was also remembering their adventures in Europe. For the first time since she had been resurrected by Victor Frankenstein, she had been—not quite home, but almost. Hearing French and German, eating food whose flavors were familiar from her childhood, she had felt closer to home than she ever did in England. Driving in the coach through the mountains of Styria, even though they had been driving into a trap set by the despicable Edward Hyde, she had felt a sense of joy from the air and altitude. And then confronting Adam again! Frankenstein's first creation, who had loved her and tortured her, if anything so cruel and desperate could be called love. In his letter to Mary, Hyde had written that Adam was dead. Justine wondered if she could believe him—she had once seen Adam die in a fire with her own eyes, and yet she had found him again, terribly injured, in Styria. But reason told her that he must be dead indeed, that he could not have survived those injuries much longer. When she had read Hyde's letter, she had felt, for the first time in her second life, a sense of release from bondage, of that peace the Bible spoke of which passeth all understanding. It was wrong to rejoice in his death, and yet she could not help doing so. Well, she would pray about it in St. James's, the church she and Beatrice attended across from Spanish Place. It would be nice to speak with Father O'Brian again!

How fortunate she was to have everything she needed: friends who loved her, a home to return to. The one thing she had truly missed had been her painting studio. That study of flowers in a blue vase was still sitting on her easel, unfinished. Would she have time to finish it when they got home? Perhaps after they had found Alice. Poor little Alice . . . where could she be? And then, like Mary, Justine worried about the kitchen maid, and Mr. Holmes, and Dr. Watson, all so mysteriously vanished.

While Mary and Justine's train drew into the station at Calais, Catherine—

DIANA: What about me? You haven't said anything about me. I was on that train too.

Diana continued to snore in her sleep. She woke only when the train lurched and she almost rolled off Justine's lap and onto the floor. The first words out of her mouth were: "Bloody hell!" Since she had been asleep for the entire journey, she had not said or thought anything worth reporting.

> CATHERINE: There, satisfied? Oh no, you don't! If you kick me again, I'm going to bite you so hard. . . .

Meanwhile, Catherine was eating a very good sausage, flavored with red pepper, in the dining room of Count Dracula's house in Budapest. Madam Zora, the circus's snake charmer, had just been thanking Mina Murray for inviting her to stay at the Count's town residence while the circus was performing.

"Don't thank me," said Mina with a smile. "I'm not the mistress here. The Count decides who stays or goes—sometimes unceremoniously! But he likes having all of you girls here—he says it gives this old mausoleum a semblance of life—and you are welcome to stay as long as you wish."

"Beatrice and I would have gone already if the circus hadn't been held over until Thursday!" said Catherine. "But Lorenzo's making so much money—he says everyone who's anyone is in Budapest right now, for the Emperor's visit. The theater is packed every night. And if anyone deserves it, he does—considering all those years we traveled around the countryside in wagons, barely able to afford food for the trick ponies or performing dogs!"

"He's giving us all double wages," said Zora with satisfaction. "But thank you all the same, Mina. Not everyone would want a bunch of poisonous snakes in their house. I didn't know what to do after one of them got loose and the hotel kicked me out. And it wasn't even one of the poisonous ones, just Buttercup! She looks impressive—most people have never seen an albino python—but she wouldn't hurt anyone, not really. I mean, unless they scared her." Although on stage Zora spoke with the accent of the Mysterious East, this morning it was evident that the east she came from was Hackney in the East End of London. She ate the final bite of her omelet appreciatively.

Just then Kati, the parlor maid, came in carrying a silver tray. She said something to Mina in Hungarian—Catherine still could not make heads or tails of that language! Mina picked a piece of paper off the tray and looked at it intently. Even from the back, it had the distinctive appearance of a telegram.

"This is from Irene Norton," said Mina, putting it down on the table. "She says she's found the warehouse in Vienna where Van Helsing was creating and mesmerizing vampires, and where they still maintain a sort of nest. She asks if we'd like to join her for a vampire hunt. You and Beatrice need to get back to London, don't you? But I could go. After all, I have developed a sort of expertise in vampires!"

"I pity Van Helsing's vampires, with two such formidable opponents to deal with!" It was Count Dracula, who had entered as silently as he always did. Catherine looked him over with satisfaction. He was such a perfect romantic hero! Not, perhaps, particularly tall, but with the easy, upright carriage of an aristocrat and military man. High cheekbones, an aquiline nose, a forehead that indicated intellect, interesting pallor, and the sort of dark, floppy hair that would have delighted Mrs. Radcliffe. And he usually dressed in black. Yes, she would have to see if she could fit him into one of her books, somehow!

Mina turned to him with a frown, not of anger but as though she were thinking hard. "I should go, shouldn't I? Irene has more resources than I do, but she has very little experience fighting vampires, whereas I—well, I've learned a great deal about them in the years since poor Lucy was transformed into one. You can't come, I suppose, Vlad? Not with the Emperor himself arriving for a state visit this week?"

The Count shook his head. "Much as I would like to see a Hungary free of Austrian influence—I was proud to stand with Kossuth, and would again, despite the failure of our cause—I have official duties to perform. I must stay and represent my country. But you might ask Carmilla. It would take her no more than a day to drive from the schloss to Vienna, and she has always enjoyed hunting—even our kind, when they prove dangerous."

Mina nodded. "I'll send her a telegram today. I'm sure Irene could use all the help she can get." She turned to Catherine and Zora. "Will you girls and Beatrice be all right here without me? You're too old to need chaperones, I think."

Catherine laughed. "I should think so! Anyway, Bea and I are leaving on Friday morning. We want to get back to London as soon as we can."

"And Lorenzo's circus is leaving too," said Zora. "We're booked all the way to Constantinople!"

Catherine could not help feeling envious. She would have liked to stay with the circus, playing her part as *La Femme Panthère*, the Panther Woman of the Andes, all the way to that fabled city. But the Athena Club needed her. How would they rescue Alice without her help?

DIANA: You're not indispensable, you know!

JUSTINE: She certainly is! You are, Catherine. We could not do without you.

DIANA: You're not going to edit that out, are you? You never edit out anything that makes you sound important.

But what were the Count and his parlor maid talking about? Kati was speaking to him in rapid Hungarian. He seemed to be arguing with her—he raised his hands and swept them through his hair in exasperation, creating even more perfect waves. She curtseyed and walked out of the room, holding the silver tray. "Kati!" he called after her; then to Catherine's surprise he followed her out of the room, still expostulating.

"What in the world was that about?" asked Zora.

Mina looked both incredulous and amused. "Evidently, young Kati has decided to go work for Ayesha! Do you remember Ayesha's assistant—Ibolya, I think her name was? Well, she and Kati were at school together, and Ibolya's going off to Zurich to study medicine, so the President of the Alchemical Society needs a new assistant—and Kati has taken the job! She just gave her two weeks' notice. You know how Vlad feels about that Ayesha—although to be honest, I think he was in love with her once, before she expelled him from the Alchemical Society. Not that I'm blaming her, considering the underhanded tactics he used in that election! I care for Vlad very much, but medieval Hungarian aristocrats don't fight according to Hoyle." She put her hand on the telegram and regarded it thoughtfully for a moment. "Sometimes I think he's still a little in love with her, despite everything. Of course she offered this position to Kati to spite him—she's still angry, and now he's going to be angry as well. Over a parlor maid! Although I admit that Kati is an exceptionally good one. Anyway, he's going to be impossible for the rest of the day. All right, I'm done with lunch. I need to telegraph Irene and Carmilla, then purchase a train ticket to Vienna. The two of you have tonight's performance to prepare for. I wonder where Beatrice has gone off to. The cook prepared some lovely goop for her, and now it will go to waste."

"She's probably with Clarence somewhere," said Catherine. "She seems to spend every waking moment with him nowadays."

BEATRICE: That is not fair, Cat! Particularly when
I was trying so hard not to spend time with him.
I wanted him to forget me, to find—well, not
someone else exactly, but perhaps something to do
other than converse with a poisonous woman.

Beatrice was, in fact, with Clarence Jefferson at that moment,
as Catherine had suspected. She looked around at the dark, paneled
walls of the Centrál Kávéház. She and Clarence had gotten into
the habit of coming here after rehearsals. She would sip an elder-
flower tisane and he would drink a dark, aromatic espresso. But
this morning she had gone to the Hungarian Academy of Sciences
for the first meeting of the Committee on Ethics in Alchemical
Experimentation, so she and Clarence had decided to meet here
for lunch and go on to rehearsals together. She was wearing the
green dress she had been given by Mr. Worth himself in Paris, for
no special reason—she had simply felt like wearing it this morning. Certainly she had not dressed up particularly for Clarence!
Not that he ever seemed to notice what she was wearing, anyway.
His attention always seemed to be entirely on her—although at
the moment, some of it was focused on stirring his coffee.

He, too, seemed to have dressed with care, but then he always
did, unless he was helping Atlas and the acrobatic Kaminski
Brothers put up or take down sets. She could see in him the lawyer
he had once been, before he had been tried and acquitted for
murder—miraculously, for a black man in America who had shot
and killed a white police officer, even before a crowd of witnesses
who could swear it was in self-defense. That evening, he would be
dressed as the Zulu Prince, who danced his native dances for an
appreciative audience—one more attraction in Lorenzo's Circus
of Marvels and Delights.

She felt, once again, a deep sense of guilt that he was sitting here with her, when he could be with any number of women who were not poisonous and with whom he could have an ordinary relationship. She had told him that once—he had replied, touching her cheek for just a moment, not long enough for his fingertips to blister, "I don't want ordinary, Bea. I want you."

Now, he reached across the table and took her gloved hand. "Honey, you look a million miles away. What are you thinking?"

"That I will miss this place. Soon, Catherine and I will be returning to London, and you will be leaving with the circus for— where do you go next?"

"Bucharest, then Varna, then Constantinople. And after that . . . maybe Athens? Lorenzo wasn't sure the last time I talked to him. I wish you could come with us. We could use a Poisonous Girl. By the way, how did the committee meeting go?"

"Well enough, I suppose. Frau Gottlieb and Professor Holly agreed that the Société des Alchimistes needs a set of ethical rules to guide alchemical research. They asked me to produce a first draft for their comments and revisions. Once we agree on a second draft, we will present it to Ayesha. What she will think of it, only Heaven knows!"

"I'd like to meet this Ayesha," said Clarence.

Beatrice looked at him with alarm. "Why? What is the President of the Alchemical Society to you?"

"Nothing, I suppose," he said, looking at her with a puzzled frown, as though trying to understand her reaction. He pulled his hand away. "You told me she was a black woman—Egyptian, you said? And she's the head of this Alchemical Society. She sounds impressive, and like someone I'd be interested in meeting, that's all."

Why had the thought of Clarence meeting Ayesha caused a sudden pang in her chest, as though she had been struck through the heart with one of Ayesha's lightning bolts? Involuntarily, she put her hand where she had felt it. Yes, Ayesha was a beautiful woman, but that did not mean all men would fall in love with her, did it? Anyway it would be good for Clarence to fall in love with someone else . . . only not Ayesha. One could not compete with someone like Ayesha.

Clarence finished his soup, chicken in a paprika broth, and wiped the bowl with a piece of bread to get at the last of the spicy red liquid. Beatrice had already finished a cucumber salad. It was a little too substantial for her—she seldom ate anything that was not in liquid form—but she had felt awkward merely drinking while he ate. She did not know what to say, so she fiddled with her fork.

"Anyway, I must help rescue Alice, if indeed she has been kidnapped," she said at last. "I am—we are all—terribly worried about her. The circus can get along very well without me, but the Athena Club—well, I would not want to abandon my friends."

"Of course not, and I'm not asking you to." Clarence ate a final piece of bread and signaled to the waiter. "I know how important the Athena Club is to—well, to all of you, including Cat. I just wish you and I could spend more time together."

"But we should not spend more time together," said Beatrice. "The more of my poison you inhale—"

"I know, I know, you don't need to remind me." He sounded impatient, annoyed. But she did need to keep reminding him, didn't she? Because she did not want him to suffer the fate of her first love, Giovanni, who had spent so much time with her in her father's garden that he too had become poisonous. He had died from drinking an antidote that he believed would return him to his natural state. No, she would not allow such a thing to happen to Clarence. It was good that soon they would be parted and he would go to Constantinople. There was no Ayesha in Constantinople. . . .

CATHERINE: So is it good or bad that Lorenzo's
circus has been offered a permanent position at

the Alhambra? You get to see him as often as you like—

BEATRICE: Which is not often enough for him! Truly, I do not know whether it is a good thing or a bad thing that Clarence and I can spend more time together. I know you disapprove, Cat—

CATHERINE: I don't disapprove. I just don't want him to die of poison. Well, at least he didn't fall for Ayesha, which would have been worse!

BEATRICE: He did, just a little. It's difficult not to, I think.

Clarence paid the bill. Beatrice had tried, the first time they had come to the Centrál Kávéház, to pay for herself, but he had said, "Honey, at least allow me to do this." So she had not insisted.

After they rose from the table, he took her manteau from the back of her chair and draped it over her shoulders. When they had first started spending time together, gestures like these had confused her. Certainly her father had never done such things, nor Giovanni, either. Slowly, she had come to realize they were the gestures men made toward women when they wished to be courteous, or romantic, or both. And Clarence was unfailingly courteous toward women, even when he was angry, as he had been at Zora for losing one of her snakes in the hotel. The entire circus had been asked to leave, but allowed to stay after Zora had promised to remove herself and her snakes to Count Dracula's residence.

Sometimes, Beatrice could not help being amused by the incongruity of it. He walked between her and the street, so her skirt would not be splashed by passing carriages. And yet she could, with her breath, poison everyone on the sidewalk! Nevertheless, she could not help feeling pleasure at being cared for in this way—she, who had always cared for others, whether her father, or his poisonous plants, or the patients for whom she so carefully concocted medicines.

They emerged into Károlyi Mihály utca, into the warmth and sunlight of Budapest. Yes indeed, she would miss this city, which reminded her just a little of her own Padua, arranged along the Bacchiglione River, as Budapest was arranged along the Danube. The streets of Budapest were busy with carts and wagons, as they always were at midday. Clarence held his arm out to her. As usual, she did not take it. Instead, with a small shake of her head, she started down the street toward the theater. Although her arms and hands were thoroughly covered, and he could not, even by accident, have come into contact with her skin, she did not want him to get used to being close to her. That would not be good for him—or her, either. Her heart had been broken once—she did not want it broken again. She had found so much in this new life of hers: freedom and friendship and a purpose. Love was not necessary.

> MARY: Are you quite sure about that? I would not say love is *necessary*—but perhaps life is not quite the same without it? We all need to be loved, in some way.

> DIANA: I don't.

> MARY: I think you need to be loved more than anyone I know! Stop that—you can't hurt me, kicking me through a petticoat. See? If I didn't love you, I would never put up with such behavior. Of course, I don't always *like* you very much.

BEATRICE: That does not change the fact that I am
poisonous. I cannot be with any man without
endangering his life. Lucinda would understand—
she is not poisonous, but her hunger for blood also
separates her from mankind.

MARY: Where is Lucinda, anyway?

CATHERINE: Playing the piano. Can't you hear it?
Good Lord, why do you primates have ears if you
can barely hear with them?

At that moment, Lucinda Van Helsing was eating a rabbit. Or,
more accurately, she was sucking its blood—later, Persephone
and Hades, the Countess Karnstein's white wolfdogs, would eat
the carcass. Magda was standing beside her in the forest glade,
looking down at her approvingly.

"*Jó, jó,*" she said, which Lucinda had come to understand meant
"Good, good," in Hungarian.

"You're doing very well," said Laura, who always came along on
these hunting expeditions—"To translate," she said, but Lucinda
had quickly realized it was as much to comfort and reassure. The
first time she killed a rabbit with her own hands, she had cried
so hard that she almost vomited up all the blood she had drunk.
Laura had taken Lucinda in her arms and stroked her hair, saying,
"Hush, hush, my dear. You'll get used to it in time."

"I do not wish to kill," she had said between sobs, stroking the
bloodstained body of the dead rabbit as though it were her childhood doll.

"But you must learn to," Laura had said. "Here at the schloss,
if you wish it, we could have blood brought to you in a glass—you
would never have to learn how to hunt for yourself, or confront

the death inherent in your mode of obtaining sustenance. But that would be both dishonest and unwise. You don't want to be dependent on others. And you are a predator—it is important for you to both understand and accept that fact. Carmilla would tell you the same herself, if she were here."

However, Carmilla was not there, but at Castle Karnstein. She had spent most of that first week at her ancestral estate, dealing with the mess Hyde had left behind. Evidently, he had left without disposing either of his chemicals or the corpse of Adam Frankenstein, which had been left lying under a sheet in the small, dark chamber where he had spent his final days. "At least I can tell Justine that he is well and truly dead," Carmilla had said to them on one of her brief visits. She had arranged for a proper burial in the graveyard behind the castle. Hyde had also neglected to pay his debts. He still owed money to the Ferenc family, which had served him so loyally while he had rented the castle. "Miklós and Dénes deserve to be horsewhipped for kidnapping Mary, Justine, and Diana on Hyde's orders," Carmilla had added angrily. "But I want to make sure Dénes can pay for his university tuition, and Anna Ferenc needs her medicine. The Ferencs have been tenants of the Karnsteins for two hundred years—I cannot let them starve. I'm sorry, Laura, but finances may be tight for a while."

Laura had just sighed—she was all too used to finances being tight, partly through Carmilla's extravagance. Now, she sighed again, but it seemed to be in relief that Lucinda had dispatched the rabbit so neatly. Lucinda simply nodded. What could she say? She was trying, as best she could, to live this new life her father had imposed on her through his experiments. She was a vampire—she would always be a vampire. She would always be able to hear the rabbit's heart beating as she tracked it in the long grass; she would always be able to climb the tallest trees, hand over hand, as though she were a squirrel. She would never grow old or become ill from the diseases to which men are prone. She would not die unless her head was completely severed from her neck or she was burned so that her body could not regenerate itself. She would always have to drink blood.

She had thought of taking her own life—she still thought of it sometimes as she lay awake, late into the night, for she no longer seemed to need as much sleep. She had thought of somehow lighting herself on fire, burning herself down to ash. She had not told Laura about these thoughts, and she could not tell Carmilla. The Countess was too formidable—she seemed old and distant, although she looked no older than Lucinda. But Lucinda could not have told her anything so personal.

Now, she followed Laura back toward the schloss. Magda came behind with the carcass of the rabbit dangling from her hand. It would provide a meal for Persephone and her brother, Hades.

As they approached the back of the schloss, which had a long terrace, Carmilla came out through the French doors. "Telegram!" she called. She was holding a piece of paper in one hand.

"Who from?" asked Laura. "And when did you get back? I didn't hear the motorcar. But then, we were pretty far into the forest. . . . *Köszönöm*, Magda," she said, nodding to the—what was Magda exactly? A coachman, a gamekeeper, a protector of the household. She seemed to serve multiple functions. And, of course, she was a vampire—the only one created by Count Dracula who had managed to retain her sanity, or most of it. Sometimes she still imagined that she was on the battlefield, and then only Carmilla could subdue and restrain her. At first, Lucinda had been frightened of her, but Magda had been so kind—they had all been so kind to her. She was grateful for that.

Nevertheless, she was so very tired, and she smelled of blood. She would go up to her room, which had been Laura's father's room, once. She sometimes wondered what her life would have been like if her father had resembled Colonel Jennings—an ordinary man who liked his books and pipe, who wore the hunting jackets that still hung in the wardrobe or the slippers in a row beneath them. But no, her father had been the celebrated Professor Van Helsing, with appointments at several European universities and a desire to breach the boundaries of life itself, to make himself and men like him immortal. With a logic that still made her so furious she clenched her fists thinking about it, he had started by experimenting on his wife. Lucinda tried not to think about her mother too often—the memory was simply too painful. Her mother had died to save her from her father's henchmen. Someday, the two of them would be reunited in Heaven, if vampires went to Heaven. If not, then in Hell. Until then, Lucinda would have to live somehow. At least, for the first time since her mother had been taken to the mental asylum, she was among friends.

Who seemed, at the moment, to be quarreling.

"But we just got home!" Laura was saying. "And you haven't even been here most of the week, but at that wretched castle—"

"I can't let Mina go into such a situation by herself, can I?" said Carmilla. "The Count won't be able to leave Budapest until after the Emperor's visit, so she's going to Vienna alone. Do you want her confronting Van Helsing's vampires without support?"

"First of all, she's not going by herself," said Laura. "She has Irene Norton there, and Irene has—well, a sort of gang, from what Mary told us. And second of all, that's an excuse, and you know it. You just want to go off on your own, in that damned motorcar of yours, like some lone figure of righteous vengeance, to fight vampires. Must you be so dramatic? Honestly, sometimes I think you're more like the Count than you realize."

"Not alone. I want to take Magda with me. She's so good at smelling out our kind. *Kedvesem*, I know you're angry with me, don't deny it—"

"Who's denying it? Of course I'm angry with you," said Laura angrily, as though to emphasize her point. "And you can't take Magda. Lucinda needs her, particularly if you're going to go off on a vampire hunt."

"—but you also know I'm right. Do you really want Mina and Irene, and a group of girls who may be very capable but have no experience hunting such monsters, to go up against a nest of vampires without our help? All right, I'll leave Magda here, but I at least need to go."

Carmilla was holding Laura's hand. Lucinda did not want to interrupt such an intimate scene—she felt a little shy even watching it. She would go up to her room, rinse her mouth out thoroughly with lavender water, and perhaps rest for a while. She still felt so awkward and ashamed about drinking blood. Would she ever get used to this new life as a vampire?

She entered through the French doors into the music room. Perhaps, before proceeding upstairs, she would play the piano for a few minutes. She sat down on the stool, which was adjusted to her height—she was the only one who played with any consistency. Ten minutes later, she did not even notice Laura tiptoeing across the room so as not to disturb her. She was so completely lost in the melodies of Shubert.

MARY: As she seems to be right now!

JUSTINE: Forgive me, Mary, but that is Chopin.

MARY: Oh. What's the difference?

JUSTINE: Why, they are not at all alike! That is like
        asking what is the difference between Ingres and
        Renoir, between Delacroix and Monsieur Monet. . . .

CATHERINE: Are you seriously interrupting my
narrative to argue about composers? "Lucinda was
playing something or other on the piano." There, I
fixed it. Satisfied?

As the cab drew up to 11 Park Terrace, Mary could not stop
looking out the window in all directions—at the gray, rainy
streets of London, the Georgian houses on either side, and the
trees waving over the housetops, reminding her that Regent's Park
was still there and now that she had returned, she could walk to it
whenever she wished.

"Stop shoving me!" said Diana, who was sandwiched between
Mary and Justine. She was awake but tired, and therefore especially cross.

The horse stopped right in front of the Jekyll residence. "Whoa,
Caesar!" shouted the cabbie. It was lovely to hear a cockney accent
again!

At Charing Cross Station, they had stopped for tea and cur-
rant buns in a tea shop—the first proper English tea Mary had
been able to order since leaving for Europe. How welcome and
familiar it tasted, although Diana complained that the buns were
stale. And then they had caught a cab. Now here they were, at
11 Park Terrace once again, a month after they had left. In that
month, she had experienced so many things! Sometimes they had
been wonderful, sometimes terrifying, sometimes merely tedious.
She would, she was sure, have such adventures again. But this was
where she belonged—no matter how far away she traveled, it was
the home to which she would always return.

She paid the cabbie, almost handing him francs by accident
and reminding herself that she would need to exchange them as
soon as possible at the Bank of England. Justine, in her incarna-
tion as Mr. Justin Frank, helped the cabbie carry the trunk to the

front stoop. Diana rang the bell an unnecessary number of times. Over it was a polished brass plaque on which was written THE ATHENA CLUB. Mrs. Poole should be expecting them—Mary had telegraphed from Calais.

But it was not Mrs. Poole who answered the door.

"What the hell?" said Diana.

Standing in the doorway was a boy—short, with ginger hair and a strange, angular face. His wrists stuck out of his suit jacket and his arms seemed strangely long.

"You rang, miss?" he said in what sounded like a foreign accent.

With a start, Mary realized who he must be: the Orangutan Man that Catherine had rescued from the British headquarters of the Alchemical Society in Soho. What had she called him? Archimedes? Archi—

"Miss Mary! Welcome home!" Ah, there was Mrs. Poole, hurrying down the hall behind him. She still had a white apron over her black housekeeper's dress. "Miss Justine! I'm so glad to see you again. And even you, Miss Scamp!" She looked just as she always did: entirely reassuring. All Mary's life, Mrs. Poole had been there, to guide and teach and sometimes reprove. She, more than anything else in that house—Dr. Jekyll's books, Mrs. Jekyll's portrait—made the Jekyll residence feel like home. Mary wondered how Mrs. Poole would respond if she kissed the housekeeper. She did not think Mrs. Poole would approve at all.

> MRS. POOLE: I most certainly would not have. I know my place, I assure you. And I trust Miss Mary to know hers.

Instead she said, as heartily as she could, "Mrs. Poole, I'm so very, very glad to see you again. It's so good to be home." But even as she said the word, she realized how different her home was now from the house in which she had grown up as the proper Miss Jekyll. Here she was standing in the front hall with her sister Diana, who was glaring suspiciously at the Orangutan Man. Beside her stood Justine, and in a few days Catherine and Beatrice would be home as well. They had all changed that house—for the better. The Jekyll residence had become the Athena Club.

And Mary herself, returning after almost a month on the continent, was not the same Mary Jekyll who had left. She had heard different languages, tasted different flavors, paid in different currencies—she had met men like Dr. Freud and Count Dracula, women like Ayesha and Mrs. Norton. She had wandered the streets of Vienna and Budapest. No wonder she felt different. Perhaps travel did that to you. Mary had come home, but she was not the same Mary who had left—not quite.

However, this was no time for reverie. They had coats and hats to take off, luggage to unpack, and friends to find—or, if Mrs. Poole's fears were justified, to rescue.

> MARY: I worry that readers who begin with this
> volume will not understand who we are, how
> we formed the Athena Club, and why it was so
> important to rescue Alice. I know you should
> begin a novel *in medias res*, Cat, but perhaps this is
> too much *in medias* and not enough *res*?

> AUTHOR'S NOTE: Reader, if you have not yet read the
> first two adventures of the Athena Club, *The Strange Case of
> the Alchemist's Daughter* and *European Travel for the Monstrous
> Gentlewoman*, I encourage you to do so before proceeding
> further. However, I understand there may be reasons
> why you are unable to do so at this time. For example,
> if you have lost your fortune, must work as a governess,

and cannot afford the first two volumes. Or if you have
been kidnapped by bandits who possess only this third
volume in their hideout, no doubt stolen from a person
of discernment and literary taste. For readers in such
circumstances, I shall briefly summarize our previous
adventures, in which Mary Jekyll, impoverished after her
mother's death, discovered that her father, the respectable
Dr. Jekyll, had engaged in experiments that turned him
into the disreputable Mr. Hyde. When he fled England
as a known murderer, he left behind a child, Diana Hyde,
who was raised by the Society of St. Mary Magdalen,
where Mrs. Raymond presided as the redoubtable director.
Mary had taken the poor, defenseless girl home with her.

DIANA: Defenseless, my arse!

But her investigations had not ended there, for her
father had been a member of the secretive Alchemical
Society, some of whose members had also produced
monstrous offspring: Beatrice Rappaccini, as poisonous
as she was beautiful; Justine Frankenstein, taller and
stronger than most men; and your author, Catherine
Moreau, a puma transformed into a woman who
retained her feline swiftness and cunning. Together,
these remarkable young ladies had formed the Athena
Club. These events are described in *The Strange Case of
the Alchemist's Daughter*, in which our heroines solved the
Whitechapel Murders with the help of Mr. Holmes and
Dr. Watson. In the thrilling sequel, *European Travel for the
Monstrous Gentlewoman,* they rescued Lucinda Van Helsing
and confronted the Alchemical Society with its crimes.
While its formidable president, Ayesha, would not agree

to halt experiments in biological transmutation entirely, she had agreed to form a committee to evaluate such experiments, with Beatrice as a member.

> BEATRICE: It does not sound very impressive when you put it like that, and yet the committee has done some very good work. The research protocols I drafted have been adopted by the society, and I believe they have changed how such experiments are carried out. What Dr. Raymond did to Helen, for example—he could not do that, under our current structure.

All of these adventures and more can be found in the first two books, offered for the very reasonable price of two shillings a volume, in an attractive green cloth cover. Copies may be purchased in most fine bookstores.

> MARY: This was supposed to be a synopsis, not an advertisement!

> CATHERINE: Well, I don't earn royalties on a synopsis, and we need money, especially now that Lucinda is staying with us.

> MRS. POOLE: Remarkably cheap she is, compared with you lot! Even goes out and gets her own food, now she's gotten the hang of it.

> MARY: About which the less said, the better.

# CHAPTER II

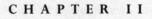

## Return to Baker Street

"C ome in, come in," said Mrs. Poole. "It's terrible damp out, and the nights are growing colder. I can't tell you how glad I am to see you all safely home! Archibald, shut the door and lock up tight. He's an excellent footman, miss," she said to Mary, "but sometimes forgetful about things like locks. I don't suppose orangutans have much use for them! Do take the ladies' hats while I take their coats—you see how nicely he does it? Now, I have a fire laid in the dining room, and I'll bring up dinner straight away. I've made pork chops for dinner, with creamed Brussels sprouts and a jam roly-poly. I'll just need to heat it up in the warming oven. I didn't know what time you'd be here, you see."

"Jam roly-poly!" said Diana. "My favorite. Well, except for all those cakes in Budapest. You made it especially for me, didn't you? Admit it."

"What nonsense," said Mrs. Poole. "They're Archibald's favorite too, you know. And I wonder those European cakes didn't make you sick, as rich as they are!"

"Mrs. Poole, have you heard anything more of Alice?" asked Justine, drawing off her gloves. Mary could hear the concern in her voice.

"Or Mr. Holmes?" added Mary. "And Dr. Watson, of course." She could not help sounding worried herself. She unbuckled her waist bag and placed it on the hall table. She must remember to take out her revolver and store it properly in the morning room desk. "I don't suppose you've had any further news."

"Not a peep," said Mrs. Poole, shaking her head mournfully. "Almost a week Alice has been gone now, and Dr. Watson, too. He vanished the same day, Mrs. Hudson tells me, without leaving her a note or anything. The gentlemen have gone off sleuthing before—but they've never been gone as long as Mr. Holmes. Why, it's almost a month now! Terrible worried she is, as am I—little Alice, what I've trained since she was a child! You'll find her, miss, now that you're home, won't you?"

"Of course we'll find her," said Mary with what she hoped sounded like confidence. They would, wouldn't they? After all, they had found Lucinda Van Helsing. Even in a city like London, with its six million inhabitants, Alice, Sherlock Holmes, and Dr. Watson could not have vanished without leaving a trace!

"Do you like playing cards?" said Diana to the Orangutan Man. "I could teach you *Écarté* or *Vingt-et-un*. Those are French words. Do you speak any French?"

Justine squeezed Mary's hand, a little too hard—it was always difficult for Justine to gauge her own strength. "We'll find them, you'll see," she said. "We are the Athena Club, remember?"

Mary smiled and nodded, but in her heart she felt a cold foreboding. The Alchemical Society was not responsible for Alice's disappearance—Ayesha had made that clear in Budapest. "The S.A. lost track of Helen Raymond before I became president," she had told Mary the day they received Mrs. Poole's telegram. "When Frau Gottlieb located Lydia Raymond, whom you know as Alice, your kitchen maid, we placed her in your household so we could keep an eye on you both. We worried that she might have inherited her mother's ability to harness the energic powers of the Earth—what you call mesmerism. From what you tell me, it seems she has grown into those powers. There are many reasons unscrupulous men—or women, like Helen herself—might want a child who is able to create illusions at will. I trust that you will do your best to find her, and apprise me when she has been found."

Apprise Ayesha! There were several things Mary would have liked to do to Ayesha that did not involve apprising. But one had to tread carefully around a two-thousand-year-old Egyptian queen who could electrocute you with her touch.

Could Alice's mother have found and abducted her for unscrupulous purposes, as Ayesha had implied? If indeed Alice had been abducted. "Mrs. Poole, you didn't give us any details. How do you know it was a kidnapping? How do you know she didn't simply leave with someone?"

"Follow me, miss," said Mrs. Poole grimly. "I'll show you."

Where was the housekeeper going? Toward the narrow back stairs that led down to the kitchen and coal cellar. Mary wondered what Mrs. Poole was about to show them. She followed Mrs. Poole down the dark staircase with a growing sense of apprehension that sent chills down her spine. Justine's and Diana's boots clattered on the stairs behind her.

> MARY: I did feel a growing sense of apprehension, but I certainly didn't have chills down my spine. What would those feel like, anyway? You're making this sound like some sort of gothic thriller, Cat. Really, sometimes I agree with Diana's assessment of your writing.

> CATHERINE: Some of my readers have wondered why I, as the author of this narrative, allow such interruptions. They tell me they find such a habit as annoying as I find Mary's, Justine's, Beatrice's,

and Diana's continual intrusions into my space and time, particularly now that Lucinda is living with us and I must do my writing in the study. No, Diana, you may not play with Omega in here! Go bother Justine up in the studio.

If you ask such a question, dear reader, it's because you have never lived in a house with six other women—seven if you count Mrs. Poole, although I'm not talking about you, Mrs. Poole. You can interrupt anytime, and also can I have some of the cold ham from yesterday? With a glass of milk, please? And there's no need to bring a fork.

I assure you, reader, that Mary and the others are just as annoying in daily life as they are on the page. If my method of writing displeases you, I assure you that such interruptions are as irritating to me, but what can I do when they insist on having their say? It sometimes makes me long for the silent peaks of the Andes, where I roamed as a puma before Moreau turned me into a woman. But then, I would not be your author, and there would be no story.

DIANA: Which might be a good thing, considering the rot you write about us.

Just beyond the kitchen were the housekeeper's suite and the small room where Alice slept—all the other servants' quarters, up on the third floor, had been converted into a studio for Justine. Mrs. Poole took a key out of her apron pocket and unlocked Alice's door. She stepped into the room and, looking around, said, "I didn't let anyone in here after I found it like this, knowing how important Mr. Holmes thinks it is to preserve the evidence, as he always says. You see? Although it's getting dark—should I bring a lamp?"

But Mary could see well enough. The narrow bed had been pulled out from the wall, the chair beside it was overturned, and Alice's clothes were scattered here and there. The basin and pitcher were lying in pieces on the floor, beside a tangle of bedclothes.

"Let me fetch a lamp from the kitchen," said Mrs. Poole. "There's something else I want to show you, but it's too dark. . . . I won't be half a moment."

While Mary could hear Mrs. Poole clattering about in the kitchen, Justine stepped into the room beside her and Diana pushed in between them, saying, "Let me see too. You never let me see. Well, at least she put up a struggle. Good on Alice."

Justine looked around the room as carefully as Mr. Holmes himself would have, but Mary had to stop Diana from kicking the clothes on the floor to see what was under them. If only the girl could restrain herself or behave with forethought just once!

MARY: Well, that has never yet happened.

DIANA: This morning I only had two eggs for breakfast.

MARY: How is that a sign of restraint?

DIANA: I could have had three, because Justine didn't want hers, but I gave one to Omega because he's been looking scrawny. I thought it would fatten him up.

MRS. POOLE: So that's what that dratted cat threw up
on the kitchen floor! I wondered what he could
have eaten that was *yellow*. Child, you will be the
death of me.

DIANA: Then who would make pudding? Mary is a
rotten cook.

When Mrs. Poole returned, she leaned over and held the lamp
down, close to the floor near the doorway. "You see?" she said. "I
wager Mr. Holmes could make something of that."

"Half a boot print," said Mary. "A man's, I think, by the size
and shape of the toe. Are there any more?"

"Just the one, and it's faint enough. I'm afraid I swept the
kitchen and corridor first thing. I always do so now those dratted
cats are bringing in who knows what! Last week I stepped on a
mouse, and it wasn't dead yet. It's likely I swept away any others
before I noticed Alice was gone. But there's something else," said
Mrs. Poole, straightening up again with one hand on her back.
"You know how prompt Alice always is. When she didn't appear
for breakfast, I knocked on the door, and when she didn't answer,
I entered this room. I found it as you see, with Archibald sound
asleep on the floor. Archibald, show them your arm."

The Orangutan Man, who must have followed them down the
stairs and crept in behind them, rolled up his sleeve. On it was a
mark Mary had seen before. It looked like an electrical burn, pink
and blistered. Around it, his ginger hair was singed. She stepped
back, startled.

"That is the sort of mark we saw on the vampires Ayesha dispatched with her energic power," said Justine. She knelt and gently
touched Archibald's arm. "This must have hurt, little one."

"Much pain," he said. "Pretty Alice all gone."

"At least they didn't take him too," said Mrs. Poole. "I'm grateful for that. I wouldn't have wanted to lose poor Archibald as well. He's such a gentle soul."

"But Ayesha's touch kills on contact," said Mary. "This—well, it certainly looks painful, but Archibald is very much alive." She turned to the Orangutan Man. "Did you see who took her?" Had he actually witnessed the kidnapping? He must have, if he had been injured by Alice's kidnappers.

He shook his head and then wrapped his arms around it, as though protecting himself from harm.

"Perhaps he is too traumatized to tell us what he saw," said Justine.

"He's telling us they covered his head," said Diana. "But you could hear them, couldn't you? And smell them? I bet monkeys have a pretty good sense of smell."

"I believe orangutans are apes," said Justine. "Look, the pillowcase is shredded. Perhaps that is what they put over his head." She held it up—Mary was shocked to see that one end was torn into long, ragged strips.

"Who the hell cares whether orangutans are monkeys or apes?" said Diana. "How many kidnappers were there? That's the important question."

Archibald held up two fingers. "Man and woman. Woman wear trousers, like me. She smell pretty, like flowers. Like Beatrice. Other smell like medicine. He put medicine in my nose."

"They must have drugged him," said Mary. "A man and a woman—who could they possibly be? Mrs. Raymond and an accomplice? Someone else entirely?" Who would want to kidnap Alice, and why? Her mesmerical powers, presumably—but how had they learned about those powers? Only Catherine's friend Martin, the mesmerist of the Circus of Marvels and Delights, had known about them. Well, at least they were developing a list of suspects! "Mrs. Poole, did you think of notifying the police?"

"The police!" said Mrs. Poole. "In a gentleman's household? That I did not, miss. Nor would I without your permission. Of course if you had telegraphed back with instructions, I would have gone straight away. If you wish me to do so—"

Should they consult the police? But that would mean Scotland Yard and quite possibly Inspector Lestrade. Mary remembered how rude he had been to her when they were investigating the Whitechapel Murders. She had no wish to see Inspector Lestrade or any of his ilk again.

"No, I think you did right. After all, we are the Athena Club. I think we can handle this matter ourselves." She looked once again around the room. Had she missed anything Mr. Holmes would see? "Mrs. Poole, if you could finish warming up dinner, I'd like to look around here one more time. Would you mind leaving the lamp?"

Once Mrs. Poole had left, followed by Archibald and Diana, who said she wanted to check on the jam roly-poly to make sure it was good and jammy, Mary turned to Justine. "Let's start at the door and go around the room systematically. That's the way Mr. Holmes would do it. Look for—well, I don't know what. Anything out of the ordinary, I guess. Then during dinner we can make plans. I have some ideas about where to get started."

Justine nodded and began examining the floor and walls to the right of the door. If there was one thing Mary had learned about Justine in her travels, it was that she could always be relied on. What a relief that was! And Diana, of course, could never be relied on. Thank goodness she was preoccupied with Mrs. Poole's pudding at the moment!

> DIANA: I can too be relied on! Who found out what
> that list of addresses in Watson's room meant? It
> was me, that's who. If it wasn't for me—

MARY: If it weren't for you, we wouldn't have been
captured in Soho!

CATHERINE: How many times do I have to warn you
not to anticipate the action for our readers?

There were no marks on the walls or the small window looking into the courtyard that separated the house from what had
once been Dr. Jekyll's laboratory. There were no marks on the
floor of the room or the passageway outside except the single boot
print. If only they could have found a cigarette butt! That was the
sort of thing Mr. Holmes always seemed to find, and it always
led him to the culprit, as though each criminal in London had his
own individual way of smoking. Finally, Mary searched through
the clothes on the floor, examining each garment, then folding it
neatly on the bed. "Alice's uniforms," she said.

"What about Alice's Sunday dress?" asked Justine from under
the bed. She looked like a quarter of a spider, with her long legs
sticking out. Suddenly, Mary felt like laughing, which would have
been most inappropriate under the circumstances.

"It's still in the chest of drawers. I can't find her nightclothes,
but I suppose she would have been abducted in those. They didn't
take anything except what she was wearing at the time."

Justine crawled back out from under the bed. "Look," she said.
"This was tangled in the sheets."

It was a pocket handkerchief of white linen, clearly a man's. As
soon as Justine held it out to her, Mary could smell the distinctive
odor of chloroform. It was monogrammed in black thread with an *M*.

"Dinner is ready!" Mrs. Poole called from the doorway. "I
want you both to stop crawling about on the floor and get something to eat. After all that gallivanting around Europe, you must
be famished for a good English dinner."

Mary *was* feeling rather hollow inside. When had she last eaten or gotten a good night's sleep? Even in the luxury of the *Orient Express*, with Diana snoring on the bunk above her, she had lain awake, worrying about Alice, Mr. Holmes, and Dr. Watson. Then, she had felt helpless—now, thank goodness, she could actually do something. The only antidote to worry was action. She would solve this mystery, just as Mr. Holmes himself would have.

"Could *M* be Marvelous Martin?" she asked Justine several minutes later when they were sitting in the dining room eating a very English dinner indeed. "Cat said he was teaching Alice to use her powers and his name starts with an *M*. I can't think of anyone else in her life with an *M*—except me." Justine was eating a roasted potato, which Mrs. Poole had made particularly for her.

"You can't live on vegetables alone, miss," she had said to the Giantess. "You've gotten thinner since you left, the both of you. It's that European *cuisine*, as they call it. Good English food will fatten you right up again!" Diana had chosen to take her dinner in the kitchen with Archibald so she could play with Alpha and Omega, who had grown in the last few weeks. When Mary had left, they were still kittens—compact balls of fluff already deadly to mice, with large green eyes. Now they were starting to look like gangly adolescents.

"Surely not Martin," said Justine, taking a second helping of Brussels sprouts. She must be feeling that hollow sensation as well—Justine never took seconds. "Martin is such a gentle man. I knew him for many years in the circus. He could not harm a fly, and anyway, from what Catherine told us, Alice knew and trusted him. He would have no need to come into her bedroom in the middle of the night to kidnap her. He could simply tell her to accompany him somewhere. We can ask him—Catherine gave me the address of the boardinghouse where the circus performers who didn't go on the European tour are staying—but I cannot believe that he would be involved."

"Then I suggest the following plan," said Mary. "Tomorrow morning, we'll go to Baker Street and see if Mrs. Hudson has heard anything from Mr. Holmes or Dr. Watson. And we should search their flat—perhaps they left clues of some sort as to their whereabouts? Then, and I hesitate to suggest this but I think it must be done, we should go to the Society of St. Mary Magdalen and ask for an interview with Mrs. Raymond. If she is indeed the woman Frau Gottleib mentioned—created by Dr. Raymond in his quest to harness the energic powers of the Earth—then she has a motive to kidnap her own daughter. Perhaps she and Martin—yes, I know you don't believe it's Martin—are working together for some purpose? But why such a woman would become director of a society for the salvation of prostitutes, I cannot imagine. Perhaps she isn't the same Mrs. Raymond at all—it's not an uncommon name. I wish I had asked Frau Gottleib more about Dr. Raymond and his experiments before we left, but there wasn't time." She should have made the time—mentally, Mary berated herself. She had been so worried about Alice and the whole situation at home that she had not gathered as much information as she should have. Mr. Holmes would not have made that mistake.

"And then perhaps after that we can see Martin?" said Justine. "I do not want him to be unjustly suspected. I'm certain he will be as shocked by Alice's disappearance as we are. He cannot possibly have anything to do with this situation."

> CATHERINE: I still can't believe you suspected Martin!
> He's the gentlest creature imaginable, and the last
> person who would chloroform anyone. Anyway,
> he treats Alice as though she were his own

daughter, I suppose, because she's the only one
he's met whose powers are even stronger than his.

ALICE: Martin has been very good to me always. But
he was a bit to blame, in his own way.

As Mary was heading down the hall to bed, after having tucked
Diana in, she met Mrs. Poole coming out of her room.

"I've turned down the bed, miss," said Mrs. Poole. "And there's
a hot water bottle at the foot. I'm sorry to raise this subject when
you're so tired, but I suppose I'd better. There's very little money
left of what you and Catherine gave me before you departed for
Europe. I've been buying groceries on credit, and the rates are
coming due. I hate to bother you—"

Mary felt mortified—had they really left Mrs. Poole with so
little? But she had not expected Catherine and Beatrice to join
her and Justine on the continent—she had assumed they would
be here, looking after the household. Instead, they had left Mrs.
Poole and Alice alone—and look what had come of that! "I'm glad
you did," she said. "And it's not a bother, of course. In my waist bag
you'll find—goodness, I don't even know how much it is without
doing conversions in my head. A bunch of francs and krone—I
spent the last of our pounds and shillings getting us home. Also
my pistol and some bullets. Could you take the foreign currency
to Threadneedle Street tomorrow and have it exchanged? And
could you please telegraph Mina and tell her we're arrived safely?
I'm so sorry, Mrs. Poole. I should have made better arrangements."
That money would carry them through—well, Mary did not know
how long. They would each need to start working again, soon. But
they would have to solve this mystery first. She thought, with a
pang, about the fact that she would not be returning to work for
Mr. Holmes tomorrow morning, but trying to locate him in the

labyrinth of London. Was she more worried about the job, or the man? This was no time to make such distinctions. The man was the job—to get back one, she would have to find the other.

"That's quite all right, miss. You can't think of everything, now can you? After all, you rescued Miss Van Helsing, and that's the important thing. Although Miss Murray's telegram didn't provide many details?"

And Mrs. Poole, epitome of a housekeeper that she was, would never ask for them! Still, it was clear to Mary that she would like to know what all of them had been doing since they left Park Terrace. After all, Mrs. Poole was human—she would never admit to curiosity, but she would certainly feel it! "I'll tell you about it tomorrow. It was Diana's doing, really, but don't tell her I said that. Oh, and she almost burned down a mental hospital in the process!"

> DIANA: But I didn't, did I? And you said it yourself—I rescued Lucinda. If it weren't for me—

> LUCINDA: For which I am most grateful, I assure you.

> DIANA: Oh. Well, it was nothing. I mean, it was something, all right—especially when we set all those sheets on fire and everyone began running out of the building, and they called the fire brigade! That was prime.

The next morning, Justine walked across the courtyard to the building that had once been Hyde's laboratory and was now converted into Beatrice's greenhouse of poisonous plants. Before she had left Budapest, Beatrice had said to her, "When you are once again in London, please look in on my plants. I do not know if Dr. Watson's ingenious arrangement of rubber tubes actually worked. I hope they are still alive—but I am anxious about them. Sometimes I think of them as my children, the only ones I shall ever have."

As she crossed the courtyard, Omega followed her, meowing at her heels. She picked up the kitten. "You can't come with me," she said to him sternly. "It's poisonous in there. *Un petit chatton* like you would not last a minute." She kissed him on the head, then put him down again and said, "Shoo! As Mrs. Poole always says, although I do not understand the reference to footwear. Go back and bother her, *mon petit*. I have no time for you this morning." He walked off disdainfully, tail in the air, as though having been rejected in that fashion, he could not be bothered with her either.

The door of the greenhouse, once an operating theater with a high glass dome to let in light, opened with a creak. The moisture inside had rusted the hinges.

Inside, it was warm, humid—and green. Justine breathed a sigh of relief. Here and there she could see patches of brown—the *Digitalis purpurea* had not survived as well as some of the hardier specimens, and the henbane was drooping. But most of the plants arranged on the semicircular wooden ledges where students had once taken notes were lush and thriving.

Justine checked all the tubes, made any necessary adjustments, and moved the *Digitalis* to a shadier location, although she was not certain if that would help. Beatrice knew more about such plants than she did, although she had done well enough raising vegetables for her own consumption during the hundred years she had spent in Cornwall.

Were they indeed the only children Beatrice would ever have? She herself was not capable of having children. When he had re-created her, Victor Frankenstein had made sure of that. When Adam had held her captive in the small cottage in the Orkneys, when he had insisted that she behave as his wife, she had been glad that she could not conceive a child. But now? She would never have the life Justine Moritz might have had, the life of an ordinary woman. There was a man who might love her—at least, she had seen marks of attention from him. The small courtesies, the poetry . . . Atlas, the Strongman of Lorenzo's Circus of Marvels and Delights, who was as tall as she was, although not as strong. How did she feel about him? She did not know. Adam's death had changed something, she was not sure what—but now she felt as though, for the first time since Victor Frankenstein's death, she could think about the future. What did the future hold for her? She had no idea.

Well, it was no use standing here in a state of uncertainty and indecision. She must go join the others—there was a great deal to do today!

While Justine was crossing the courtyard from Beatrice's greenhouse to the tradesmen's entrance, Mary was waiting in the parlor for her and Diana. She paced back and forth, then paused and looked up at the portrait of her mother over the fireplace. She had not come into this room last night—the fire had not been lit, and it had been a cold, dark cave. But now, morning light streamed in through the windows, illuminating the sofa and armchairs Beatrice had re-covered in a floral pattern, the Turkish rug she had bought at a church sale. Mary looked up at the painting of her mother over the mantel, between two Chinese jars that, yes, Beatrice had chosen. The Poisonous Girl was, after all, their resident aesthete and decorator. There was Mrs. Jekyll, with her golden hair and cornflower-blue eyes, dressed in the romantic and slightly ridiculous fashion of a previous generation. Mary walked to the fireplace and stood beneath the painting.

*Mother, if you could have been there,* she thought. In that castle in Styria where her father—well, Edward Hyde—had told her the terrible story of his experiments: how he had tried to become his better self, how he had fallen to his lower impulses. And while he was still trying to become the higher man, a more rational, evolved human being through chemical experimentation, he had given his wife something, some drug created through his experiments, that allowed her to have the child she had so long desired. *He experimented on you too. And I was the result of that experiment.* If her mother were here now, what would Mary tell her? She did not know. Perhaps it was better, after all, that Ernestine Jekyll was lying in the graveyard of Marylebone Church. What characteristics had Mary inherited from that version of her father? No wonder she and Diana, who was born of her father's lower, more bestial self, were so different. But the higher man—could he not be as inhuman as the lower? She was, perhaps, as much of a monster as her sister.

DIANA: Oy! Anyway, you're worse than me any day. At least I'm never a sanctimonious prig.

"Mary, are you ready?" asked Justine. There were Justine and Diana in the doorway, both dressed in men's clothes—well, boys' clothes, in Diana's case.

"Is it absolutely necessary for you to dress like that?" said Mary. "Where in the world did you get that suit anyway, from Charlie? You look like one of the Baker Street Irregulars. Indeed, there's no need for you to come at all. Why can't you just stay here and do something or other with Archibald?"

"You never want to include me!" said Diana, putting her hands in her pockets and planting her feet wide, like Charlie Sutton or another of the Baker Street boys. "Well, I'm coming—nohow."

"I am not certain that word means what you intended," said Justine.

"Words can mean whatever you want them to," said Diana. "You just have to pay them enough. Anyway, what do you know about English? You're Swiss."

Mary had no time to waste on such nonsensical chatter. "Come on, then. Honestly, half the reason we bring you anywhere is that it's usually more trouble to leave you behind!"

She walked at a brisk pace out the front door of 11 Park Terrace, then across Regent's Park, annoyed at Diana and anxious about what she would find at Baker Street. In the park, the trees and shrubs, which had still been green before they left for Vienna, were draped in their autumn finery. A few leaves, yellow and orange, already littered the ground. The roses of summer had turned into red hips, and the ducks and geese on the river looked ready to depart for warmer climes.

BEATRICE: That's lovely writing, Catherine.

CATHERINE: Thank you. I must have rewritten that
  description three times. I wasn't sure about
  "climes"—it may be too Wordsworthian? But
  "climate" sounded so ordinary. I wanted it to sound,
  you know, poetic.

At 221 Baker Street, Mrs. Hudson greeted Mary with voluble joy. "Oh, Miss Jekyll, I'm so glad to see you safely back!" she said. "No, I'm afraid I don't have anything more to report. Nor hide nor hair I've seen of either Mr. Holmes or Dr. Watson since I spoke with Mrs. Poole. Sometimes the gentlemen are away for long periods of time, but they generally let me know where they're going, although Mr. Holmes can be secretive, to be sure. Yes, of course you may search their rooms—I know they wouldn't mind *you* doing so. And this is Miss Frankenstein! I wouldn't have thought you were a lady, in that getup—look quite gentlemanly, you do. But Mrs. Poole told me all about you, miss. Such a nice time we have on her days off—we go to the Aerated Bread Company for tea, and then on to Harrods or a walk down Piccadilly to look at the shops. And Miss Hyde, too, of course. She's told me all about you!" Mrs. Hudson looked at Diana disapprovingly. "Mind *you* behave yourself upstairs! No monkey business." She took a large set of keys from her apron pocket. "I'll just unlock the flat for you, shall I? How were your travels on the continent?"

"Very well, thank you," said Mary. So Mrs. Hudson and Mrs. Poole went out for tea and shopping! Mary would have liked to be a fly on that wall so she could overhear their conversations. She wondered what they said to each other about the Baker Street and Park Terrace households. "We went to Vienna and Budapest. It was—well, it was an adventure."

"I've never been to Europe myself," said Mrs. Hudson, "although I traveled with my husband when he was in Her Majesty's army. We were in Lahore for a while, and then he was posted to Goa. Ah, we were so young! It's easier to travel when you're young, I think. You don't mind the inconveniences so much."

Mr. Holmes's residence at 221B looked exactly the way it had the last time Mary had seen it. Books lay scattered over every surface. There was the long table with its scientific instruments, the camera on its tripod sporting a top hat, the shelves of glass jars containing—she scanned them quickly—yes, mostly ears, and she thought back to the monograph Mr. Holmes had been dictating the last time she had seen him. It had focused on the distinctive characteristics of ears and their use in criminal investigation.

"What are we looking for?" asked Diana.

"I'm not sure. Any indication of where Mr. Holmes might be. If he's on a case, he may have left notes of some sort. He usually makes notes to himself. I'll start with the desk. Justine, could you start—well, honestly, any place is as good as another. And Diana, could you stay out of the way for a while? Maybe you can sit on the sofa—oh, it's covered with books. Well, find a place anyway."

Mary sat down at the rolltop desk, which was spilling over with papers. That was where she usually worked as Mr. Holmes's assistant, although she had kept it so much neater! However, the papers she could find were simply notes for his monograph and some of her typescripts. At one point she called Diana over to unlock the hidden drawer.

"Easy peasy," said Diana, putting a thin metal tool of some sort back into a compact leather case filled with similar tools. "See? You want me out of the way until you don't. What would you do without me?"

"Where did you get that case?" asked Mary, sliding open the drawer.

"It's the one Irene gave me. Why?"

"I've just never seen it before, that's all. I mean, I've seen you pick locks, but I've never seen the instruments all together like that. Like some sort of nefarious manicure set!"

"You only see what I want you to see. Anyway, I usually only carry around what I need, but I didn't know what would be needed this time, did I? Also, what does 'nefarious' mean?"

Mary sighed. If only Diana were less annoying! She could be so useful sometimes—and she never failed to point that out or let you forget it!

The hidden drawer held only the photograph of Irene Norton—Irene Adler, as she had been then—that Mr. Holmes had shown her before their European trip, and a stack of letters postmarked from Vienna with the Baker Street address written in violet ink. Those must be from Irene. Mary remembered what Dr. Watson had told her the day they had received Mina's telegram, as they were hurrying back through Regent's Park to the Jekyll residence: *I believe she was the love of his life.* And yet Irene herself had said that she and Sherlock were fundamentally incompatible. Would Mr. Holmes agree with her assessment? And did it even matter? Mary still did not know him as well as she would have liked, but she suspected that he would be perfectly capable of feeling an unrequited passion for many years, like one of those rivers that run deep underground, giving no evidence of its presence—but there nonetheless.

"Don't misjudge Holmes," Dr. Watson had once told her when she remarked on the imperturbable way he had approached a brutal murder. "He may seem like a thinking machine, but he is capable of great depth of feeling. When he learned that my wife was dead—that day he appeared again, like a magician's trick, after his supposed death at Reichenbach Falls—you cannot imagine his kindness and compassion, Miss Jekyll. I assure you, there is more to him than what you see on the surface." But would she ever see below that surface?

"I have found something." Mary turned around to see Justine standing at the door to Dr. Watson's room. "Come look."

Unlike the parlor, Watson's bedroom was as neat as a pin, with a narrow cot in one corner, a wardrobe and chest of drawers, and a desk under the window. Everything was folded and tucked away. A wool blanket at the foot of the bed and a pair of boots by the door waited for when their master might need them. Of course, he had once been a soldier. It made sense that he would keep his personal space tidy.

"Here, on the desk," said Justine. She pointed to the leather blotter—one of the flat kind that covered the desk, rather than a handheld device. The sheet of blotting paper on top was relatively new—there were few marks. But close to one corner was what looked like a list of addresses. Watson's handwriting was neat, and even backward, Mary could make them out.

"There's a date on top," she said. "September 21, a little more than a week ago. Thank goodness Dr. Watson is used to recording Mr. Holmes's cases so meticulously. He must have written this just before he disappeared. Justine, would you mind copying these down? I'd like to look in Mr. Holmes's room as well."

Mr. Holmes's room! It was so easy to say, but she put her hand on his door with some trepidation. She had never, of course, been in either of the bedrooms before. Dr. Watson's was impersonal enough that she had felt no compunction in entering. But Sherlock's room . . .

She was right to have worried. Everything in that room—the violin in the armchair by the window, the pipe on the bedside table, the slippers under the bed, their heels worn down, spoke of him. The room was a mess. An infernal mess, Mrs. Hudson would probably have called it.

It felt so strange searching through his personal possessions! Looking through the bedside table drawer and in the pockets of his waistcoats and suit jackets in the wardrobe, which was identical to the one in Dr. Watson's room. She felt as though she were invading his privacy. Would he be angry with her when they met again? But first she had to make sure they would meet again, and that meant finding him. Which meant looking everywhere she could think of for clues as to where he might be.

Here, too, there was a desk, but it contained nothing enlightening. The blotting paper was crisscrossed with fragments of sentences, but none of them seemed to have any bearing on this case. On one corner of the desk was a sheaf of papers entitled *Notes for Mary*, but they had to do exclusively with ears. Was that, after all, what she meant to him? Was her value simply as a transcribing machine? Mary felt tired and despondent. *Pull yourself together, my girl,* she thought. *It's almost lunchtime, and you're getting hungry, that's all. There's no time for thinking like that, not right now.* Would they find anything at all useful in this mess?

At last, she found something that might be of use—a card in the pocket of his greatcoat, which had been tossed onto a chair. On it was engraved: MR. MYCROFT HOLMES, THE DIOGENES CLUB, and on the back in Mr. Holmes's handwriting—she had seen it so often that she could pick it out from a hundred others, as she could pick his face out of a crowd—was written: *10 a.m. urgent.* Dr. Watson had mentioned that just before Mr. Holmes's disappearance, he had gone to meet his brother Mycroft. *Urgent*—that sounded as though he had been summoned for some reason.

"Have you found anything?" asked Justine, standing in the doorway.

"Just this." Mary held the card out to her. "I think we'll need to visit the Diogenes Club, as well as those addresses you wrote down. Do you have the list?"

Justine patted her jacket pocket.

"All right then, I think we've probably done all we can here. What worries me is that Mr. Holmes doesn't seem to have taken his clothes. I mean, as far as I can tell." She had examined his clothes thoroughly—she had opened a drawer full of socks and felt her cheeks grow red from embarrassment. And the drawer of underclothing . . . well.

> MARY: Could you please not mention to the general public that I looked through Sherlock's underclothes?

> CATHERINE: Don't worry, I'll take it out before publication.

> MARY: That's what you kept saying about the last book, but you didn't take out any of the things you promised to.

CATHERINE: Didn't I? That must simply have been an oversight on my part. I promise to this time. Cross my heart.

MARY: Thank you, Catherine. I expect you to keep that promise.

DIANA: You are *so gullible*.

They headed back to Park Terrace with Justine's list and the card in Mary's purse, as well as a basket of scones fresh from the oven, with the compliments of Mrs. Hudson to Mrs. Poole. The search had taken them longer than anticipated. By the time they returned, Mrs. Poole had already set the table for luncheon. "I thought the morning room would be best, seeing as there are only three of you," she said. "Mrs. Hudson's scones! Really, Adeline is so thoughtful. You know, she trained as a cook originally, before marrying a military man. Have you found anything—any clues, as you call them?"

Over lunch, Mary showed Mrs. Poole the list of addresses and the card they had found that morning.

"I don't know as you girls should be roaming the streets of London, going to all corners without protection of some sort," said Mrs. Poole, looking at the list of addresses and shaking her head dubiously. "Jamaica Yard, Fishmonger's Mews, Oyster Lane. What sorts of names are these? Who knows where they might be. In some disreputable part of town, like as not, inhabited by murderers and thieves."

"But that sounds exactly like the sort of place one might find kidnappers," said Mary. "After all, we're not dealing with Sunday School teachers, are we?"

Mrs. Poole said nothing more, but continued to look concerned.

"All right," said Mary after finishing her Welsh rarebit. "Here's the agenda for the afternoon: We need to go to the Magdalen Society first, to figure out if Mrs. Raymond is involved in Alice's kidnapping in any way. After that, we'll tackle Martin. These addresses may need to wait until tomorrow. We still need to figure out where they are, and I think we had better go in disguise. Agreed?"

Justine nodded, but Diana leaned back in her chair and said, "No way am I going back to the Society of Mary Blooming Magdalen. I'll go anywhere in London, but not there. You two enjoy yourselves. I've got other fish to fry."

"What sorts of fish?" asked Mary suspiciously. She did not particularly want Diana going with them—there would be no locks to pick at the Magdalen Society, and she did not want her quarreling with Mrs. Raymond. They had not parted on amicable terms. But she also worried about leaving Diana behind. What sort of mischief could she get into?

> DIANA: Not amicable! That bloody bitch—

> ALICE: Remember that you're talking about my
> mother.

"I'm going to teach Archie a new card game," said Diana. She looked at Justine's plate. "Are you going to finish that, or can I have it?"

"I do not think he likes being called Archie," said Justine. She placed her knife and fork neatly on the side of her plate, then put her napkin on the table. She had eaten only half her lunch. "Mary, I'll go change my clothes now. I think they would not let me into the Magdalen Society dressed like this! I shall have to once again be an exceptionally tall woman." She smiled wanly, as though she had made a joke—and she probably had. Justine's jokes were seldom actually funny.

"That's why I call him that," said Diana, grinning. "To annoy him! Seriously, if you're not going to eat anymore . . ."

Mary just sighed and rose. Well, Mrs. Poole would have to deal with Diana that afternoon. She was not at all sorry to relinquish the responsibility for a while. What would they find at the Magdalen Society? She remembered the dour stone edifice in which magdalenes—reformed prostitutes—in gray gowns and white caps sat in silent rows, endlessly sewing linens for wealthy patrons. She had no desire to enter its cold gray halls again, and she was certainly not looking forward to another meeting with Mrs. Raymond.

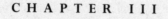

# CHAPTER III

## *Adventures in Soho*

Mary rang the bell on the gray stone wall. The sound echoed around the forbidding courtyard of the Magdalen Society. It had not changed at all since the last time she had seen it—how long ago was that now? Four months? No, five. Not quite six. Had it truly been such a short time ago that she had found Diana, and then Beatrice, Catherine, and Justine? It seemed as though she had known them much longer than that. Through the gate, she could see that the courtyard was still bare, except for a row of dark green yews by the stone wall of the building, and the building itself still looked as though it had come out of a novel by Sir Walter Scott.

"Should we ring again?" asked Justine. For the first time in a month, she was attired in women's clothes. They felt strange—not uncomfortable, but as though she could no longer move freely and easily about in the world. She was aware of restrictions, limitations. Perhaps Beatrice was right, and our clothing did impact the way we thought and felt. And yet, there was a beauty to women's garments that was lacking in modern men's clothes. As a painter, she could see that. It was all rather confusing.

Mary raised her hand to ring again, but a woman—or rather a girl, because she looked only fifteen or sixteen—rushed out from the shadowy arched doorway of the building. She was halfway to the gate when the white cap on her head fell off and began rolling over the flagstones. Quickly, as though in a panic, she picked it up, put it back on her head, and ran the rest of the way, with one hand on top of her head to hold it on and another under her chin, clutching the ribbons. Surely it would have made more sense to stop and tie it? Mary remembered the sharp-featured and sharp-tongued Sister Margaret who had opened the gate for them last time. This was certainly a very different sort of greeting!

"I'm so sorry," said the girl, panting, with one hand on her side. "I'm supposed to be the porter today, but I was in the lavatory, and I didn't hear the bell until one of the other girls shouted. I came as quickly as I could. McTavish would be so angry if she knew I was away from my post! You must be—looking for linen to purchase? Or perhaps you wish to make a donation?" She looked at them curiously, as though wondering what two ladies were doing here. They were not fancily dressed, but nevertheless clearly ladies, and with these philanthropic young women you could never quite tell how wealthy they were by their clothes.

"Yes, that's exactly right," said Mary. "We're considering a donation, but we would like to make certain that your organization is a worthy cause. Could you please tell the director that a Miss Jenks and a Miss Frank would like to see her?"

She had been wondering exactly how they would get in to see Mrs. Raymond. Well, this seemed as good a way as any! She hated lying, of course, but she thought it was justified under the circumstances.

"Follow me," said the girl, unlocking the gate. "My name is Doris. I've been here six months. The society has become like a second home to me. At first I thought it was terribly gloomy, and the food bland though plentiful, but it's been so much more jolly in the last few weeks."

Mary looked at Justine and shrugged. How anyone could describe the Magdalen Society as jolly, she did not know!

They crossed the courtyard behind Doris. There was

the ivy-covered wall that Diana used to climb when she was a resident—

DIANA: A prisoner, you mean!

—of the Magdalen Society. It was the same wall Catherine had climbed down the night she learned that Hyde was involved with the Whitechapel Murders. That night Alice had been kidnapped for the first time, drugged by Mrs. Raymond, and taken away by Hyde to the warehouse by the Thames.

CATHERINE: You do seem to have a habit of being kidnapped, don't you?

ALICE: I've been kidnapped exactly twice! I would not call that a habit. And the first time was purely a coincidence—I was following you and trying to find out who you were, since you were clearly in disguise. It had nothing to do with me.

CATHERINE: Well, try not to be kidnapped again, if you can help it.

Once again, they stepped through the forbidding doorway of that gothic edifice. When they were inside, Mary was startled to hear . . . was that laughter?

"What in the world?" she said.

"Oh, them's just the girls in the workrooms," said Doris. "You see, miss, we sew linens of all sorts here—bed linens, linens for the kitchen, and even children's clothes, leastways the simple things like smocks. Come this way. The director's office is up the stairs, on the second floor."

"Did you not say the society was very strict?" whispered Justine as they followed Doris up the stairs.

She had, and it had been, the last time Mary was here. But now they passed a group of women sitting on the stairs—just sitting and talking, as though they hadn't a care in the world. Several of them were wearing the regulation white caps, but the rest had taken theirs off.

"The director will be mad if she sees you sitting here chatting and not working," said Doris with a frown.

"Then let her High and Mightiness be mad!" said one of them, who threw back her head and laughed. She was still young, with pretty blond ringlets, but was missing several teeth.

Doris shook her head. "They ought to treat her with more respect, they really ought to. After all, someone has to run this place and get donations, and arrange for us to sell our work. She tries to be strict, but the girls ain't scared of her, as you can see. Though they're good girls really, and they don't break too many rules. No sneaking gentlemen visitors in or anything like that, I assure you! Just a bit of gin now and then, and cigarettes, and maybe a card game for pennies—all in fun. I hope I'm not shocking you, miss. Not so as you'll decide not to donate, anyway. We're all liable to temptation, and all sinners in our own way, ain't we? I assure you that we truly repent our old profession, and would much rather be here than out on the streets!"

Mary did not quite know what to say to this, but now they were at the door of the director's office. She steeled herself to meet Mrs. Raymond once again.

Doris knocked on the door, was answered with a "Come in!," and pushed it open.

"A Miss Jenks and a Miss Frank here to see you," she said. "They want to donate to the institution." She let them through, then closed the door again behind them.

The director rose from her desk, smiled graciously, and walked out from behind the desk toward them. "Miss Jenks and Miss Frank, is it? If you'll just take a seat—*You!*" The exclamation sounded like a cork popping from a bottle. "What in blazes—I mean, what in the world are you doing back here?"

The director was dressed like Mrs. Raymond, in a plain gray merino, with a chatelaine at her waist. Her hair was pulled back into a tight and very respectable bun at the back of her head, so tight that it stretched her skin a little. But it was not Mrs. Raymond.

"Sister Margaret!" said Mary. "Are you—"

"You will please address me as Matron McTavish," said the woman who had been Sister Margaret. "Mrs. Raymond, my predecessor, resigned abruptly almost a month ago, causing no end of trouble and considerable inconvenience to me. The trustees asked me to step into her place temporarily, until a new director can be found. Of course, I told them I would help in any way I could." Miss McTavish, as we must now call her, looked both aggrieved and gratified, as though the thought of being inconvenienced rather pleased her. "But your name isn't Jenks," she said, looking at Mary suspiciously. "What was it now?"

"Doris must have misheard our names," said Mary. "I'm Mary Jekyll, and this is Justine Frankenstein." Goodness, she was getting just as bad as Diana, with all these lies! "We most particularly want to speak with Mrs. Raymond. If you have any idea where she might have gone—"

"I haven't the faintest," said Miss McTavish coldly. "She left without giving notice or leaving a forwarding address. So you see, I cannot help you at all." She smiled tightly, with pursed lips, as though not being able to help was the first thing that had given her pleasure all day. "Now, I have a great deal of work to do."

"Thank you," said Mary, mentally adding *for nothing*. "Come on, Justine. I don't think we need trouble Matron McTavish further."

As soon as they had left the director's office, they saw Doris, halfway down the hall, talking to another of the magdalenes—a girl, short and slight—in a gray dress. As Mary approached, the girl turned to her.

"Miss Jekyll? Do you remember me?"

She was not a girl after all—her face was marked by fine lines, and she had obviously once had smallpox. But she had a pair of sharp, clever brown eyes.

"Kate Bright-Eyes!" said Mary. "What in the world are you doing here? This is my friend Justine." She turned to Justine and continued, "Kate was a friend of Molly Keane's. You remember, she helped Catherine make herself up to infiltrate—well, this place, when we were investigating the Whitechapel Murders." Kate looked almost the same as the last time Mary had seen her, except of course for the absence of rouge and whatever it was that certain women—those in Kate's profession—used to blacken their eyelashes. Her eyes were all the more birdlike without it.

"It's a pleasure to meet you, Miss Bright-Eyes," said Justine, offering her hand.

Kate shook it vigorously. "It's a pity the Whitechapel Murders were never solved, ain't it? Though I'm sure you and Mr. Holmes tried hard enough. I'm not blaming you, don't think I am."

"But they were solved," said Mary. "I mean—we found out who did it, but he—well, he escaped to the continent, so he could not be brought to justice. And he died there—a painful death, I assure you. As painful as the deaths he brought on all those poor girls." She remembered Adam Frankenstein in that bare room, on that small bed, dying of his burn wounds. Of course, Hyde had not been punished—he was still out there somewhere, free to continue his nefarious career. Well, if there was any justice in the universe, he would get his own comeuppance, someday.

"And it wasn't in the papers?" said Kate. "Well, he must have been someone high and mighty, to keep it all so quiet. Connected to the Royal Family, maybe? But whoever he was, I'm glad he got what was coming to him. Anyone who did what he did to Molly deserves to rot in Hell. Talking about high and mighty, Doris tells me you're looking for Mrs. Raymond."

Mary looked at her, startled. "How did you know——"

"Keyhole," said Doris. "Not very proper, I know, and my mum would scold me about it, but it's important for us to know what's going on around here, so we take turns eavesdropping. No one dared, while Mrs. Raymond was here—she always seemed to know what we were up to, I don't know how. She must of had eyes in the back of her head. But McTavish doesn't notice half of what goes on."

"A completely necessary and understandable practice," said Mary. "And yes, we are looking for information on Mrs. Raymond. Do you happen to know——"

"Not here in the hall," said Kate. "Come on, follow me."

She led them to a small room that was apparently used for storing the products made by the Magdalen Society, because there were shelves stocked with tea towels, aprons, and children's smocks. Through a narrow window, Mary could look down to a dismal garden behind the building, with a few privets and an unkempt lawn.

"This is all I know, and it ain't much," said Kate. "Maybe Doris knows more—she's been here longer than I have. I came because I caught the influenza, and when I got out of St. Bartholomew's, I was too sick and tired to work—say what you will about this place, they do give you hot meals you don't have to pay for! Anyway, about a week after Mrs. Raymond admitted me, we were told she was gone, and Sister Margaret—Matron McTavish, as she insists on being called—was in charge. There were plenty of rumors going around, I assure you—like that she wasn't Mrs. Raymond after all, but a Mrs. Herbert. Do you remember the Herbert murder case? It was more than ten years ago—Mrs. Herbert was accused of murdering her husband, although they never could figure out how she done it, so she was acquitted for lack of evidence. They say she killed him to be with her lover!"

"The trustees found out about it—at least, that's what we think—and she had to go," said Doris. "Agnes insists that one night, about a week before Mrs. Raymond disappeared, she saw a man in her office. He was tall, with dark hair. Maybe that was her lover, come back for her? Or maybe he was blackmailing her and she refused to pay up? Then he told the trustees. . . ."

"Agnes has the most vivid imagination," said Kate, shaking her head. "What she probably saw was the shadow of a hatstand—if anything at all! Anyway, some say Mrs. Raymond was the one who wanted to leave—the trustees were fair begging her to stay. Either way, one morning she was gone, and nothing has been heard of her since."

"When was this?" asked Mary. "When did she disappear?"

"Around the end of August," said Doris. "I'm sorry, miss, I wish we had more information for you. The truth is, no one really knows where she went, or what became of her."

Mary sighed. Rumor and conjecture, that was all. Well, at least it was something! Mrs. Raymond had vanished about a month before Alice was kidnapped. Could the two disappearances be connected? She had no idea.

"Thank you both," she said. "And Kate, if you ever need help, you know that you can come to us: 11 Park Terrace in Marylebone. If we're not at home, tell Mrs. Poole who you are, and she'll admit you." She held out her hand, which had a shilling in it.

"That's very good of you, miss," said Kate, taking the shilling and then pressing her hand.

"Particularly if you need medicine," said Justine. "Beatrice cannot cure the influenza, but her plants can help you recover from it sooner. She's away from home, but should be back in a few days. Her medicines are as effective as anything you'll receive at St. Bartholomew's."

> BEATRICE: I am so thankful to Dr. Watson for his
> system of rubber tubes. Without it, my plants
> would certainly have perished while I was away.
> Even the datura, which I was so worried about,
> survived magnificently. While our activities as the
> Athena Club are important, it is also important
> that I supply the hospital from my pharmacopeia.

> CATHERINE: I'm trying to tell an adventure story, and
> you're talking about an irrigation system?

With another shilling for Doris, Mary bade them farewell, grateful for the information they had provided, although wondering if it truly helped them at all. Once she and Justine were walking away from the Society of St. Mary Magdalen along the streets of Soho, she said, "If Mrs. Raymond was Mrs. Herbert, maybe she's not the woman we're looking for after all. If Raymond was simply an assumed identity, she may have nothing to do with Dr. Raymond or his experiment. The name may simply be a coincidence. . . . After all, there are plenty of Raymonds in London!"

"Could we find out more about this murder?" asked Justine. "Frau Gottleib said she did not believe in coincidence. I would not discount the role of chance in human affairs—however, in a situation as tangled as this one . . ."

"There should be more information in Mr. Holmes's files," said Mary. "He's cataloged the details of every murder in London since he became a consulting detective—and many before that!

If it's not there, we might have to ask Inspector Lestrade." She shuddered.

"Where to now?" asked Justine. "Shall we proceed to the boardinghouse where the performers of Lorenzo's circus are staying? Although as I told you, I cannot believe that Martin would hurt or even frighten Alice in any way."

Mary nodded. She did not share Justine's confidence in the Marvelous Mesmerist.

They were both tired, and walked without speaking. Had they really arrived home only yesterday? Mary felt as though she had never left the fog and grime of London. The bright sunlight of Vienna, the pink and green and ocher buildings of Budapest, seemed like a dream, rather than things she had actually seen for herself. How quickly the human mind adjusted to new circumstances! Or, in this case, old ones. She was glad to be back, but she wished they could have had some rest, some time to spend at home in Park Terrace, before starting on yet another adventure. If only their friends were not in peril. . . .

On Whitechapel High Street, they caught an omnibus toward Clerkenwell. The boardinghouse was not difficult to find, but when Justine asked for Martin, the landlady, who smelled of cabbages, told them that he had moved out a week and a half ago. There were still circus performers staying at the boardinghouse, but they did not have much more information. Maisie the bareback rider told Justine that he had not said much about where he was going. "He said he'd found a better place, and didn't want to be a circus mesmerist anymore. And then he was gone, just like that." She snapped her fingers. "Do you have any news of Lorenzo? We heard the circus is doing a grand tour and making lots of money."

"Yes, how is everyone?" asked Daisie, who was Maisie's sister and also rode bareback. "I wish we could have gone with them—but you can't take the horses all that way, can you?"

Justine told them as much as she could, while Maisie regaled her with all the gossip from the circus performers who had stayed behind. She and Daisie were appearing in a horse show at the Alhambra, temporarily—it didn't pay quite as well, but then a job was a job, wasn't it, particularly in these difficult times? Mary sat on a sofa in the boardinghouse parlor, lost in thought. She interrupted their conversation once to ask if Martin was tall and had dark hair. A tall, dark man had been see in Mrs. Raymond's office. Could it have been the mesmerist? Of course Justine did not want to believe anything bad about her fellow performer, but he remained Mary's prime suspect.

"Very tall and very dark," Daisie replied. "Why, do you know him, miss?"

Mary just looked at Justine meaningfully, while Justine shook her head. Well, she might not want to admit it, but this disappearance was suspicious. Alice, Mrs. Raymond, and Marvelous Martin were all gone. That must mean something?

Half an hour later, she and Justine were once again on the streets of London, heading back toward Park Terrace.

"I suggest we stop at an ABC and have afternoon tea," said Mary. "I don't know about you, but I'm famished. Well, at least Diana had a nice, quiet day, although I'm sure she drove Mrs. Poole quite mad, what with asking for jam and teaching Archibald to gamble!" But at least Diana was out of mischief.

BEATRICE: If only there were more places like the
　　Aerated Bread Company stores, where women
　　could go by themselves for a meal or to meet
　　a friend! Where they were not liable to be
　　importuned or insulted, as in a pub.

CATHERINE: If anyone tried to importune or insult you,
　　I'm sure they would get what was coming to them!

BEATRICE: But, Cat, not all women have my natural defenses. Women ought to feel safe in public spaces, even if they are not poisonous.

CATHERINE: So you admit that being poisonous can be a good thing?

BEATRICE: Well, sometimes . . .

When Mary and Justine reached home—

DIANA: Wait a minute! You're not going to talk about what I did? It was much more important than that trip to the bloody Magdalen Society. Don't shake your head at me! You're not much of an author if you leave out the most interesting parts. Not a patch on the bloke who wrote *Varney the Vampire*, anyway.

CATHERINE: Fine, I'll write about you. Then will you go somewhere else for the afternoon? The *whole* afternoon. And don't slam the door behind you as you go out.

In a particularly disreputable part of Soho, Diana knocked on the door of a dilapidated house, *rat-a-tat-tat*, in a specific pattern.

"Who's knocking?" came the rough cry from inside.

"It's Charlie," said Charlie, who was standing slightly behind her. "I need to see Wiggins." The door opened, and a small, sharp face peered out. It belonged to a boy a little younger than Diana. His face was covered with strawberry jam.

"What the—" he said when he saw her.

"This is Diana," said Charlie. "Diana, this is Burton Minor. His older brother, Burton Major, brought him several weeks ago." Charlie looked at Burton Minor disapprovingly. "Clean yourself up, man. What sort of guard are you, looking like that?"

"Are you really Diana?" asked Burton Minor, eyes wide, the way he might have asked if she were really the Loch Ness Monster or the Feejee Mermaid.

"What do you think?" she said rudely. She had no time today for underlings. "And that's Miss Diana Hyde to you. Tell Wiggins I want to see him. *Now.*" She stepped over the threshold and into a large room with peeling wallpaper. Burton Minor retreated before her.

"He's powerful mad at you," said Charlie doubtfully when Burton Minor had turned and fled up the stairs on his errand. "He says you left without saying goodbye."

"Well, I'm back now, so he'd better get over it," said Diana. But she smiled, feeling rather pleased that Wiggins had been angry at her sudden departure. She liked making people angry—at least then they weren't so dull! Not that Wiggins was dull. Indeed, he was the least dull person she knew. Still, it was gratifying.

For a few minutes, she sauntered around that shabby room. It had a broken sofa against the far wall, with horsehair showing through the upholstery, and in one corner were a set of bowling pins and balls. Clearly someone had been bowling along the floor, because the planks were scuffed and the baseboard was marked with dents where balls had hit it. However, despite these signs of decay, there was no dust in the room, no dirt in any of the corners. The windows were covered with tattered curtains that kept a casual passerby from peering in, but they were washed. It would have been easy for Burton Minor and his ilk to keep a watch over the street through the holes in the curtains.

Burton Minor clattered back down the stairs. "All right, Mr. Wiggins will see you. He says come on up."

Diana nodded. Of course he would see her! If he had refused, she would soon enough have given him what for.

She followed Burton Minor up the narrow staircase. On the second floor there were two doors opening from the hall. Neatly painted on one were the words:

MR. WIGGINS

OFFICE

The other, she knew, was a sort of storage room. Wiggins himself had given her the grand tour the day Charlie had first brought her here. "Wiggins wants to meet you," he had told her. "And I think you should get to know the boys."

She remembered that first day—how they had all looked at her, either suspiciously or with an expression of incredulity. What in the world had Charlie told them about her? He would not say.

Wiggins' office had been filled with boys of all ages from nine—which was the youngest you were allowed to join—up to fifteen. Wiggins himself had been seated behind a large desk. He had risen in a casual way she found insulting and had made her a mocking bow. Charlie had said, as politely as though he were addressing the blooming aristocracy, "Miss Hyde, may I introduce Mr. Bill Wiggins? Wiggins, this is Miss Diana Hyde."

*Rat-a-tat-tat.* It was the same knock, executed by the fist of Burton Minor on the office door.

The door was opened from within.

"Hallo, Dennys," said Diana to the freckle-faced boy holding open the door as she passed inside. He looked at her with wide, innocent blue eyes, as though butter would not melt in his mouth. Those blue eyes had once gotten him out of a pickpocketing charge—the woman who had accused him, a grocer's widow, had decided he was a poor orphan who did not know better but could be taught, so instead of being transported to Australia, he had been adopted. Officially, he worked as a grocer's clerk. Unofficially, he was Wiggins' right-hand man.

Which probably made Buster his left-hand man? He was standing behind Wiggins, leaning against a windowsill. Unlike slim, fair, energetic Dennys, Buster was a big boy, fully grown despite his fourteen years. He looked slow and a little stupid, but he was in fact remarkably quick, both in movement and intellect. Diana reflected once again on the advantage it gave you to not look like what you were. That was the benefit of being a girl. If you dressed right and lowered your eyes convincingly, no one ever suspected you of anything.

She had demonstrated that, the first day she had come here.

"If you'll forgive me asking, *Miss* Hyde, why should we pay any attention to you?" Wiggins had asked her, with a smirk on his face. "From the way Charlie described you, I expected you to be six feet tall, and as strong as an ox. You're nothing but a little girl."

Five minutes later, she had been standing behind him with a knife at his throat. A roomful of Baker Street Irregulars had looked at her with equal parts horror and trepidation. She had shown them, all right! After that, they had treated her with respect.

Now, the office was empty except for Wiggins and his lieutenants. Wiggins himself was sitting behind his desk, leaning back in his chair with his feet up, crossed at the ankles. His face was sullen, his brows drawn together in a frown. Had his father really been a Lascar pirate, and his mother a governess who had run away to sea for love of him? Or was that more of the legend of Bill Wiggins? He did not look quite English—more like a distillation of the various populations of the East End, wherever they originated. He was the oldest of the Baker Street Irregulars, and their leader. Every one of them would have died for him, which would have been preferable to disappointing him. He was not as tall as Buster, nor as handsome as Dennys, but there was something about him that compelled attention and loyalty. Not from Diana, of course! She had no loyalty, unless it was to the Athena Club and its members. Justine was prime, and Catherine had some admirable qualities. Beatrice was annoying, but at least she could poison people. And Mary—well, Mary was a pill and a sourpuss, that was all. But at least they were family.

Wiggins glared at her, and for a moment it looked as though he would not budge from his chair.

Diana walked up to his desk and stood in front of it, feet planted, hands in her trouser pockets. "Hallo, Bill," she said.

He looked at her for a moment, then put his feet on the floor, stood up, and said, "So you're back, are you?"

"I am, and I need your help."

He crossed his arms. There was that smirk again! "Gracious, Miss Hyde! Admitting that you need our help?"

She shrugged. "Why shouldn't I?"

He scowled again and looked at the floor. "You prefer to play a lone hand, or so I noticed."

She frowned. Oh, so he was going to be like that, was he? As though he had a right to be angry with her. Well, he didn't. She didn't answer to Bill Wiggins. "I get it. You're mad I didn't tell you I was going to Europe. Well, I had to make my plans pretty damn quick—I didn't even pack! Anyway, why should I tell you anything? I'm not Buster, here, to go where you want me to, or Dennys, to bring you information. Where do you get off—"

"Boys, get out," said Wiggins, waving his hand in a motion of dismissal. "This is between me and Diana." Reluctantly, Charlie and the others filed out of the room. As he closed the door behind him, Charlie gave her a last, worried glance.

"Now what?" She glared at him. "If you're going to try to lecture me, Bill Wiggins, I'll hit you so hard . . ."

"All right! All right!" Wiggins raised his hands in front of his face, as though fending off blows. "You've made your point. Don't look at me like that—"

"Like what?" Diana put her hands on her hips. What *look* was he talking about?

"Like you're going to kill me with your eyes." He glanced at her ruefully. "I was just worried about you, that's all. Charlie said you'd disappeared, but he didn't know where—finally your housekeeper told him you'd run away to Europe. That's all I—all we knew. Do you blame me for worrying?"

"Yes." She put her hands back in her pockets and paced around the room, stomping her feet a little as she spoke. "Because it means you think I can't take care of myself. I can take care of myself perfectly well, Bill Wiggins, and you know it. I forbid you to worry about me!" *I forbid you*—she liked the way that had come out. It sounded rather grand.

"Forbid me! You can't forbid me from doing anything." He looked at her from beneath lowered brows. Oh, didn't he look angry! Like a thundercloud. She enjoyed making him angry.

"And you can't forbid me from doing anything either. I'm not one of your Baker Street boys. You may be the high and mighty Mr. Wiggins to them, but you're nothing to me!"

"Nothing, Diana?" Now he looked pained. "Am I really nothing to you?"

If she were Mary, she would have felt guilty. If she were Beatrice, she would have attempted to comfort him. But she was Diana, so she felt a deep sense of satisfaction.

"Well, not nothing. I've come for your help, haven't I? But then you go on about how I left without telling you, as though I was supposed to report to you—I don't report to anyone, and don't you forget it!"

He looked down at the floor sheepishly. "All right, Diana. You don't have to go on and on. What do you need help with? You know I'll help you any way I can."

"I don't know, unless you tell me! I'm not Dr. Freud, am I? Here——" She reached into the inside pocket of her jacket and pulled out a piece of paper. "I need to know what these are."

It was the list Mary had so carefully locked into her mother's desk that morning.

MARY: Don't you leave *anything* alone?

DIANA: If you want me to leave something alone,
         don't put it in a locked desk, where it's just lying
         for me to take!

Wiggins looked at it for a moment. "I think these are in Limehouse, but Cartwright will know for sure." He looked at her more gently than he had so far. "Are we friends again, Diana?"

"Speak for yourself. I was never not friends. You're the one who's been kicking up a fuss." She looked at him scornfully for a moment. Really, what was wrong with boys? If she had been given a choice, she might have preferred to be one herself. Life was so much easier as a boy! No one telling you to behave yourself, or forbidding you from going out at night, or climbing trees, or getting into any kind of mischief. And it seemed as though everything the least bit fun in the world counted as mischief. But then, boys were so emotional! Even Wiggins, with all this fuss about her going on a trip . . .

"All right, I'm sorry. I won't do it again. Apology accepted?" He held out his hand.

She shook it a little too hard, to show that she was still angry with him. Seriously, she had no time for this! "Accepted. Now, those addresses? I want to get home before Mary does." Wiggins' fussing was annoying, but Mary's was going to be ten times worse. She didn't particularly feel like facing the wrath of Mary today.

MARY: My wrath! When do I ever get wrathful?

CATHERINE: It's your particular kind of wrath. You don't shout—you just get precise and icy.

MARY: That's not wrath. I don't think that counts as wrath.

DIANA: It's Mary wrath. Your particular kind, as Cat said. Not that I'm scared of it, mind you. But it's worse than being shouted at.

MARY: I have no idea what either of you are talking about. Alice, am I ever wrathful?

ALICE: Well, yes, actually. If you don't mind my saying so, miss. When you learned what the Order of the Golden Dawn had done to me and Mr. Holmes—

CATHERINE: Oh no, you don't! We have chapters to go before you can talk about that. Really, not one of you has any idea of narrative timing.

MARY: And I think you can stop calling me miss now, Alice.

ALICE: Oh, right. Sometimes I forget. Sorry, miss—I mean Mary.

Wiggins opened the door. "Buster, can you tell Cartwright to come down? I want him to look at something."

Through the doorway, Diana could see Buster, Dennys, and Charlie looking in apprehensively. What did they think, that she and Wiggins might have had some sort of fight? As though he would try anything so stupid!

A moment later, Cartwright clattered down the steps from the third floor. He was a small boy with spectacles and tangled hair.

"Cartwright! Jam on your nose. What have you been doing, man? You look like a circus clown." Wiggins sounded disapproving.

Cartwright wiped his nose with his sleeve. "Sorry, Mr. Wiggins," he said with consternation. "Me and the boys upstairs were having our tea."

"Well, I want you to identify these addresses. You can take them upstairs and consult the maps if you like."

Cartwright glanced down the list. "There's no need, sir. I know these right enough. They're in Limehouse, down by the docks. They're all opium dens. Oh, they don't advertise themselves that way—some of them look like warehouses or regular shops, in front. But you go inside, and they're opium dens right enough."

Diana grinned. "Well, well. So there's where Dr. Watson was searching for the great detective! And him so prim and proper all the time. I bet we'll find him in one of those places, smoking an opium pipe. Wait until Mary hears about this!"

Wiggins looked at her with alarm. "Is that what this is about? If you'd told me you were looking for Mr. Holmes, I would have ripped this list up as soon as looking at it. He said he was going to disappear for a while, and gave us instructions not to look for him, no matter who asked—not even Dr. Watson! He said it was too important, and too dangerous. Diana, give me that list!"

"Not on your life!" said Diana, scrunching the piece of paper up into a ball and putting it in her mouth. "You try to get it from me, Bill Wiggins, and I'll skewer you until you scream like a pig, see if I don't!" Her little knife was already in her hand. She had the wall to her back, and she would die, or more likely kill him, rather than give it up. Of course, the addresses were still on the blotter, and Justine could copy them again—but it was the principle of the thing. Wiggins was not going to tell her what to do, nohow!

> JUSTINE: Ah, that is why the paper was so damp when you showed it to us later! It is good that I wrote the list in pencil rather than ink.

> MARY: Why must you always do things in the most disgusting way imaginable?

Fifteen minutes later, Diana sauntered back through the streets of Soho with Charlie by her side. In her pocket was the list of addresses and Cartwright's handwritten instructions for how to get to them, together with a map he had marked with red crosses. She could be very persuasive when she chose, even with someone as pigheaded as Wiggins. Mary was Mr. Holmes's personal assistant—whatever rules applied to the Baker Street Irregulars didn't apply to her, did they? As Wiggins had finally conceded, although Mr. Holmes had told the boys not to follow him, he had not said anything about the Athena Club—and could Diana put the knife down now please? It was tickling his throat.

Mary would be so impressed! Of course, Mary was never sufficiently impressed by her cleverness.

"Do you want to hear about how I rescued Lucinda Van Helsing from an insane asylum?" she said to Charlie.

His look of admiration and prompt "Cor, did you really?" was all she could ask for.

She did not know, she could not know, that at no great distance from her, in the tangled streets of Soho, Alice was sitting on a cellar floor, gnawing on a crust of bread and drinking a cup of weak tea. The dim light of a single lantern shone on the shackle around her ankle and the chain by which it was affixed to the wall.

What was that sound? Footsteps approaching along the corridor! She stuffed the bread into her mouth, chewing as quickly as she could so she would not have to taste it, and gulped down the tea. Then she crawled back to the wall, beside the thin mattress she had been sleeping on, and put her arms around her knees. Having the wall at her back gave her no particular protection, but it made her feel safer.

The footsteps stopped right in front of her prison door—they must be coming for her again. Twice now she had refused to help them. The key turned in the lock. She wondered what they would do to her if she refused a third time.

# CHAPTER IV

## The Order of the Golden Dawn

The cellar door opened with its customary creak. Mrs. Raymond entered. Alice expected her to be followed by the man who called himself Professor Moriarty. She had first seen the professor on the night she had been woken by a sound and a light in her bedroom, the night a piece of cloth saturated with some pungent liquid had been held against her nose until she had passed out.

She had woken here, in this cellar, still in her nightgown, already chained to the wall. She had a mattress on the floor to lie on, a scratchy wool blanket to cover herself with, and a chamber pot in one corner that she could just get to, chained as she was. Light came from a single lantern hanging on the wall that was periodically refilled with kerosene by the woman who brought her food. The streaks of soot on the walls, and on her bare feet, indicated that this had once been a coal cellar. She was not sure how long she had been in this place, without a window to tell her when it was day and night.

Periodically the woman brought her porridge and tea for what she assumed was breakfast, then bread and a thin stew, with scraps of meat in it, for a dinner of sorts, again with tea. It was weak tea, without milk or sugar, but Alice drank it eagerly enough. Once, the woman had brought a slice of apple tart, and Alice had almost cried—it tasted like Mrs. Poole's apple tart, although with walnuts in it, and Mrs. Poole would never have used walnuts. How it made her long for the house at

Park Terrace! She might only be the kitchen maid, but it was still her home.

Several times, she had tried talking to the woman, who was dressed like a respectable domestic: a housekeeper, or perhaps a superior housemaid. But the woman had simply shaken her head. Once, she had said, "No Anglich," with an apologetic smile. It was obvious that she was a foreigner of some sort. Once she had set down Alice's food, she usually scurried away as quickly as she could. She had a frightened look in her eyes.

Alice's only other visitors had been Mrs. Raymond and Professor Moriarty. Twice they had come. Twice, the professor had said the same thing: "If you will help us in our endeavor, Lydia, all this will be over—you will join us upstairs, as a member of our company. Show me that you are your mother's daughter." Was Mrs. Raymond truly her mother, as she claimed? She had demonstrated her own mesmeric powers, dissipating Alice's illusions as though they were smoke. But would a mother treat her daughter like this?

Lydia Raymond. That was, evidently, her name—the one she had been christened with. That was who they wanted her to be. Well, she was *not* Lydia Raymond, she would never be Lydia Raymond, no matter how they tortured her—although so far there had been no actual torture, only hours and hours of tedium and the weight of the shackle and chain. In the books Alice liked to read, printed on cheap paper and sold for only a penny at newspaper stalls, beautiful young girls were frequently captured and imprisoned. Mrs. Poole often told her to stop reading such nonsense. "They are nothing at all like real life," Mrs. Poole said, and Alice had to admit that Mrs. Poole was right. Being kidnapped was neither as exciting nor as terrifying as those books made out, but considerably more boring and painful. She was so tired of sitting all day or pacing in the short circuit the chain allowed her! Also, she felt dirty all over. And she smelled.

To amuse herself, she created small illusions—sometimes she sat in a forest grove, with a stream running through it. She could hear the wind in the trees above her, and the notes of bird-song dropping down like rain. It reminded her of the walks in Regent's Park. Sometimes she sat in a palace out of a fairy tale, with windows overlooking a garden, and delicate painted furniture scattered about, and a chandelier overhead, blazing with a hundred candles. That was inspired by a theatrical production of *Cinderella, or the Little Glass Slipper* that Mrs. Poole had taken her to at a theater in the West End. "I don't hold with theater in a general way," Mrs. Poole had said. "But there's no harm in Shakespeare or fairy stories, even for a girl like you, Alice." Once, she had tried to re-create the kitchen at 11 Park Terrace, with its black iron stove, the long table on which Mrs. Poole rolled out pastry, the capacious sink . . . but the sight of it had made her so sad that she had allowed the mesmerical waves to dissipate. It was better, after all, not to think too much of home.

What must Mrs. Poole think of her disappearance? She had disappeared once before—would Mrs. Poole assume she had run away? And what about Miss Mary, so far away in Europe? Would she be angry that Alice had left without giving notice?

That was another way in which her penny tomes were not particularly accurate. There would be no handsome young hero coming to rescue her! She must figure out how to rescue herself.

She had decided that when she next saw Professor Moriarty, she would agree to help him with whatever he was planning. It would be a lie, of course—she had no intention of helping him. But at least it would get her out of this cellar, and then she could get a better sense of what this was all about and why they had kidnapped her. Surely that was what Mary would do?

But this time it was not the professor who entered the room. Instead, accompanying Mrs. Raymond was a woman—tall and very beautiful, with a pale face and masses of black hair piled on top of her head in the most fashionable style. She was wearing a black walking suit and still had a hat pinned to her coiffure, as though she had just arrived and not yet taken it off. The feathers curled down and almost touched her cheek. In one hand she was still holding a pair of gloves.

"Oh, for goodness' sake!" she said. "What were the two of you thinking? I would expect this sort of thing from Moriarty, but you should know better, Helen. Your own daughter!"

She strode across the cellar to Alice, who could not help scurrying back against the wall—not so much from fear as from surprise.

"My dear Lydia, I do apologize. If I had been here, you would never have been treated so shamefully. Come, show me your ankle. Shackled! How ridiculous and unnecessary. Here, let me unlock it."

With a key she was holding in her slender, manicured hand, she unlocked the shackle from Alice's ankle.

Oh, how good it felt to have that weight off! Her ankle itched terribly. There were red marks all around it where the skin was rubbed raw.

"No, don't scratch," said the woman. "I'll put some cold cream on it. Come, my dear. Can you stand up? You must be so stiff!"

Mrs. Raymond frowned. "I assure you, Margaret, the intent was not to harm her. We were simply trying to convince——"

"And you thought this was the way to do it?" The woman, who must be named Margaret, shook her head incredulously.

Mrs. Raymond looked disapproving. "Lydia, this is Miss Margaret Trelawny. Evidently, she believes I have mistreated you. Well then, do whatever she directs. I am not used to having my actions questioned, but if she believes this is the wrong way to proceed, we shall try her way. Go on, Margaret—I will follow you. We shall see if you get better results than I have!"

Miss Trelawny smiled. "You are all vinegar, my dear Helen. I believe in the judicious application of honey."

Alice looked at the two of them—Mrs. Raymond in her gray dress, with her gray hair up in a net, looking as grim as always, and the woman she had called Margaret Trelawny, who looked as though she had stepped out of a fashion magazine. Who was she, and why was she involved with Mrs. Raymond and the professor? But there was no time for such questions now, for Miss Trelawny had taken her hand and said, "Come on. I'm going to doctor that ankle, then take you upstairs."

Since she had woken up in the coal cellar, Alice had wondered where she was. Still in London, she supposed—why would Mrs. Raymond and the professor want to transport her elsewhere? But of course she had not known for certain.

As soon as Miss Trelawny pulled her out of the room in which she had been confined, she thought, *I've been here before.* She recognized the long hallway with its half-moon windows at both ends. On one side would be a large kitchen, on the other a butler's pantry. In the kitchen would be two dumbwaiters that ascended to the rooms above. She knew because she and Catherine had used them to listen in on a conversation between Dr. Seward, his associate Dr. Raymond, and Mr. Prendick about reestablishing the English branch of the Alchemical Society. Could this be the same house? Or did it just resemble that one? After all, houses in certain parts of London were much alike.

Miss Trelawny pulled her down the hall and into a kitchen. The woman who had brought Alice's food looked up from her cooking, startled. A man in a suit, who was sitting at the table eating some bread and cheese, stood up and said something—what language was he speaking? Alice could make neither heads nor tails of it, but it was obvious, from his clothes and bearing, that he was the butler, just as it was clear, now, that the woman was both housekeeper and cook. *"Setzen Sie sich, Mandelbaum, setzen Sie sich,"* said Miss Trelawny. The man nodded, then sat and continued his meal, looking at them curiously from under thick eyebrows.

"Sit here," she said to Alice, pulling out one of the kitchen chairs. "I'll ask Mrs. Mandelbaum to get our medical supplies." Then she said something to the housekeeper in what sounded like the same language, except that Mrs. Mandelbaum did not seem to understand her. The man turned to her and explained whatever it was—in the same language or another? His name must be Mandelbaum, so they were husband and wife? This was becoming very confusing. Miss Trelawny leaned down, took hold of Alice's ankle, and raised it to show the woman the bruise that the shackle had left. She mimed putting something on it.

The woman nodded, then went to one of the cabinets and pulled down a large tin box. From it, Miss Trelawny took a bottle of alcohol, a roll of linen, and a jar of cold cream. Mrs. Raymond looked on with a frown.

The alcohol stung Alice's ankle terribly, but the cold cream felt soothing going on. Once her ankle was properly bandaged, Miss Trelawny said, "All right, that's better. Come on, I'll show you to your room." Alice followed Miss Trelawny up the stairs to the ground floor, limping a little. Mrs. Raymond walked behind them, still grim and disapproving.

Yes, this was the English branch of the Alchemical Society. Alice recognized it now for certain. But how different it looked from the last time she had been here. Then, dim light had come through cracks in the boarded windows. Everything had been covered with a layer of dust. Clearly, the building had not been used in a long time. Now, sunlight filtered through the lace under-curtains, and the damask over-curtains were bright from washing. Everything had been dusted—wooden tables gleamed, and the gilding on the picture frames shone with a soft luster. They were ugly pictures, Alice decided as she followed Miss Trelawny along the front hall. Most were of men wearing wigs, presumably members of the Alchemical Society from the last century. Surely the English branch had been around that long?

The house still seemed empty, and silence reigned over all, although when they passed the entrance to the large common room, Alice could smell a cigar and hear the murmur of male voices.

As they passed, one of those male voices called out, "Miss Trelawny, is that you?"

Miss Trelawny stopped so abruptly that Alice almost bumped into her. "What does he want?" she said to Mrs. Raymond, so low that Alice could barely hear.

"It's always best to humor them," said Mrs. Raymond in the same low tones.

Miss Trelawny sighed with what seemed to be exasperation. "Come on," she said to Alice. "This won't take long, and then we'll go to your room and make sure you have a proper bath."

She took Alice's hand and pulled her into the common room. Mrs. Raymond followed behind them. Three men rose from armchairs drawn up to the fireplace, although there was no fire. One of them moved toward her.

"My dear Dr. Seward," she said, holding out her hand and shaking his when it was extended. Her voice sounded like treacle, rich and sweet. Alice looked at her, startled. She was smiling, and seemed pleased to meet him. So this was Dr. Seward, the director of the Purfleet Asylum, who had helped Professor Van Helsing perform experiments on his daughter Lucinda! And who had confined Archibald to the same coal cellar where Alice had been held captive. She looked at him with a frown. He seemed ordinary enough—of average height, with middling brown hair that was starting to recede, and a not particularly noticeable face. Strange, that evil should look so bland.

"How lovely to see you again." Miss Trelawny turned to the other two men. "Lord Godalming, a pleasure as always. And this must be your friend Mr. Morris. One cannot mistake the American adventurer." Lord Godalming bowed. He was a handsome man, with golden hair just starting to turn gray at the temples and a mustache that reminded Alice of a nailbrush. His companion was clearly Mr. Morris. So this was what Americans looked like! He had dark brown hair curling down to his shoulders, and a long mustache that made Alice think of the walrus from *Alice's Adventures in Wonderland*. His jacket and trousers were made of leather, with a leather fringe. Hanging from his waist was a long sheath—Alice could see the hilt of a knife sticking out from the top. It must be a large knife! He looked so theatrical that she felt an impulse to laugh. It did not seem a very practical outfit for walking around London. His face was brown from the sun, and his blue eyes crinkled up at the corners. It was he who had been smoking a cigar, which was now in an ashtray.

"Hello, little lady," he said to Alice. She stared at him without answering.

"This is my daughter, Lydia," said Mrs. Raymond.

Alice looked at her, startled. She had never been introduced as anyone's daughter before! But she was even more startled by Mrs. Raymond's appearance. Gone was the gray hair—now it was entirely black, piled in an elegant chignon, and her plain gray dress had become a watered silk afternoon gown. It was still gray, but with lace at the low bodice and around the cuffs. She could have been Miss Trelawny's sister!

Alice looked down at herself, ashamed of her nightgown, but she too had miraculously changed clothes. She was wearing a blue silk dress with an apron of white lawn, and on her feet were button boots. Goodness, she had never worn such an outfit in her life! The dress was far too fine for a kitchen maid, and what would she have done with such an apron? Why, it would have torn almost immediately, if she had worn it for her daily work. But none of this was real—she could still feel the wooden floor beneath her bare feet.

"It's a pleasure to meet you, Miss Raymond," said Lord Godalming, bowing to her. She could not tell whether it was a mocking bow—he seemed sincere? After all, gentlemen did bow to young ladies like Lydia Raymond. "I assume you're all here for the meeting this afternoon?"

"Of course," said Miss Trelawny. "Who else are we expecting?"

"Just Harker and Raymond," said Seward. "I don't suppose you'll have some time later for a walk? Although we are not in a prepossessing area of the city, there is a park. . . ."

Alice could not help looking at him with a startled expression. The Raymond he had mentioned must be Dr. Raymond! So he was involved with Mrs. Raymond and Moriarty. She truly was in the lion's den. Luckily, at this particular moment no one seemed to be paying attention to her.

"I'm afraid not," said Miss Trelawny. "Mrs. Raymond and I have a great deal to do—you understand, I'm sure." She smiled at him again, but Alice thought there was something dismissive in her smile. Could Dr. Seward see it? She thought not. Miss Trelawny held out her other hand to Mr. Morris, who took it in his large brown one. "It's such a pleasure to meet a man who has traveled to all corners of the earth. You must tell me more about your travels at dinner. I'll make certain we're seated together, shall I?"

Mr. Morris bowed over her hand, looking inordinately pleased, while Dr. Seward glared at him.

"Come, Lydia," said Mrs. Raymond, taking Alice's other hand and pulling her back toward the hall. She did not look like Mrs.

Raymond anymore. Should Alice still think of her as Mrs. Raymond? But she could not think of her as Mother.

She felt herself tugged between the two women. Inadvertently, she pulled Miss Trelawny along behind her.

"Must you provoke them?" Mrs. Raymond asked when they were standing in the hall again. Miss Trelawny seemed to be laughing to herself.

"Divide and conquer, my dear Helen," she responded with a smile. It was the same treacly smile she had given Dr. Seward, but now it seemed just a bit sinister. What in the world was going on in this house? Was this once again the Alchemical Society at work? It must be—after all, this was the headquarters of the society in England, and Dr. Raymond, who was expected later, had been the head of the English chapter. But what did Professor Moriarty have to do with the Alchemical Society? And who were those other men—Lord Godalming, Mr. Morris, and that other one, the Mr. Harker they had mentioned? Were they alchemists as well?

Alice was frightened, of course. But then, she had been frightened most of her life—of the bigger girls at the orphanage, who would steal food from the smaller ones because they were so hungry themselves; of Mrs. Poole finding out that she was just an orphan, rather than a respectable girl with a family in the country; of starving on the streets of London after Mary had let the servants go; of dying in the warehouse from Beatrice's poison. Fear was familiar, almost comfortable, like an old coat. And in addition to being afraid, she felt terribly curious. What was going on here? Why had she been kidnapped?

She climbed the stairs behind Miss Trelawny. The upper hall was filled with sunlight—it must be around noon. They walked down a corridor with closed doors on both sides—bedrooms, Alice remembered from the last time she had been here. Suddenly, from one of the rooms, she heard a faint groan. Which room had it been?

"Walk on, Lydia," said Mrs. Raymond in her cold tones. For a moment, Alice had stopped, and Mrs. Raymond had almost tripped over her.

Obediently, Alice—who would never, she mentally swore, think of herself as Lydia—walked on, following Miss Trelawny to the end of the corridor. There, Miss Trelawny opened the last door.

"Your room is right next to mine. If you need anything, just knock on the wall and if I'm there, I'll come right over." Miss Trelawny smiled at her, encouragingly. Then, she stepped into the room and pulled Alice along with her.

The room was not large, but light and airy, with white lace curtains. The last time Alice had seen these rooms, they had been bare, but now fresh linens had been put on the bed and there was a vase of flowers on top of a bookshelf filled with books, next to a comfortable chair for reading. A wardrobe, chest of drawers, and washstand completed the furniture of the room.

Mrs. Raymond entered behind her, walked to the wardrobe, and opened the doors. Inside were dresses, hanging in a row. She pulled out one that looked exactly like the blue dress she had conjured for Alice out of energic waves.

"I think this will do for today," she said. "I want you to look respectable for our meeting."

Alice glanced down at herself. She was once again wearing the dirty nightgown. But Mrs. Raymond still had on her gray silk dress, and her hair was still a luxuriant black. Which was the real Mrs. Raymond? Alice could see the energic waves roiling about her head—Martin had taught her how to see them. She could see them about Miss Trelawny as well, but only faintly—most people, meaning people who were not mesmerists, had waves just like that. But Mrs. Raymond—well, it had been clear from the first moment Alice had seen her in the cellar that she was a mesmerist, much stronger than Martin. There would be no fooling her with illusions.

"There is a bathroom at the end of the hall," said Miss Trelawny. "I'll have Gitla bring up hot water and towels. She'll take you there so you can bathe. And then I want you to get dressed in that pretty dress Helen—your mother—has chosen for you. You can do that, can't you, my dear?"

"Yes, miss," said Alice. It was the first thing she had actually said in—how many days? Her voice sounded like a rusted hinge.

"Please call me Margaret. I think you and I are going to be good friends. Now, your mother and I have some things to take care of. We'll see you in a couple of hours."

"Do you understand, Lydia?" said Mrs. Raymond. "You are to bathe and get dressed. We will come for you when your presence is required."

"Yes, I understand," said Alice. Miss Trelawny—Margaret—had put it so much more nicely! She had at least pretended that she was not ordering Alice, but asking her to get ready for some sort of meeting. What sort of meeting? And why would Alice need to be there?

Mrs. Raymond just nodded. A moment later, Alice heard a key turn in the lock behind them. Once again she was alone and locked up, but at least it was in better circumstances! What now? Really what she wanted to do was lie down on the bed, pull the covers around her, and cry. But how would that help? The last time she had been kidnapped, Mary had come for her—well, for Justine and Beatrice really, but she had been rescued as well. This time, no one was coming. Mary and the other members of the Athena Club were far away, in Europe, which might as well be the antipodes. Mr. Holmes was off somewhere on a case—unless he had returned already? But even if he had, there were probably more important things to occupy his time than chasing down a kitchen maid! She could certainly not expect the great detective to come after her. Alice had always been comforted by her own insignificance. If she was *just* a kitchen maid, she would be safe. No one would bother her or ask much of her. Well, now she was Lydia Raymond, or so they told her, and she did not feel safe at all. Surely Mrs. Poole would do something? But what could Mrs. Poole do? If she went to Scotland Yard and reported that her kitchen maid had been kidnapped, she would likely be told that kitchen maids ran away from their employers every day, and she should simply find a new one. After all, who kidnapped kitchen maids? Who would want them? There were thousands of girls just like Alice in London, who could scrub floors and sinks and dishes, who could stir soups and watch to make sure cakes did not burn. There was nothing unique about her—except her mesmerical abilities, which seemed to be what had gotten her into all this trouble!

She would lie down on the bed after all, just for a moment, to have a good cry.

It lasted for more than a moment. She had not cried so hard since the night after Mrs. Jekyll's funeral, when Mary had told the staff they would have to be let go. She had known, then, that it was either going on the streets or back to the orphanage for her. She had never felt so alone. And here she was again, as alone as she had been that night. But no, she was not completely alone. She had friends, even if they were far away. And she herself was not as lost and uncertain as she had been back then. After all, she had participated in the escape from the warehouse, even if her part had been a small one. And later, she had helped Catherine rescue Archibald, hadn't she? She would be fourteen years old in February. That was Diana's age, and look at all the things Diana did! Of course, she did not actually want to be Diana, because Diana annoyed everyone. And yet, how handy the ability to pick locks would be right now!

No, the person she really wanted to be like was Mary.

DIANA: Why in the world would anyone want to be
like Mary? She's *so boring*.

Mary was logical. Mary could break a problem down into its component parts and solve them one by one. What was the central problem, then? She needed to escape. There was either the window or the door. Alice stood up and walked to the window. It was a sheer drop to the ground. Nothing to climb down, not even some ivy growing up the wall, and she wasn't a monkey like Diana. The door, when she tried it, was most definitely locked. The key was not in the keyhole—Mrs. Raymond must have taken it.

While standing there, she heard a groan again—it was coming, faint but distinct, from down the hall. Then there was another sound—boot heels! Was Mrs. Raymond or Margaret Trelawny coming back for her? A moment later, when a key turned in the lock, Alice was sitting back on the bed, with her feet tucked under her, crying into her hands—but this time the tears were false. If whoever came in thought she was distraught, it might be easier to escape somehow.

When the door opened, she looked through her fingers and saw a girl, not much older than she was—perhaps fifteen or sixteen?—in a maid's uniform. Alice sniffed and dried her nonexistent tears. It was a waste of time pretending to cry for a maid, and anyway, maids, in her experience, were more perceptive than other people. The girl might be able to tell that she had not really been crying.

"Hello," she said tentatively.

"Hello," said the maid back, smiling in a friendly fashion. Her "Hello" was heavily accented. She had dark brown hair and wide cheekbones that reminded Alice of the old woman who had brought her food in the coal cellar. Could this be her daughter?

"My name is Alice." She scooted over to the edge of the bed and put her bare feet on the floor. "I'm in service, just like you."

The girl shook her head and said something that sounded like a stream of gibberish—but of course it must be another language. It sounded nothing at all like English. "I have no Anglich," she repeated, more slowly.

"You don't speak English?" said Alice.

The girl nodded, smiling again. So much for trying to communicate with her or elicit her sympathy!

The maid pointed to herself. "Gitla," she said. "Gitla Mandelbaum." Yes, then she must be the Mandelbaums' daughter. The mother a housekeeper, the father a butler, and daughter a maid—that was often how it worked when entire families were in service.

Well, if they were reduced to pantomime—"Alice," said Alice, pointing to herself.

Gitla nodded, then said something in that foreign language of hers, and gestured for Alice to come along. This must be her promised bath?

Sure enough, Gitla led her to a bathroom at the end of the hall. The bath was already filled with water. Beside it stood the bucket in which Gitla must have carried the water—several trips up and down, since the water was comfortably deep. On a stool beside the bathtub were a towel and robe. Gitla gestured toward the bath, then curtseyed and walked back out into the hall, shutting the door behind her.

Alice listened intently, but there was no sound of footsteps receding. She tiptoed to the door and peeked out through the keyhole. Yes, Gitla was still standing there, leaning against the wall. So she wasn't just a maid—she was a guard as well! There was nothing to do now but take a bath, and goodness, she needed one! Mrs. Poole would have been shocked by how dirty and, yes, smelly she was.

She immersed herself in the bathwater, which was still deliciously hot, and scrubbed herself with a bar of Castile soap she found on the towel. Just for good measure, she washed her hair as well. There was no vinegar to rinse with, but she rinsed her hair as well as she could in cold water from the tap.

She put on the robe, leaving the soiled nightgown neatly folded on the chair, then called out, "I'm ready!"

Gitla opened the door and gestured for her to come out, saying something incomprehensible. It was strange not being able to talk to someone! This was how Mary must feel in Europe, where everyone spoke different languages. But Mary had Justine and the others to translate, whereas Alice must do her best without a translator. Somehow, communicating by pantomime, Gitla led her back to the room, then combed her hair and dressed Alice in the blue silk frock that Mrs. Raymond had picked out. There were stockings to go with it—goodness, silk stockings, with embroidered clocks! And a very fine pair of button boots that Gitla fastened with a boot hook.

By this time, her hair was almost dry. Gitla patted it once more with a towel, then braided it and tied it at the bottom with a blue silk ribbon. Alice had never worn such fine clothes in her life. Evidently, Lydia Raymond was not a kitchen maid! Alice felt like a perfect fraud.

"*Ślicznie Panna w tym wygląda,*" Gitla said, looking at Alice as though pleased with her handiwork.

And then Alice was left alone again. With an apologetic smile, Gitla locked the door behind her. What now? There was nothing she could do until Mrs. Raymond or Miss Trelawny came to get her, so she looked at the bookshelf—*The Cuckoo Clock* by Mrs. Molesworth, *The Water-Babies* by Mr. Kingsley, *The Little Lame Prince* by Miss Mulock. . . . She had read all those books at the orphanage, where they had been considered improving literature. Someone had planned this room for a child. But what child? It took a moment for the truth to dawn on her. *She* was the child. All that time she had been locked in the coal cellar, this room, with its clothes that were a little too large for her, its books that were a little too young, had been waiting for her. Planned by whom? Mrs. Raymond? She could not imagine Mrs. Raymond planning any such thing, and yet who else could have done it? Sometimes, at the orphanage, she had imagined that she was not an orphan after all, that one day her mother would come for her. Who would she be? A soldier's widow reduced to penury who had been unable to keep her daughter? A fallen governess who had sought to hide her shame? In her dreams, her mother had always loved and wanted her, but had been forced to give her up due to unfortunate circumstances. As she had grown older, she had put such dreams aside. And now her mother had come for her—kidnapping her, imprisoning her, wanting her to work for a man such as Moriarty, who was, she could tell, what Mrs. Poole called a *wrong 'un*. She did not know what to think.

She was quite hungry by the time a key turned in the lock again. This time, it was Margaret Trelawny. She was no longer dressed in a black walking suit. Now she had on a very attractive black afternoon gown with a neckline that was, Alice thought, a little too low for mourning attire—after all, she must be in mourning, or why would she be wearing black? Around her neck was a magnificent gold necklace with a pendant that looked like a large ruby carved in the shape of a beetle. Surely that was not proper under the circumstances either? In mourning one wore a set of jet beads, or perhaps a locket with the braided hair of the beloved dead inside. But it certainly did look striking on her white neck, framed by the black collar.

"Why, Lydia, don't you look lovely!" she said. "Come on down. The meeting is about to start, and there will be tea—I'm sure you'd like some. I asked Mrs. Mandelbaum to send up some of those little cakes she makes so well. At least, I think I did. The Mandelbaums don't speak English at all—well, Gitla knows a few words, but they're recent immigrants. And of course I don't speak any Polish. But Abram Mandelbaum speaks a little German—he was a school teacher in his own country—and my father taught me German so I could help with his research. At any rate, there will be food of some sort. Now, here's what I want you to do. . . ."

Alice nodded. As she followed Miss Trelawny down the hall, she mentally repeated to herself what Margaret had told her: Don't speak unless you're spoken to; when you are spoken to, answer clearly but briefly—no need to volunteer more information than you are asked for; listen carefully to the conversation and remember what you have learned; make sure to eat and drink, so you can keep up your strength. She was not at all sure whether she should like Miss Trelawny. Certainly, she was much kinder than Mrs. Raymond or Professor Moriarty—after all, she had gotten Alice out of the coal cellar. And yet she was in league with them. In league to do what? Alice had no idea. Well, for now she would follow Margaret Trelawny's instructions to listen and learn.

As she put one foot on the stair, she heard it again—a groan, this time from behind her. It was long and drawn out. Someone was in pain. Should she ask Miss Trelawny about it? But Margaret Trelawny was already halfway down the stairs. *Listen and learn,* she reminded herself. Listening and learning had gotten her out of bad situations in the past, at the orphanage for example. Whoever was groaning so piteously, she would have to find out about it later.

At the bottom of the stairs, Miss Trelawny led her to the common room, with its plush chairs, dark paneling, and brocade curtains. Portraits of solemn old gentlemen looked down from the walls. Seated in the armchairs gathered around the fireplace, in which a fire had been lit, was a collection of gentlemen much younger than the ones in the portraits. Among them, in the armchair closest to the fireplace, was Mrs. Raymond. She was still in her soft gray dress, with lace falling over her shoulders and arms, and her black hair was swept up in the most modern style. She looked quite romantic, like a duchess in a society magazine.

When they entered, all the men rose—Alice felt quite intimidated by this spectacle of male courtesy. If she could have, she would have shrunk down into a small blue heap and crept out of the room like a mouse. Lord Godalming said, "Miss Trelawny, if you please," and gestured toward his armchair.

"Thank you," said Margaret Trelawny, smiling a particularly charming smile. She steered Alice to the armchair, then pulled her down until they were sitting side by side. There was just room enough in the armchair for the both of them. When they were seated, the men sat—all but one of them, who stood in front of the fireplace as though about to make a speech.

It was Professor Moriarty. He put one hand on the back of Mrs. Raymond's armchair, beside the antimacassar. He frowned at Alice—or maybe he was just frowning in her general direction, because he did not seem to see her. She shrank back a bit. Yes, she was frightened of him—why shouldn't she be? He had been there when she had woken up in the coal cellar, already shackled to the wall. He had asked her to demonstrate her mesmeric powers, and then told her that she would be let out as soon as she agreed to use those powers as he directed. Twice she had refused, before Margaret Trelawny had released her. Now that he had seen her, would he order her back in that dungeon?

But he scarcely seemed to notice her presence. "Where is Raymond?" he asked, of no one in particular. "I thought you told him we would be starting at four." That statement was aimed specifically at Mrs. Raymond.

She raised her eyebrows and responded coldly, "I told him, but I am not his keeper. He has farther to come than any of us, except Mr. Harker." She nodded at one of the men—presumably Mr. Harker? He looked young, and rather stupid. "However, having come all the way from Essex, Mr. Harker probably took an early morning train to make our meeting. Dr. Raymond no doubt took the latest one he could—he usually does."

"I'm here," came a voice from the doorway. In walked an older man, by far the oldest in the room, thin and stooped. He had a halo of white hair around a bald, wrinkled brow, and leaned on an ornate cane that was evidently as functional as it was ornamental, for he limped as he walked. "Hello, Helen. Lord Godalming. And Seward—we should have traveled from Purfleet together. Now then, what's all this? Godalming has told me part of your purpose, Moriarty. I am in general agreement with your aims, or I would not have rented you this building—rather, the Alchemical Society would not have rented it to you. As there is no official branch of the Alchemical Society in England at present, I function as its de facto representative. But who are these other gentlemen—and ladies?" Here he bowed to the ladies and peered at Alice curiously. "I do not have the pleasure of their acquaintance."

His voice took Alice back to the day she and Catherine had hidden in the kitchen below, listening to Raymond and Seward discuss Van Helsing's plan to take over the Alchemical Society. Were these all members of the society, planning some new mischief? And had Van Helsing managed to gain power, or had Miss Mary and the others foiled his plans? She had no way of knowing. If this was some new plan of the society, how was her mother—or, rather, Mrs. Raymond, for she did not wish to call that woman her mother—involved?

"These are the members of our organization," said Moriarty. "Welcome, gentleman . . . and ladies"—he bowed to Mrs. Raymond and Miss Trelawny—"to the new headquarters of the Order of the Golden Dawn."

# CHAPTER V

## The Delirious Man

"Let us begin with introductions," said Professor Moriarty.

*Listen and learn,* Alice reminded herself. She would be just like Mary, who was just like Mr. Holmes himself. She would observe and remember, so that when she got out of here—and she *would* get out of here, she was determined—she could tell Mary and Mr. Holmes all about it. She leaned forward a little so she could see all the men in the room. Now Professor Moriarty was introducing them. She must remember their names. How would she describe them to Mary?

They reminded her of the characters in one of her penny dreadfuls. There always seemed to be a group of men who fought the monsters and saved the realm. Mentally, she cast them in their proper roles. Lord Godalming was the Peer of the Realm. He was handsome, not young anymore but still boyish, despite the gray in his hair and mustache. He had a pair of very blue eyes. Mr. Quincy Morris was the American, with what she assumed was an American accent. Despite her trepidation and discomfort, Alice could not help being amused by his fringed leather outfit and the large knife at his belt. Was this what Americans wore all the time, or only in the Wild West? As for Jonathan Harker, what was he, exactly? Quiet, deferential, clean-shaven. He looked younger than the others, and had an air of not quite knowing what was going on. She would not assign him a role yet. Seated on the other side of Lord Godalming was a heavyset man whom Moriarty introduced as Colonel Moran. As Moriarty mentioned his name, he rose and joined his leader by the fireplace, leaning on the mantel. He was obviously the Enforcer. His jacket did not hang quite right. When he moved, Alice could see there was something underneath, the approximate shape and size of a revolver. Dr. Seward was of course the Alchemist, a member of the Alchemical Society and the director of the Purfleet Asylum. And Moriarty was the Mastermind. He was so clearly in charge, so clearly the leader of this group. As for Dr. Raymond—well, she was not quite sure how to describe Dr. Raymond. Was he just another Alchemist, like Dr. Seward?

"This is Miss Trelawny, daughter of the late Professor Trelawny, the Egyptologist," said Moriarty. "No doubt you have heard the name."

"Indeed," said Dr. Raymond, bowing in Miss Trelawny's general direction. "My condolences, Miss Trelawny, on your father's untimely death. I saw his obituary in *The Times* and was shocked, quite shocked, at the loss of such a brilliant mind. It will set our efforts in Egypt back significantly. I understand that the artifacts from the tomb of Queen Tera are about to go on display at the British Museum."

"Thank you," said Miss Trelawny. "Your words bring me comfort, Dr. Raymond." Although she made this statement in the same pleasant, genteel tone with which she said everything, Alice glanced at her, puzzled. Somehow, it did not ring true. The energic waves around her head did not look quite right.

"And this," Miss Trelawny continued, "is your granddaughter, Lydia."

Granddaughter! Suddenly, all eyes were on Alice. Oh, if only she could sink down into the chair cushions, or hide herself in the folds of Miss Trelawny's dress! She did not want their attention on her, particularly after such a revelation. Nevertheless, she could not help looking at Dr. Raymond curiously. This was her grandfather? This man whom she knew to be cruel and callous, who had allowed Archibald to remain locked up in the dark? Mrs. Raymond her mother, Dr. Raymond her grandfather . . .

"Indeed," said Dr. Raymond, peering at her. He took a pair of spectacles out of his jacket pocket—they had no earpieces and simply sat on his nose—to examine her better, as though she were some sort of interesting insect. "So you found her again, after all these years. And is she—"

"Almost as skilled at manipulating the mesmeric waves as I am, and she will no doubt surpass me someday," said Mrs. Raymond coldly. If they were father and daughter, there was no love lost between them! She did not seem particularly happy to see him, had not risen or greeted him in any way. *So this is my family,* thought Alice. She would much rather have been related to Mrs. Poole.

> MRS. POOLE: Well, I did raise and train you, my dear, after you came to us from the orphanage. I think you can consider me family.

> ALICE: Thank you, Mrs. Poole. You don't know how much that means to me.

> DIANA: We're family too! Don't forget about us. I mean, you're annoying and insipid, but then so is Mary, and she's my sister.

"If we could have a small demonstration of her powers . . . ," said Dr. Raymond, looking at Alice in a way she did not like. Gleefully? Avariciously? Catherine would have known the right word.

"This is neither the time nor the place," said Mrs. Raymond with a frown. Her voice was contemptuous. "You will have plenty of opportunity to observe the results of your experiment. This is a business meeting."

"But what sort of business?" asked Jonathan Harker. "I'm grateful, of course, that Lord Godalming has included me in this enterprise, but thus far I have only the vaguest notion of what we are aiming for, or how we are to achieve it. If you would enlighten me—"

"Of course, Mr. Harker," said Moriarty. "That is precisely why we are holding this meeting today. Lord Godalming and I want to make certain you gentlemen understand and are in agreement with our goals. We have given you an inkling of them—now we shall explain ourselves fully. Allow me to—ah, here is Mandelbaum."

Alice had not noticed the butler standing just outside the circle of armchairs with a tea tray in his hand, but of course that was the defining characteristic of good butlers—one did not notice them. Ah yes, Margaret Trelawny had said there would be food. In her fear and consternation, Alice had almost forgotten.

"If someone would move the tables—" said Moriarty.

"Here, if you please," said Miss Trelawny. "I shall do the pouring out."

Mr. Harker placed one of the small tables beside Miss Trelawny's chair, where she could reach it easily. The butler proceeded to put the tea tray on it, then went to the place in the wall that opened onto a dumbwaiter and took out what had been raised from the kitchen below—teacups and saucers, and two trays: one with pastries, the other with a selection of small sandwiches. Alice looked at them hungrily. How long had it been since she'd had a proper meal?

The others did not seem particularly interested in the pastries or sandwiches. Once the butler had left and most of the men, as well as Mrs. Raymond, had teacups in their hands—Mr. Morris declined and was drinking something out of a flask he had produced out of an inside pocket—Miss Trelawny loaded a plate for her. Alice tried not to eat too quickly, worried about making herself sick after the meager diet of the last few days, but it was difficult not to gulp down the sandwiches, which were very good.

Shrimp paste! She had always liked shrimp paste. And some sort of cream cheese with cucumber. She did not recognize the pastries, which were quite different from the kinds made by Mrs. Poole. Some of them were filled with chocolate, some with apricot jam.

"Now," said Moriarty. "Where were we? Ah yes, why I have brought us here together. The nine of us come from different worlds. Mrs. Raymond and Colonel Moran have been in my organization for many years. It is, shall we say, a commercial enterprise of sorts. We import and export various goods that fetch a high price on private markets. We provide services of the kind more, shall we say, conservative businesses are unable to provide. The good doctors"—here he nodded at Raymond and Seward, who were seated next to each other—"are members of the Alchemical Society, who have very kindly rented us their former London headquarters. Lord Godalming was at one time a member, until the English branch was disbanded and he resigned in protest. Mr. Harker is his solicitor and trusted representative. Mr. Morris is the famous explorer—we have all heard of his travels up the Amazon, his hunting expeditions in Africa. And Miss Trelawny represents her late father, whose discovery of the tomb of Queen Tera at Philae has brought us what we need to effect our central purpose."

"Which is?" asked Harker. He looked as though he still did not understand what was going on. Well, Alice didn't either.

Moriarty smiled. She did not like his smile—it reminded her too much of how Mrs. Raymond smiled. Whatever jollity their mouths expressed did not reach their eyes. "Mr. Harker, I invite you, Dr. Raymond, and Mr. Morris to join the Order of the Golden Dawn. The rest of us here are already members. The German branch of the order has repudiated us—indeed, I received a letter just this morning asking us not to use that name for our organization. But no matter. Golden Dawn we are and shall remain, because that is what we propose to bring to England.

A glorious new dawn for this country, and the true English men and women in it."

He put his teacup on the mantel, clasped his hands behind him, and leaned forward a little—it was the stance of a man in front of a lecture hall.

"As we meet here in the magnificent city of London, the greatest city in the world, a modern rival to the glory of ancient Rome, we might assume that we stand at the heart of a powerful empire. But you know, gentlemen—each of you knows—that we have been invaded. Look at our docks! They team with the outcasts of Europe and beyond. Why, there are places in this city where no English is spoken! Our markets are a cacophony of languages, of nationalities. Where, anymore, but in the highest halls of polite society can we find the pure, the Anglo-Saxon, strain that made this country great? At the same time, we send our young men off to India and Africa, to water foreign lands with their blood. And what does this get us? An empire, to be sure, but at the cost of the purity of our race, the stability of our nation. At the cost of our traditions—the cost, I tell you, of our very souls! What we propose—the purpose of our Order—is no less than the restoration of England, for Englishmen—and women, of course." He bowed to Mrs. Raymond. "You all know of Galton's *Hereditary Genius* and his later writings on what he has called 'eugenics'—the good, pure, noble birth. English society is headed in the opposite direction, that of 'dysgenics.'" The poor give birth like rats, immigrants fill our cities with the refuse of a hundred shores, and the flowers of English manhood and maidenhood are swamped in the tide. We must regulate our borders so that we no longer accept immigrants and refugees, regulate births so that only the best, the highest intellects, are allowed to perpetuate the race— although we must of course allow a certain number of the lower classes to continue breeding, or we shall have a servant problem indeed!" Here he smiled as though he had said something amusing. "What we need is a group of men, true Englishmen, who are not afraid to fight for their vision of what this country could be. A small group of dedicated men, with the proper resources at their disposal, can do what mobs cannot. As the Spartans held off the Persians at Thermopylae, so too must we stop the tide that is threatening to overwhelm us. And we have resources—Godalming brings to us his position in the House of Lords and considerable fortune. Raymond and Seward bring scientific knowledge. Moran has connections in what is sometimes called the underworld of London that have already served us well. Together with Morris, he also brings us, shall we say, a certain amount of firepower. And you, Mr. Harker—your knowledge of the law will add to our arsenal. We shall form the central core of the Order. As for the ladies, they too have much to contribute. Helen, my dear, perhaps this is the time for a demonstration?"

Everyone looked at Mrs. Raymond. There she sat, a beautiful woman of middle age, her black hair not yet touched by gray, the white lace falling from her snowy shoulders over the gray silk bodice of her gown. She gave a small, grim smile—and suddenly, she was not there anymore. Instead, sitting in her chair—

"What the devil!" said Morris.

Harker sprang up and almost tripped over his chair. "Your Majesty . . ."

Alice would have cried out in astonishment, but Miss Trelawny had gripped her arm, as though in warning.

The woman who rose from the chair in which Mrs. Raymond had been sitting was as familiar to her as her own face in the mirror. She had seen that countenance all her life, on coins and stamps, in photographs in the newspapers. It was the Queen herself, a compact figure in black crepe, with a lace cap on her head and an expression on her face of determination and resolve. This was the woman who ruled the greatest empire the world had ever known.

And yet—the mesmeric waves swirling around her were recognizably those of Helen Raymond. The illusion would have been perfect, except to a mesmerist.

"Rest easy, we have not whisked Her Majesty from Buckingham Palace to this room," said Moriarty with a dry chuckle. "Helen, if you would reveal the illusion?"

Before their eyes, Queen Victoria seemed to swirl like smoke— a column of black, gray, and white that reformed into the semblance of Mrs. Raymond.

"That, gentlemen, is the power of mesmerism," she said. "I was able, for a time, to convince you that you were seeing the Queen herself. It was, of course, merely a kind of trick. If you would like me to demonstrate again—"

"Not for the world!" said Harker. "Can such a power truly exist? I thought mesmerists were merely charlatans."

"Most of them are," said Mrs. Raymond. "But some of them can truly manipulate the mesmeric waves that surround us like an invisible ocean. By manipulating those waves, I can determine what you see—for a time."

"Then you did not truly become Her Majesty?" He still sounded disbelieving.

Mrs. Raymond sighed, as though wearied by his questions. "Mesmerism does not change the physical world—it merely alters our perception of it. Actually changing material reality is theoretically possible, but would take more power than I currently have. And there is a limit even to the visions I can create. I could not sustain this illusion if there were hundreds of spectators present, rather than the nine of you in this room."

"Which is of course the problem," said Moriarty. "Over the past decade, my organization has infiltrated government at the highest levels. Colonel Moran and I have assembled a dossier that could bring down half the cabinet. Once we tell certain powerful figures what we know about them, they will beg us to command them, and willingly do our bidding. But the Queen herself, sitting above the daily fray of politics, is nevertheless sharp-eyed. She keeps a watch over matters of state and has her own shadow cabinet, as it were, whose members are loyal only to Her Majesty. While her role appears ceremonial, in reality she is far more than a figurehead. If we are to effect true change in this country, we must replace her with another, more amenable, version of herself—whom you have seen! That version will reign long enough for us to put our members into the government. Lord Godalming will be our new Prime Minister. And then she will abdicate in favor of Prince Edward. From what I have been told by reliable informants, he will be much more sympathetic to our cause. All of us here are loyal to the Crown—that goes without saying. But the Crown is not necessarily the Queen. She shall not be harmed, I assure you. However, she is old, and it is long past time the throne passed to her son. He will understand the problems of the new century, which is almost upon us. What say you, gentlemen? Are you ready to join the Order of the Golden Dawn?"

"Is this not treason?" asked Harker. "What will happen to Her Majesty during this—this interregnum you are describing?

"She will be kept in the Purfleet Asylum," said Dr. Seward. "I assure you that she will be both safe and comfortable. If she claims to be the Queen of England, she will be seen as yet another madwoman. And when we return her after her abdication, any mention of having been abducted or confined will be treated as evidence of incipient dementia. Either way, she will not be believed."

"Jonathan, consider," said Godalming, turning to the solicitor. "You and I have talked about how someone needs to take things in hand. This country is going to the dogs—with this depression, and beggars even in Pall Mall, and Fenians bombing whenever they please. India in rebellion, war coming in Africa . . . Someone needs to *do* something. Why should that someone not be us? If we abduct the Queen—for yes, that is what Moriarty is suggesting, let us have no illusions about that. She will be well taken care of, with the comforts that her age and station require, but this is nevertheless an abduction. If we do so, we will be doing it for a higher purpose, a greater good. Is that not true patriotism, to serve one's country and one's race, even if no one will ever know what we have done? Even if we earn no praise, receive no accolades, for our actions? Once we are in power, we will close our borders to the unwashed masses that pollute our cities. England for Englishmen! We will administer our empire with a firmer hand—no more rebellions, or at least not ones that go unpunished. No more concessions to native populations who have no idea what is good for them. I assure you that in public policy, mercy is an overrated virtue. Come, man, do you not want to save your country?"

Alice, who still had an uneaten sandwich on her plate, put it aside. She was shocked by what these men were planning to do. Kidnap the Queen? And then hold her prisoner in a mental institution where she would not be listened to or believed while they rearranged the government to suit their purposes? Impose this system of "eugenics," whatever that meant, on the English people? She did not understand all the details of their plan, but what she did understand horrified her.

Harker still looked undecided, but Morris said, "I'm in, gentlemen. This is about as dangerous as hunting lions in Rhodesia, I reckon. Tell me what we do next."

"As you can see," said Moriarty, "Helen has considerable power—but not enough, not yet, to effect our purpose. Initially, we thought that if we found the most powerful mesmerists in England, they could, as it were, augment her power—but they turned out to be poor specimens, after all. One of them led us to Helen's daughter, whose power I have seen with my own eyes. Helen, show us what Lydia can do."

What had he just said? Was he expecting Alice to do something, in front of all these people? She shrank back even farther into the cushions of the armchair.

"Here? Now?" said Mrs. Raymond. She sounded surprised and angry. "I thought perhaps later, when Lydia has recovered a little—"

"Yes, here and now," said Moriarty. "We need to see what abilities she can add to our cause. Or are you not as committed to that cause as you have told me?"

Mrs. Raymond glared at him. He merely looked back at her, imperturbable. "All right," she said after a moment. "Lydia, come here."

What in the world was Alice supposed to do? She felt like Galatea before Aphrodite brought her to life—as though she were a statue incapable of motion.

"Go on," whispered Margaret Trelawny, pushing her just a bit, so that she slid to the edge of the armchair. "Go to your mother."

Feeling numb, Alice stood up and walked over to Mrs. Raymond. She had no idea what to do. Mrs. Raymond grabbed her wrist and pulled her over, more roughly than necessary. "Just open your mind," she hissed under her breath. "I can't do this unless you open your mind to me. Do you understand?"

Open her mind how? Alice did not even know that it was closed. But then she felt it—another presence in her head, tugging at her consciousness, pulling her spiritually rather than physically. She looked down at her arms in wonder. The mesmerical waves—she could see them flowing from her to Mrs. Raymond. Their waves were merging. Suddenly they were no longer seated in the common room of the Alchemical Society. Columns were rising around them, coming together into pointed arches between walls of white stone with statues of saints in carved niches, and then windows of stained glass, letting in multicolored light, and then up until the illusion knit itself together into a high domed ceiling, gilded and painted. Alice had never seen anything so magnificent in her life.

"The dome of St. Paul's!" said Harker in wonder, like a visitor from the country seeing it for the first time. "How is this possible?"

"Well, damn," said Mr. Morris. "Now that's impressive."

And then, like the illusion of Queen Victoria, it dissipated, the cathedrals and statues and stained glass swirling away like smoke. Once again they were standing in the common room. Alice's arm hurt where Mrs. Raymond had gripped it.

Dr. Raymond rubbed his hands together gleefully. "Wonderful, wonderful," he said. "You see, Helen, this is what I always wanted. This is what I suffered and sacrificed for. Look what you and little Lydia can do together. Surely this will allow us to implement Professor Moriarty's plan."

"No," she said coldly. "It will not. Even drawing upon Lydia's powers, I can only maintain such an illusion for a limited period of time. We need to fool hundreds of people over a period of weeks."

"And for that, we need something more," said Moriarty. "What we need, gentlemen, is to summon the Great God Pan!" He said it dramatically, as though it might mean something important. However, the only response was Dr. Raymond's sharp intake of breath and Mr. Harker's "I'm afraid I don't understand. What does classical mythology have to do with all this?"

"Dr. Raymond, if you will explain?" said Moriarty, looking irritated.

Raymond took a deep breath and said, "I'm not quite certain what you mean by it, Moriarty—whether you mean what I think you mean. But it's an alchemical procedure that I myself . . . well. It's a metaphor, of course. The alchemical sciences have long used metaphors to express the inexpressible, or what, for practical purposes, must be kept hidden from the ignorant public. As you know, the god Pan was the Greek deity of the natural world. To summon Pan means to summon the energic powers of the Earth and contain them within a host. That is what I tried to do, long ago, to a girl—a beautiful young girl, my wife, Helen's mother. Unfortunately, her mind could not support such an influx of power, and she went mad. At the time, unbeknownst to me, she was with child. You see the result." He nodded toward Mrs. Raymond. "My wife died in a mental hospital, so I sent Helen to be raised in the country, which I thought would be healthier for her. Besides which, I did not want to be reminded of my dear departed. Since my experiments were not yielding the results I wanted, I gave them up and pursued other studies. And then, after many years, for we had become estranged, I heard from Helen again. I'm sorry that we did not speak for so long," he said to Mrs. Raymond. "And I'm glad to see that you have grown into such a fine woman. You have your mother's eyes, my dear."

Mrs. Raymond did not respond.

"Well," he said after a moment. "When Helen contacted me, she told me something I could scarcely believe. I am still not certain whether to credit her account. . . ."

"And yet it is entirely accurate, Dr. Raymond," said Miss Trelawny. "As I'm sure you all know, for it was featured prominently in *The Times*, six months ago my father discovered the burial chamber of Queen Tera. That was not surprising—such discoveries seem to be made every year, now that we have men such as Flinders Petrie in Egypt and the support of the Egypt Exploration Fund. What did surprise us was the intact state of the chamber, which had never been looted, and the paintings we found on its walls. Queen Tera was the High Priestess of the Temple of Isis at Philae. On the walls of her burial chamber, in faded hieroglyphs, was described a ritual for raising the energic powers of the Earth and imbuing the High Priestess with such powers. For those of you not familiar with Egyptian history, Tera was the second wife of Ptolemy Auletes and mother of Cleopatra, whom you know from Shakespeare. After Ptolemy's death, she was sent as far away from Alexandria as possible—to Philae, near the first cataract of the Nile, on the border between Egypt and Nubia. There, she became High Priestess of the Temple of Isis. She died in 30 B.C., when Augustus invaded Egypt. After he had secured Alexandria, he sent his soldiers south, to attack Philae—most likely because Tera was there. Cleopatra was already his captive—he was planning to parade her through the streets of Rome. It would have been imprudent to leave her mother, the former queen, behind in Egypt, where she might try to ascend the throne and challenge the Roman forces."

Miss Trelawny leaned forward and looked at each one of them, as though addressing them directly.

"We know what happened at Philae because those who survived recorded it on the walls of Tera's tomb. The priestesses defended the temple, and many of them were killed. Tera herself died leading the defense. The survivors ordered a tomb to be built for Queen Tera. Its walls were covered with friezes carved into the stone. Among them, my father found rituals and recipes—medicines long lost to civilization, ways of performing surgical procedures—as well as an account of that final battle with the soldiers of Augustus. They showed lightning coming out of Tera's left hand. They also depicted a ritual for raising the energic powers of the Earth and containing them within a living host, who was intended to be the High Priestess herself. Once these powers were contained, they could be redirected and used—for whatever purpose the host desired. This ritual, my father attempted to perform, with himself as host. Also present were Eugene Corbeck, my father's assistant, and my fiancé, Malcolm Ross—a solicitor like yourself, Mr. Harker. You will no doubt have heard of the terrible accident that took my father's life, as well as those of Ross and Corbeck. But it was no accident. There was, indeed, an explosion in the room where he housed his collection, but it was not set off by bitumen, as reported in the papers. Rather, it was the ritual itself that killed them. You see, the ritual demands a sacrifice—as it fills a host with power, it must drain power from another. Someone must die. My father did not realize that—he had not read the original Egyptian hieroglyphs as carefully as he should have. Alas, I realized it only after his death, when it was too late. This ritual can indeed give you gentlemen power—but do you truly want to attempt it? The two men I loved most in the world perished in the quest for knowledge. Do you, too, wish to risk your lives for the power and wisdom of ancient Egypt?"

She looked around at the men in the room. Alice, cradling her arm where Mrs. Raymond had gripped it, looked around at them as well. Mr. Harker seemed apprehensive, but the rest of the men appeared to be eager, even cupidous. Dr. Raymond was rubbing his thin, dry hands together. If Miss Trelawny's words had been meant to deter them, she had not succeeded.

"And who is to be our host?" asked Seward. "Who is to wield these powers? You, Moriarty?"

"I am," said Mrs. Raymond. "I already know how to wield energic power, and I am willing to risk my life in this endeavor."

"The danger of this ritual will be primarily to her," said Moriarty, putting a hand on her shoulder. "However, she is willing to undertake that danger to further our cause." What was the relationship between him and Mrs. Raymond? Clearly she was his subordinate— he told her what to do and she obeyed. And yet his attitude toward her was more intimate than such a relationship implied. Whatever it was, it made Alice feel a little sick. She did not particularly care about Mrs. Raymond—why should she? What sort of mother had she been? But Moriarty, despite his high, white forehead, which should have signified intellect, reminded her of a devil in human form. As imperceptibly as she could, she returned to her seat beside Margaret Trelawny. She wanted to get as far away from Moriarty as possible. Fortunately, no one seemed to be paying attention to her.

"Well, gentlemen?" said Moriarty, looking around at all of them. "Are you with us?"

"Of course we are," said Godalming. "What man would draw back from such a challenge?" He smiled his charming, sincere smile, which Alice was beginning to distrust. Better a cold smile like Mrs. Raymond's than Lord Godalming's deceptive warmth! Harker continued to look dubious, but Alice could see the other men nodding.

"Excellent," said Moriarty. "Now that Dr. Raymond and Mr. Harker have agreed to join us, we have everything we need for the ritual."

"Well, I don't know . . . ," said Harker, but Lord Godalming glanced at him in a meaningful way, and he did not finish his sentence.

"Which are what?" asked Seward. "What do we need exactly? And how do we know that what happened to Trelawny and his assistants won't happen again?"

Mrs. Raymond rose and walked over to Miss Trelawny's armchair. The men who were seated rose when she did, and did not sit again until she had seated herself on the arm of the chair, next to Alice, who looked up at her uncomfortably. She hoped she would not be called upon to demonstrate her mesmerical powers once more. Her mother and Miss Trelawny looked like sisters, with Mrs. Raymond as the elder. Alice felt very small between them.

"The ritual was meant to be enacted by the priestesses of Isis," said Mrs. Raymond. "They were accustomed to manipulating the energic powers of the Earth. That is why the ritual will be conducted by myself, with the assistance of my daughter." She put one hand on Alice's shoulder. Suddenly, all eyes were on Alice again. She wished that she could sink down into the cushions—down, down, through the stuffing and then the common room floor, back down to the cellar where she had been held captive. "Of course, we will be acting under the direction of Miss Trelawny."

"And we will have the seven of you to light the lamps," said

Miss Trelawny. "Seven lamps, carved to resemble the seven incar-
nations of Hathor, were found in the tomb. My father lit them one
by one—I believe they need to be lit simultaneously, and at the
correct moment, for the ritual to take effect. Furthermore, when
my father conducted the ritual, he did not realize it required a
source of energy before it could draw upon the energic powers of
the Earth—as one needs to prime a pump. It drew power out
of him rather than imbuing him with it. We will have a source
of power to draw on—a battery, you could call him. Or, if you
prefer, a sacrifice, as Professor Moriarty said. You see, we have
planned very carefully. We do not intend to repeat my father's
mistakes. The exhibition opens on Monday—we are planning
on conducting our ritual on Sunday, while the British Museum is
closed and we have Queen Tera's artifacts all to ourselves."

"This sacrifice . . . ," said Harker. "Are you speaking of a
human being?"

"An old enemy of mine," said Moriarty with satisfaction. "A
man I have been trying to get rid of for years, and who almost
managed to get rid of me at Reichenbach Falls! I do not know how
he survived in the turbulent waters—if Moran had not dragged
me out of the pool below the falls, I would have drowned myself.
He is a man the world would be better off without. It will, indeed,
be a mercy to rid the world of such a meddling, sanctimonious—
well. Are you satisfied, gentlemen? If so, I suggest Lord Godalming
and Dr. Raymond continue this conversation in my office. We
have some logistics to discuss. The rest of you may smoke—Helen
and Margaret won't mind, I'm certain. And the child can go back
to—wherever you've put her."

"Come on," Margaret Trelawny said to Alice, taking her hand.
"I'll bring you back to your room. And put some of those little rolls
in your pocket—you need something nourishing, after that diet
of dry crusts!"

Alice took three of the pastries, put them in her apron pocket, and followed Miss Trelawny, dodging the gentlemen who were milling about now, talking among themselves and paying no attention to her. Once they were in the hall, Miss Trelawny said, "Gitla, just a moment! *Einen Moment!*" The maid was halfway up the stairs, carrying a water jug. "Can you take Lydia back to her room?" She pointed to Alice, then up, toward the second floor.

*"Jawohl, Madame,"* said Gitla, nodding. She gestured for Alice to follow—with her head, because she had no hands free.

"I'll make sure Mrs. Mandelbaum sends up some supper," said Miss Trelawny. "You'll be all right, won't you, my dear? No one will mistreat you, now that I'm here. And you must not think too hard of Helen—of your mother. Her life has been difficult in ways you cannot imagine. Now, go on. I won't see you again tonight, but tomorrow we shall have a great deal to do."

Miss Trelawny leaned down and kissed her on one cheek. Alice was so startled that she could only nod. Then, she ran to catch up with Gitla on the stairs.

As they walked along the second-floor corridor, Gitla said something incomprehensible, then stopped in front of a door that was not Alice's. She placed the water jug on the floor, unlocked the door, turned to Alice, and held up her hand—clearly, Alice was supposed to wait outside—then opened the door and carried the jug in.

Through the open door, Alice saw a room that resembled hers, with afternoon light streaming through the window. Someone was lying on the bed, under a blanket. As Gitla entered, the form on the bed turned toward her, murmuring weakly, "Watson, is that you? Watson . . ."

There, on the pillow, was the pale, damp, feverish face of Sherlock Holmes.

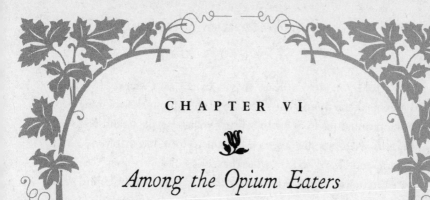

# CHAPTER VI

## Among the Opium Eaters

W hat do you mean you don't want to come with us?" said Mary. "You always want to come with us. And it's *opium dens*."

"Yes, and where are you going first?" asked Diana, leaning back into the sofa cushion as though she was not about to budge. Alpha was curled up on the sofa beside her. Mrs. Poole insists that cats are not allowed on the furniture. Evidently, the cats do not listen to Mrs. Poole any more than Diana does.

They were in the parlor, waiting for Justine to join them. She had insisted on checking Beatrice's greenhouse to make sure some sort of plant, with a name Mary could not remember except that it reminded her of fingers, was flourishing where she had put it.

BEATRICE: That was the *Digitalis purpurea*, what you would call foxglove. It almost died while I was away.

CATHERINE: I don't think our readers need to know that. This isn't a horticultural manual.

BEATRICE: But it is always best to be precise, particularly with poisons.

"I told you, to see Kate Bright-Eyes," said Mary. "I've never been inside an opium den, but one of the inmates of the Magdalen Society must have. She can tell us what to expect, and Kate can help us with our disguises. We want to look like habitual opium eaters, and I have no idea what that looks like."

"I'm not going anywhere near that blasted society," said Diana. "Never again. You can bloody well go without me. I told you those houses were opium dens, didn't I, and gave you directions for where to find them? So I think I've done my bit. Anyway, who cares whether we find the Great Detective? If he can't take care of himself, what good is he?"

Mary resisted the urge to slap her sister. "And what will you be doing all day while we're gone?" she asked suspiciously. What mischief was Diana up to this time? First she had run off to Soho when she was supposed to stay home, and now when she was being offered a chance to participate, she refused to go. The girl was insufferable.

"I thought I would help Mrs. Poole scrub the kitchen range," said Diana. "It's very dirty, you know." Her eyes were limpid pools of innocence in her freckled face.

Did she actually think that would fool anyone? Mary crossed her arms and waited. For a moment, the parlor was very quiet. Diana did not like silence—Mary had learned that the best way to get her to tell you something was to merely wait.

"All right, fine, if you must know," said Diana impatiently. "The Baker Street boys aren't allowed to look for Holmes, but no one said anything about Mrs. Raymond. Charlie says they'll help us find her. They know every corner of London, so if anyone can find her, they can. And Wiggins says I can be in charge of the search. If they find her, they'll also find Alice, and I can rescue her, just like I rescued Lucinda. I'll have saved the day, as usual! And then we'll send Mrs. Raymond to Newgate, where I hope she hangs."

Diana looked very satisfied with herself, as though she had already accomplished this feat.

Should Diana be trying to find Mrs. Raymond among the slums of London with a bunch of street urchins and ragamuffins? But then, she would be as safe with the Baker Street boys as in opium dens, and perhaps their search would not find anything after all. Mary would rather they came up empty-handed than have Diana confront Mrs. Raymond by herself, as no doubt she would! In Diana's mental world, Mrs. Raymond was a kind of demon incarnate.

"Oh, all right!" she said. "Go off with Charlie if you must. At least I'll know you're with him this time, which is better than running off without telling anyone. I wish you were helping Mrs. Poole scrub the kitchen range! She misses Alice terribly."

"Archie can do that," said Diana. "Can't you, Archie?"

The Orangutan Man was standing at the parlor door.

"You rang, miss?" he said.

Had she? Oh yes, just a minute ago. In this verbal altercation with Diana, she had almost forgotten.

"Yes, could you fetch my coat and hat, please? And my purse—the black one." It was large enough for her pistol. She did not want to go into an opium den unarmed.

He moved away in his awkward fashion, half the lope of an ape, half the walk of a man. And yet, Mary had to concede that he was an excellent footman—and maid, for he also did the work that Enid would have done, without once breaking the bibelots on the mantelpieces.

"Mary, I am ready." Justine was standing in the doorway.

Mary looked at her judiciously. "Yes, you'll do. I don't know what it is exactly—perhaps that floppy purple beret and the matching cravat—but you look exactly like *Punch*'s idea of a degenerate artist."

"Thank you," said Justine. "They're Beatrice's. The cravat is actually one of her belts. I think they are a little feminine, but not so much that a gentleman would not wear them."

BEATRICE: They are the clothing of the New Woman. They are meant not to be feminine, but practical.

CATHERINE: On women they look like men's clothing, on men they look like women's clothing. That's where the New Woman meets the Dandy.

BEATRICE: Why is it necessary to categorize people in that fashion? Why can we not all wear whatever we wish, whatever is useful and aesthetically pleasing? I believe that someday we shall all wear garments that are light and of a pleasing texture, easy to put on and take off. At the same time, they will express the aspirations of the spirit. They will be like the garments of the Greeks, both graceful and functional. Why can we not dress in such a fashion now?

MRS. POOLE: Because this is England, and you would all catch your deaths of cold.

Mr. Justin Frank stared across the street at the perfectly ordinary house they knew to be an opium den. "You do not need to come in. I can do this by myself, if necessary."

"Well, it's not necessary," said Mary crossly. "I'll be fine. I just don't feel comfortable looking like this, that's all. What in the world would Mrs. Poole think?" She looked down at herself, wearing a cheap, shabby dress that revealed more of her décolletage than modesty would have dictated, despite the shawl she had wrapped about her shoulders. It had come from the storage room of the Magdalen Society, where the clothing of recent penitents were kept before being turned into rags. Kate Bright-Eyes had chosen it for her, and fixed her hair, and put rouge on her cheeks and lips as well as a little lampblack on her eyelashes. She was supposed to be a—well, a prostitute, there was no other way of saying it—accompanying Mr. Frank to an opium den. "I know you wanted to be a working woman, Miss Jekyll," Kate had said. "But working women have better things to do with their time than smoke the pipe of sweet dreams. A woman of the profession—my profession that is—would accompany a gentleman there if she were paid to do it. The way to be least conspicuous is to accompany Mr. Frank as his, shall we say, paid companion, I assure you." She had even put an artificial flower into Mr. Frank's buttonhole to complete the effect.

How in the world did one act like a prostitute? Mary had no idea. All the ones she had met, like Kate and Doris, were simply ordinary women trying to get by without family to support them, or friends to offer them help, or the training required for more respectable employment. But she had never seen them in action, as it were, plying their disreputable trade. Well, she would have to do the best she could.

The door was opened by a perfectly ordinary woman, a shopkeeper's wife perhaps, who asked what they wanted, but when Mr. Frank explained in hushed tones that they had come for the drug and put something that clinked in her hand, they were admitted into a chamber that looked as though it had been decorated for a theatrical performance set in the fabled, fantastical East. A "Chinaman" with a long beard, in an embroidered robe, greeted them by putting his hands together and bowing, then led them into a second chamber where, on low sofas and cushions spread on the floor, sat and sprawled dreamers in the land of Opium. They were gentlemen, most of them, with a few sailors and less reputable-looking fellows, as well as a few women who looked, Mary thought, thoroughly fallen indeed. Beyond was another room of dreamers, and another, three altogether. Dr. Watson was not in any of them.

"Well," said Mary when they were once more standing outside on the street. "That was an experience." She could still smell the sweet, cloying odor of the opium pipes. She felt a little sick. "On to the second address on Diana's list."

At the second address, only a few streets away, it was the same—the exotic rooms, the bowing Chinaman, who could have been a brother to the first, and rooms of men and a few women smoking opium pipes, lost in dreams.

The third had a beggar sitting out front, and when Mary saw him, she exclaimed, "Poor Richard!" Yes, it was the beggar who had spent the night beside the dead body of Molly Keane, the third victim in the Whitechapel Murders. He was looking just as ragged as the last time she had seen him, with a long multicolored scarf wound around his throat.

> CATHERINE: Readers who do not remember Poor
> Richard should consult their copies of *The Strange
> Case of the Alchemist's Daughter*, the first volume of
> these Extraordinary Adventures of the Athena
> Club. If they have not yet read that most excellent
> book, it is available for two shillings at booksellers
> and railway stations, or direct from the publisher.

> MARY: Will you stop that, already?

"I seem to remember you from somewhere, lassie," said Poor Richard, looking up at her. "But I don't rightly know where. My memory ain't what it used to be."

"I was with Mr. Holmes and Dr. Watson," she said. "I wasn't dressed like this, and I don't think we were ever introduced—I'm Mary Jekyll." She leaned down and held out her hand. He shook it, looking searchingly up into her face. He had rheumy eyes and the veined, bulbous nose that accompanies a life of habitual drunkenness, but his smile was as gentle and gap-toothed as a child's.

"Ah, that was a terrible morning, to find I'd been sleeping all night beside a corpse! It's good to see you again, miss. You'll be looking for Dr. Watson, then?"

"What do you know of Dr. Watson?" asked Justine. "Do you know his location—"

"Oh, aye," said Poor Richard. "He's here, in this den of iniquity, or house of merciful dreams as some calls it. Mr. Holmes said to me—Richard he said, I think they've discovered who I am, and if they have, then they'll come for me, most likely tonight. You go tell Dr. Watson where you saw me, and tell him the man who kidnapped me is an old enemy of ours who we thought dead. Or something to that effect—I don't remember his words exactly. He would not give me a note, he said, in case they found it on me. He wanted me to remember, despite my memory not being so good, as I said. So I went to find Dr. Watson, but I had a bit of a tipple first to get my courage up, and on the way to Baker Street a copper stopped me for begging and vagrancy, so I spent a week in prison before the warden got around to my case and realized it was me—we're old friends, the warden and I. He said there was no harm in me, and anyway they needed the cell for another, so he let me go instead of sending me before the judge. Then I made my way over to Baker Street and told Dr. Watson what Mr. Holmes had told me, but I could not remember exactly where I had seen Mr. Holmes, except that it was one of the opium dens in this part of town. So I offered to lead Dr. Watson here, feeling badly for having forgotten which one I had seen Mr. Holmes in, and for being in gaol for a week, though it weren't my fault. That was—it must have been yesterday, or maybe the day before that—I don't rightly remember."

"More than a week ago," said Mary. Evidently, Poor Richard did not have a very firm grasp of time. That was when Dr. Watson had disappeared—he must have been going from opium den to opium den ever since, trying to find news of Mr. Holmes. Mary hoped Poor Richard was right and Watson was inside this particular establishment. The beggar might mean well, but his memory was not to be trusted. "An old enemy of ours, that we thought dead—whom could Mr. Holmes mean by that?" asked Mary. "Does it have something to do with the opium trade? Each of these houses seems to be run by a Chinaman. . . ."

"Oh, that's just for show," said Poor Richard. "Like them gold dragons on the walls and the Chinese furnishings. People expect a Chinaman, so the proprietor supplies them. It's part of the image, you see. But all the opium houses in these streets belong to an Englishman—Colonel Moran, they call him. He's a big fellow that looks as though he could break bones. He's a toff, he is—I've seen him come down in his fancy brougham. I called him 'Your Lordship' once, hoping to get a few pennies. He said, 'Out of my way,' as though I weren't nothing but a bit of refuse blowing about the streets, and his lieutenant pushed me so that I fell in the mud." He looked as scornful as a fundamentally gentle man can look. "He makes a bundle out of these houses, I'll be bound. A lot of gentlemen come here to forget themselves and their sorrows."

"And you say Dr. Watson is inside this establishment?" said Justine.

"Indeed, and you'd best talk with him yourselves—I've told you all I know. I ain't seen Mr. Holmes since that day he gave me the message for Dr. Watson."

Mary had no money—she had given it all to Mr. Justin Frank,

who was more likely to have a full purse than Mary Mulligan, which was the name she had chosen for herself. "Give him a shilling, won't you?" she whispered to Justine, although if she was going to keep tipping informants at this rate, she would soon run out of money! Detecting was an expensive business. "And come on. We need to find Dr. Watson."

> MRS. POOLE: I cannot believe the two of you went into such a place! With all those men lying about on the floors and whatnot.

> MARY: It really wasn't that different from any gentlemen's club, Mrs. Poole. Except for the lying on floors bit. Although they weren't on floors, but on cushions mostly, the kind they call ottomans I think. But you could smell the opium—a thick, heavy smell.

> MRS. POOLE: What your mother would think, I simply don't know.

Once again they were greeted by a Chinaman, although this time instead of bowing silently he said, "Welcome, honorable visitors, to this humble house." No doubt it was supposed to sound foreign, but his accent was decidedly cockney.

This opium den resembled the others, as though they had all been decorated by the same person who had been told to leave out no detail that could refer to the East, but in an even more sumptuous style. There were gilded sculptures of dragons guarding the doorways, and screens with dragons on them partitioning the rooms, and dragons embroidered on the cushions. The light was dim, the decor opulent, the air heavy with the smell of opium.

Mary kept almost tripping over low tables on which were placed opium pipes, cups of tea without handles, and plates with a selection of biscuits and sweets. The clientele was well dressed: These were gentlemen, for the most part. Of course, working men could not afford such a place, nor the release that opium provides.

"He's not here," said Justine, looking around the first room and behind the screens. "We must venture deeper."

Dr. Watson was not in the second room, either, but in the third room—there he sat, looking dejected, next to a fair-haired man from whose fingers dangled an opium pipe. Mary was so relieved to see him that she almost forgot her disguise. But no, she must remain Mary Mulligan, at least for now. It would not do to call out to him, and he could not see them—he was looking steadily at the floor, and talking to the fair man in low tones.

Mary walked across the room and sat down next to him on an ottoman. "Hello, love," she said in what she hoped was a convincing Whitechapel accent but was probably not—our Mary is not very good at accents.

> MARY: I did the best I could! I'm sorry that I'm not as good at acting as Diana. I'm not used to *lying* about myself.

Dr. Watson looked up at her, startled. But he looked even more startled when he saw her face and recognized Miss Mary Jekyll, of 11 Park Terrace, under the rouge and lampblack.

"I'm Mary Mulligan," she said rapidly, before he could make a fuss. "And this is Mr. Justin Frank, who brought me here. He's a friend of yours, remember?"

"Of course, of course," said Dr. Watson, looking up at Justine. "This is Mr. Gray." He gestured toward the fair-haired man who was looking at them curiously. When Mary saw his face, she was

startled by its youth and beauty. He had a look of perfect innocence, as though a vile or unworthy thought had never entered his
head. What was he doing in a place like this? "He has been provid-
ing me with information. I am not partaking of the drug, I assure
you. I am here trying to locate Holmes, who has been missing for
some time. I've looked for him in several of these places—this is
the first time I have been able to hear anything of him. But what
are you doing back from—well, this is not the time. Mr. Gray,
this is Miss Mary Mulligan. She is also an associate of Mr. Holmes."

"Is she now?" said Mr. Gray, looking at her curiously, no doubt
wondering why Mr. Holmes would have such an associate. He
glanced at Justine, and his eyes widened just a little, as though in
surprise.

"What sort of information?" asked Mary. She looked around—
no one seemed to be paying attention to them. Could they talk
freely here? She was not sure. And who was Mr. Gray? Was he
involved in this matter somehow?

"Sir, if you'll take a seat," said Mr. Gray to Justine, indicating
a place beside him on the ottoman. He smiled—it was a particularly engaging smile—and his eyes expressed frank admiration.
Well, Justine did make a particularly handsome man, after all!
Mary, a little annoyed to be overlooked, sat down on the other
side of Watson.

"Among other things, he has told me that Holmes was here
more than a week ago, and that he left in the company of the proprietor of the place—and not willingly."

"The proprietor?" said Mary. "Do you know who he is? Poor
Richard told us he was not the Chinaman who greeted us at the
door, but an Englishman—a Colonel Moran."

Mr. Gray gave a low laugh. "That Chinaman isn't even Chinese,
although he enjoys playing the part. Mr. Bintang is from Sumatra,
although he's lived in London for twenty years. He goes by Bobby

and plays cricket on his days off. And no, Moran is merely an agent of a higher and more sinister power. The proprietor is a man named Moriarty, who styles himself a professor, and a poisonous man he is. Moran is simply his chief henchman. I would not come here myself—but it's one of the few places in London where I'm still welcome."

"Moriarty—I have heard that name before," said Justine. "But I cannot recall where?"

"You are French!" said Mr. Gray, looking at Justine with curiosity as well as admiration. "I cannot quite place your accent. I myself adore the French—their fashions, their novels, their *jeu d'esprit*. Do you ever go to Antibes? I have a house there. If you ever wish to visit . . ."

"I am Swiss," said Justine, looking both pleased and a little confused. "I have never been to the south of France. I have heard it is very pleasant, and a wonderful place to paint."

Oh, for goodness' sake! They were sitting in an opium den, trying to find two of their friends who had, it now seemed, both been kidnapped! This was no time for a flirtation.

Mary leaned forward. "You've heard that name because Catherine read us Dr. Watson's stories in *The Strand*, remember? While Mrs. Poole was teaching me to knit, and Beatrice was doing some sort of intricate embroidery, and you were—I don't remember what you were doing. But Professor Moriarty died at Reichenbach Falls. At least, that is what Dr. Watson wrote." She looked at Watson almost accusingly.

"That is what Holmes himself told me," said Watson. "But then, I believed Holmes to be dead as well. I was astonished when he revealed that he had not died in the waters of the falls but found a small ledge to stand upon. It seems Professor Moriarty also escaped the falls alive, and has been conducting his nefarious operations here in London for some time. Miss—Mulligan, I think I had better get you and your friend home. I came here because Holmes was last seen in one of these places—the beggar Poor Richard conveyed this information to me. Mr. Gray has confirmed that Holmes spent considerable time in this establishment—he saw Mr. Holmes here himself about a fortnight ago. But I have been here three days without finding out any more, although Mr. Gray has been very helpful—he has, among other things, informed me that Professor Moriarty is still alive. We can conjecture that Holmes's old enemy Moriarty, as well as his lieutenant Moran, are somehow involved in his disappearance. I am surprised to see you back from Budapest, but now that you are here, perhaps we had better regroup and recalibrate. You know I hesitate to involve you in such a dangerous enterprise, but this is a matter of Holmes's life. I would be most grateful for your help."

"And I for yours," said Mary. Should she tell him about Alice? No, not here—she was not at all sure whether to trust Mr. Gray, and anyway, they still did not know if Alice's kidnapping had anything to do with Mr. Holmes's disappearance. It could be a separate matter altogether.

"You will call upon me, will you not?" Mr. Gray was saying to Justine. "At my house in Grosvenor Square, I have some art I would like to show you—lovely pieces. Sculptures as well, tapestries . . . I am a collector, you see. And remember, you are always welcome in Antibes."

"Thank you," said Justine, lowering her eyes. How utterly ridiculous—she was actually responding to his advances! Although Mary had to admit that if the force of Mr. Gray's charms had been turned on her, she might well have behaved in the same way.

> MARY: I would most certainly have not! Mr. Gray was
> not at all my type. Who was he, anyway? A man
> we met in an opium den! Imagine what sort of

dissolute life he must lead, although indeed he did not look like the sort of person one would expect to see there. He had a sort of choir boy look about him, as though one might meet him at a Sunday School outing.

BEATRICE: Do you truly not know who he was? Mr. Dorian Gray, the lover of Mr. Oscar Wilde, who was sent to Reading Gaol for—well, for holding opinions that society does not approve of! For believing in beauty, and art, and love. What guilt and remorse he must feel, for causing the downfall of the greatest playwright of the age! It was Mr. Gray's dissolute parties, the antics of his hedonistic friends, that exposed Mr. Wilde to scandal and opprobrium. No wonder he has fallen prey to the narcotic.

MARY: Or he could just like opium. He didn't seem particularly remorseful, Bea.

JUSTINE: Mr. Gray is not what society deems him to be. He has been greatly misunderstood. He assures me that he had no intention of harming Mr. Wilde.

MARY: He *would* say that.

CATHERINE: Can we not discuss the Wilde scandal in the middle of my book? You're going to get it banned in Boston, and such other puritanical places.

BEATRICE: I think we must stand up for what we believe to be right. Surely you do not think that

Mr. Wilde should have been confined in such a barbaric fashion, for so trivial a reason? I've heard that his health is entirely ruined. We cannot help whom we love.

JUSTINE: Are you speaking of Mr. Wilde, or of yourself and Clarence?

MARY: So it's *your* book, is it? I thought you said it was *our* book. Why is it always *your* book when you want to leave something out, but *our* book when you want us to contribute?

"Thank you, my friend," said Dr. Watson, gripping Mr. Gray's hand. "If you do hear anything more of Holmes, you'll contact me, won't you? And remember that the inhabitants of 221B Baker Street are at your service."

"I will, Dr. Watson," said Mr. Gray. "And thank you—your conversation over these last few days—your friendship—has meant a great deal to me. There are not many men in England who would speak to me as kindly as you have. I am an outcast in this country—for a short time, you made me feel as though I were an Englishman like any other. I hope to see you again, in a better place than this."

"Why not come with us?" said Watson. "You are welcome to lunch—or is it dinner? I've lost track of time in this place. You would feel better for fresh air, and exercise, and Mrs. Hudson's cooking."

"You are most kind," said Mr. Gray, with a melancholy smile, "but I think I will remain here for some time at least. I have a great deal—more than most men—to forget. And, Mr. Frank, remember, I count upon you for a visit."

Dr. Watson shook his head, but took his leave of Mr. Gray.

Mary and Justine followed him back though the rooms of the opium den, to the entrance where the supposed Chinaman—Bobby who played cricket and spoke with a cockney accent—accepted a rather large sum of money from Watson and bowed them out ostentatiously. Mary felt so much better when they were out on the street again, away from all those fumes. They had given her a headache!

It was already midafternoon by the time they reached Baker Street. Mrs. Hudson sighed with relief to see Dr. Watson, then exclaimed over the state of their clothes—none of them looked particularly reputable, Mary least of all! "I'll bring up some tea," she said. "Surely you all need it, after whatever adventure you have been on." She looked once again surreptitiously at Mary, who drew her shawl more closely around her borrowed dress.

"Tell me what you know of Mr. Holmes and this mysterious errand of his," Mary said once they were seated in the parlor, waiting for tea and sandwiches from Mrs. Hudson.

"Very little, I'm afraid," said Watson. He ran his fingers through his hair. Mary had never seen him look so perplexed or put out. "He disappeared shortly after you left for Europe, saying his brother Mycroft had sent him on an errand of such secrecy and urgency that he could not even tell me about it. After that I heard nothing of or from him until Poor Richard came to me with his message. I was terribly worried, but did not wish to betray his trust by attempting to track him down—he would not have welcomed my interference. However, when Poor Richard told me that Holmes had requested my help, I knew that I had to act. But what are you, Miss Jekyll and Miss Frankenstein, doing back from Europe? How did you come to be in that den of iniquity?"

As succinctly as she could, Mary told him about the telegram they had received and Alice's disappearance, as well as what they had discovered up to that point—what little they had discovered, because they still knew so very little about where Alice might be.

"So you see," said Mary, "we followed the clues we had—the list of addresses on your blotter—as Mr. Holmes himself would have done." She did not apologize for intruding into his room. Surely Holmes would have done the same? "But we must also look for any clues as to Mrs. Raymond's whereabouts. Or Mrs. Herbert's, if indeed they are the same woman. Do you remember—"

"The Herbert murder case?" said Watson. "Yes, vaguely. I'm certain Holmes has the files—he has records of every murder committed in London for the last twenty years. So Mrs. Raymond may be Mrs. Herbert! Well, with her notoriety, she would have had to leave the country or hide under another name. Half of London believed she was innocent, while the other half was calling for her blood. But let me see if I can find the case file."

"Allow me," said Mary. After all, she was the one in charge of the files, was she not? She was Mr. Holmes's assistant. She had never seen that particular case, but guessed where it might be—there was a box of cases in his room that she had not yet filed. She would look in there.

By the time Mrs. Hudson brought up tea and sandwiches, they were already deep into the files of the Herbert murder case, which had indeed been in that box. No wonder Mary had never seen it before, or she might at least have remembered the name.

"Third gentleman found dead in the vicinity of Paul Street." Mary looked down at a notice clipped out of *The Times*. "That was on June third, 1883. The account in *The Daily Mail* says he appears to have died of fright, like the other two men—but you know these sensational papers. You can't trust a thing they say!"

"August seventeenth, Herbert himself was found dead. Look here—" Dr. Watson pointed at another article that had been neatly clipped and filed. "*The Herald* contains a particularly gruesome description of the victim—evidently, his face was frozen in a ghastly expression of fear, as though he had seen something too terrible to be borne. That's *The Herald* for you—an objective account isn't enough. It must be embellished with all sorts of gothic flourishes. It says his widow is suspected of doing away with him for the insurance money. *The Times* again, October seventh: 'Mrs. Herbert, who was recently acquitted in the murder of her husband, Mr. Charles Herbert of Paul Street, has been reported missing. The Metropolitan Police are particularly anxious to find her, as she is with child.' I'm not sure this enlightens us at all, Miss Jekyll. Even if Mrs. Raymond had a disreputable past—even if, as Mrs. Herbert, she murdered her husband and those other three fellows—what does that have to do with the disappearance of little Alice?"

"Pardon me, Dr. Watson, but remember that little Alice is also Lydia Raymond," said Justine. "Or so Frau Gottleib told us, and we have no reason to disbelieve her. If Mrs. Raymond was with child, perhaps that child was Alice? Perhaps she kidnapped Alice because she wished to be reunited with her daughter."

"I rather doubt that Mrs. Raymond is overflowing with maternal instincts," said Mary. What sorts of sandwiches had Mrs. Hudson brought up? Ham and cucumber. She felt in need of ham. She was not entirely recovered from the miasma of the opium dens. A ham sandwich and very strong tea—that was what she needed. Luckily, Mrs. Hudson's tea was always strong and hot. She added sugar, which she did not usually take, to revive her spirits, and then a slice of lemon. "If she kidnapped Alice, it may be because of her mesmerical powers, as Ayesha suggested. After all, according to Frau Gottleib, Mrs. Raymond had those powers herself, as a result of Dr. Raymond's experiments."

"But for what purpose?" asked Watson. He looked down at the file folder on his lap and rifled, once again, through its contents. "What use is the power of creating illusions? They cannot alter empirical reality."

"Nevertheless, they can frighten a man to death," said Mary. "What if the newspaper accounts of men being frightened to death are not mere sensationalism? Imagine if a tiger were coming at you—or a giant serpent, or something even more terrifying. Could that not be what happened in these cases? We cannot know what frightened these gentlemen to death, but surely Mrs. Raymond can produce such an illusion."

"Poor Alice!" said Justine. "She must be terrified if she is in the power of a woman like Mrs. Raymond. How can we find her? And Mr. Holmes, of course. Does her disappearance have anything to do with Mr. Holmes? I think not—we have found no connection between them."

"Then we should pursue two lines of inquiry," said Mary. "We need to find out more about Mrs. Raymond—if we find her, we will also find Alice. We don't know if Diana has found out anything—the Baker Street boys are resourceful, but this inquiry may be beyond their powers. They are only boys, after all."

> DIANA: Only boys! The Baker Street boys, only boys? Oh, if Wiggins heard you say that . . .

> MARY: That was a long time ago. I have since seen for myself what courageous and resourceful young men they are. Mr. Wiggins knows how much I respect him and his organization.

> DIANA: Well, all right then.

"I hate to suggest it," continued Mary, "but might this be the time to go to Inspector Lestrade? I honestly don't know if he will agree to answer any of our questions, but Scotland Yard was keeping an eye on Mrs. Raymond because of the Whitechapel Murders.

If we tell him she was also Mrs. Herbert, he may be able to tell us something about where she has gone, or is likely to go."

"And I would like to ask him about Moriarty," said Watson. "Before his death—well, his supposed death, as we now know— Moriarty was a mastermind of London's criminal underworld. It seems as though he has resumed his illegitimate activities. I would like to know more about what he's doing now. However, before we go to Scotland Yard, I suggest trying once more at the Diogenes Club. It may be that Mycroft has returned from wherever he's been this past week. I would like to consult him—or rather, confront him, because it is clear that he has put Holmes in danger. He should at least be willing to tell us what sort of danger!"

"Well then, let us meet tomorrow morning," said Mary. "Dr. Watson, could you lend me a coat or jacket of some sort to cover this dress? If I return to Park Terrace looking like this, Mrs. Poole will have a fit."

> MRS. POOLE: When have I ever had fits? You girls
> dress in all sorts of ways—as ministers of
> the Lord and circus performers, as women in
> unfortunate circumstances. . . . Someday, you'll
> go out looking like chimney sweeps, for all I
> know! I have never once had a fit, no matter what
> you have looked like.

> CATHERINE: You're right, Mrs. Poole. We don't give
> you nearly enough credit.

> MARY: We really don't, Mrs. Poole. If it weren't for
> you, the Athena Club could not function—and
> none of us would ever get our breakfast! We are
> most grateful, I assure you.

DIANA: Speak for yourself! I think we would get along just fine without Mrs. Busy Body bothering us to take meals and baths and go to bed because it is past our bedtime. . . . Who invented the idea of bedtime, anyway?

MRS. POOLE: Which it is—past your bedtime, I mean. So off with you! And don't make that face at me, young lady! Or start with your endless complaining. When have I taken notice of it? Never, that's when.

# CHAPTER VII

## The Scarab Necklace

What had Alice been doing all this time? The problem with being imprisoned, she had discovered, was that it was just so boring. Usually, her days were filled with activity from dawn to dinner. There were fires to lay, and breakfast to get, and then the washing up, and a few hours for dusting and general cleaning before lunch, and then she and Mrs. Poole would sit down to do the housekeeping accounts—Mrs. Poole was teaching her how—and plan their afternoon. Trips to the grocer's, the butcher's, the baker's, sometimes the fishmonger's or fruit seller's—there was always a great deal to do, things to see and learn. Now all she could do was sit on her bed reading *The Water-Babies*—could this book be any more dull?—and wait to be summoned. Really, she felt about ready to tear her hair out!

It was another hour before Gitla came, unlocked the door, and mimed something that looked like eating. Finally, she was going to have breakfast! Goodness, it must be nearly ten o'clock. Breakfast at Park Terrace was always served at eight sharp. Everyone in this house must be terribly lazy. She had been up and dressed, in another of the fancy dresses from the wardrobe, this time a green-and-blue plaid one, for hours.

As she followed Gitla down the hall, she reminded herself: *You have a plan. Follow the plan, no matter what happens. Don't be afraid, or at least don't show you're afraid. You must help Mr. Holmes.* Was he ill, or under the influence of some powerful narcotic? Alice thought the latter. After all, how else would Moriarty be able to imprison a man like the detective? If she could figure out where the drug was kept and how it was administered, perhaps she could do something . . . although she did not, at this particular moment, know what.

She was worried that she might have to endure a meal with those men again—she no longer thought of them as gentlemen. Perhaps it was not her place to judge—well, it was not the place of a kitchen maid to judge, although Alice knew her own mind of course—but she had found them both rude and frightening, especially Professor Moriarty. Despite Lord Godalming's handsome countenance, she did not trust him an inch. Mr. Morris had been ridiculous in that American getup. She could tell he was the sort of man who was constantly posturing for others. Dr. Seward had looked like a turnip carved for All Hallows, and Dr. Raymond had reminded her of a dried-up prune. They might have fancy initials after their names, but she knew them for what they were—the sorts of men who imprisoned helpless Beast Men. Colonel Moran had been, quite simply, a bully. She knew the type well from her years at the orphanage, where the headmistress's son had been exactly the same way. He had been large for his age, and enjoyed lording it over the smallest children. Mr. Harker had been a nonentity—even she could tell that he simply did not matter, that he was there because seven men were needed for whatever ritual they were planning. And Professor Moriarty—thinking of him sent shivers down her spine. There had been a light in his eyes that she had seen before in the eyes of a hellfire and brimstone preacher who had come to the orphanage and told the girls, who had not two pennies to rub together, that most of them were going to Hell. The rows of orphan girls, with holes in their stockings and nothing in their pockets, had watched him in stony silence, until one of the little ones started wailing and had to be taken away by a matron. And his plans for England—she had not entirely understood what he was saying. There were foreign words in his speech—she suspected they were Greek, and she knew only a little Greek. Nevertheless, she knew that they were *wrong*. Would she have to share another meal with them?

But no, when Gitla opened the door at the end of a passage-way on the ground floor, she saw only Mrs. Raymond and Miss Trelawny. They were sitting in a small, pleasant room that looked quite different from the rest of the house. Its walls were papered in a floral pattern. It had a desk in one corner, a sofa, and a com-fortable reading chair in front of the fireplace. In front of the window was a round table set for breakfast, and seated at the table were the two women, quite alone, thank goodness.

"Good morning, Lydia," said Miss Trelawny. "We're about to have breakfast. We hoped you would join us. Did you sleep well?"

"Yes, thank you," said Alice. Now was the time to implement her plan. Could she do it? She steeled herself for the most difficult thing she had done in her life. She walked up to Mrs. Raymond, leaned forward, said, "Good morning, Mother," and kissed her on the cheek.

Mrs. Raymond turned as though startled and looked at her with astonishment.

"I've been thinking since yesterday, just alone in my room," Alice continued. "And . . . well, I've decided to help you, Miss Trelawny. With mesmerism, you know. Like Professor Moriarty and my . . . mother wanted."

"Oh?" said Miss Trelawny. "Were you persuaded by Moriarty's diatribe—that is, argument—yesterday?"

She was smiling, but there was something in her expression . . . and the energic waves around her head were darker than usual. What should Alice say? That she had been convinced by Moriarty, even though his idea of an England for Englishmen was the stupid-est and most frightening thing she had ever heard? After all, Mr.

Byles, the butcher, was English right enough, but what about Mr. Patel, the grocer, who always saved the best vegetables for Mrs. Poole, so she would go nowhere else, or Mrs. Jablonski, who made the best bread in Marylebone? Or Mr. Nolan, who was a groundskeeper in Regent's Park and always greeted her so kindly when she walked through the park on errands? He was Irish. Did that count as part of the professor's England? Alice rather thought not. And what Moriarty had said about the Queen—well, that was blasphemy! What in the world would Mrs. Poole do if she heard such a thing? She would hit Professor Moriarty with a rolling pin, and he would deserve it. Could she convincingly tell Miss Trelawny that she thought his ridiculous plan was a splendid idea?

"No, that's all rot," she said. "But I want to spend more time with my mother. After all, we haven't seen each other since I was a baby. She may have abandoned me in an orphanage"—here she looked at Mrs. Raymond accusingly—"but she's still my mother. Or so she tells me."

"You don't understand," said Mrs. Raymond, frowning—but not as though she were angry, simply as though she were displeased at having to remember what had happened so long ago. "I had been accused of murdering my husband—your father. Although I was acquitted for lack of evidence, the police would not give up— there was a young sergeant who was convinced I was guilty. I had to get away from London. How could I do that with a child—an infant? You were only three months old. And I would have been putting you in danger as well. Besides, I was not fit to be a mother, not then—perhaps not even now. Some women are born to be mothers; some are not. I am the latter sort."

"Fit or not, you are a mother—my mother," said Alice. "So I'd like to get to know you better. Also, I'm hungry."

Miss Trelawny laughed. "Come sit down, Lydia." She patted the chair next to her. "Mrs. Mandelbaum may not speak English, but she can certainly make an English breakfast! Toast and marmalade, eggs, sausage—" She was heaping these on a plate as she spoke. "Milk and sugar in your tea? You look like the milk and sugar type. And please do call me Margaret. We're friends, are we not? There's no need to be formal among ourselves."

The breakfast was indeed excellent, and Alice had been right— she was hungry. She had not realized how very hungry until there were sausages and eggs and toast on her plate, under her nose. Then, despite her best effort to remain ladylike—as ladylike as Mary would have been under the circumstances—she began to eat with a sort of restrained ravenousness.

"Are all the items for the ritual properly situated?" asked Mrs. Raymond, turning to Miss Trelawny—or rather Margaret—and continuing whatever conversation they had been having before Alice entered.

"I believe so," said Margaret. "That's where I was yesterday morning, or I would have come sooner. I measured between the altar and sarcophagus myself."

"As *she* directed?" asked Mrs. Raymond, whom we may as well, at this point, call Helen. After all, she was not quite the woman Mary had met at the Magdalen Society anymore. She was younger, less harsh in her manner—and she was Alice's mother. "They have to be placed correctly for the energic waves to flow through them."

"Of course." Margaret put her hand up to the ruby beetle at her throat. "I assure you, I've followed directions precisely. I'm going back again this afternoon. I want to check the Hathor lamps one more time. When we get to that part of the ritual—"

"Little pitchers have big ears," said Helen, warningly.

"What—oh, you mean Lydia? I don't think she's even listening. Lydia?"

Alice looked up from a deliciously runny egg she had been trying to get onto a piece of toast. "Yes, ma'am?"

"There's no need to ma'am me. Do you agree with Helen?"

Alice tried to look startled and innocent. "Um, yes, of course."

"About the fact that Professor Moriarty resembles a fish?"

"Oh yes." Alice sighed with what she hoped was obvious relief. "He does, a little. A flounder, I should say. Not that I've been acquainted with many flounders, except the ones at the fishmonger's." *Listen and observe. And don't let them know you're doing it.* She had received valuable training in that at the orphanage.

"There, you see? Lydia agrees with you," said Margaret. "Would you like another cup of tea, Lydia? Eat up, there's a good girl. I need to be back at the British Museum at noon. The exhibit opens next week, and there are still boxes to unpack, artifacts to arrange. We want the tomb of Queen Tera to be set up just right, so visitors can see exactly what we saw when we opened the tomb."

"Were you with your father in Egypt?" asked Alice, astonished. She knew, of course, that Egypt was a real country—after all, it was mentioned in the Bible. But actually going there seemed only slightly less fantastical to her than going to the moon.

"Of course!" Margaret smiled. "I was my father's unofficial assistant—his amanuensis. I did his research for him, wrote down all his findings—indeed, I often wrote the first drafts of his papers. He would revise them, of course, adding all sorts of technical phraseology I did not know. I had raised the possibility of going to university myself—Girton would have been my first choice—but he did not believe a university education was suitable for women. 'You will get married and have children,' he said. 'And then it will all have been a waste of your time and my money.' But when we entered the tomb of Queen Tera, it was I who deciphered the hieroglyphs on the walls. The inscriptions were in both the hieroglyphic writing of ancient Egypt and the Greek used in Alexandria during the Ptolemaic Dynasty. Do you know anything about the Ptolemaic Dynasty, Lydia? I don't know how much you were taught—"

Alice just shook her head. Beatrice had taught her the natural sciences, and a little Latin and Greek. Mary had taught her history and geography. Justine had taught her philosophy, which she did not particularly understand. Catherine had taught her literature, and Mrs. Poole had taught her arithmetics. But no one had taught her anything about ancient Egyptian dynasties.

"Well," said Margaret, with evident pleasure—she seemed to enjoy explaining to someone who knew nothing about the subject, "there were many Ptolemies, so we distinguish them by epithets. Tera was a queen before she was a priestess of Isis, the second wife of Ptolemy Auletes. His first wife, who was also his sister, bore him a daughter, Berenice, but was too sickly afterward to bear another child, so he set her aside and married Tera, the daughter of the High Priest of Ptah at Memphis. For generations, the Ptolemies had not married outside their own family. Brother married sister, uncle married niece, with terrible results—deformity and madness in the family line. Tera was a popular choice—the Egyptians were rebelling against Macedonian rule, and she was a native Egyptian. She bore Ptolemy three healthy children— Cleopatra, Arsinoë, and his son Ptolemy, called Philopator. She ruled Egypt for several years while her husband was exiled in Rome, then ceded the throne again on his return. When he died, his son Philopator and daughter Cleopatra ascended the throne. Cleopatra said the Goddess Isis had come to her in a dream and told her that Tera should become the High Priestess of Isis at Philae. It was, of course, to get her out of Alexandria so she would not try to assume the throne again herself. She would certainly have made a better ruler than her daughter!"

Miss Trelawny sounded like a university professor. Mrs. Poole had once taken Alice to hear a professor of literature speak about *Wordsworth: Our English Bard* in a lecture at the Working Women's Institute, and he had sounded exactly the same way. Would

Margaret have liked to be a professor? If women could become professors—Alice was unsure on that point.

"You know the rest from Shakespeare," Margaret continued. "Cleopatra lost Rome to the armies of Augustus. After conquering Alexandria, Augustus sent a contingent of his soldiers to Philae, to the temple of Isis. He was hoping to capture the High Priestess, because he feared that she might once again claim the throne and lead a rebellion against Roman rule. The priestesses resisted his soldiers, and many of them were killed, including Tera. A tomb had already been prepared among the rocky hills that flanked that portion of the Nile, for Egyptians planned carefully for the after-life. The remaining priestesses interred her in that tomb, sealing the entrance and covering it with desert sand. There it remained undisturbed until my father discovered it a year ago."

"Your father! As though he had anything to do with the dis-covery." Helen snorted. "You're the one who discovered that tomb—and did he give you credit? Of course not."

"Well, you could say that I stumbled upon it," said Margaret. "You see, I had gone out to see the sunrise over the Nile—I had been awakened early by the call to prayer, which was chanted by the leader of our Arab bearers five times a day. As I climbed a sandy cliff, my foot slipped on the sand, and I felt something hard beneath it. For no reason other than idle curiosity, I leaned down and started to dig with my bare hands. When I realized it was a door set into the underlying rock, I went to get my father and Eugene Corbeck, a weasely little man my father employed to find him genuine artifacts in the markets of Cairo, where they were often sold by grave robbers. The three of us were the first to open that door—and then Corbeck went to fetch our bearers, to help us clear the rest of the sand from the tomb. It was carved directly into the cliff. Once we had cleared the entrance, I followed my father down a long passageway illuminated only by the light of our lanterns. We were excited, of course—it seemed to be a new tomb that had never been found by robbers. Any Egyptologist would be excited by such a discovery. But we did not expect what we would find at the end of that passage." Here she paused for a moment, her hand on the beetle at her throat, as though remembering.

"And what was that?" asked Alice. She could almost see it—the desert sand, the bright light of the Egyptian sun, and then the darkness of the passageway, illuminated only by lanterns. For the first time in her life, she wondered what it would be like to travel to faraway lands, to see such sights. Yes, she was just Alice the kitchen maid. Nevertheless, she would not mind seeing Egypt, or Greece, or the lands of the Bible. Perhaps someday . . .

Helen smiled and raised her left hand. She waved it like a con- ductor gesturing for the orchestra to begin. Suddenly, stone walls rose around them, covered in pictures unlike any Alice had ever seen—scenes of what life must have been like in ancient Egypt, as well as rows of hieroglyphs, which looked like small pictures them- selves. The room was growing dimmer. The three of them were standing beside—what was it? A large, oblong box made of stone, with a stone slab to cover it, carved and painted. Around them, set into the walls, burned seven lamps. By the walls stood furniture of various sorts: a narrow bed with a platform of woven reeds, several folding chairs and small tables, a cabinet with drawers, and what looked like a game board, all beautifully carved and painted. Along one wall was a narrow table on which was placed a series of intri- cately decorated boxes. Next to them was a mummified cat, with almond-shaped eyes and a whiskered smile painted on its wrappings.

"Have I gotten it right?" asked Helen, looking at Margaret. "This is how you described it when we first planned . . . you know."

"Close," said Margaret, looking around at the tomb of Queen Tera with pleasure, as though glad to be back there. "It was darker, of course. The lamps were not lit, not then, and we could not see as clearly by the light of our torches. The paint was worn, and some of the plaster had fallen. But you must show Lydia what we saw when we opened the sarcophagus itself."

Helen waved her hand. Suddenly, the top of the oblong box was gone. Inside the box was another, without a top, and inside that lay a woman. She was old—her face was covered with a web of wrinkles—but she must have been very beautiful in life. She had light brown skin, high cheekbones, and delicate features. White hair flowed past her shoulders, as fine as thistledown.

She was wrapped in white linen, with only her left arm outside the linen wrappings, placed over her chest, her hand where her heart would be. In it she held an ankh, the Egyptian symbol of life. Alice saw, with a start, that she had seven fingers! On her neck was a gold necklace with a ruby pendant in the shape of a beetle, just like Margaret's.

"Very beautiful," said Margaret. "But that was not how we found her."

Suddenly, the woman's wrappings turned brown. Her fine features shriveled up, until she looked positively ancient. The white hair fell out until there were only a few tangled strands. Her seven-fingered hand curled into a claw clutching the ankh. Only the necklace with the beetle on it stayed the same, glowing on her breast.

"That's more accurate," said Margaret. "It's a good re-creation. I wish I could show it to the visitors who will be flocking to the museum to see the exhibition. Instead, they will have to imagine it, based on the artifacts themselves."

"Is that the necklace you wear?" asked Alice, looking down at the one on the wrinkled brown neck of the mummified queen.

"It is," said Margaret. "Temporarily, of course, since Queen Tera may wish it back some day!" She smiled, as though making a joke. "It's a scarab—a beetle sacred to the Egyptians. The scarab beetle rolls its dung up into a ball, like Ra rolling the sun across the sky each day, from dawn to sunset—therefore, it was seen as a symbol of resurrection. The equivalence may seem strange to us—we are not accustomed to thinking of the sun as a dung ball! But the Egyptians did not scorn such humble things as beetles, or even their dung. The dung of the scarab beetle fertilized the fields of Egypt." She looked down at her wristwatch "Goodness, look at the time! I think we've been talking long enough. Now I had better go check on Queen Tera herself! If you will excuse me, Helen—"

The illusion swirled around them, like paints in a jar of turpentine, then melted into the floor. They were back in the pleasant room in the considerably less pleasant headquarters of the Order of the Golden Dawn, with the remains of breakfast in front of them.

"Go on, Lydia," said Margaret. "You can find your way back to your own room, can't you? Now that you have joined our cause, I don't think there's any need to keep you confined."

"Are you quite certain?" asked Helen, sounding surprised. "Of course, I could tell if Lydia tried to leave the environs of this house—I can sense her energic waves, as I can sense yours. And she would not make it past Moriarty's sentries. But I think it would be best if her room were kept locked."

So that was how her mother still thought of her—as a prisoner who might escape. *What does she mean that she can sense my energic waves?* Alice wondered. How far could this ability extend? Throughout the entire house? Beyond it? Well, it did not matter, because she was not planning to escape, not anymore. Now there was something more important than her personal safety involved. First, she needed to help Mr. Holmes, to get him out of this place. And after that, she needed to stop Moriarty, somehow. She had never imagined that it might be up to her, Alice the kitchen maid, to save the Queen, but there was no one else, was there? So she would have to do. If her mother could sense her energic waves— *Could I sense hers, if I tried?* She could see the waves, swirling around her mother's head. Would she be able to sense them at a distance?

"Yes, I'm certain," said Margaret. "You can't keep your own daughter locked up. Even you should know that! Lydia said she was on our side. I trust her—don't you?"

"It's for her own safety," said Helen, frowning. "Lydia, pay attention! You look as though you're a million miles away. Harker is a harmless idiot. Godalming and Seward are unlikely to concern themselves with you. But I don't trust Moriarty out of my sight. Moran does whatever Moriarty tells him, and as for my own father—well, he's far too interested in resuming his old experiments. Moriarty was delighted when one of the mesmerists we located told us about you. He suspected at once who you must be. I was skeptical—until I saw you myself. Then, of course, I knew. One cannot mistake the resemblance in our powers, or our energic signatures. I only wish I had noticed that night at the Magdalen Society—we could have become acquainted sooner. But I was not paying attention to you. My mind was entirely on Hyde, whose requests I was fulfilling as a representative of Moriarty. He is, among other things, in the business of supplying young women—he does not ask for what purposes. And while I'm glad to have found you again"—she did not look particularly glad, but perhaps it was the only way she could look glad?—"I'm concerned they might have plans for you that they haven't shared with me. Moriarty does not tell me everything— he is secretive, and a very dangerous, man. I will be glad when this ritual has been successfully completed."

"One of the mesmerists you found told you about me?" said Alice. It could only be Martin. Had he betrayed her? She had thought of him as a friend and teacher!

"Yes, Marvin I think his name was. A circus performer of some sort." Helen's voice was scornful. "These mesmerists are poor specimens—of all the so-called practitioners of mesmerism we found in London, only five of them proved to have any mesmerical abilities at all. This Marvin was the most powerful, and he said he knew of one more powerful than he was, a young girl with significant natural abilities although little training. Of course he did not know what we wanted mesmerists for—he thought we were putting on a show of some sort—*The Wonders of Mesmerism*!"

"Where are these mesmerists now?" asked Alice. "You haven't hurt them, have you?" At least, if Martin had betrayed her, he hadn't known he was doing it!

"No, we may have some use for them later. They are being, shall we say, stored where they cannot escape, under the watchful eye of the man who found them for us—a mountebank showman who calls himself Professor Petronius." Helen pushed her chair away from the table. "That's enough questions. I have important work to do, as does Margaret. All right, child, we'll do this her way—find your room, stay there, and don't get into trouble!"

> BEATRICE: Oh, that Professor Petronius! I wish I had
> never seen or heard of him again, after the way he
> treated me. But I am glad that, during our battle
> in Southwark, I was able to—

> CATHERINE: Oh no, you don't! All of you did this in
> the last book as well. I warned you about it then,
> and I'm warning you again now. No discussing
> important events before we actually get to them!

Alice waited a while in her room before sneaking out. It wasn't really sneaking, was it? She had permission now to roam around the house. But she did not want to run into Moriarty or any of the other men. She was frightened enough of them without her mother's warning.

There was no one in the hall, so she tried the door to the room where Sherlock Holmes was being held. It was locked. Once again she wished that she could open locks like Diana.

> DIANA: You see? You never want me until you do, and
> then if I'm not there, you're stuck!

What else could she do? Whatever drug he was being given would likely be kept in his room—or would it? Not if they wanted to keep it away from him. Then where? The bathroom! She walked back down to the end of the hall, to the room in which she had taken her bath. Yes, it contained a cabinet. In it were all the usual things one found in bathrooms: Dr. Lyon's Tooth Powder, Lloyd's Cocaine Toothache Drops, Dalton's Nerve Tonic, Bruceline Hair Restorer— that must be for Moriarty, whose hairline was certainly receding! Tweezers, a pair of small scissors, a mustache comb. What was that on the top shelf? A brown bottle—yes, it was marked BAYER HEROIN HYDROCHLORIDE. She unscrewed the top—sure enough, the bottle was half full of white powder. Next to it was a leather case. Alice took it down and opened it—there was the hypodermic. Presumably whoever gave him the drug mixed it with water in some sort of vessel—the tooth glass? Could she perhaps hide the bottle? No, another could easily be purchased at the nearest apothecary. Then could she dilute it somehow? What would be safe to substitute? She tried to remember what Mrs. Poole had taught her. *A woman is the nurse and doctor of her household,* Mrs. Poole had said. *Whether as wife, mother, or housekeeper, she should know how to treat an injury or illness. You never know when a doctor may be unavailable, or not arrive in time. All right, Alice, if a child had jaundice, what would you give him?* What would Mrs. Poole do in this case?

Salt. She could substitute salt, which should be indistinguishable from the powdered heroin. In water, it would make an ordinary saline solution. And where could she find salt? In the kitchen, of course. She would have to go downstairs and brave the Mandelbaums.

She returned the hypodermic case to the cabinet, exactly as she had found it, and screwed the top securely back onto the bottle of heroin. Then she walked along the hall as quietly and inconspicuously as she had been taught a maid should walk. How useful her training turned out to be in these difficult circumstances!

It was early afternoon. The headquarters of the English branch of the Alchemical Society—and now the Order of the Golden Dawn—was quiet and empty. On the second floor, she heard someone snoring in one of the rooms. On the ground floor, two male voices were quarreling behind a closed door. She put her ear to the keyhole for a moment as she passed, but could not make out what they were quarreling about.

She walked down the back stairs to the kitchen. Mrs. Mandelbaum was at the large black range, while Gitla was seated at a central table, peeling potatoes. Presumably for dinner? Clearly, no one had thought about Alice's lunch! Well, she was glad to be forgotten for a while. When they saw her, Gitla stood up and curtseyed, and Mrs. Mandelbaum, managing to look both friendly and apologetic at once, waved her in. *"Niech Panna usiądzie,"* she said, then put a plate of small pastries in front of Alice. They were the same kind that had been served the day before in the common room, when Moriarty had held his ridiculous meeting. The memory of that meeting still frightened Alice—she did not want to think about it. But her mouth began to water as soon as she saw the pastries. She must be hungry after all.

As she ate, she watched the Mandelbaums, mother and daughter, work. It felt strange to be sitting idly and not peeling potatoes herself. She almost offered to help Gitla, then reminded herself that, first, Gitla would not understand her, and second, she was supposed to be Lydia Raymond now, not Alice the kitchen maid.

Mrs. Mandelbaum took a pot off the stove and poured a dark brown liquid into a cup—ah, she had made coffee, and Alice had not even noticed! Her attention had been on those potatoes. Surely any minute now she would have the opportunity she was waiting for. . . .

Mrs. Mandelbaum added milk and sugar, then put the coffee cup on a saucer in front of her. Alice sipped it cautiously. In the Jekyll household, coffee had always been for visitors—she and Mrs. Poole had drunk good English tea. It was better than she expected, although very strong, despite the milk and sugar Mrs. Mandelbaum had added to it.

"Thank you," she said, not sure if Mrs. Mandelbaum would understand, but the housekeeper smiled and nodded. She seemed relieved not to be bringing Alice dry bread and water in a coal cellar! She still had a frightened look about her—as well she might, living in such a household! But she seemed a little more at ease than the last time Alice had been in this kitchen.

Gitla rinsed the potatoes, then salted them from a large salt shaker—a kitchen salt shaker, not one of the dainty silver shakers that sat on dinner tables. Was it too large? Alice was not sure. She hoped to goodness that her apron pocket would be large enough! It was such a silly apron, useless for any real work. Real aprons had two deep pockets, not this single ornamental one—but it would have to do. This was the moment. . . . Oh, how she hated to do this! All her training under Mrs. Poole rose up against the thought. But quickly, before she could think twice, she stood with the coffee cup and saucer in her hands, as though about to give them to Mrs. Mandelbaum. Suddenly, she tripped over nothing at all and stumbled forward. The cup and saucer dropped from her hands and crashed on the tiles. Pastry crumbs scattered, and drops of coffee spattered all over the place. Porcelain fragments flew through the air, littering the kitchen floor.

Alice gave a little scream, then raised her hands to her mouth and burst into tears. Truth to tell, she had wanted to cry all morning, although not perhaps as torrentially as the day before. This time, it had nothing to do with being a captive. Could it have to with what had happened at breakfast—when her mother had described leaving her at the orphanage? But what good would crying have done? Mary would not have cried, so she had tried not to, and had succeeded admirably. Now, as though a dam had burst, all those tears spilled out. Now they would serve her well—now she could cry.

Mrs. Mandelbaum said something she could not understand, no doubt telling her that it was all right, that she should not cry over broken dishes. Gitla sprang up and went to fetch a broom and dustpan. As soon as Mrs. Mandelbaum turned around, searching for something or other, Alice slipped the saltcellar into her apron pocket. Yes, the pocket was just large enough. In a moment, Mrs. Mandelbaum had handed her a clean dishcloth to cry into, and Gitla had returned to sweep up the mess. Alice stayed in the kitchen just long enough to finish crying convincingly, then thanked them and, still wiping her eyes, made her way out into the hall. Now to get back upstairs to the bathroom!

But wait, what was that? She could smell tobacco. . . . It was coming from the window at the end of the hall. Like all the other windows on the basement level, it was set high up in the wall and shaped like a half moon. One of the panes was open. Could that be one of Moriarty's guards smoking? Through the window, she could see—no, it could not be—but yes, it was. The back of a pair of bare, scrawny, bowed legs. They were covered with dirt.

Quickly and quietly, she walked to the window. "Pssst! Over here!" she whispered. She was taking a chance—but one had to take chances in life, didn't one? At least that's what Catherine was always saying.

Suddenly, the legs bent at the knees and knelt down. A startled and very dirty face appeared at the window. It was, as she had guessed, a boy about her own age, smoking a forbidden gasper.

"Cor blimey!" he said. "You nearly scared the life out of me, you did!"

"Be careful," she said in as low a voice as she could. Mrs. Mandelbaum and Gitla were all the way down the hall in the kitchen, but she did not want them to hear. "There are guards around the house. How did you get past them?"

"Oh, there are only two of them, and they're playing poker. It's not them I'm worried about. You're not going to tell Mum that you saw me smoking, are you? She'll wallop me if she finds out!"

"Of course not," said Alice. "I'm not a rat. How would you like some more of those, and better? Gentlemen's cigarettes. I'll make sure you get them if you do something for me."

"And what's that?" He looked at her suspiciously. As well he might—girls dressed as well as Lydia Raymond did not consort with the likes of him, or offer cigarettes for doing them favors! *But I'm not Lydia Raymond,* thought Alice. *I'm a Londoner born and bred, and I know a thing or two.*

"Do you know where to find the Baker Street boys?"

"Of course. Every chap in these parts knows about them! I'd like to be one myself, if Wiggins would take me. But you don't get to be a Baker Street boy just for the asking. They're very particular who they associate with, if you know what I mean."

"Can you get them a message for me? Tell them that Mr. Sherlock Holmes is being held prisoner in this house. He's being drugged with heroin so he won't escape. Tell them that Alice, Mary Jekyll's kitchen maid, sent you. Can you remember all that?" If he could tell the Baker Street boys, they could get a message to Dr. Watson, perhaps even Inspector Lestrade. And they would come to the rescue—or, at least, she hoped they would.

"Blimey! Mr. Holmes himself? This is like one of those *Boy's Own* adventure stories. I'll ask to see Wiggins himself. . . ."

"Yes, but get going, and don't let the guards see you," she said, impatiently.

"Right. I'm off!" He ground out the gasper under one boot heel, and for a moment she could see his bare legs running away. Then he was gone.

For a moment, she was tempted to run away herself. If the guards really were playing poker . . . But her mother had said she would be able to tell if Alice tried to leave, and Alice believed her. She was much more afraid of her mother than of the guards! And anyway, she still needed to adulterate the heroin. If she poured it down the sink and substituted the salt, whoever injected the drug into Mr. Holmes's veins would be injecting harmless salt water. He would, slowly but surely, recover from the drug—wouldn't he? Besides, she couldn't leave while there was a threat to Her Majesty. It was Alice's duty as an Englishwoman to stay and do her best in this situation, whatever the result.

As quietly as she could, since she did not want to attract the Mandelbaums' attention, Alice made her way back along the corridor. Would her message reach the Baker Street boys? Would Dr. Watson come to rescue Mr. Holmes—and her? Would he arrive in time? She had no idea. As she climbed back up to the second floor, where the great detective lay drugged and inaccessible, she hoped against hope that someone would come to save her and Mr. Holmes—soon.

## CHAPTER VIII

### Ayesha's Story

"W hy in the world did you bring Clarence?" Catherine whispered to Beatrice. They were standing outside the door of Ayesha's office in the Hungarian Academy of Sciences. She hoped he could not hear her—he was speaking to Frau Gottleib about something or other.

"He asked to meet Ayesha," said Beatrice, raising one hand in a gesture of helplessness. The other was holding the sort of portfolio used by legal clerks. "If I had said no, it would have seemed—strange, would it not? What reason could I have for refusing him? And she said that she would like to meet him, after I mentioned that we were having a meal together at the Centrál Kávéház."

"No reason, other than the fact that she's inhumanly beautiful, and can tell him what life was like in ancient Egypt based on personal experience. And that you don't want him falling in love with her, the way all sorts of men—and probably women—seem to."

"You are not being helpful!" whispered Beatrice.

Just then, the door opened. "Come in," said Leo Vincey. He sounded as sour and unwelcoming as ever. He still had four red scars on his face where Lucinda had scratched him, but they seemed to be healing well. He obviously did not like Catherine—and she did not particularly like him either. But he could at least be courteous! She and Mary had warned him and Professor Holly about Van Helsing's attack on the Alchemical Society, and he had not listened. Ayesha was probably angry with him, which was not Catherine's fault. It was easier for him to dislike her than to blame himself—she could understand that. It was just human nature—cats were so much more rational!

Ayesha's office looked exactly the same as the last time they had been here—the wooden desk, now with papers scattered over it, the plain wooden chairs, the shelves with back issues of the *Journal de Société des Alchimistes*. It was a utilitarian space, although behind Ayesha, who was seated at the desk, Catherine could see a magnificent view of the Danube and the Buda hills.

She rose when they entered. "Hello, Beatrice. And Catherine—it's a pleasure to see you again. Do come in." Today she was looking her usual self, which was unfortunate for Beatrice. But surely if anyone could resist Ayesha's charms, it would be Clarence! Ayesha was dressed in the same dress she had worn for the opening ceremony of the Alchemical Society meeting, a cloth of gold gown that Beatrice had identified as a House of Worth model from the fall collection, whatever that meant—Catherine did not speak Fashion. She was tall, as tall as Clarence, and her hair hung down in a hundred black braids. Her eyes were outlined with kohl. Also in the room with her, sitting around a table with documents piled on it, were Professor Horace Holly and Kati, Count Dracula's former parlor maid. Kati smiled and nodded at them. Professor Holly scowled, but that seemed to be his usual expression—indeed, he was scowling in a more welcoming way than usual.

"We were just sorting through the latest submissions to the journal of the society," said Ayesha. "Many of the members bring their submissions directly to the meeting to save on mailing costs. Have you come for any particular reason, or merely to visit?" Although her voice was gracious, they were clearly interrupting.

"I've brought the research protocols for the committee," said

Beatrice. She held out the portfolio she had been carrying. So that was what she had been so laboriously typing in Mina's study! "They contain the criteria for our approval of research in biological transmutation. Frau Gottleib thought it would be best if we made the criteria explicit, so alchemists who wished to perform such research could know ahead of time what the committee required for approval."

"Did she indeed?" Ayesha looked at Frau Gottleib skeptically.

"You appointed me chairwoman of the committee," said Frau Gottleib in her heavy German accent. "Did you expect me not to take that role seriously? Beatrice came up with some excellent proposals. You know I always believed in curtailing—or at least controlling—those experiments."

Ayesha opened the portfolio, took out a sheaf of closely type-written papers, and rifled through them. She shook her head and sighed. "You modern young people, with your scruples! But who is this?" She looked at Clarence.

"Clarence Jefferson, ma'am, at your service." He bowed.

"I don't need your service at present, Mr. Jefferson," she said crisply. "But if and when I do, I shall certainly call upon it. You are the Zulu Prince in the circus Beatrice has spoken about, are you not? She has told me about you. I was curious to meet a fellow African who has lived among these colonial powers."

"Yes, ma'am, that's me," he said. "At least, that's what I am, not who. It's a job, is all."

"Yet you are not a Zulu. You remind me of the people of Kôr—the Amahaggar. They too were tall and strong and comely, like the Nubians, my father's people. They too had lost their great civilization, which lies beneath the jungle. By the time I came to Kôr, it was already a city of the dead, and the Amahaggar had become a tribe rather than a great nation. Your ancestry is East African, is it not?

"I don't know," said Clarence. "All my mother could tell me was that her people came from Virginia. Her mother was a slave on a plantation there. Her father was a freedman, a blacksmith who had to buy her to marry her. And I don't know about my father's family. He died before I was born of typhoid fever. He was working for one of the railroad companies in Colorado, building the railroad, trying to make enough money to send back home, when he caught sick and died. He never told my mother where his folks came from, so that's all I know."

Ayesha frowned in anger. Catherine worried for a moment that she was going to start zapping someone! "How can this century pride itself on progress, when it perpetuates the barbaric institutions of the past in even baser form? Someday, the depredations of the European nations will end, and the land above the Zambezi will be free once more. If it happens within your lifetime, I will show you the land of your ancestors, Mr. Jefferson. Alas that I could not be the one to free it! But I was one woman against the British East Africa Company and its soldiers."

"Beatrice told me that you were a priestess in Egypt, a land I would like to visit," said Clarence. "How did you come to be here in Budapest, if you don't mind my asking?"

Ayesha smiled. It was the first genuine smile Catherine had seen her give in—well—ever. "Would you like to hear my story, Mr. Jefferson? Or Clarence, if I may? We were going to stop for coffee in about an hour, but perhaps this is as good a time. Sit down, all of you. Kati, could you fetch us some coffee? And perhaps some *kifli* to go with it."

"I'll help her," said Frau Gottleib. "I've heard this story, and I have more important things to do than hear it again."

"Thank you, Eva. If the rest of you would care to sit? That is, if you have nothing more pressing."

Well, they did have to finish packing! They would need to

catch the *Orient Express* to Paris tomorrow morning, and Catherine had not even started yet. She always seemed to put packing off until the last minute. Soon, they would be rejoining Mary and Justine—and Diana, of course. Hopefully Mary and Justine had already found Alice! But they could certainly spare an hour, and anyway, Clarence had already sat down. From the way he was looking at Ayesha, it was obvious that he wasn't going away without hearing her story, and Beatrice would not want to leave without him. Catherine was amused by Beatrice's jealousy. Not that Beatrice was vain, of course, but she was used to being the most beautiful one in any room.

> BEATRICE: I was not jealous! I was merely concerned
> that his fascination with Ayesha would put him in
> danger. Do not misunderstand me—I have great
> respect for our Madam President. But she has lived
> so long that she no longer understands human
> morality. Those around her must remind her of
> the need for empathy and compassion.

> CATHERINE: Oh, so "concerned" is now a synonym for
> "jealous," is it? And she's certainly not *my* Madam
> President!

Ayesha, Princess of Meroë, Priestess of Isis, Queen of Kôr, and now President of the Alchemical Society, sat down on a corner of her desk and, with a faraway look in her eyes, began to speak.

"When my mother left me at the temple of Isis at Philae, I became just another of the postulants—that is the closest equivalent in English, I think—of the Goddess. In my father's palace, there had been servants to tend to me and my sisters—but at the temple, we were all servants of the Goddess. The girls came from every corner of Egypt and beyond—the sophisticated salons of Alexandria, the temple complexes of Memphis, the merchant houses of Damascus and Tyre. There were girls from Athens and Carthage and Babylon, for Isis was worshipped throughout the known world. We were all equal—that is, servants in the house of the Goddess—and the priestesses did not let us forget it! Indeed, I was considered rather slow and old, for I had come to the temple on my twelfth birthday, and some of the novices had been there since they were seven. We woke at dawn and bathed in cold water, then oiled our skin and hair. For an hour before breaking our fast, we cleaned the temple, so it would be fresh for each day. After a breakfast of barley bread with butter and honey, and a mug of beer for each of us, we studied for the rest of the morning. I missed my mother, my sisters, and brother—but to learn as we were learning! No school now teaches as we were taught in the temple of Isis.

"The greatest of our teachers, the one whose image even today I hold in my heart, was an Assyrian named Heduana, the priestess in charge of novices when I myself was one. She had been a princess in her own country, but at the temple such worldly distinctions meant little. We were all equal in the sight of the Goddess, except for those ranks established within the temple itself—the novices, junior priestesses, senior priestesses, and of course the High Priestess herself. Even she, despite her power, was simply called Tera.

"You know—or perhaps you infants of the modern age do not know—the story of Isis, how she healed her husband, Osiris, after he was murdered by his brother Set, who had cut his body into pieces and scattered them across Egypt. Isis searched for his body parts, keening with grief like a falcon. Her tears flooded the Nile, which is why the Nile floods to this day. When she had found all the parts of his body, she assembled the pieces and brought Osiris back to life with herbs and spells. She was, in a sense, the first physician. When I grew older and was inducted into the mysteries of the temple as a priestess myself, I learned that the gods were metaphors, names for energic forces—that all the world, from the stars down to gems hidden in the rocks, was filled with these energic forces, and that we could use them to heal. As novices we studied all the plants in the temple garden, learning their names and properties, their uses in medicine. We helped the priestesses treat the sick and poor who came to the temple.

"So I grew up in that place, under the tutelage of Heduana, and of Tera herself. She had been a queen—the wife of foolish Ptolemy, called by his friends Auletes and his enemies Nothos, which means bastard, for he was illegitimate, and she was the mother of ill-fated Cleopatra. When her husband died, she had been sent to the temple to serve as High Priestess, for Cleopatra considered her own mother a rival for the throne. She had a curious physical feature—seven fingers on her left hand. Now it would be considered a deformity, a congenital abnormality. Then, it was seen as the mark of Isis, whose sacred number was seven. She was an effective, if exacting, High Priestess. She ruled the temple as efficiently as she has once ruled Egypt while her husband was in exile. The novices were frightened of her, but the priestesses treated her with respect. Heduana always told us that she was not as frightening as she appeared to inconsequential beings such as ourselves. But she said this with a smile, for she loved us and we loved her in return. Heduana was our leader and guide. She never allowed us to slack in our studies or shirk our responsibilities to the sick who came to see us. 'You are serving the Goddess,' she would say. 'See that you do it well.' I remember, once, a novice who used her energic powers to kill a mouse that had been bothering her at night, squeaking about her room. The next day she was sent back home to Thebes. All of the novices were assembled to watch her walk out through the lion gates, wearing the clothes she had arrived in rather than the white linen of the Goddess. It would, Heduana said, be a lesson to us all never to abuse our powers."

"Yet you used your power to kill those vampires," said Beatrice. She sounded both perplexed and accusing.

Ayesha turned to her. "I am not the girl I was then. I have lived and learned a great deal, and I do not value life as I did. What would Heduana think of me now? I do not know." She looked grim.

Just then the door opened. In walked Kati with a coffee tray, followed by Lady Crowe bearing a plate of crescent pastries. "Hello, Catherine, Beatrice," she said. "How nice to see you again. Do give my love to Mary and Justine, and of course little Diana, when you see them. Ayesha, can I borrow Kati for a while? I need help sorting through the receipts from the conference. Based on how much was eaten, you'd think we had put on a conference for elephants!"

"If she doesn't mind, I don't," said Ayesha. "We're taking a sort of break, as you see. *Kati, tudsz segíteni Lady Crowe?*"

"Well, *some* people have time to," said Lady Crowe, but she was smiling. "*Gyere, Kati.* Let's leave these ne'er-do-wells to their break."

DIANA: *Little* Diana! I'll little her. . . .

Catherine poured herself a cup of coffee, then looked inquiringly at Beatrice. Beatrice held up two fingers, so she poured out two more. She was surprised—Beatrice did not ordinarily drink coffee, just green goop. But she supposed coffee beans were plant matter as well? Beatrice would not want cream or sugar, Clarence would want sugar, and she wanted hers with a great deal of cream. She prepared each cup, then passed two to Beatrice. Ah yes, that was better! As for the pastries, pumas did not eat such things. Professor Holly took several and poured himself a cup of coffee, but Leo simply shook his head.

MARY: You never drink coffee here at home! Or even
tea, unless it's one of those goopy green tisanes.

BEATRICE: I do not like the taste of it. But that
day, somehow, I wanted to seem more normal,
more like an ordinary woman. Yes, Catherine, I
suppose I was a little jealous. Clarence seemed so
fascinated by Ayesha's story, and of course with
Ayesha herself.

CATHERINE: Leo Vincey was looking daggers at him!
If it were physically possible, he would have killed
Clarence with his eyes.

MARY: And yet, Bea, you know that Clarence loves
you. I can't think of anyone more constant, more
faithful under difficult circumstances.

BEATRICE: Alas, that I myself am the difficult
circumstance.

"This Tera was Cleopatra's mother?" said Clarence, taking his
coffee cup from Beatrice. "Then you must have been there when
Egypt was conquered by Augustus."

"Augustus!" Ayesha said the name with contempt. "Of course a
man as vain as Octavian would call himself Augustus and declare
himself a god! He detested Egypt, and he destroyed Rome. At
first we thought the war would have nothing to do with us. After
all, we were in Philae, far away from the turmoil in Alexandria.
But his soldiers came for the High Priestess—either because Tera
had been respected as a queen, or because of the knowledge she
possessed as High Priestess of Isis, who knows? They stormed the

temple, and we fought back with everything we had, except the powers that would have made the only difference, but that we had been taught never to use for harm. I was a junior priestess by then and in charge of the novices, the eight- to fourteen-year-olds. Heduana herself, who had risen to senior priestess, had recommended me as her replacement. Before the fighting started, I was able to get the novices out through a passageway known only to the priestesses, which led down to the river. I put them in reed boats and fled with them to my father's household. My mother took charge of the girls and arranged to send them back to their families. Therefore, I was out of the battle and heard about it only afterward.

"Knowing that they were about to be defeated, Tera ordered the priestesses to fight back using their energic powers. Heduana argued against it, saying it was better to die than betray their oaths to the Goddess. Many of the senior priestesses, particularly those who were close to Tera, in her inner circle, followed the High Priestess, but the ordinary priestesses followed Heduana. They could not imagine breaking their oaths, and anyway did not know how to use their powers in battle. If they had all followed Tera and fought back, could they have prevailed against the Roman forces? I do not know. As it was, the temple itself was sacked and the remaining priestesses, those who escaped or surrendered and were allowed to live, scattered—to other temples or back to their home countries. One of them told me that rather than being captured, Tera had drunk poison before the altar of Isis. So perhaps the price of Heduana's idealism was the destruction of our order. You see, Beatrice, I have become a realist, or what you might call a cynic.

"Suddenly, everything that had been my world since I entered the temple was gone. My father said he would try to find me a husband—at eighteen, I was past the age when most princesses married, but I came from the royal house of Meroë, and there were men who would have wanted my hand for an alliance with my father, particularly since Rome was flexing its might. But what did I want with a husband, I who had been a priestess of Isis? No, I wanted to *learn*. Only learning would assuage my grief and anger. So I left Meroë and began to travel—up through Egypt, then by ship to Greece, trading my knowledge of medicine for food and shelter. In Sparta, then Athens and Corinth, I studied with physicians, learning about new medicines, new methods. In Ithaca I met a Greek man, Kallikrates. We became lovers."

Catherine looked over at Leo Vincey. He was staring at Ayesha intently, with a peculiar look on his face. What was it? Not jealousy, which she had expected. No, it was a kind of longing.

"Kallikrates was a physician, the best I have ever known. He had a school of medicine in the hills above Ithaca, where he trained young men and a few women in his methods. They came from all over the known world. I asked him to teach me all he knew, and when he learned that I had come from the temple of Isis at Philae, he asked me to teach him as well. I became one of the teachers at his school, and slowly we began to care for each other. I had never been in love before. It was a new and delightful experience for me. He was the great love of my life—" She paused for a moment. "Until Leo, of course."

Catherine glanced over at Leo again. Now he was staring down at his hands.

"But even then our aims were different. He wanted simply to heal. I wanted to continue learning what I had been taught by the priestesses of the temple—how to manipulate the energic powers of the Earth. It seemed to me that if I could gain enough power, I would be able to heal the body by a touch and a thought—I would knit bone to bone, turn the tumor back into healthy tissue, restore vitality when disease had enervated the patient. I might even defeat death! Kallikrates had no such ambition. 'Death is the natural end of all life,' he told me. 'We practice medicine to provide a good life, and eventually a good death—that is our duty to Asclepios, Ayesha. But beside Asclepios walks Thanatos, and we must not deny or disrespect either of those gods. What would life be without death? It would not be life.'

"I did not listen to him. One summer, when the olive flowers were blooming on the hillsides around his medical school, I traveled back to Egypt, to the library of Alexandria, to consult all the ancient scrolls I could find on the energic powers. The philosophers had written of them centuries before, in metaphor and myth. Then I traveled to Nineveh, to consult the library of Ashurbanipal, or what remained of it, for much of it stood in ruins. Then down to Arabia Magna, where I traveled with the Arabian tribes, consulting their healers and elders. I went, by caravan, as far as Kandahar, always searching for wisdom and knowledge.

"It was two years before I returned to Ithaca. I was still young— despite the destruction of my temple, I knew little of life's losses, of how time is the one thing we can never regain, until our understanding of the energic powers is much greater than mine. I am convinced that time itself is only energy . . . but you want to hear my story, not scientific theories. I came back to find that Kallikrates was dying of a cancer, which had already spread too far for any of his students to heal.

"'Let me try,' I said, kneeling beside his pallet. 'I have learned so much since I left you! Let me use my new powers and abilities, the knowledge I have gained, to make you well.' I have never been one to weep, but at the sight of his emaciated body, my tears flowed like the Nile.

"'No, beloved,' he said to me. 'I feel the wings of Thanatos beating the air—can you not hear them? He has come for me. It is my time, and it would be ungrateful of me—ungrateful to Hera who watched over my birth, to Hades who is waiting to welcome me into the land where all must go—to ask for more. Place obols on my tongue and over my eyes so I can pay Charon. Put a biscuit in my hand so I can placate Cerberus. In my other hand put a sprig of olive flowers so I can present them to Queen Persephone. And let me go.'

"Three days and nights I did not leave his side, but sang to him and slept beside him. On the third night, he crossed the river over which no mortal returns. I had lost my beloved."

Ayesha grew silent. There was no sound in the room, until Catherine heard a sniff. It was Beatrice, her eyes swimming with tears. She took out a dainty linen handkerchief and wiped her nose with it. Clarence reached over and held her gloved hand. Vincey was still looking down at the floor. Holly took another of the crescent pastries and poured himself a second cup of coffee. He was barely paying attention, as though he had heard this story before—as no doubt he had.

After a moment, Ayesha continued. "What did I have left but my studies? I returned to them. Finally they led me to Delphi, where in a storage chamber, still intact among the ruins of the ancient temple of Apollo, I found a manuscript written by the priestess Themistoclea, who had been the teacher of Pythagoras. It was her writing that allowed me to unravel the final mystery of extended—perhaps eternal—life. I took that manuscript and placed it in the library of Alexandria, where I hoped it would remain safe. But Aurelian set fire to the library in order to defeat Queen Zenobia, and spread, once again, the power of Rome. Then came Constantine, convert to the new religion, and Theodosius, who destroyed the temples of the old gods. By then, I was almost five hundred years old. I had lived as a wanderer, a healer traveling from village to village of the Roman Empire, applying my skills, teaching where I could. But the world was changing around me.

The government in Rome was growing more corrupt. Faith and fanaticism had replaced philosophy and science. Ignorance and superstition were spreading throughout the civilized world—when I healed, the villagers called me a witch. Outside it, Germanic tribes were waiting to break through the gates. I could stand it no longer, so I returned to Egypt, now simply another Roman province. Even there, I saw the disintegration of all that had been. The temple of Isis was deserted—no one practiced the healing arts in those halls anymore. Only the descendants of the temple cats remained. I saw one sleeping in the stone chair where Queen Tera had once sat with her black cat curled in her lap, welcoming me to the temple. Sick at heart in a way even I could not heal, I traveled south. For the first time since I had left my father's house, I went home to Meroë. The city had been sacked by King Ezana of Aksum, and was a shadow of its former self. That was when I determined I would no longer live among men.

"I continued southward, into the kingdom of Aksum, and then beyond kingdoms. At last I came to the banks of the Zambezi River. It reminded me of my own river, the Nile. From the tribes along the riverbank, I heard stories of an ancient civilization that had flourished inland, in a mountainous country. I followed these threads of story, traveling from tribe to tribe. At last I reached the tribal lands of the Amahaggar. It was the chief himself who led me to the entrance of that kingdom within the mountain. 'We do not go here anymore,' he told me. 'We do not wish to disturb our ancestors' ghosts. But you, priestess of the River Goddess'—for that is how they understood my description of Isis, who resembled their goddess of the Zambezi—'for you it may be the home you seek.' And so it was. Among those silent halls I found, not papyrus scrolls, but stone tablets filled with ancient wisdom, for the Kôrites had their own philosophy, their own alchemy. They had been great miners, and I studied their knowledge of the Earth, of minerals and rocks. The stones of the Earth have their own energic powers, which modern civilizations are beginning to understand. That is why, after millennia, the British came, and the Belgians, and the Germans—those savage tribes, the Gauls and Franks and Goths, now in Africa to ravage an ancient world they did not understand. And one day, they brought me Leo and Holly."

"I had been asked to go by the British East Africa Company," said Professor Holly in his deep voice. He looked down into his coffee cup as though it contained something of import, but Catherine could see that it was empty, except for the dregs of his coffee. "They had stumbled upon some of the ruins of Kôr among the foothills, including the tomb of a Kôrite queen. On her head was a crown made of gold, with rough diamonds in it as large as those found in the mines of South Africa. They hoped that if they could translate some of the texts in the tomb, they would find information about ancient mines—particularly of gold and diamonds. I am a linguist—they had heard of my work deciphering the languages of the ancient world. So they paid for me to take a leave of absence from Cambridge and travel to Africa. I brought Leo, who had been my ward since he was a child. He had been the son of my best friend, who died, alas, too young. Leo was no scholar—indeed, if I had not continually urged him to attend to his studies, I believe he would have spent all his time on the cricket fields or sculling along the Cam."

Leo Vincey smiled—the first genuine smile Catherine had seen on his face. For the first time since she had met him in the Café New York, when she and Mary had tried to warn him and Horace Holly about Professor Van Helsing's dastardly plans, he looked human and likeable.

"Poor Horace," he said. "I was such a disappointment to you. I could never concentrate on learning my Greek declensions—and when you wanted me to study Sanskrit! No, there was only one thing that interested me at university, besides sports. . . ."

"What was that, Mr. Vincey?" asked Beatrice.

*Girls,* thought Catherine. *I bet that's what he's going to say. He looks just the type.*

"Geology, Miss Rappaccini. Even as a boy, I had been fascinated by the theories of Charles Lyell. I had climbed all over the rock formations around Cambridge, studying strata. Our housekeeper had to dust around my collection of rocks. I took my degree in geology, much to Horace's chagrin. He would rather I had been a sedentary scholar, like himself, but I preferred to climb things. I was working for a mining company in Wales when he was offered the opportunity to travel to East Africa. I immediately threw up my job and offered to accompany him. It was my fault we were captured by the Amahaggar, but I wanted to explore the caves of Kôr without the interference of the East Africa Company representative, who was interested only in prospecting. He did not give a damn about the history or geology of the region except to the extent there was gold or diamonds involved. So at my insistence, we rode into the hills by ourselves, with only a pair of sturdy ponies—directly into an ambush!"

"The Amahaggar initially welcomed the British," said Ayesha, frowning at him—but Catherine thought it was an affectionate frown. "They had an ancient tradition of hospitality. But when they realized that their forests were being burned for coffee plantations, that the animals on which they depended for food were being shot by big game hunters who would cut off trophies and leave the meat rotting in the fields, they became significantly less welcoming. They started fighting back. They were right to capture you," she said. "You were encroaching on their land."

"I conceded that long ago, my love," he said. "And I thanked you, if you remember, for saving our lives."

"I should have let them run their spears through you," she said, shaking her head and smiling with pursed lips. "Except they would not have done that. The Amahaggar had no tradition of killing except in war. Criminals were exiled, not executed. Not knowing what to do with these two, they brought them to the caverns deep in the Earth where I lived and studied the ancient teachings of Kôr. And then I saw Leo. . . ."

She looked at him. For a moment, it was as though they were the only two people in that room. It felt so intimate that Catherine wondered if she should turn away.

"He was the image of Kallikrates—as though my beloved had come back to life. I do not know what happens to the spirit after death. I know that the energy of which we are made returns to its source. Can it be embodied again, thousands of years later? Pythagoras thought so. It seemed to me that, just as I was beginning to feel old and tired, just as I was thinking of ending my life upon this Earth, Kallikrates had returned from the dead."

"What do you think, Mr. Vincey?" asked Clarence. He was looking at them both closely. Well, he had his own complicated romance to figure out—no wonder he was interested in this one! He too was in love with a beautiful, dangerous woman.

"When I saw you," Leo said to Ayesha, "it was as though I had seen you before, in a dream or another lifetime. I recognized you at once as the woman I loved, and would love until the day I died."

This was getting . . . intense. Catherine felt a little uncomfortable. Should they really be listening to this?

"So you came back with him to Budapest?" said Clarence to Ayesha.

"To Vienna, where the Société des Alchimistes was headquartered at the time. The Amahaggar were being driven away from their traditional hunting grounds, into the mountains of the interior. I knew that even if we stood together, we could not prevail against the British—there was little we could do against the guns and explosives of the British East Africa Company. Before I left, I told the chief and his counselors to head north to Ethiopia, where European rule had not yet encroached. I hoped that there the descendants of Kôr could survive the depredations of the European powers. And I was intrigued by Holly's descriptions of the scientific advances that had been made in the last century. It seemed to me that the age of darkness had passed, and men were once again studying the world empirically. The knowledge of the ancient world was being regained, and discoveries were being made that even the priestesses of Isis had known nothing about. Holly was giving a paper at the annual meeting of the Société des Alchimistes on the ancient sciences of Kôr, so Leo and I accompanied him. The former President of the Alchemical Society was about to end his term. He was old and did not wish to seek reelection. Count Dracula wanted to be the next president. I decided to run against him—and won. And now here I am. The world I knew disappeared a long time ago—my mother, my father, my brother and sisters. The priestesses of Isis, Heduana, and Tera. My city of Meroë, the kingdoms of Nubia and Egypt. Even my gods have passed away from the world. But I have Leo and Holly, and Lady Crowe, and Frau Gottleib, and now Kati to keep my company. I have my work as President of the Société des Alchimistes. It is enough."

*Was it?* Catherine wondered. Ayesha's hair had no gray in it and her face was unlined—she appeared eternally young, like the statue of a woman rather than a living one. But in that moment she seemed as ancient as the Earth itself. Catherine thought, for the first time, that it must be terrible to never grow old and never die.

"And these energic powers," said Beatrice. "What are they? You have told us that all the things which seem so solid, the table, these chairs, the stones of this building, are made of energy. But how do you draw upon that energy?"

"Watch," said Ayesha. She raised her hand, and suddenly they were in a garden, with a circular pool where the table used to be. It was filled with lotus flowers, and dragonflies flitted above its surface. They were standing on the paved area around it. On three sides, the garden was surrounded by stone walls over which they could see palm trees. Beneath the walls were long beds filled with a profusion of plants: trees and shrubs and flowers. On the remaining side rose a large stone building, brightly painted in ocher and yellow and blue, with pillars that terminated in lotus blossoms. The sky was blue overhead, with a scattering of white clouds. The sun fell warm on their faces.

"The temple of Isis at Philae," said Ayesha. "And my home for many years. Reach out—touch something with your hand."

Beatrice leaned down and tried to lift one of the lotus flowers from the pool. Her gloved hand went right through it.

"Illusion," said Ayesha. Suddenly, they were back in her office. "Parlor tricks that a circus mesmerist might aspire to."

"But—how did you do it?" asked Clarence.

"Consciousness is not only in the brain," said Ayesha. "It is in the body and beyond the body. Each of you is surrounded by the energic waves you generate. I reached out with my own consciousness, and I altered those waves. They transmitted not what your physical eyes saw, but what I directed you to see. However, that is not true power. This is true power."

She walked over to the table, reached out her hand, and put it on a stack of manuscripts. "These are the ones you've rejected, are they not?" she said to Holly.

"Yes, but is this absolutely necessary?" He shoved his chair back several inches. Its legs screeched on the floor.

"You would have discarded them anyway. Why not use them for a demonstration? Watch," she said to them all. Under her hand, the stack of manuscripts burst into flames. In a moment, all that lay on the table was a pile of gray ash.

"God damn!" exclaimed Clarence, and immediately looked chagrined at the outburst. "Excuse me, ladies. I didn't mean—"

"Even that," Ayesha continued, "is not true power. This is true power." She reached out to Leo, who had not moved his chair back, and touched his cheek where Catherine could see the scratches left by Lucinda's fingernails. "In another day or two, these scratches will be completely healed, and Leo's cheek will once again be unblemished. If I had not healed them, he would have borne those scars until the day he died." She stroked his cheek. He put his hand over hers and held it there. It was strange to see the two of them looking so tender.

"Now," she said in her usual crisp tones, turning and moving away from the table, "our break is over. Holly, Leo, and I have work to do, and no doubt you do as well. Beatrice, as a member of the Société des Alchimistes, I expect you to report back to me on your progress in locating Lydia Raymond and dealing with her mother. This is yet another experiment of the society let loose upon the world. I believe you and your fellow members of the Athena Club are capable of dealing with it—I have great confidence in your abilities—but if you find that you need the support of the society, call upon me, and I shall do my best to assist you. Dr. Raymond was, and perhaps still is, a dangerous man—your world is not ready for the power he seeks. The priestesses of Philae trained to use the energic powers of the Earth from the time they were children. They did so within an intellectual framework and for a spiritual purpose. Dr. Raymond attempted to produce the same results through surgery, with none of that training or preparation. It is no wonder that his experimental subject went mad. I want to make sure that he and the results of his experiments are stopped. Mr. Jefferson, it was a pleasure to meet you. If you wish to speak again about the ancient world, in which you seem to have a particular interest, come see me. Now Leo, if you could escort our guests out? And if any of you would like more *kifli*, do take some with you. There is plenty left."

Dutifully, they trooped back out, following Leo Vincey. Clarence had taken several more of the *kifli* and was chewing on one, with his hand beneath it to catch any crumbs. As they walked down the hall, Catherine heard him say to Beatrice, "You told me about her, but you didn't really *tell* me about her."

At the front entrance of the Academy of Sciences, Catherine turned to Leo and asked, "Have you ever wanted to live forever?"

He smiled at her—his second genuine smile of the day! It was a sad one. "Ayesha has not offered to make me immortal, and I would not ask her. Kallikrates did not. I know very well, Miss Moreau, that I shall grow old while she stays eternally young. I shall die, while she endures as long as she herself wishes. But perhaps, if Pythagoras is right, someday my spirit will come back and be reunited with hers. At least, I choose to believe so."

She shook his hand. "Goodbye, Mr. Vincey. You're not the conceited ass I thought you were."

He threw back his handsome, golden head and laughed. "Thank you, Miss Moreau. I think that may be the most refreshingly candid thing anyone has ever said to me. I will do my best not to be a conceited ass, at least in your vicinity, so I may continue to earn your approbation."

Catherine looked at him quizzically, wondering if he was mocking her, but he seemed entirely sincere.

> MARY: Although he is a conceited ass, most of the time. I don't really know what Ayesha sees in him.

> CATHERINE: But at least he's honest about it.

It was Catherine who decided that they should go to the

Centrál Kávéház afterward. "This is our last day in Budapest," she said. "We don't have to be at the theater for a couple of hours— our final show! That should give us just enough time for lunch. Unlike Clarence, I can't stuff myself on—what were those things called? *Kifli*. And unlike Beatrice, I actually need to eat. Where is that place the two of you always go?"

While an excruciatingly correct waiter was bringing them what they had ordered—roast goose for Catherine, stuffed cabbage for Clarence, and a linden-leaf tisane for Beatrice, who was feeling sick from the coffee—Lucinda was staring down at a cup of blood. Sometimes, she missed the taste of food. She could smell Laura's lunch—an omelet and grilled tomato, with a cup of strong coffee. She found the scent both alluring and nauseating. She herself was having what was now her usual liquid meal. Pig, today, for a pig had been slaughtered on one of the surrounding farms, and for once Laura was not making her hunt. It was strong and rich—this particular pig had rooted in the forest, rather than feeding exclusively on slops.

"I still can't believe Carmilla left for Vienna." Laura attacked her omelet with a knife and fork. "We had been home seven days! Seven! I know Irene Norton and Mina need her help—I understand that. But when was the last time we got to spend a quiet evening together, without vampires to hunt or insane alchemists to fight? Do you know that tomorrow is our tenth anniversary?"

Lucinda shook her head and took a sip of blood.

Laura speared another piece of omelet on her fork, as though for emphasis. "We've been together ten years, and they've been wonderful years, filled with excitement and adventure. Still, I would like, just once in a while, to spend a quiet evening at home. What in the world is that?"

It was a cacophony of barking.

"Persephone! Hades! Stop that at once! For goodness' sake, what has gotten into those dogs?"

"I hear a motorcar," said Lucinda.

"A motorcar! Carmilla must have changed her mind." Leaving her omelet half-eaten, Laura sprang up and rushed out of the room, too quickly for Lucinda to tell her that it was not Carmilla's motorcar. The roar of it sounded quite different.

Should she stay or go see what was happening? Uncertain, as she usually was even about the smallest matters, such as what dress to wear on any particular day, she rose reluctantly and followed Laura into the hall, then out the front door of the schloss. There, on the circular drive, sat a motorcar—similar to Carmilla's, but not the same. Next to it stood a woman in an outlandish outfit—a close-fitting leather cap, a long canvas coat that went all the way down to her ankles, and leather boots. On her hands were thick leather gloves, and over her eyes were a pair of round goggles that made her look like a frog. She took off the gloves, put them on the seat of the motorcar, then lifted the goggles so they sat on her forehead, over the leather cap.

"*Liebe* Laura!" she said. "How wonderful to see you! What do you think? Is she not a beauty? But I remember you do not like automobiles. Where is Carmilla? I must show her my newest creation." Who was this woman with the German accent? What sort of woman drove alone through the countryside in a motorcar?

"Well, you can't, because she's not here. She's gone off to Vienna in your previous creation," said Laura crossly. She kissed the woman on both cheeks. "It's lovely to see you, Bertha, but really, she's left again and I have no idea when she'll be back." She waved Lucinda forward. "Lucinda, this is our friend Bertha Benz. Bertha, this is Lucinda, who is staying with us for—well, a while, anyway. Bertha is the brains behind Benz and Cie Gasmotoren-Fabrik, her husband's motorcar company."

"Do not—what is the word—shortchange Karl," said Bertha, smiling. "He is a brains as well. He is not very good with money, but he is wonderful with automobiles. What a pity that Carmilla is not here! I wanted to show her the newest Phaeton—I have made such improvements. And also, I hoped she would accompany me. I intend to show some timid gentlemen who do not wish to invest in our company that the automobile is the vehicle of the future. But to do so, I must drive a long distance—in fact, I am going all the way to England! Carmilla would have made the perfect travel companion—she is such a good mechanic. And you are welcome as well, Laura, although I know your distaste for this mode of travel."

"To England!" said Laura. "How in the world? I mean, there happens to be some water in the way. . . ."

"Yes, that is what will make it so spectacular. Imagine the headlines—Benz automobile crosses the English Channel! I have arranged to drive straight onto a boat at Calais. After all, if boats can transport race horses from England to France, and French carriages to the English nobility, why not Brunhilde here?" She put her hand on the carriage of the motorcar.

"I take it Brunhilde is the name of this contraption?" said Laura. She walked around to the other side of the motorcar, then to the back, looking it over.

"Yes, the Benz Phaeton III, built to my own specifications," said Bertha. "Isn't she a beauty?"

By this time, Laura had circled all the way around the motorcar. "Lucinda," she said, "how would you like to go to England? I've always wanted to go. Not this way of course—I imagined a comfortable train trip from Vienna to Calais, and then the channel crossing by ferry! But when will I have the opportunity again? And it will serve Carmilla right for leaving so abruptly! She'll come back, and we'll be gone. . . ." She turned to Bertha. "I know that I'm not Carmilla—I'm certainly not as good a mechanic. But would you consider taking me even if Carmilla can't come? And if Lucinda wants to come as well—"

"Of course," said Bertha. "I would welcome the company. Can you leave in—oh, an hour or so? That will give me time to drink a cup of Mrs. Madár's excellent coffee."

Lucinda stared at both of them wide-eyed. "You mean we are leaving for England—today? In one hour?"

"Yes, today! Carmilla is always doing things like this—going off impulsively. Why shouldn't I do it for once? That is, if you wish to come. You can stay here quite comfortably, you know. Magda can take care of you without me. Thank goodness she didn't go with Carmilla." She turned to Bertha Benz, who was taking off her leather cap. Under it, her brown hair was coiled up around her head in a tight braid. "Come on, there's coffee in the morning room, and breakfast as well, if you want some. I'm just going to throw some clothes in a suitcase. How much room is there?"

Plenty, as Bertha demonstrated. Behind the closed carriage was a boot where they could tie suitcases or a small trunk.

As Lucinda followed Bertha back into the schloss, Laura took her by the arm. "My dear, forgive me for springing all this on you so suddenly. You don't have to come, you know. You don't have to deal with the fatigue and uncertainty of travel. I only offered it because I did not want you to feel as though you were being left behind. You would be quite right to tell me that I am being an idiot, and that I should stay home quietly working at my embroidery and waiting for Carmilla to come back. After all, she's much better at such adventures than I am—which is perhaps why I would like to go on my own adventure for once! Say the word, and I will not mention it to you again but leave the schloss in Mrs. Madár's excellent care, with particularly directions that Magda should take care of you."

Did Lucinda want to stay here, where it was safe? She had gone through so many changes recently. She had lost her mother, and in a sense her father, and in an entirely different sense her very self. Who was she now? Who was this girl dressed in white who still played the piano, but also drank blood, and could climb up walls, and hear the heart of a hare beating in its chest? She had no idea. She did know one thing—she did not want to be left behind. "I would like to go," she told Laura. As soon as she had said the words, she wondered if she had made a terrible mistake.

Three hours later, for packing had taken longer than expected, as it always does, Lucinda was sitting in the back seat of Brunhilde, driving through the Styrian countryside in a cloud of dust and gasoline fumes, wondering what in the world she had gotten herself into.

> LUCINDA: It was a silly, impulsive thing to do. I
>     should probably have stayed in Styria with Magda
>     and Mrs. Madár. . . .

> CATHERINE: If you had, I'm not sure any of us would
>     be here today, and I would not be writing this
>     book.

> LUCINDA: Thank you, Cat, but I did very little—it was
>     Laura whose actions were most important, at the end.

> DIANA: And mine! Don't forget what I did.

> CATHERINE: As though you would let us . . .

The next morning, Catherine and Beatrice boarded the *Orient Express*. Catherine had almost blanched at the price of the tickets— she and Beatrice needed to travel in separate cabins, because she could not spend the night breathing *La Belle Toxique*'s poisonous fumes. Why in the world would anyone pay so much, simply to get from one place to another? Luckily, they had all their earnings from Lorenzo's Circus of Marvels and Delights, and before they left, Count Dracula had handed them a purse. "I think Mina would have wanted you to be fully supplied with funds," he said. "Travel safely, and know that you are always welcome in my house." Then he had bowed to them with the courtesy of a four-hundred-year-old Hungarian nobleman, his hair flopping attractively over his face. Catherine had once again wondered whether he did anything to it, or it just naturally fell that way.

Clarence had come to the Nyugati railway station to see them off, and waited on the platform until the last moment. Beatrice was standing out in the corridor, with the window pulled all the way down, talking to him when the whistle sounded, indicating that they were about to depart. Catherine heard him say, "If Ayesha and Mr. Vincey can make it work, we can make it work, I know we can." She could not hear Beatrice's reply, because just then the train started moving. They were on their way back to London, to rejoin Mary, Justine, and Diana—and hopefully Alice. Had the others found her yet? Of course, it had only been a few days. Even Mary and Justine, as resourceful as they were, could scarcely have solved the mystery of her disappearance that quickly! But if they had not found her by the time Catherine arrived, she would search all of London for her. And when she found out who had kidnapped Alice, she would tear out his throat.

As the *Orient Express* pulled out of the station, a Benz Phaeton III, the only one of its kind in the world, roared through the Austrian countryside, upsetting chickens on the road and farm-wives who thought that perhaps the Beast of the Apocalypse had arrived to signal the end of the world. They crossed themselves as it passed and muttered prayers to the Blessed Virgin. Inside the motorcar, Lucinda, who was starting to feel sick from the constant motion, wondered once again what in the world she had gotten herself into, and what would be waiting for her in England—at the Athena Club.

# CHAPTER IX

## A Visit to the Diogenes Club

M r. Holmes has not been here for several weeks," said the porter of the Diogenes Club. He was a venerable-looking man, with a full head of white hair and side-whiskers. If you had seen him walking down the street, you might have assumed he was a duke.

"Thank you, my good man," said Watson. He turned away, looking downcast. "I suppose Mycroft is off doing something terribly important and hush-hush," he said to Mary and Justine. "What next? Shall we try Inspector Lestrade at Scotland Yard?"

"If you would like me to flag down a cab . . . ," said Justine. She was the best of them at getting the attention of cabbies, probably because of her height.

"If you would," said Watson.

Mary frowned, not at him but to herself. Mr. Holmes—Mr. Sherlock Holmes, that is—had told her that instinct was unreliable, that it must always be checked and corrected by the application of rational thought. But she had an instinct that something was not right.

She reached into her purse, then turned back to the porter. "If you would just check," she said, holding out her hand. When he placed his hand beneath it, she dropped a guinea into his palm. There, that was unobtrusive, wasn't it? Just as though she had been bribing porters her whole life! "And if you discover that he is there after all, could you tell him that Mary Jekyll wishes to see him?"

A guinea was a lot of money, and she might be wasting it on the porter after all, but this was the sort of thing Irene Norton would have done. She wanted to be just a little more like Irene— smarter, bolder, more courageous.

"Very good, miss," said the porter, with the perfectly impassive face of a discreet servant. "I will certainly check to see if I have somehow overlooked him, although he is not an easy gentleman to miss."

In ten minutes, he returned. "I must apologize, Miss Jekyll. Mr. Holmes is indeed in the club—I cannot think how I missed him. He will meet you in the Strangers' Room, where conversation is permitted. If you will follow me?" He looked at her so directly, with such steady blue eyes, that she could almost believe he had truly not known Mycroft Holmes was in the club.

She followed him through the front entrance and into the precincts of the Diogenes Club, the most secretive gentleman's club in London. Once she, Justine, and Watson were standing in the entrance hall, with the large wooden doors shut behind them, it was so quiet that they could not even hear London traffic. The porter led them past a large, luxuriously furnished room in which a number of gentlemen were sitting in armchairs upholstered with crimson plush, which had high sides so they could not see their neighbors reading *Punch* or the novels of Anthony Trollope. At least, Mary could not see what they were reading, but those were the sorts of things gentlemen read in red plush armchairs. None of the chairs was turned toward any other, and there was no conversation.

The porter stopped at a door on the right. He opened it, stepped inside, and held the door open for them. "Miss Jekyll, sir," he said to the man who was waiting within, seated in a particularly large, comfortable armchair. It had to be large, for he was a large man. Only by the height of his forehead and the sharpness of his nose could Mary have guessed that this was Sherlock's brother.

"Miss Jekyll," he said. "Come in, and your companions as well. Ah, Watson. How are you?" He seemed to feel no shame for having asked the porter to lie about his whereabouts. "And you must be Miss Frankenstein," he said to Justine. "You see, my brother has told me about you and the Athena Club, as well as the Société des Alchimistes. When Jackson mentioned that you were asking to see me, I was curious enough that I instructed him to admit you."

"And yet you would not see me before," said Watson bitterly. "I'm dreadfully worried about your brother. What sort of errand have you sent him on? We have learned that Professor Moriarty is still alive. If so, he will no doubt make an attempt on Sherlock's life. If you have any information——"

"If I did, I would not divulge it," said Mycroft with a bland stare. "You do not understand the gravity of the situation. It is a matter of state that must be kept entirely secret from the public. If the large, ignorant, easily panicked body politic had any idea that its titular head was in danger, its limbs would begin to writhe——"

"By titular head, do you mean the titular head of state? Do you mean the Queen?" asked Justine.

"Her Majesty in danger!" said Mary. "How is that possible?"

"There, you see, I have already said too much. Her Majesty is being protected as well as she can be, I assure you. Nevertheless, the danger is real. There are forces out there, in the great, dirty thoroughfare of humanity that is London, seeking to destabilize the government. We are keeping track of them as best we can. We do not yet have enough information to apprehend Moriarty, and arresting his underlings would merely alert him to our presence. He himself is too powerful to arrest on incomplete evidence. We believe he is receiving financial backing from a member of the House of Lords."

"What lord of the realm would betray the Queen?" asked Watson, looking shocked.

"Your faith in humanity is as refreshing as it is ridiculous," said Mycroft. "Miss Jekyll, you look like a sensible young woman. Where Sherlock has gone, I cannot—and will not—rescue him. That would betray my hand prematurely in this affair. My position is both my power and my weakness. I can get in where other men cannot, and cannot get in where other men—or perhaps young ladies—can. I did not give much credence to Sherlock's description of your abilities—he is obviously biased by his affection for you. But Irene Norton thinks very highly of you, so I am going to tell you this: Find my brother. Sherlock and I are not alike—he is far too emotional, has always been since he was a child. Our father was a philosopher of sorts, a purely theoretical scholar who spent his days in his private library. I take after him. Our mother was, as women are, a creature of fire and feeling. Beautiful, intelligent, but driven by instinct and emotion. Sherlock adored her and was devastated when she died. He was only fourteen at the time, and impressionable as all boys are. I believe that is why he has never married, and why he pursues this hobby of being a private detective. He wishes to impose order on the chaos of the world, and so he approaches life as a series of clues, a puzzle to be solved. He aspires to a rationality that is not natural for him. He is, after all, our mother's son. Well, I hope you find him and get him out of this situation—alive. I am not an emotional man myself, but Sherlock is the only family I have left. Now, I have considerable work to do. Run along, rescue Sherlock if you can, and do not visit me again. I shall not be in."

"Can you give me no information as to his whereabouts?" asked Mary. "How can we rescue him if we do not know where he is?"

Mycroft Holmes looked at her impassively. "If you cannot figure that out for yourself, then you are not as competent as Mrs.

Norton said you were, and you are of no use either to me or to Sherlock. The more I tell you of this matter, the more you can tell Moriarty and his men if you are captured. I have given you as much information as I care to, or as you require. You are reputed to be an intelligent young woman, Miss Jekyll. I look forward to seeing whether you succeed in your inquiries."

When they were once again standing out on the street, Mary said, "Well, that was—"

"Interesting?" said Justine.

"Infuriating," said Watson. "How could he leave his brother in peril, when he was the one who *put* his brother in peril? Mycroft has no notion of human sympathy."

"I suspect that he can't afford to," said Mary. "I don't know what sort of work he does for the government, but Irene Norton said he was her counterpart. She is a spy for the Americans."

"Is she indeed?" said Watson, looking astonished. "I wonder if Sherlock knows. He has always held her in such high regard. She was a lovely woman, with rich auburn tresses. . . ."

MARY: Is there any woman Dr. Watson hasn't fallen in love with at one time or another?

JUSTINE: Mrs. Hudson, I imagine.

MARY: Oh, you know what I mean. Any woman of the appropriate age. Irene, Beatrice . . .

CATHERINE: You, although he was too loyal to Holmes to continue that particular infatuation.

MARY: I think it was the appearance of Beatrice on the scene. As soon as Beatrice shows up, all male attention shifts to her. Which can be very useful, sometimes.

BEATRICE: That is absolutely not true! And once they find out I am poisonous, they lose interest.

CATHERINE: There is that. Only someone as foolhardy as Clarence would completely overlook the fact that you could kill him with your breath.

BEATRICE: Alas . . .

What had Mycroft Holmes meant by his brother's affection for her? Mary took off her gloves again in the front hall of 11 Park Terrace. Watson and Justine were already in the parlor. Of course they had fewer accoutrements to remove—their hats came off quickly, without having to pull out pins!

"You were gone long enough." Diana was standing at the top of the stairs, dressed in boys' clothes. For goodness' sake, why could the girl not comb her hair? It looked like a bright red bird's nest. And why could she not dress properly, like the young lady she was—or should be?

"I hope you didn't get into any mischief with the Baker Street boys this morning," said Mary.

"Hello to you too, sister dear," said Diana. "I haven't been to headquarters yet. I was getting ready to leave when Charlie showed up with a message.

"You didn't say hello either." Mary had not felt cross until right this moment, but Diana always had the power to put her back up.

"I have important things to tell you," said Diana. "Do you want to hear them, or not?"

"Yes, all right, what is it? And come into the parlor, so Justine and Dr. Watson can hear them as well." Mary assumed whatever Diana wanted to tell them had to do with either Alice or Mr. Holmes.

Diana clambered down the steps, then jumped over the final few to make a resounding *thud* that annoyed Mary—her boots always seemed louder than anyone else's somehow. Once they were in the parlor, with Watson looking at them quizzically and Justine saying, "Hello Diana, I hope you had a good morning," Diana said, "Sherlock Holmes is being kept drugged in the house where those alchemical blokes used to meet. You know, in Soho. Alice is there—she sent a message through the Baker Street boys."

"Are you absolutely certain about this?" asked Mary.

"Charlie told me Wiggins told him, and some boy I don't know told Wiggins that Alice told him herself. She promised him that Watson would give him cigarettes. Charlie's around here somewhere—I think Mrs. Poole is giving him something to eat. That boy has an insatiable appetite."

As one might say of Diana herself! "That scarcely sounds reliable," said Mary, frowning. "Who was this boy? Can he be trusted to tell the truth? Although if he says he spoke with Alice . . ."

"It's the first lead we've had," said Watson. "We have to follow up."

"Of course we shall follow up," said Justine. "Mary, should we—"

"Go to the headquarters of the English branch of the Société des Alchimistes in Soho? Of course," said Mary. "We have to find out if this story is true. I guess we'll have to put off our trip to see Inspector Lestrade at Scotland Yard." About which she was not entirely sorry. "Justine, if you and I went to reconnoiter—"

"I'm coming too," said Diana.

"And I," said Watson.

"I don't think that's a good idea, Dr. Watson," said Mary. "If Professor Moriarty or Colonel Moran are involved, would they not recognize you from the last time Mr. Holmes went up against them? If Justine and I—all right, and Diana, stop kicking at my ankle, you can't reach it anyway through my petticoats—go, we will be able to reconnoiter without being recognized."

"What shall I do?" asked Watson. "Should I go see Lestrade and ask for the assistance of the Metropolitan Police? But Lestrade would never believe me on the say-so of a random street urchin. We would need solid evidence that Holmes is being held captive in the Alchemical Society headquarters."

"Then we shall get that evidence," said Mary, with grim determination.

"In the meantime, you could come with me, gov'nor." Charlie was poking his head—he still had a cap on, and smears of jam around his mouth—through the parlor door. "Wiggins is organizing a rescue. He's sent out a signal—all the boys should be at HQ by this afternoon."

Mary looked at the both of them with alarm. "Charlie, you are not to launch any sort of rescue attempt before Justine and I—and yes, Diana, I see you glowering at me—can return with enough evidence to convince Lestrade and enlist his help. Dr. Watson, please go with Charlie and try to prevent the Baker Street boys from doing anything foolish! We don't know enough yet about how Alice and Mr. Holmes are being held or by whom. We need more information before we can take any action. Diana knows the way to the headquarters of the Baker Street boys, which I understand is in Soho? She, Justine, and I will meet you there at—" She looked at her watch. "Oh goodness, it's almost lunchtime. I think we'd better get something to eat, or we'll all fall over with hunger. Maybe Mrs. Poole can make some sandwiches, so we can take them with us? I don't want to lose any time. One for you too, Charlie."

"Thanks, but I'll eat with the boys," said Charlie. "They'll have fish and chips ordered, with so many showing up. Not that I don't like Mrs. Poole's cooking—she gave me one of her jam tarts for elevenses—but it ain't fish and chips. Come on, Dr. Watson. You can eat with us. Wiggins has already started planning for the raid, but you were a soldier—I bet you could teach us a thing or two!"

"Well, a doctor in the army, but yes, I was sometimes in the thick of the fight," said Watson. "If you need my assistance, it is yours for the asking."

"No raid!" said Mary. "Dr. Watson, I'm counting on you to be the figure of authority here. Wait for us to return with more information. Then we can decide on a course of action and contact Scotland Yard."

"Of course, of course," said Watson. "Moriarty is a dangerous man, Charlie. You are all brave, resourceful boys, and you have helped Holmes in many ways in the past. But this is a different situation. I would not want any of the Baker Street boys to get hurt."

> MARY: Of course it was Dr. Watson who got hurt, in the end.

> CATHERINE: He always does get hurt, doesn't he? Whether it's shot, or stabbed, or bitten. Someone needs to teach him to run away from bullets and Beast Men, not toward them!

> BEATRICE: You are not being fair to Dr. Watson. He is good, kind, and always loyal.

> MARY: Oh, I know. I'm questioning his judgment, not his character. If he had listened to me, he would not have ended up in the infirmary!

DIANA: Because you always know what's best.

MARY: Not always. Just most of the time.

It was early afternoon before Mary, Justine, and Diana reached Potter's Lane in Soho and surveyed number 7, which seemed completely deserted.

"I don't know," said Mary. "It doesn't seem as though anyone lives there at all. I mean, look at the condition it's in." The paint on the front door was peeling, and the bricks of the building were covered with soot. The door number had long ago fallen off—they could tell it was number 7 only because the buildings on either side were 5 and 9.

"No," said Justine. "There is someone living there. Look, the windows have been washed. It appears dilapidated on the outside, but someone has been caring for the interior."

"Oh, you're right," said Mary. "I wonder why I didn't notice that?"

"Remember that I was once a maid," said Justine. "It is not the sort of thing the lady of the house would notice. If you'll forgive my saying so, Mary—you have never cleaned windows."

"No, she's better at bossing people around," said Diana. "Aren't we going to *do* anything?"

Mary sighed. If only they could have left Diana at home! She put her hand on her waist bag. It has served her well in Europe, and would be more convenient, she had decided, than carrying a purse. She could feel the shape of her revolver. It was reassuring.

"I suggest we examine the exterior of the house," said Justine. "Perhaps we can find some indication of where Alice and Mr. Holmes are being kept. I assume they are both prisoners of Professor Moriarty? Perhaps they are in a cellar of some sort. Catherine mentioned a coal cellar where Archibald had been imprisoned."

Once, Justine would not have made such a suggestion—she

had been more timid, more retiring, when she had first joined the Athena Club. Being Justin Frank seemed to have made her bolder. Mary liked this new Justine. Had she, too, changed as much in their European travels? She did not feel quite like the old Mary anymore. Should she draw her revolver? No, not yet—not until they saw some sign of danger. Until then, they were just a man, a woman, and a boy wandering down the alley that led to the back of the house.

At the back was a patch of overgrown grass and weeds. The brick wall rose as it had in front. At ground level were several demilune windows, and then two stories of windows above. "I don't see anything unusual," said Justine. "Unless—what is that?"

Hanging down from one of the windows on the second floor was a handkerchief. It must have caught in the sash at one point.

"What? Oh, it's just a piece of cloth," said Diana. "It could have been there forever."

"No, it's still white," said Mary. "If it had been hanging there for more than a few days, it would be covered with soot. Justine may know windows, but I know handkerchiefs. It's exactly the sort of thing someone might leave as a signal, hoping anyone not looking for a signal would assume it had gotten there accidentally. Diana, can you climb up to that window?"

"Oh, *now* you need me!" Diana looked up at the wall. "I can't climb straight up the bricks. I'm not Carmilla, you know. But there's a drainpipe over there, and a smaller window above it. I bet that's a bathroom. I could climb up that pipe, go through the window, and get into the other room that way."

"Are you sure you can open the small window?" asked Mary. "It may be latched."

Diana gave her a pitying look. Then she walked over to the drainpipe, which came right down to the patchy grass and then disappeared back into the bricks again, took off her shoes, and began to climb.

"Honestly, you'd think her toes were fingers!" said Mary. Diana really was Hyde's daughter. But then, Mary was Jekyll's daughter, and was that any better? She remembered the moment, in the castle in Styria, when her father had revealed that she was as much the result of an experiment as Diana. Resolutely, she pushed the thought away. This was not the time to think about such things.

"Diana has climbed inside," said Justine.

Yes, Diana's feet were just disappearing through the window. Would she be able to locate Alice and Mr. Holmes? Five minutes passed, then ten, then fifteen.

"I'm worried," said Mary, looking at her wristwatch. "If she doesn't give us a sign of some sort in the next five minutes, I think we need to go in ourselves."

Suddenly, a face appeared at the window with the handkerchief. It was Diana.

"Thank goodness," said Mary breathing a sigh of relief.

And then another face appeared at the window, above hers. Although she was one floor up, Mary could tell immediately who it was—that grim face was unmistakable. Holding Diana by the arm was Mrs. Raymond, just as Mary remembered her from the Society of St. Mary Magdalen.

"Oh no!" she cried. She was about to draw her pistol—although what good was that going to do?—when behind her, she heard an all-too-familiar click. She turned. There stood a large man with a revolver, a much larger revolver than Mary's, in his hand. With him were two underlings—one could tell at once that they were underlings and he was the one in charge. Both of them had pistols pointed at Justine.

"Inside," the large man said, in a harsh voice. "Front door, and step to it, missy!"

Mary had no choice but to walk back down the alley to the

front door, cursing under her breath, with Justine following behind her.

DIANA: Were you really cursing?

MARY: I hate to admit it, but yes, I was!

DIANA: Sometimes you aren't completely hopeless.

"Well, that didn't go as planned," said Mary an hour later. She looked down at her wrists, which were tied together in front of her. She was sitting on a mattress on the floor of what appeared to be a windowless coal cellar. The only light came from a lantern hanging on a hook, high on the wall. Her waist bag was, of course, gone—they had taken it from her, first thing. Not that a pistol would have helped in her current circumstances.

"I was as quiet as a mouse," said Diana defensively. "I don't know how that—that—" She appeared to be searching for an epithet scathing enough for Mrs. Raymond. "How she knew I was there. All the sudden, I turned and there she was. I bit her hard before she caught me too! If I could have reached my knife—"

"It's no use discussing what-ifs," said Mary. "We have to decide what to do now. I hope Justine is all right."

Diana's wrists were also tied together. She was sitting at the other end of the mattress. Justine was lying beside it on the floor, unconscious. If only they had not drugged Justine! The large man, whom the others called Colonel Moran, had held a piece of cloth over her mouth until she passed out. It had taken a full fifteen minutes, with his lackeys holding their pistols to Mary's and Diana's heads the entire time. Mrs. Raymond had stood by the door, overseeing the proceedings.

"Tie her hands as well, and put that shackle around her

ankle," Mrs. Raymond had said. "She is the female creation of Victor Frankenstein. If you were not threatening her friends, she would tear you apart, limb from limb." As a result, in addition to tying her wrists, as they had done to Mary and Diana, Moran's men had also placed the shackle connected to a staple in the stone wall around Justine's right ankle. It was the same shackle, Mary deduced, as the one Dr. Seward had used to imprison Archibald.

> JUSTINE: I would not have torn anyone limb from
> limb. I have never killed anyone unless absolutely
> necessary, and never in such a savage fashion. I am
> not an animal.

> DIANA: Well, you should have. They deserved it!

"Miss Jekyll," Mrs. Raymond had said after Justine was lying unconscious on the floor. "What a pleasant surprise to receive another visit from you. I still remember our previous encounter at the Society of St. Mary Magdalen. If I had known that my daughter Lydia was working as a scullion in your household, I would have removed her at once. She is with me now, and no longer subject to your mistreatment."

*"Mistreatment?"* said Mary. "When have I ever mistreated Lydia— I mean Alice? And what have you done with her?"

"Yeah, I bet you have her locked up too!" said Diana. "If you hurt our Alice, you old sow, I will bite you so hard—"

"Harder than this?" Mrs. Raymond held up one arm. On the wrist were two semicircular marks that looked like Diana's teeth. Mary had seen such marks before—all the members of the Athena Club had, although they were usually not as deep as those on Mrs. Raymond's wrist! Without meaning to harm them exactly, Diana had inflicted such wounds on each of them at one time or another—except for Beatrice. Not even Diana would bite the Poisonous Girl, who was usually called upon to doctor the wounds. In Mrs. Raymond's hand was Diana's lockpick kit. "I'm sorry to tell you that you will not get that opportunity. Did you really think you could come into this house without my knowing you were here? I could sense your presence—your energic signature—as soon as you climbed through that window. I would know it anywhere, my girl. Each time you climbed out the window at the Magdalen Society, I hoped some mischief would happen to you, so I could tell Hyde you had come to an unfortunate end. Evidently, living with Miss Jekyll has failed to teach you manners. If Sister Margaret were here, I would direct her to fetch the switch, forthwith!"

"What do you intend to do with us?" asked Mary, before Diana could open her mouth again. Insulting Mrs. Raymond was not going to help them, or Alice, or Mr. Holmes.

Mrs. Raymond smiled. It was a cruel smile. "Do you truly expect me to tell you that? As far as I'm concerned, the best place for you is where you are—right here, where you cannot interfere. Come, Colonel. We have more important things to do than converse with our guests. I hope you're comfortable, Miss Jekyll. You will be here for quite some time."

As she turned and opened the door, Diana shouted, "Go to hell, you bloody bitch!"

Suddenly, the floor of the coal cellar was alive with snakes. Mary screamed and scrambled back, while Diana kicked at them, trying to stamp first one, then another.

"What the hell?" she said. Her boot stamped on the floor of the coal cellar. There was no squish of snake flesh beneath it.

"They're an illusion," said Mary, her heart still racing. "Just an illusion—just mesmerism. They're not real."

"They bloody well looked real," said Diana. Once again, the floor was bare, the door was shut, and they were alone. "That bitch. That bloody bitch. I'd like to see *her* frightened for once. Not that I'm frightened, you understand. Not of a bunch of snakes! What happens now?"

Diana might say she was not frightened, but Mary had never seen her so discomposed before. She reached over and squeezed her sister's hand. For a moment, Diana squeezed back, before slapping her hand away. Mary looked around at the bare, soot-stained walls of the cellar, and then at Justine, still unconscious. "I have no idea."

> DIANA: I'm never frightened. I wanted to kill her, and if I'd had my little knife in my hand instead of my tool kit, I would have. I bit her so hard before she hit me! I wish I'd bitten her even harder.

> ALICE: Remember that you are talking about my mother.

> DIANA: Well, excuse me! You all say nasty things about my dad all the time, and do I make a fuss about it?

> MARY: Usually, yes.

For what felt like an eternity, nothing happened. The light from the lantern flickered around the room. Mary sat on the mattress, her back against the wall, feeling a greater sense of despair than she had felt since they had been held captive in Styria by Mr. Hyde. At least they had not been in a coal cellar, and they had not been tied up! Yes, there was help close at hand—somewhere in Soho, Watson was with the Baker Street boys, waiting for her to contact them. When she did not, hopefully he would go to Lestrade and ask for help. And hopefully, Lestrade would believe his story. She knew that he did not like her or Diana any more than he liked Holmes, but surely he would not let three young women disappear without investigating? She comforted herself with a vision of the Metropolitan Police breaking into the coal cellar and leading them all to safety.

Meanwhile, with the part of her mind she was not using to worry about their situation, she was playing a game that Diana had decided to call "Guess What I'm Thinking."

"Is it bigger than a breadbox?" Diana asked.

"Yes."

"Is it a person?"

"Yes."

"Is it Sherlock Holmes?"

"Yes."

"Oh God, why are you so *predictable*? You owe me another shilling. That's thirteen shillings in my favor. My turn."

"All right. Is it an elephant?"

"No. That's a stupid way to begin. I'll give you a hint. It's larger than an elephant."

"Is it the Alps? I mean, is it smaller than the Alps?"

"Yes, it's smaller than the Alps."

"Is it alive?"

"Yes and no."

"You can't answer yes and no. It has to be yes or no."

"But I can't answer that if it's not accurate."

"I wish someone would rescue us so I wouldn't have to play this stupid game!"

It took Mary another thirty-seven questions to answer *"Orient Express."*

"See?" said Diana. "It's not alive because it's a train, and it is alive because it has people in it, and they're alive. I think you should lose that one—you took so bloody long to guess!"

"But I didn't give up," said Mary. "I thought you only lost if you gave up?"

Finally, thank goodness, Diana fell asleep. Mary did not want to fall asleep—someone should stay awake, in case anything happened. In case Mrs. Raymond came back again, or the Metropolitan Police came to rescue them . . . She was so tired! And getting hungry. No one had come to give them food or water. She would stay awake, she was determined. She would not allow Mr. Hyde to keep them here, captive in Styria. Lucinda was dying—they must get her to Budapest. Where were Justine and Diana? Mary could not find them. She walked and walked through the long stone passages of Castle Karnstein, lit only by streetlamps. It was so dark here among the streets of Soho—it must be past midnight. Mr. Holmes was late. She looked down at her wristwatch and paced back and forth impatiently. What was that? Gunshots, off in the distance. She began walking toward them, but did not seem to get any closer. *Oh,* she thought. *I'm in Looking-Glass Country.* She sighed with relief that finally everything was making sense.

MARY: I still can't believe Dr. Watson was so stupid. Why didn't he go to Lestrade?

CATHERINE: Do you really think Lestrade would have believed him? Anyway, Wiggins was partly to blame as well. He wanted a raid and he got a raid. Men and boys—honestly, I don't think there's much difference between them, except for the length of their pants. They like playing soldiers.

DIANA: Don't you dare say anything against Wiggins!

CATHERINE: Why? You do all the time.

DIANA: That's different.

"Hold my hand, Lydia," said Helen. "I'm not going to let them take you away from me."

Alice was standing at the window with her mother and Professor Moriarty in the common room of the Order of the Golden Dawn. It was difficult to tell exactly what was going on outside.

"Dr. Watson and a group of ragged boys!" Professor Moriarty had said, sounding incredulous. "Do they really think they can get in here, past Moran and his men? Helen, I don't have time for this. Get rid of them."

Alice looked up at her mother, worried. She had felt so hopeful, ever since she had sent that message to the Baker Street Irregulars and hung the handkerchief out the window, in case anyone might notice. Perhaps they would understand that it was a signal. Then, last night, Helen had come into the room where she was sitting with Margaret Trelawny, checking items on a list Margaret had given her against an exhibition catalog. "Well, my dear," she had said, "you will be glad to know that we captured Mary Jekyll, that devil Diana, and a confederate of theirs, the monster Justine Frankenstein. I always assumed she had been destroyed, as Mrs. Shelley described, but it seems not. I shall have great satisfaction, eventually, in taking her apart, to see how she was assembled. But there's no time for that now. We have more important work to do." It had taken all of Alice's effort not to break down and cry in front of her mother and Margaret.

"You do not look as pleased as you should, daughter," Helen had said. "These are the people who relegated you to being a kitchen maid. You should be glad that we have them safely locked up so they can't interfere with our plans. You do not understand those plans yet—I will tell you more when the time is right—but in the end we will have such power as you cannot imagine. You and I and Margaret—will that not be grand?"

"Yes, mother," Alice had said. She had tried to smile, while Margaret had looked up at her sharply. She did not want either her mother or Margaret to suspect her betrayal. That night, she had barely slept. No matter how she tried, she could not keep from sobbing. If Mary, Justine, and Diana were here, that meant they had returned from their mission in Europe and were trying to rescue her and Mr. Holmes. If they had been captured, it was her fault.

In the middle of the night, she had tried to sneak all the way down to the coal cellar. She was sure the door would be locked, but perhaps she could knock on it quietly and contact them? Perhaps she could help them escape in some way? Diana was with them, and Diana could pick any lock that had ever been made, couldn't she?

DIANA: Damn right I could!

But when she got down to the bottom of the back stairs, she had seen that the cellar door was guarded by one of Colonel Moran's men. After that boy had told her there were only two of them guarding the house, she had tried to observe them surreptitiously, to figure out any weaknesses that might be important if one were trying to escape. Surely that was what Mary would do? *Observe and learn. . . .* This was the younger one, with shaggy dark hair. The older one was bald and had a broken nose. He must be guarding the house outside. This one was sitting in front of the door, playing some sort of solitary card game by the light of a single lantern. There was no way she could get past him. She waited a while to see if he might go to the kitchen for some food, or perhaps to use what she thought of as *the facilities*, but he had not moved. Finally, she crept back up the dark staircase to the second floor. She paused by the door of the room where Mr. Holmes was being kept and put her ear to the keyhole, but all was silent. As far as she knew, no one had noticed the substitution of the salt for heroin, although she had replaced almost half the bottle. She hoped a lower dose of the drug would have some effect. Then she had gone back to bed and cried herself to sleep, feeling useless.

Now here she was, watching through the window as Dr. Watson and the Baker Street boys attempted a rescue.

"Give me your hand," said her mother again. Reluctantly, Alice put her hand in Helen's. Once again she could feel the tug of mesmeric power being pulled out of her. What was her mother trying to do? What did she need Alice's power for?

Suddenly, there were men standing in front of the house— men with pistols in their hands. Where had they come from? Of course—they were only an illusion. But that one—no, he was no illusion. That was the older guard, the bald one. And, yes, there was the younger, with his shaggy hair. Now Alice could see boys running across the street toward the front of the house. Those must be the Baker Street Irregulars! They were carrying knives, slings, what looked like pieces of lead pipe. She could hear their cries through the closed windows. They sounded like war whoops. Did those boys think this was some sort of game? Did they not realize the gravity of the situation? Two of the guards shot—no, they were illusory guards, and the bullets were illusions as well. The boys hesitated. Some of them kept running forward, some of them retreated. One of them cried out to those who were retreating and waved them forward. Had they realized the bullets weren't real? They were rushing forward again, and there was Dr. Watson, who had run to the front, leading the charge, a pistol in his hand. Something struck the window—a rock thrown from a sling, she guessed, because cracks spread across the glass. Another of the guards shot—illusion again? No, it was the bald one. That shot was real. Dr. Watson was down! The Baker Street boys would not be able to tell which of the shots were real and which ones weren't.

Horrified, Alice pulled her hand from her mother's.

"What is it, Lydia?" said Helen, looking down at her. "Are you afraid those boys will get in here somehow and harm you? You should not be—I will protect you. I learned very young that life is a struggle. What matters is how much power you have in that struggle. The more power, the better. You and I will emerge from this particular struggle triumphant, you shall see. And then we shall have enough power so that no one will ever harm us again. Now, let me finish this, and then we can have—breakfast? Have you breakfasted yet? No?"

Outside, the Baker Street boys seemed to be retreating. Where was Watson? Alice could not see him. The illusory guards were still there, alongside the real ones, although they seemed to be growing fainter, more translucent, and they were no longer shooting their pistols. Helen must not be paying as much attention.

"I had coffee and toast early, with Margaret. She has already gone to the British Museum to prepare for our ritual. We shall join her tonight, after the museum closes. It will be closed tomorrow as well—it is always closed on Sundays—so we shall have plenty of time to complete the ritual without fear of interruption. Fortunately, the director himself gave her a set of keys so she could complete work on the exhibit after hours, which means we can come and go as we please. Now, I think the situation outside has been resolved satisfactorily. Mr. Hoskins and Isaac can handle any remaining disturbance. I'll order an omelet and—what else? Potatoes and sausage? Some sort of compote? You're so skinny, my dear. And you need to keep up your strength—this will be a busy day."

Feeling heartsick, and dreadfully worried about the people she loved, Alice followed her mother out of the room. She had no idea what to do. Somehow, she must try to rescue her friends. But how?

CATHERINE: Do you know what happened to that set of keys? I would love to be able to get in and out of the British Museum whenever I pleased.

MARY: I haven't the faintest idea. That wasn't at all what we were focused on at the time!

CATHERINE: Could they be somewhere in the Alchemical Society headquarters? Or would Margaret Trelawny have taken them with her?

MARY: You're interrupting your own narrative for this stupid question?

BEATRICE: Forgive me, Mary, but it is not a stupid question. A person who had such a set of keys would have access to one of the most magnificent collections of art and artifacts in the world. Imagine being able to roam among the Elgin Marbles without interruption!

ALICE: Or study the mummies. I've been trying to learn about the Egyptians. Ancient history means so much more when it actually happens to you. . . .

CATHERINE: All right, we'll start by searching the Alchemical Society, and then if that doesn't work, who's up for a trip to Cornwall and Kyllion Keep?

MARY: You are all quite mad.

DIANA: Barmy, the lot of them.

Mary sat up groggily. Had Mrs. Poole come in to tell her that breakfast was ready? She was terribly hungry! It took her a moment to realize that she was still in the coal cellar. The lamp had burned low, and she could only see dimly, but Diana was still asleep, thank goodness. She heard a groan. Who was that? Of course—Justine. Was she all right? Mary managed to sit up again. What time was it? Automatically, she looked at her wrist, but they had taken her wristwatch.

Justine groaned again. *"Où suis-je?"* she asked. "Mary—where are we? I'm am so—*étourdie*. My head, it does not feel well."

"We were captured, remember?" said Mary. Was Justine all right? In the dim light, she looked even paler than usual—almost a little green. Mary probably looked that way herself.

"In Styria?" Justine raised her hands to her head, then seemed startled to see that they were tied together. She looked at her bound wrists, and at the shackle on her ankle, in wonder.

"No, that was—well, ages ago. We're in London. We've been captured by Mrs. Raymond, and I suspect Professor Moriarty, although we haven't seen him yet. You were chloroformed. I don't know how long we've been here—I fell asleep. Are you all right?"

"No. My head—it is swimming, as though I were underwater."

"I suspect that will wear off after a while. I'm just glad you're awake at last!"

Justine sat silently, with her head in her hands. The minutes passed. Mary looked at her, worried. Would Justine be all right? Finally, she raised her head, looked at her hands, and pulled her wrists apart. Mary expected the ropes to start fraying and then break—after all, this was Justine! But they did not.

"I am still too weak," said Justine apologetically. "Perhaps when I have recovered a little more . . ."

Diana rolled over and opened her eyes. "Is breakfast ready yet?" She sat up groggily. "Oh, bloody hell. We're still in here, aren't we?" She looked around. "I need to piss."

> MARY: Do you *have* to include such details in our book?

> CATHERINE: Oh, it's our book now, is it?

Just then, the door opened—slowly, tentatively. In came an older woman in the black dress and apron of a housekeeper. In one hand she was carrying a pitcher of water.

"Hello," said Mary. "I'm Mary Jekyll."

The woman simply nodded, then walked up to her with the pitcher. *"Wasser,"* she said. She held the pitcher out to Mary. Should she drink? It could be a trick of some sort. Perhaps the water was poisoned, or contained some sort of drug? She looked at it with suspicion.

*"Ist gut,"* said the woman, holding out the pitcher as though urging her to drink.

"You speak German," said Justine. *"Verzeihung, sprechen Sie Deutsch? Sind Sie aus Deutschland?"*

*"Nein, nein,"* said the woman. *"Bisschen. Gut Wasser."* Again, she seemed to be urging Mary to drink.

Justine replied with what seemed like a stream of German phrases, but the woman shook her head, as though trying to indicate that truly, she did not understand. She seemed apologetic.

Mary was so thirsty! She could not take hold of the pitcher with her wrists bound, but she steadied it with her hands and then drank. The water was deliciously cold. Not too much—she had to leave enough for Diana and Justine. After she had drunk, the woman carried the pitcher to Diana, then Justine. And then Diana again, because Justine drank only a little. "I need less than the two of you," she said.

When the pitcher was empty, the woman carried it to the door, as though about to leave. But as she opened the door, she turned back to them. *"Hilfe kommt,"* she said solemnly. Then she walked out and closed the door behind her.

"Help is coming," said Justine. "What do you think that means?"

"Probably that someone is coming to help us," said Diana. "Turn around—I'm going to use that chamber pot."

> MARY: Oh, for goodness' sake! Are you going to give a detailed account of all our bodily functions?

> JUSTINE: While I agree that it is indelicate, I understand what Catherine is trying to do. In those penny dreadfuls Alice is continually reading, imprisonment is often described as some sort of adventure, but in truth it is tedious and painful. We sat for hours with nothing to do. The ropes rubbed the skin on our wrists raw. Our muscles ached. We were hungry—that is, you and Diana were hungry. I can go for a long time without food. And of course there were bodily needs, as well as a lack of privacy. Catherine is trying to be truthful and accurate about our experiences. I think that is an admirable goal, for a writer.

> CATHERINE: Thank you! Unfortunately, truthfulness and accuracy don't pay as well as Rick Chambers, exemplary English gentleman, facing giant spider gods in the Cavern of Doom! I'm proud of my

Astarte books, but you can't say they illuminate human nature.

MARY: Perhaps they illuminate spider god nature.

CATHERINE: That's supposed to be a joke, right? It's
sort of remarkable that your jokes are never funny.

After what felt like hours, Justine said, "I think perhaps I am strong enough now." She held her hands up in front of her. Then, she began to twist and turn them, one way and then the other. The ropes strained, then began to break. Mary could see blood on her wrists, and almost told her to stop and rest for a little longer—but Justine looked so determined, and surely she was the best judge of her own actions? Justine twisted and pulled, the ropes continued to strain—a strand broke, and then another. Suddenly, with a shredding sound, the final strands broke and Justine's hands were free. Now, if she could break the chain that bound her to the wall, she could free Mary and Diana as well. Then they could smash their way out of this pit. . . .

Again Justine pulled, this time at the chain that bound her to the wall, close to the shackle around her ankle. Yes, she was regaining her strength, Mary could see that. And then with a snap, the chain broke. Justine was free! At that moment, the door opened. Standing in the doorway was Colonel Moran. With him were more of his lackeys—three of them this time, different from the ones who had captured them, all armed. "I don't think so, missy," he said when he saw what Justine had done. "You won't get away from the professor. But you've saved me some trouble with the lock. Mr. Fletcher, would you mind tying this young lady's hands together again? And quickly, if you don't mind. The professor wants to see them upstairs, *toute suite*."

JUSTINE: I am not a *missy*. We are not, any of us, *missy*. And that is not the correct pronunciation of *toute suite*.

As the three of them filed upstairs, Mary felt a sense of despair, as well as a burning anger at how they were being treated. The anger was useful—the despair was not. She must try to put it away for now, lock it in some sort of box so she would be calm and collected and resolute for whatever was about to happen. After all, she was her father's daughter—Jekyll's, that is—born of his most rational self, or so Hyde had told her in Styria. She must be that person now.

They followed Colonel Moran, and were followed by the men with revolvers pointed at them, up the stairs and into a large room. It appeared to be some sort of common room, like the one at the Diogenes Club—there were armchairs and small tables scattered about. By the light coming through the window, it was late in the day. How long had they been in that cellar?

Standing at the front of the room was a tall man, almost as tall as Holmes, with sharp features. That must be Professor Moriarty. Next to him stood—was that Mrs. Raymond? Her features were the same, but she looked so much younger, with black hair piled on her head, in a stylish gray walking suit. Beside her, holding her hand, was Alice. She did not look like Alice anymore. She was wearing the sort of fancy dress Alice had never worn, and would probably never have worn if she had a choice. It was blue, with all sorts of frills and furbelows. It seemed—impractical? Alice stared at her with wide, wary eyes.

"Well, well," said Professor Moriarty. "So here are our honored guests. Greetings, Miss Jekyll, Miss Frankenstein. I've heard a great deal about you, Miss Hyde—none of it good. I hope you have enjoyed your stay here. Dr. Watson dropped in for a visit this morning, but could not stay. I believe he took a bullet to the leg. He's an old soldier, used to such wounds, so I hope it causes him no inconvenience. He seemed to be with a group of boys—I was not aware that he had become a scouting master?"

Oh, he was so smug! Mary despised him. And she felt a sense of dismay. So those shots in her dream must have been real shots after all? Watson must have tried to stage a rescue with the Baker Street boys—against her express orders! Damn his sense of chivalry. But what, exactly, was going on with Alice? Why was she dressed that way, and why was she with Mrs. Raymond? She did not look like a captive. . . .

"I'm afraid you're in for a long night, but it should be instructive. After all, we are going to the British Museum!" Moriarty chuckled, as though he had said something amusing. Mary was not amused.

"Is it really necessary to bring them?" asked Mrs. Raymond, frowning. Whereas before her frown had looked formidable, now it seemed petulant. "You're taking a risk—"

"Oh, I doubt Miss Jekyll and Miss Frankenstein will do anything foolish," said Moriarty. "After all, they would not leave without Holmes, and he is coming with us. Isn't he, Colonel?" He looked toward the door behind them. Mary turned, then drew in her breath sharply. There was Colonel Moran, with two of his underlings holding up Sherlock Holmes between them. Those were the two men who had captured them—so altogether there were five guards, all armed. Mary noted their number automatically. Holmes was upright, but not standing on his own feet—slumped forward as though drunk, with his knees bent, hanging from the arms of the two men on either side of him. What in the world was wrong with him? Behind them came another man, rather nondescript—she barely noticed him. Her attention was on the detective.

Instinctively, she took a step toward him. Holmes looked up and said "Mary . . ." in a slurred voice. He tried to take a step forward, but stumbled so the men on either side had to hold him up more firmly.

"What have you done to Mr. Holmes?" asked Justine.

"Nothing he hasn't done to himself before, I assure you," said Moriarty, with a sort of sneering satisfaction. "Or were you not aware of his less reputable activities, Miss Jekyll? Of his, let us say, addictions?"

"What do you mean?" Mary balled up her fists. She wished she were close enough to hit him.

Moriarty looked at her in mock surprise. "Why, Miss Jekyll, you don't seem to know as much about Mr. Holmes as I assumed, judging by your intimacy with him."

Intimacy? What in the world did he mean by that?

"In the depth of his drugged sleep, he called out your name. 'Mary, Mary,' he called, over and over again. Evidently, you're said to be his *assistant*, or so my associates have determined. You see, I have done some research since we captured you and your friends. That's a novel and interesting use of the term. I'm sure he will want to see your face before he dies, just as I'm sure you will want to be there for his last moments."

Oh, the man was odious! If only Mary could—what? Nothing, she could do nothing. She imagined sending a bullet, neatly and precisely, through the center of his forehead.

Moriarty laughed. "If looks could kill, Miss Jekyll! But they can't, can they?"

"Mr. Holmes doesn't look right," said Mrs. Raymond. "He should be—I don't know. He's too conscious, considering the dose."

He didn't look conscious to Mary! He raised his head for a moment and stared at her, but his eyes seemed glazed over, as though he could not recognize what was in front of him. Alice's message had said they were keeping him drugged. This must be the effect of the narcotic. Well, it was better than him being sick, or perhaps injured! But it hurt her to see him in that condition.

"You bloody bastard!" said Diana. "You're damn right we're not leaving here without him—or Alice." She sprang toward Moriarty, as though about to attack him, despite the fact that her hands were still tied together. Justine was just quick enough to catch the back of her jacket, although her own hands were tied as well. Oh, stupid Diana! What in the world was she trying to do, get herself killed? She struggled—but suddenly her forward momentum ceased. Justine had picked her up by her jacket collar, as a mother cat might pick up her kitten.

Diana kicked and flailed in Justine's grasp. "Put me down, you oversized scarecrow!" She continued to struggle for another moment, then hung limp and defeated. With a little shake, as though in warning, Justine put her down again.

"I suggest you keep Diana under control," said Mrs. Raymond in icy tones. "Colonel Moran will not hesitate to shoot her. As for Alice—by which you mean my daughter Lydia—she has no desire to return with you. Do you? Tell them, Lydia."

Alice looked up at her, and then at Mary. For a moment, she seemed uncertain what to say. "No, Mother," she said finally. "I would like to stay with you and Miss Trelawny." Her voice sounded sincere enough, but her eyes looked cautious, as though she had to be careful of what she was saying. At least, that is how they looked to Mary. Was Alice truly declaring her loyalty to Mrs. Raymond, who was, after all, her mother? Or was she being coerced?

"You ungrateful little rat," said Diana. "How could you? We came here to rescue you!"

"Be quiet, Diana!" said Justine. Mary had never heard her speak so forcefully.

Abruptly, Diana shut up. *Thank the Lord for small mercies,* thought Mary.

"That's quite enough," said Moriarty. "Come, it is time we left. Margaret will have everything prepared. The others are meeting us in the exhibit hall. Mr. Harker, your client, Lord Godalming, and Dr. Seward are already there waiting for us. I suggest you take your umbrella. We expect to be there all night, and it may rain when we return tomorrow morning."

Mr. Harker! Moriarty must mean the nondescript man, who was now nervously putting on his hat and placing an umbrella under one arm. So this was Mina's husband? He was attractive, in a washed-out, weak-chinned sort of way. Quite the opposite of Dracula. Would Mina be any happier with the Count? Mary did not know. But at least the Count would not have looked so thoroughly cowed by Moriarty! She imagined, with pleasure, Count Dracula drinking the professor's blood.

> LUCINDA: I believe the Count would have spit it out in
> distaste. He is most particular about his source of
> nourishment.

"As for Miss Jekyll, Miss Frankenstein, and Miss Hyde," continued Professor Moriarty, "I suggest you ladies walk in the middle of our little group so the inhabitants of Soho, should we pass any, do not notice that you are my prisoners. As it is dinnertime, I suspect we shall parade through the streets largely unnoticed. If you attempt to escape, Mr. Hoskins will immediately shoot Mr. Holmes. But why would you want to miss the spectacle that awaits? You are about to witness the greatest scientific experiment in modern times. It will alter the world we live in more than any vaccine, more than the steam engine or telegraph. It will give us a source of unlimited power, and with it, we will change the world! Tonight, we will summon the Great God Pan."

"Bollocks," said Diana, but under her breath, so only Mary, and she imagined Justine, could hear it. It was very much what she would have liked to tell Moriarty herself. Instead she followed him and Mrs. Raymond out the front door. They walked, in a sort of armed cavalcade, into the London evening toward the British Museum where Moriarty would do—what? What in the world did it mean to summon the god Pan? He was the Greek god of nature, was he not? Surely he did not actually exist. Was it another of those ridiculous metaphors alchemists used for their experiments?

Alice was ahead of her, walking with Mrs. Raymond. Had she truly betrayed them? Surely not. And yet Mary could not be certain. She stole a quick glance behind, where Mr. Holmes was being half-dragged, half-carried between Colonel Moran's men. He had called her name in his delirium. . . . If only she could help him! But there was nothing to do but follow after Moriarty and Mrs. Raymond. The sun was beginning to set above the rooftops, turning the buildings of Soho red and gold. She walked on beside Justine, who had a firm grip on Diana's jacket so she could not launch some sort of sudden attack, and wondered what that night would bring.

**W**hat should she do? Alice had no idea. Should she somehow try to help Mary? Or Mr. Holmes? But there was no way she could help them, not at the moment.

Mary, Diana, and Justine were sitting together, guarded by Colonel Moran. At least his henchmen had left—she imagined they were patrolling the museum, making certain no one interfered with the ceremony that was about to begin—a ritual to summon the Great God Pan, or what Helen had described as the energic powers of the Earth. So far it did not look like much of a ceremony. No one was wearing special robes, no one was chanting an ancient litany in spectral tones. Compared to the books Alice liked to read at night, by candlelight before she went to sleep, the scene before her was not particularly impressive.

MRS. POOLE: You'll ruin your eyes doing that, my girl.

They were in one of the large exhibition halls of the museum. It was filled with what she presumed were Egyptian artifacts, including a great many pots, most of them broken in one place or another. She would have liked to fix them with a bit of glue. She recognized some of them from the vision of Queen Tera's tomb that Helen Raymond had conjured up. Just to make clear where they had all come from, there was a large sign by the door:

THE TRELAWNY EXHIBIT
VISIT THE TOMB OF QUEEN TERA
SPONSORED BY THE BRITISH ARCHAEOLOGICAL ASSOCIATION
AND THE EGYPT EXPLORATION FUND

Underneath was some information on the Ptolemaic Dynasty and the Temple of Isis at Philae. Alice had glanced at it briefly as they entered. She would have liked to read more, but there was no time now. She had only been to the British Museum once before, with Mrs. Poole, and wished she could wander around, looking at all the exhibition rooms—she had seen some very large statues of winged, bull-headed men that looked interesting. If she got out of this situation alive, she would most certainly have to come back. There was so much to see and learn! She did not want to be an ignorant kitchen maid all her life. *I hope I live through this,* she thought, looking at Margaret Trelawny dubiously. Thirteen seemed awfully young to die.

"Welcome, welcome," Margaret said when they all entered, although she had looked with astonishment at the addition to their party of Mary, Diana, and Justine. She was wearing her black gown with the low neckline that showed off the scarab necklace to perfection. There had been a brief whispered conversation between her and Helen. Then she had nodded and gone back to bustling around the raised wooden platform at the center of the room, on which rested the stone sarcophagus of Queen Tera. It must have been difficult to get that large stone box all the way from Egypt to London! The lid was lying on the platform so you could see the painted carvings on it, and also look inside the sarcophagus to see the mummy of Queen Tera lying in her coffin. Alice had looked in quickly. Queen Tera was there all right, but she did not look as she had in the vision produced by her mother. This was a real mummy—all wrapped up in bandages that had been dried and darkened by the centuries.

Strangely, however, as in the vision, her left hand had been left out of the wrappings. It had long ago turned into a wrinkled claw. It was still holding the golden ankh Alice had seen in the vision.

At the corners of that platform, and centered on three sides, were wooden pillars carved to resemble the lotus-topped columns of the Temple of Isis, seven in all. At the top of each pillar was a curiously shaped bowl. Margaret called them lamps, and she kept fussing with them, as though they needed to be positioned in just the right way.

The gentlemen were milling around—Lord Godalming talking to Dr. Seward, Dr. Raymond focusing intently on how Margaret was arranging the lamps, no doubt trying to memorize her movements for some Pan-summoning of his own, and Jonathan Harker sitting in the chair ordinarily occupied by a museum guard, looking a bit lost. Colonel Moran was standing beside Mary, Diana, and Justine, who were sitting on the floor, their wrists still tied together. He and Mr. Morris were showing each other their firearms, as though comparing their relative merits. Seriously, at a time like this, all they could think of was their guns? And Moriarty was pacing impatiently up and down, asking Margaret every five minutes if it was time yet. Alice was not a violent person, but she would have liked to smack him and tell him to stop. The noise of his boot heels clacking back and forth on the stone floor was distracting.

Alice cast an agonized glance down at Mr. Holmes. He was lying on the platform, where Moran's henchmen had placed him. He seemed to be unconscious. Had her trick with the salt not helped him at all? Or perhaps there had been something wrong with the salt, some sort of impurity, and she had inadvertently poisoned him! She felt sick with worry. If only she could talk to Mary, tell her everything she had found out, everything Moriarty intended to do! Then Mary could advise her. Mary always had such useful, sensible advice! But if she betrayed Helen and Margaret in any obvious way, she would be tied up with Mary, Diana, and Justine, which would be no help to them at all. It had been horrible, letting everyone think she was in league with Mrs. Raymond, knowing what her friends must think of her. Diana had made her opinion perfectly clear!

What should she, what *could* she, do? Nothing, for the moment. She must just bide her time.

"We're about to begin," said Helen finally. How long had they been there? It already felt like hours. She took Alice's hand. "You and I will help Margaret draw upon the energic powers locked in Queen Tera's sarcophagus. You don't need to do anything—I shall draw upon your power to amplify mine, as I did in the fight against those Baker Street ruffians. Do you understand, Lydia?"

"Yes, Mother," said Alice, not at all sure what she was saying she understood. The energic powers in the tomb? Were they not drawing on the energic powers of the Earth itself?

"Place the sacrifice on the lid of the sarcophagus," said Margaret.

Lord Godalming and Seward stepped forward, lifted Holmes by his hands and feet, and placed his body on the sarcophagus lid, spread-eagled so that his hands and feet were at the four corners. Holmes did not awaken.

Alice wished she understood more about what they meant. Were they going to drain the life out of him, as Professor Trelawny's life had been drained? Would it take some time, or would it happen immediately? Would there be time for Alice to do anything? Involuntarily, she started moving toward Holmes, but her mother's hand held hers as though in a steel vise.

"Please take your places, gentlemen," said Margaret. "It is almost midnight. Let us begin the ceremony inscribed on the walls of Queen Tera's tomb. In a moment, we will summon a power stronger than man has ever known. Are you ready?"

"Get on with it, Miss Trelawny," said Moriarty impatiently. Like each of the other men, he was now standing by one of the seven pillars.

"As you wish," said Margaret. She seemed to be smiling a particularly catlike smile. It reminded Alice of the smile painted on the mummified cat in Tera's tomb. Margaret stepped onto the platform, stood next to the sarcophagus, and said, "Light the lamps."

> MARY: What was it about those lamps, anyway? Why were they so special?

> BEATRICE: Ayesha told me it was not the lamps themselves, which were merely ceremonial objects, but the oil they contained. Certain substances have the power to amplify energic waves. Some crystals will do it, as will certain kinds of musical instruments. And there is a combination of cedar and other aromatic oils that the priestesses of Isis would use for that purpose.

> ALICE: Also cod liver oil, believe it or not.

What were they doing with Mr. Holmes? Mary leaned forward to see. Perhaps if she stood up . . . Moriarty and Colonel Moran were now standing by two of those strange pillars, which were shaped like lotus flowers. There were seven pillars in all, and on top of each one was a bowl of some sort. One flared up—ah, they were lamps! Each of the men stood behind a pillar—one by one, they were lighting the lamps, which burned with a strange white flame. She had heard their names earlier, when Moriarty had told them what to do: Lord Godalming, Dr. Raymond, Mr. Morris, Mr. Harker, whom they had walked over to the museum with, and of course Dr. Seward. She was afraid Dr. Seward might recognize her as Miss Jenks from when she had visited the Purfleet Asylum with Mr. Holmes, but he had scarcely glanced at her. So that was the infamous Dr. Raymond? It did not surprise her that he was involved in this absurdity as well. There, now the last of the lamps were lit. Were they about to start the ritual?

No one was paying attention to her, Diana, or Justine. They had simply been left sitting beside one of the exhibition cases, as though they were no longer important. Well, that was a relief! Mary stood up and tried to see what they had done to Mr. Holmes.

He was lying on the lid of that large stone box—the sarcophagus, she believed it was called. Lying spread-eagled like that, he looked more than ever like a spider. But not a dead spider! He was still alive—he must still be alive, mustn't he?

In front of the sarcophagus stood a beautiful woman with upswept black hair, looking down at a scroll she held in her hands, saying something in a foreign language, her voice rising and falling, almost as though she were intoning a chant. She wore a black gown with a low collar, and around her neck was a magnificent gold necklace with a ruby pendant dangling from it. Earlier, when they had first entered and Moriarty called the women over for a hurried consultation, Mary had noted that it was in the shape of a scarab. He had called her Margaret—she must be Margaret Trelawny, who would be performing whatever strange ritual was being enacted here. On the other side of the sarcophagus stood Mrs. Raymond, holding Alice's hand.

"What language is that?" Mary asked Justine. She did not think anyone would overhear them—the participants were too far away, and too occupied with those strange-looking lamps, whatever their purpose.

"None that I recognize," replied Justine. "There is no one watching us. I will attempt once again to break this rope."

"That will not be necessary," said a low voice behind them. Mary turned around, startled. There, crouched in the shadow of a display case, was one of Colonel Moran's lackeys. He spoke with a foreign accent that sounded almost, but not quite, German. She felt a sense of satisfaction that, after her European adventures, she recognized the intonation.

"Here," he said, holding out a knife. "Free yourselves and flee while it is still possible."

Diana snatched the knife out of his hand and sawed through the rope around her wrists, then quickly cut those around Mary's and Justine's wrists as well.

"Who are you?" asked Mary in a voice as low as his. At the center of the room, Margaret Trelawny was still reading from the scroll. The scarab on the necklace she wore was now glowing red.

"My name is Isaac Mandelbaum," he said. "You have met my mother, the housekeeper for Professor Moriarty. She asked me to help you, to get you out before the—what is the word—the engagement. The combat. Soon, I hope, the Metropolitan Police will be here. They shall arrest Moriarty and his men for breaking and entering into the British Museum, with the intent to steal the artifacts from this exhibit. And then, once he is in custody, he will be brought up on other charges. He has been careful, very careful, but now we have evidence of his crimes—the opium dens, the houses of prostitution, the smuggling of goods and people."

"What is *we*?" asked Diana skeptically. "Who are you working for, anyway?"

"That I cannot tell you," he said. "But I am loyal to your British government, and I have been instructed, if possible, to save Mr. Holmes." He drew a pistol from behind his back—it must have been in his belt. It was the same pistol that had been pointed at them only an hour ago, but now, apparently, he was a friend. Mary was not sure whether to trust him.

"Did Mycroft Holmes send you?" she asked. Who else in the British government knew about Moriarty and his criminal enterprises? It must be Mycroft—despite his apparent indifference in the Diogenes Club, he must be trying to save his brother. But Isaac Mandelbaum did not answer. He merely crouched in the shadows, pistol drawn, waiting. For what? He had said that help was on the way. . . .

Suddenly, Margaret Trelawny's recitation ceased. Mary looked at the central platform. Margaret was no longer holding the scroll. She was standing still, turned toward Mrs. Raymond, who had her hands raised. Alice was leaning over, rubbing the hand Mrs. Raymond had been holding, and looking down at Mr. Holmes.

As Mary watched, the air around Mrs. Raymond shimmered. It looked as though she were surrounded by multicolored waves. Were these the energic waves Ayesha had described? They swirled around her, rising and falling, shifting with her motions. She looked like a conductor before an orchestra, but her orchestra was the air itself. Mary felt a cold wind rise and begin to blow around the room.

Around the platform, the seven men stood at the seven pillars. The wind whipped Mr. Morris's long hair about his head.

"It's time for the sacrifice!" shouted Moriarty, with a sort of triumphant glee in his voice. "This will be the last of you, Sherlock Holmes! You will be drained of your life, your essence, like a battery. This time there will be no resurrecting you from the waters of Reichenbach Falls!"

They were going to sacrifice Mr. Holmes in this insane ritual! For what purpose? Mary had no idea, but she knew that she had to save him.

"Help me!" she said to Justine. "I have to get to Sherlock!"

"Mary, what are you going to do?" asked Justine. She had to raise her voice to be heard above the wind.

"I don't know!" said Mary. "I'll think of something!" She had no plan—she always had a plan, but now she simply did not know what to do. She just knew that she had to get Sherlock Holmes off that platform.

Her skirt was whipping in the wind, which was rising and getting stronger. Justine nodded and stood up beside her. Together, somehow, they would get to Mr. Holmes. Could they reach him in time?

"No!" shouted Isaac Mandelbaum, reaching toward her. "You must not. You will simply endanger yourself."

Suddenly, Mary was blinded by a bright flash of light. It had come from the sarcophagus itself. She peered at it, blinking. Were those multicolored swirls the energic waves, or the aftereffect of that flash on her irises? She rubbed her eyes to try and clear them.

Something was rising from the sarcophagus, some form. She could see it, a shadow against the brightness. It stepped out of the sarcophagus and onto the platform. What in the world was happening? Mary rubbed her eyes again. They were tearing up from the light, and stung as though she had gotten some caustic substance into them. She blinked and tried to see as best she could. The shadow appeared to be the figure of a woman, wrapped like a mummy, as though Queen Tera had risen and stepped out of her tomb. But that was impossible—this must be another of Mrs. Raymond's illusions. She was being mesmerized—but it seemed so real! The mummy stood in front of the sarcophagus, next to Margaret Trelawny, whose necklace was blazing like a red eye through the shifting waves. Mrs. Raymond was still conducting her orchestra of lights. Mary could see that the waves were rising in accordance with her gestures.

"Justine!" She clutched Justine's arm. "Can you see—tell me what you see!"

"I do not know," Justine shouted back, almost into her ear. "Is that—"

"It's the mummy!" Diana's voice was almost a shriek. So Diana could see it as well! Either it was not an illusion, or they were all being deluded at the same time.

"What are you doing? What's happening?" shouted Moriarty. "This isn't—"

"Priestess of Isis, Queen of Egypt, accept our sacrifice," shouted Margaret.

The mummy turned and held out its left hand, which appeared to be unwrapped. Curiously, it seemed to have seven fingers. From those seven fingers came seven beams of light that spread to the seven lamps.

"Helen! Don't do this!" That was the man they had called Dr. Raymond. The flame in his lamp sprang up, up, until it was as tall as the pillar. The light from the mummy augmented the flame, raising it higher and higher, like a giant candle. The flame began to dance in the wind that was still whipping around the room. And then it turned, bent down, and wrapped itself around Dr. Raymond. He threw back his head and screamed.

All of the flames were rising, all of them were dancing, all of them were reaching for and enveloping the men who stood behind the pillars. And now they were aflame! Moriarty and Moran, Godalming and Seward, Morris and Harker—all screaming and writhing as though they were on fire. They were human torches, surrounded by a blazing white light that shot multicolored specks, like a Catherine wheel. Mary heard a scream—was it Alice? It sounded like Alice. But the flames were nowhere near her, thank goodness. Around the platform, the seven men were being consumed by flames.

"*Mój Boże!*" shouted Isaac Mandelbaum. "What is happening?"

Mary could barely hear him over the sound of the wind. "Justine!" she cried. "Can we try to save them? How can we save them?" Those men might be her enemies, but they were dying in agony. She must do something.

"I do not know," Justine shouted back. What could they do? The wind was swirling all around them. Now it carried the smoke of the burning men, a white smoke like fog, with multicolored glints in it. She could still hear their screams. This was terrible! It was the most terrible thing she had ever experienced. It was worse than the night in the warehouse when Adam Frankenstein had gone up in flames, because she had not been able to see him burn. But these men were dying right before her eyes. Through the smoke, she could see clothes disintegrating, flesh charring and melting. For a moment, she hid her eyes, sickened at the sight.

But she must not turn away. Perhaps she could not save those men, but Sherlock and Alice were still in there, in the noise and smoke. She must try to save her friends. She turned and grabbed Isaac Mandelbaum's revolver. He stared at her, too stunned to resist.

"No," shouted Justine. "You cannot go in there. It is too dangerous. I will go."

Before Mary could protest, Justine had sprung up and rushed into the swirling fog. It seemed to be part smoke, part flames, part multicolored lights the colors of sunrise: blue and yellow and pink. It rose and fell around the platform, where she could still see the figure of the mummy—but now it too was bathed in a bright white light, with flames dancing around it. Those flames gave off no heat, only light, the brightest light she had ever seen, so that she had to cover her eyes again from the sheer pain of it. She squinted between her fingers to see Justine running toward the platform.

Suddenly, as though someone had turned down a Bunsen burner, the flames burned down, and there was only a low fog, rising and falling like waves, along the floor. On the platform stood Margaret Trelawny and Mrs. Raymond. Between them stood the mummy. But as Mary watched, its wrappings fell off, turned to dust, and blew away in the wind. The wind itself fell, so that for the first time since the waves of light had appeared, it was quiet.

Where the mummy had been stood a woman. She was entirely naked. Her skin shone like burnished copper in the light of the seven lamps, which now burned only with low, flickering flames. She was entirely hairless, even on her head. Mary was so astonished at the sight of her that for a moment she forgot entirely where she was or what she was doing. She just stared at this apparition— was this the mummy, somehow brought back to life? It must be an illusion. They must all simply be witnessing the same illusion. But could an illusion have killed all those men?

"Queen Tera," said Isaac next to her. "They have resurrected Queen Tera from the dead. This is not what Moriarty planned."

His statement brought her back to herself. What was happening now? Justine had almost made it to the platform. Where was Alice? Ah, there—crouched by Mr. Holmes! And he was sitting up, speaking with her. Thank goodness, at least he was no longer unconscious. If Justine could reach them . . .

The woman Isaac had called Queen Tera raised her left hand. Lightning sprang from it, as white as the light of the lamps, hitting Justine in the chest. The Giantess crumpled to the ground. Mary could see Alice raising her hand to her mouth, stifling another scream. Holmes reached toward her weakly, as though to comfort her. Mary almost screamed herself. What had happened to Justine?

As casually as though nothing had happened, Queen Tera turned to Margaret Trelawny and Helen Raymond. Margaret Trelawny unclasped the scarab necklace from her neck, knelt before Queen Tera, and held the necklace out to the naked woman. "Hail, Priestess of Isis, once Queen of Egypt, soon to be Queen of England. Your loyal subject greets you."

Queen Tera took the scarab necklace and clasped it around her own neck, where it glowed briefly for a moment, then dimmed to a dull red hue. She said something that Mary could not understand. Was it in the same language Margaret had been reading from the scroll? Then she turned to Mrs. Raymond.

"Are you a loyal subject to me also, child of this new age?" Her voice was hoarse, like a rusted pulley. It sounded as though she had not used it in two thousand years. She spoke with a heavy accent. But how was she speaking English at all? Was she indeed Queen Tera? Or was this some sort of charlatan's trick? Those men—they had truly burned in the flames. And Justine was truly lying on the floor. Mary rose, prepared to run forward to where she was lying.

Isaac grabbed her wrist. "No. She will kill you, too. Can you not see that she has powers beyond what Moriarty dreamed of? You will not help your friends by dying yourself."

Mary wrenched her wrist from his grasp and crouched down again. He was right, she had to admit he was right, but she could not just stay here, doing nothing! Her wrist ached where he had grabbed it.

"I am, my queen," said Mrs. Raymond, replying to Queen Tera. Instead of kneeling as Margaret had, she bowed low for a moment. "I have waited all my life for a glimpse of the powers you wield, and to avenge myself upon my father, who gave me just so much, and no more, of them."

"Do not call me Queen until I sit upon the throne of your British Empire, heir to the Roman Empire of old. Call me Tera. Your language falls strangely on my tongue—it is an ugly language, without the mellifluous tones of Egyptian or Greek. So did the Roman tongue sound to my ears, when Octavian's soldiers came."

She looked around at the exhibition hall. "Shall we remain here, Margaret? Rise, and let us plan for the conquest of the known world."

"No, Tera." Margaret stood up again. "My house by the ocean is prepared for us, and we have a plan—Helen and I have it all figured out. If only Moriarty could have known what we were going to pull off! I would have liked to see his face when he realized—well, maybe he did, in those final moments. We're putting his plan in motion, but for an entirely different purpose. It will be England not for Englishmen, but for us and whoever decides to join us—your loyal followers, my Queen. Within a week you will sit upon the throne in Buckingham Palace."

Mrs. Raymond had once again grabbed Alice's hand. She paid no attention to Sherlock Holmes. Although he was sitting, he still seemed unsteady, as though the effect of whatever drug he had been under had not yet worn off. "Come, Lydia. Meet your future Queen. She will rule this country better than it has ever been ruled, make it stronger than it has ever been. It will become the greatest empire the world has ever known."

"And what of them?" Queen Tera was looking at Mary and Diana.

"They are irrelevant," said Margaret. "I suggest you burn them up in your fire, leaving their ashes to scatter through these halls, as the ashes of Moriarty and his followers are doing even now."

"No!" cried Alice. "You can't do that! Not to Mary!"

At that, Holmes sprang up. He no longer seemed so unsteady on his long spider's legs. It looked as though he was going to leap at Queen Tera! No, he must not—the Egyptian Queen would strike him down, just as she had Justine.

Mary lifted Isaac Mandelbaum's revolver and pointed it at the platform. It was a .32, not her usual small but very effective .22 caliber revolver. She would have to aim carefully, adjusting for its harder kickback. She had Queen Tera in her sights. She did not want to injure either Alice or Sherlock Holmes. Carefully, carefully, she squeezed the trigger.

*Bang! Bang!* What was that? She had not yet fired. No, it was the doors of the exhibition hall, which had burst open and hit the walls behind them. Pouring through the doorway were the Baker Street boys, led by a tall, wild-haired boy who was yelling, "Charlie! Dennys! Get Mr. Holmes. Some of you fellows go to Diana. She'll tell you what to do. The rest of you, with me!"

Here was the cavalry, come to save them in the shape of a group of ragged street urchins and ragamuffins! For a moment, Mary blessed all the poor, dirty boys of London. Then she thought, *Queen Tera is going to kill them all.* She must take out the Egyptian Queen. She aimed again—but now there were Baker Street boys in the way. She could no longer get a clear shot.

"It's Wiggins!" said Diana. "Well, he took his bloody time. Wiggins, get Holmes and Alice, and don't forget Justine! She's on the floor—get her out of here! And then we're going to tear that naked mummy limb from limb."

On the platform, Queen Tera looked with astonishment at the stream of dirty boys rapidly spreading across the floor of the exhibition room. Holmes sprang toward her, but she waved her hand in his direction and he was hurled back, as though by a wave that had struck him in the chest. Mary could see Alice kneeling down beside him. Then, Queen Tera raised her hands. Multicolored waves rose around her. They swirled as though a wind were blowing them about. Mary heard a roar like the waves of the ocean. A rising tide of light surged around the platform, sparkling and flaring with all the colors of the rainbow, like small firecrackers going off.

Startled, the Baker Street boys fell back, staring at one another and then at Wiggins, wondering what to do. Was Tera going to blast them all?

If Mary could not shoot, then she must join the melee. If she and Isaac Mandelbaum both rushed Queen Tera, perhaps the mummy would only be able to take out one of them at a time and the other could get through? Although Mary remembered lightning coming out of her seven fingers at once . . . Nevertheless, they had to do something.

"Come on," she said, but suddenly realized that Isaac Mandelbaum was not there. Only Diana sat beside her. The coward had run away! Perhaps he was not working with Mycroft after all? Perhaps he had simply been one of Moriarty's henchmen, and had left to betray them to his other confederates.

"I'm with you!" said Diana. She had Isaac's knife in her hand. "Let's go get that Egyptian bitch!"

But the wind had grown so high and loud that Mary felt as though she were in the middle of a tornado. When she rose, it almost knocked her down again. Even if it were a good idea for her and Diana to rush the platform, they could not have.

"Bloody hell!" shouted Diana. Her hair was whipping in the wind like a red halo around her head.

Mary grabbed Diana's hand. "Hold on!" she said. "Just hold on to me."

Suddenly, the sound of rushing waves ceased. The waves of light that had surrounded the platform died down. Lower and lower the waves fell, finally swirling around the floor like water going into a drain, until they disappeared entirely. The exhibition room looked exactly as it had when Mary first entered it, except that now it was filled with Baker Street boys, looking around the room, puzzled.

Justine was still lying on the floor, in front of the platform with Queen Tera's sarcophagus on it. Wiggins was standing beside her. Queen Tera, Mrs. Raymond, Margaret Trelawny, Mr. Holmes, and Alice were all gone.

There was a noise outside the door. In burst Isaac Mandelbaum, followed by a group of men in the blue uniform of the Metropolitan

Police. "I have brought help!" he said. He looked around the room, now filled with boys. "What has happened here?"

"That was exactly what I was wondering," said the man who walked in behind them. He had bright red hair and a frown that seemed to have permanently creased his forehead. "What are you doing here, Wiggins? And where is Mr. Holmes?" Then he saw Mary and Diana. "Oh, it's you again. As soon as I got out of bed this morning, I knew it was going to be a bad day. Why don't you explain to me what sort of mischief you've been up to this time?"

That was the very last thing Mary wanted to do. She was tired and heartsick. Once again, they had lost Alice and Sherlock, and Justine was—wounded? Dead? She braced herself for the interrogation she knew was coming, and said, "Good morning, Inspector Lestrade."

MARY: He hates me. He absolutely hates me.

CATHERINE: But probably less than he hates Sherlock Holmes.

MARY: Is that supposed to be a source of comfort?

CATHERINE: No, not really.

"I don't expect that hellcat to know any better," said Inspector Lestrade, looking pointedly at Diana. "But you, Miss Jekyll. Why don't you stay home quietly, embroidering or whatever it is ladies do all day? Mrs. Lestrade says she finds needlework very soothing. The next time Mr. Holmes asks you and your friends to help him with one of his investigations, I hope you will find a more productive way to spend your time. Involving those Baker Street boys is bad enough, but how he can put you young ladies in such a dangerous situation is beyond me."

"Yes, Inspector," said Mary, biting her tongue. She could have told him a thing or two about what young ladies were capable of. After all, she had spent the better part of the last two days locked in a dungeon—apparently it was Sunday afternoon, and she had once again missed going to church. She was tired, hungry, and dirty. But he had helped her transport Justine back to 11 Park Terrace in a police wagon, so that she was now lying in her own bed upstairs, still unconscious. Mary was desperately worried about her. She was so grateful to Lestrade for helping them that she merely nodded, as though agreeing that embroidery was the appropriate occupation for any young lady, no matter her ambition or intellect. At least he had believed her story that they were merely helping Mr. Holmes investigate a ring of thieves stealing ancient artifacts!

They stood in the parlor, by the mantel with Mrs. Jekyll's portrait over it. Mrs. Poole had not yet had time to light a fire. Should she? Did Lestrade intend to stay for a while? She had no idea.

Diana was lying on the sofa, half asleep. No wonder she was so quiet! But in response to his comment, she opened her mouth—oh goodness, she was about to say something, wasn't she? Something obnoxious, no doubt. That would only make Inspector Lestrade more angry.

Like the angel of perfect timing, Mrs. Poole bustled in. She was carrying a tray with a bottle and two glasses. "Would you care for some port, Inspector? Dr. Jekyll's best bottle. I know you officers of the law don't drink while working, but surely after the events of this morning . . . If I may be so bold as to suggest a medicinal quantity? And I cannot thank you enough for bringing the girls safely home. You don't know how I worry! I know their behavior is not quite what one might wish, but they are all poor, motherless orphans, with no one to teach them better—just me. I do my best, you know, but I am no substitute."

"I'm sure you do your best, Mrs. Poole," said Lestrade, looking at her approvingly. Apparently, the one member of the 11 Park Street household who met his standards of proper behavior was the housekeeper. "It's not your fault if they go running around London at all hours. And that one"—he glared at Diana—"I don't know who or what could contain her."

Diana stuck her tongue out at him. Oh, Mary would have liked to slap her!

"Ah well, she was brought up badly," said Mrs. Poole. "She was under the care of Mrs. Raymond—you know whom I mean, of the Magdalen Society. A terrible woman."

"Who may also have been Mrs. Herbert, of the Paul Street Murders," said Mary. "Do you know anything about her?"

Lestrade looked at her disapprovingly. "Don't you go getting mixed up in any more murders, Miss Jekyll. If Mrs. Raymond is Mrs. Herbert, then she's a dangerous woman. The men who died in Paul Street—we never could connect the murders to her. There was no apparent motive, you see, and no murder weapon. They seemed to have died of sheer fright. But I believed then, and I believe now, that she was responsible. Poor Charles Herbert was completely taken in by her. Spent his fortune on a house in London for her, with fine furniture, a fancy carriage, fabulous jewels— everything a woman could want. I thought we might get her for his murder at least—juries don't like women who kill their husbands. But she looked so young and innocent on the witness stand, as though butter wouldn't melt in her mouth. She was a beautiful woman, with masses of wavy black hair—it reminded me of Medusa's snakes! She was acquitted of all charges, but she was as guilty as sin, I can tell you that."

"And after the trial, she disappeared?" said Mary.

Mrs. Poole poured a glass of port for Lestrade, who did not refuse it, then another for Mary, who took a small sip. She did not usually enjoy alcohol, but today the warmth of it was welcome.

"What about me?" asked Diana petulantly. She sat up on the sofa. Well, at least she was no longer sprawled all over the place!

"Roly-poly pudding on the kitchen table," said Mrs. Poole.

"Right-ho." Diana sprang up, and in the moment she was out the door. Once again, Mary mentally thanked the Lord and his angels for Mrs. Poole. What in the world would they do without her?

MRS. POOLE: You would get by, miss. You are all resourceful young women.

BEATRICE: We might get by, but it would not be the same. We could not possibly do without you, Mrs. Poole.

JUSTINE: Indeed, we could not. It would not be at all the same.

CATHERINE: I hate to join the chorus, but we would be a complete mess. Don't even start, Diana. You know perfectly well we would be.

DIANA: I wasn't going to say anything. Why do you always assume I'm going to say something nasty?

MARY: Because you always do?

"Yes, Mrs. Herbert disappeared after the trial," said Lestrade. "Several years later, there was a set of murders in high society. I was called in when Lord Argentine was found dead in his bedchamber.

Each of the men—peers of the realm, barristers, surgeons, even an orchestra conductor—was found dead in his home. There seemed to be no connection between the murders, except that each man had an expression on his face of sheer terror, which was what made me suspicious. I discovered that before returning home on the evening of their deaths, each had been at the house of a Mrs. Beaumont, who hosted literary and artistic salons. I went to Mrs. Beaumont's house in Mayfair. That house—well, she was getting money from somewhere, living like a duchess. But it was empty—Mrs. Beaumont was gone. She must have been frightened off by the investigation into Argentine's death. In her parlor, I saw a portrait over the mantelpiece. It was by Mr. Sargent, the society painter. She was slightly older, but I could see that it was a portrait of Mrs. Herbert. I never heard of her again—until now."

"This information was not in Mr. Holmes's files," said Mary.

"Well, sometimes the police know things that interfering private detectives don't," he replied, in acidic tones. "The public blames us for any murders left unsolved, and gives them credit for the few they manage to solve—through lucky guesses, like as not! But you say Mrs. Herbert is also Mrs. Raymond?"

"Yes," said Mary, taking another sip of the port. She would *not* remind him of all the times Mr. Holmes had helped him and taken no credit for it! She would simply continue to bite her tongue. It was going to feel awfully sore after this conversation, in a metaphorical sense. "Mrs. Raymond was associated with Professor Moriarty and Colonel Moran."

"Moriarty!" said Lestrade. "He's a gent I've wanted to get my hands on for a while now. We thought he was dead, but a month ago Mr. Holmes tipped us off that he was back, though keeping a low profile. He's responsible for half the crime in London—in low places and high, but we've never been able to prove it. He's too clever by half, and Moran does the dirty work for him. I thought

we'd be able to catch him tonight at the museum—we got word
from an informant that he would be trying to steal artifacts from
one of the Egyptian exhibitions, and he must have succeeded,
since a mummy seems to be missing. We were disappointed to
find only yourselves and a bunch of boys on the scene! Indeed, you
must have frightened him off and lost us our quarry. If you have
any information as to his whereabouts, Miss Jekyll—"

What was she going to say, that Moriarty and his lieutenant
were small piles of white ash on the floor of the British Museum?
Lestrade would never believe her.

"If I hear anything of Professor Moriarty, I will certainly
inform you." Mary could say that with a clear conscience—she
knew perfectly well that she would not be hearing anything of
Moriarty again. This time, he truly was dead.

Lestrade nodded approvingly. "That's right, Miss Jekyll.
Scotland Yard is the proper authority to handle a matter of that
sort—not some interfering private detective!"

Once again Mary had to bite her tongue in the metaphorical
sense. But there was another piece of information she wanted
from him. "Inspector, there is a death I'm curious about, that of
Professor Trelawny, the Egyptologist. Do you know if anyone
investigated—"

"Outside of my jurisdiction," said Lestrade. "The Professor
died in his house in Cornwall, where he kept his collection. That's
the one in the museum, isn't it—the Trelawny Exhibit? It must
be Trelawny's mummy that's gone missing. I told you to stay out
of this case, Miss Jekyll. At any rate, his death was an accident.
He was using some electrical apparatus and it malfunctioned, or
so I gathered from *The Times*. You should not concern yourself
with deaths, whether deliberate or accidental. It's morbid, and
no young lady should be morbid. Embroidery, I tell you! Now, I
must be on my way." He drank the last of his port. "Thank you,

Mrs. Poole. I'm glad to see a nice, respectable woman such as yourself in charge around here. You'll keep these girls in order, I'm sure. Good God, what is that?"

It was Archibald, dressed in his footman's uniform. It had once belonged to Mary's footman Joseph, who had married Enid, the housemaid. Now, they kept a public house together in Basingstoke. Mrs. Poole had cut the uniform down considerably for the Orangutan Man. He was carrying Lestrade's overcoat and hat.

"Just a poor boy we took in from the streets. We're training him to be a footman," said Mrs. Poole. "He's very teachable, although not very bright and a bit odd-looking, poor lad. Do come again, Inspector. It's such a pleasure to meet a member of the Metropolitan Police. I'm sure we should all be grateful that you and your men are out on the streets of London, enforcing the law."

"We are here to serve, dear lady," said Lestrade, putting on his overcoat and looking at Archibald dubiously. "And do try to keep these girls from getting into any more mischief. I won't always be there to save them, you know. It was irresponsible of Holmes to get you involved in the first place, and now he seems to have disappeared—along with the mummy that was supposed to go on display tomorrow. I don't understand this fascination with mummies myself—they're just dried-up corpses. But people seem to be going barmy over anything Egyptian nowadays! I even caught Mrs. Lestrade reading a book called *The Mummy's Curse*. Sheer nonsense, I told her. 'Stolen mummy! Stolen mummy!' all the newsboys will be crying tomorrow morning. And of course we will be expected to do something about it. If, as you say, Mr. Holmes is pursuing the thieves, his first duty is to communicate all he knows to the Metropolitan Police. If you hear from him, Miss Jekyll, you tell him so."

"Of course, Inspector," said Mary, doing her best to look humble and obedient. There was no point in antagonizing Lestrade further. He was angry enough at them as it was.

After Mrs. Poole had let him out and returned to the parlor to gather up the tray, Mary said, "*Girls!* I'm twenty-one. I am not a girl."

"Of course you're not, my dear," said Mrs. Poole. "But sometimes it's best to let gentlemen talk. If you had argued with him, he would not have given you so much information about Mrs. Raymond. Honey catches more flies than vinegar, you know."

MARY: That reminds me of poor Mr. Renfield. How is he? Does anyone know?

CATHERINE: He's doing better under the new director of the Purfleet Asylum. They asked Dr. Hennessey, the old associate director, to come back from Ireland, and he has all sorts of ideas about how to treat the mentally ill, as he calls them. He's letting Renfield catch his flies, which makes him very happy, and Joe Abernathy has been promoted to head day attendant. Also, Florence can speak again—Joe says it was a new treatment from Vienna that helped her. I suspect Dr. Hennessey is implementing the ideas of Dr. Freud. She's going to be discharged next month. But Lady Hollingston is as mad as ever!

Justine was lying in bed, her head almost touching the headboard. Once, this had been Dr. Jekyll's room—his bed was the only one long enough for her. Mary sat down beside her and took her hand. It was cold, but then Justine's hand always was.

Well, at least she was breathing! She looked asleep, but it was a deep sleep—they had tried putting a bottle of *sal volatile* under her nose, bathing her face with *eau de cologne*, even shaking her. Justine had not woken up.

"You have to eat something, miss," said Mrs. Poole, putting a tray on the bedside table. "I have some cutlets here, potatoes, and carrots—everything's cold I'm afraid, since I didn't know when you would be coming back. Where in the world have you girls been since Friday afternoon? Why did Inspector Lestrade think you were investigating a robbery in the British Museum? And why are there coal smudges all over your clothes?"

As clearly and rapidly as she could, Mary explained the events of the past two days while picking at her carrots. She felt too sick to eat, even though a hollow feeling in her stomach told her that she must. Where were Alice and Mr. Holmes? How in the world was she going to find them now?

"Well, I don't believe for a moment that Alice was helping that woman," said Mrs. Poole after Mary had described what had happened in Soho. "I trained Alice myself—she would never do such a thing."

"Then why was she holding Mrs. Raymond's hand, and why was she all dressed up like that?" Diana came into the room and plopped herself on the bed. "Mary, can I have one of your cutlets?"

"No, you may not," said Mrs. Poole. "I'll bring you a plate of your own. Don't you dare take Miss Mary's food. And can't you wipe your face? Come here and stand still for a moment—I'll do it. You have jam all over your cheeks, and a little in your hair, mixed with coal dust." She wiped Diana's face with Mary's napkin.

"What in the world are we going to do?" asked Mary. She was so tired! The glass of port had probably not helped, although it had certainly felt good going down. "I can't believe Queen Tera reduced those men to ash. I don't think even Ayesha could do that. I just don't know how we're going to find her now—or rescue Alice and Mr. Holmes!"

"They're going to some house, right?" said Diana. "Some house the one they called Margaret has all prepared. So we have to find that house, wherever it is in London. Mrs. Poole, if I take one of Mary's cutlets now, she can have one of mine when you bring it up." She took a cutlet from Mary's plate and dodged Mrs. Poole's ineffectual slap at her hand.

"Cornwall," said Mary. "Miss Trelawny said 'my house by the ocean' is all prepared." She hoped she remembered that correctly. "Professor Trelawny had a house in Cornwall where he died, and I bet it wasn't because of an electrical malfunction. That would be her house now." Although she was so tired, in her head a plan was already coming together.

Once again, they would be packing for a journey, but this time it would not be to Europe. They would go to Cornwall, they would find Alice and Mr. Holmes, and then they would rescue their friends from the clutches of Queen Tera. How, she did not know.

# VOLUME II

# The

# Mummy

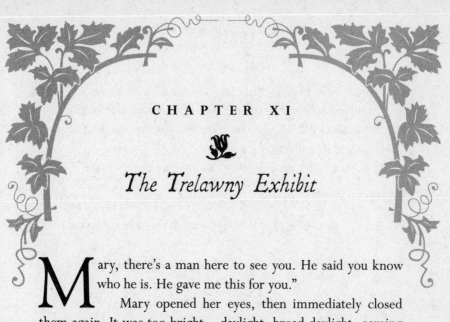

# CHAPTER XI

## The Trelawny Exhibit

"Mary, there's a man here to see you. He said you know who he is. He gave me this for you."

Mary opened her eyes, then immediately closed them again. It was too bright—daylight, broad daylight, coming through the open curtains of her bedroom. What time was it? She opened her eyes again, tentatively. At least it was not the strange white light with multicolored sparkles in it that she remembered from the night before! Mrs. Poole was sitting on the side of her bed, holding her waist bag. She could tell immediately, by the shape, that her revolver was in it.

"Isaac Mandelbaum?" she said, sitting up. Her revolver had been confiscated by Professor Moriarty. Isaac was the only person she could think of who might have known where it was or retrieved it for her.

"He didn't give a name," said Mrs. Poole. "A handsome young man with quite a lot of dark hair. He had a foreign accent."

Yes, that described Isaac exactly. Mary rubbed her eyes. "How is Justine? I need to go check on her."

"Still the same, I'm afraid. She has not woken up yet. Archibald is sitting with her, and has strict instructions to let me know as soon as she so much as turns her head. Diana is asleep, of course. That child never gets up until I've summoned her at least twice. But you should probably see this young man first. He said he could only stay for a little while."

"Right," said Mary, sitting up. "I'll see him in the parlor."

"He wouldn't come farther than the kitchen. He knocked at the back door, like a tradesman, and said he would wait for you down there, if that was all right. Is it?"

"I guess so. Is it proper for me to see him in my wrap?"

DIANA: Why the hell wouldn't you be able to see him in your wrap? It covers you all the way to the neck.

MARY: Is it *any* use asking you to stop swearing?

JUSTINE: For once, I must agree with Diana. There is modesty, and there is propriety. The former is a natural instinct, given to us when Adam and Eve left the garden and realized their nakedness. The latter is merely a social construct. Although as human beings we wish to consort with our fellows, and therefore yield to their judgments in matters of dress and behavior, surely we may break the rules of propriety when they interfere with the important matters of our lives, so long as modesty is not thereby wounded.

DIANA: It sounds like you're going to write a book! Who cares if modesty is wounded? How do you wound modesty anyway? It's just a word. Mary needed information. Why shouldn't she meet a man in her nightgown if she wants to?

MARY: I would never do such a thing! Meet with a man in my nightgown? Mrs. Poole would be shocked.

DIANA: More than when Lucinda drinks blood? Or
   when Kate Bright-Eyes and Doris come over for
   tea? Is that proper?

MRS. POOLE: Kate and Doris are good women, and
   don't you forget it! It's not their fault they've fallen
   off the path of virtue. And Lucinda can't help what
   she eats.

LUCINDA: I do not wish to give trouble, Mrs. Poole. If
   my diet discomfits anyone—

MRS. POOLE: It's no trouble at all, not any more
   than making Beatrice's teas. Most of the time
   you provide for yourself anyway, and if we have a
   dinner party or some such, I just go to Mr. Byles. I
   tell him one of the young ladies is anemic, and he
   gives me nice fresh blood. So don't you fret—and
   don't listen to Diana!

At the kitchen table sat Isaac Mandelbaum.

"Ah, Miss Jekyll." He rose when she entered. "I have only a
little time—I must get my family out of the city. Mr. Hoskins does
not understand how Moriarty and other gentlemen disappeared
from the museum. He is leading a search through Bloomsbury,
but soon his attention will turn back to the house in Soho. My
mother and father, my sister—they are brave. They survived in
Poland, and when it became too dangerous to stay, they left their
lives behind to make the arduous journey here to England, where I
hoped and prayed they would be safe. But there are hazards here as
well, almost as great as those in my own country. I will take them
to the countryside, where I hope they can stay until Moriarty's

confederates have been rounded up and they can once again return to London."

"I don't understand," said Mary. "How did you come to be working for Moriarty in the first place?"

He looked at her earnestly. She could not help noticing that he had beautiful eyes, with long, dark lashes. "You do not know—the English do not know—the history of pogroms in my country. Many of us have attempted to flee to the West. There are men, some of them good, some unscrupulous, who help families like mine—they provide transportation, food, shelter along the way. They charge a great deal. Those who have money, pay. Those like my family who have no money go into debt. Colonel Moran was one of those men. He suggested that to repay our debt, we work for Moriarty. We were happy to do so—until we realized what sort of criminal enterprise he was running."

"Wait," said Mary. "Moriarty was making money off transporting refugees to England?"

"Among other activities—gambling, prostitution, narcotics, all preying upon the weak to enrich himself. I could see what an evil man he was, the men and women whose lives he ruined. Many of my compatriots had to work off their debt indentured to sweatshops or butchering yards. He was, among other things, a hypocrite—a nationalist and racial supremacist making money off people he regarded as vermin. I will be glad to get my family out of his clutches."

"Do you need any help?" asked Mary. "I don't have much money, but if you need—"

Just then, the teakettle began to whistle. Isaac started, turned around, saw that it was only the kettle, and breathed with visible relief. "Thank you, but I have enough, and can get more if necessary. My employer has been quite generous."

"Your employer—your real employer. Do you mean Mycroft Holmes?"

Mrs. Poole put two teacups on the table, then the sugar bowl and a small plate of lemon slices.

Isaac smiled. He had a very attractive smile, kind but also mischievous. Mary scolded herself—how could she be thinking about such things when Mr. Holmes had once again been kidnapped, and was probably imprisoned somewhere—she knew not where? "Then you know that peculiar gentleman as well. When he—I think the word is *recruited*—when he recruited me, he told me that above all we must work in secret. That we must protect this country, but that no one must know who we were or what we did. Perhaps I have told you too much already. Despite the danger—not to me, which I disregard, but to my family—I was willing to help him. I asked my parents, should I do this thing? My father is a school teacher, Miss Jekyll. He has never done an immoral thing in his life. He told me that I must fight evil wherever I see it. My mother and sister agreed with him. So I told Mr. Holmes that I would join his network of—should I call them spies? Or, rather, informants. I was not to expose myself, or become involved in any way, only to watch and report. But last night, I knew I had to do something, so I sent a message to Scotland Yard that a robbery was taking place at the British Museum and that Moriarty was involved. I hoped the presence of the police would at least frighten Moriarty and his men from doing whatever they planned. And if he was arrested, we finally had the evidence to convict him, assembled over many months. As for what happened—"

"What *did* happen?" asked Mary. "They were going to summon the energic powers of the Earth, and instead—Queen Tera rose from the dead. How? Why?"

Mrs. Poole put the teapot between them. "It's good and hot," she said. "Would either of you care for milk?"

"Yes, please, Mrs. Poole," said Isaac. "You remind me a great deal of my mother. I believe you would like each other, although she speaks only a few words of English."

"She would still be more understandable than half the people who were born and bred here!" said Mrs. Poole acerbically. "Sometimes the costers and cabbies mumble so, and speak so fast, one can't hear a thing they're saying."

She put the milk jug on the table, then poured some milk into a bowl and put it by the door. In a moment, two cats, one gray, one orange, were lapping loudly and contentedly at the milk.

Isaac laughed. "They have a good appetite."

"The orange one is Alpha, the gray one is Omega," said Mary. "And yes, they're growing fast. They were scrawny little things when we found them abandoned in the park. But about Queen Tera—"

"I don't know any more about it than you do," said Isaac. "Moriarty's plan, what I overheard of it, was to abduct the Queen herself during her visit to Cornwall. How exactly, I do not know. But he was going to stay in a town named Marazion on the coast— Moran asked me to write for reservations at an inn there."

"Marazion!" said Mrs. Poole. "Her Majesty will be in Marazion on Thursday. She is scheduled to tour St. Michael's Mount."

Mary looked up at her, startled. "How do you know that, Mrs. Poole?"

"Why, it's right in the newspaper. Now, where did I put . . . I was going to use it for the fire." Mrs. Poole leaned down and rooted through a box of kindling by the large iron stove. "Ah yes, here it is. But it's got dirt all over it and I just washed the table! Ah well, I can certainly wash it again." She put a copy of that morning's *Daily Telegraph* on the table, by the teapot. "There, you see?" On the first page was an article titled "Her Majesty to Visit Cornwall," next to one about Bertha Benz, the lady motorist, and her spectacular attempt to drive from Budapest to London in the new Benz motorcar.

"It says she'll be touring the coast in the royal yacht," said Mary. "Stopping at St. Ives, Penzance, then a special tour of St. Michael's Mount, Falmouth, St. Austell . . . Mrs. Poole, I've never been to Cornwall. I have no idea where these places are. But it looks as though St. Michael's Mount is the only place she'll actually be disembarking. Otherwise, she'll stay on her yacht and greet distinguished visitors. Well, she's quite old after all. It sounded as though Mrs. Raymond and Margaret Trelawny were going to carry out Moriarty's plan to kidnap the Queen, for their own purposes. If they make that attempt, the obvious place would be during the tour of St. Michael's Mount."

"What a Godless, heathenish thing to do!" said Mrs. Poole. "I hope to goodness you're going to stop them, miss."

"Of course we are," said Mary. "I don't know how, not at the moment, but no Englishman or woman would hesitate in such a circumstance. Mr. Mandelbaum, should we attempt to join forces?"

"I don't believe that will be possible," he said, shaking his head regretfully. "Much as I would like to, Miss Jekyll, I do not think Mr. Holmes would permit it. He works only in secret, and while I work for him, I must as well. But I will let him know of your plans, and perhaps he will be able to help you in some way? Now, I must go—I must get my family to the train. It has been a pleasure meeting you."

"Mr. Mandelbaum, won't you take something with you? Biscuits, perhaps?" said Mrs. Poole.

"Thank you, but I would not take your breakfast—"

However, Mrs. Poole was already holding a bag out to him. "For your family, to eat on the train. Food purchased on a train is seldom satisfactory. One never knows about its quality, or how long it has sat in the heat. And these are not breakfast—I make a proper breakfast, I assure you!"

"You are one of the good angels who walks this Earth, Mrs.

Poole," said Isaac. "And, Miss Jekyll, I hope we will meet again in the not-too-distant future."

Mary held out her hand to shake his, but he leaned down and kissed hers. *"Do zobaczenia, piękna,"* he said.

Well, he was European, after all! Mary had gotten more or less used to this hand-kissing business in Europe. She was startled by it here in England, but he was only being polite. "I hope so too, Mr. Mandelbaum," she said.

And then he was gone, out the back door. Alpha slipped out at the same time.

Omega, who was more shy than his sister, looked up at her inquiringly. She picked up the cat and scratched him under the chin. He purred loudly and nuzzled against her shoulder.

"Mrs. Poole, could you——"

"Look up the trains to Marazion? I'll do that as soon as I've washed the table. Just look at this dirt, and these little splinters of wood! One of those will go in Archibald's finger if I don't wash up now. He's not as careful as Alice. I'll have breakfast for you girls in half an hour."

"Thank you. I'll check on Justine, and then I'll need to go to the headquarters of the Baker Street boys, wherever that is. I need to figure out what happened to Dr. Watson. He was wounded in an attack on the house in Soho, but I don't know how badly. I assume he's in a hospital somewhere? And I have to thank Wiggins for his rescue attempt—well, both rescue attempts. You know, I don't think I appreciated those boys enough before. They may be foolhardy, but they're certainly brave. Then I think another trip to the British Museum is indicated. We need as much information as possible on Queen Tera and Margaret Trelawny. I hope the exhibit itself will tell me more about—well, who Queen Tera is, and how in the world they resurrected her. There's so much I don't understand!"

"I'm with you, miss," said Mrs. Poole. "Resurrecting ancient Egyptian mummies who want to become Queen of England? It's beyond me."

"Empress of the world, it sounds more like, from the way she was speaking," said Mary.

"Either way, it's the strangest adventure you girls have had yet. I can't quite wrap my head around it."

"Neither can I. Nevertheless, we have to do something—the Queen herself is in danger. Do you think we could be packed and ready to go to Cornwall tonight, or first thing early tomorrow morning? If we're right in our conjectures, this kidnapping attempt won't happen until Thursday, but I think we should get to Marazion as soon as possible. Perhaps we can stop Queen Tera before the attempt is made."

"Don't forget that Catherine and Beatrice will be arriving sometime this week. Catherine sent me a telegram—now, where have I put it?" Mrs. Poole sorted through a neat stack of what looked like receipts on the counter. "Yes, here it is. I received it on Friday, while you were being captured in Soho. Goodness, I sound like a penny dreadful, don't I?" She put a telegram on the table. Mary leaned over and read what was written on the thin, cream-colored paper:

LEAVING ON ORIENT EXPRESS BE HOME SOON
SAVE SOME ADVENTURES FOR US CAT

"You see, she doesn't say when she's departing or when she expects to arrive." Mrs. Poole shook her head. "That girl has no sense of time. . . ."

CATHERINE: I'm a puma, remember? Pumas don't
wear wristwatches or consult train timetables!

"It will be such a relief to have them home," said Mary. "All right, I'm going to get dressed. Then I'll go wake up Diana. Always let sleeping Dianas lie as long as possible, isn't that what Catherine says? But I'll have to get her up eventually. Down you go." She put Omega on the floor. "You're a good kitty, you know that?"

"Humph," said Mrs. Poole. "He's no better than he should be. All cats are scoundrels."

But before she left the kitchen, Mary saw her slip Omega a bit of ham.

> MRS. POOLE: I did no such thing. Those cats are here to catch mice. I would no more give them ham than the time of day.

> CATHERINE: Mrs. Poole, you do it all the time. Give them ham, I mean. I don't know what cats would do with the time of day.

> MARY: Schedule their naps? They seem to sleep half the time.

"Dr. Watson is in the infirmary," said Wiggins. "He was shot in the leg. He's fine—he'll live, if he just stays put instead of trying to get up and go home, as he's been threatening!"

The infirmary? What sort of infirmary could there be in this run-down, rather dusty old house? Mary looked around, confused. Surely Dr. Watson should be in a hospital, particularly if he had a gunshot wound. Mary did not take such an injury as lightly as Wiggins seemed to.

"This way," said Diana. "I'll show you. And you don't need to come with us," she said to Wiggins, rudely. "I know where I'm going."

"I'm coming to make sure you don't annoy him," said Wiggins. "The way you annoy everyone else!"

Mary stared at him in astonishment and admiration. She had not thought there was anyone in London as rude as Diana, but here he was, her equal in lack of manners! She thought that she was going to like Mr. Wiggins.

She followed him and Diana up another flight of stairs. There, at the top of the house, Wiggins opened the door to a long, sunlit room with six narrow iron beds in it, all with white sheets and pillows. Unlike the rest of the house, this room was immaculately clean. Three of the beds were occupied: in one was Charlie, in another was a Baker Street boy she did not recognize, and in the farthest from her, she saw Dr. Watson talking to a man with a stethoscope around his neck.

"Charlie!" said Diana. "What happened? And that looks like Buster. Why isn't he moving? What did they do to you?"

"Nothing," said Charlie disgustedly. "When we got close to the house, all these men came out with pistols—it looked like maybe twenty of them! We started running, and then someone shouted that they weren't real, just an illusion. The bullets flew right through you. So we turned around again, but then Buster went down—he was close to the front, and he's the biggest target. So we knew that at least some of the bullets were real. Anyway, we started running away again, but I twisted my ankle on a stone and fell. And now Dr. Radko says I have a sprained ankle. Bloody ridiculous!"

"And you, Dr. Watson?" said Mary. "I heard you were hit by one of those real bullets."

"Grazed, Miss Jekyll. It's just a flesh wound," said Watson. "Dr. Radko has been taking excellent care of me. We've been discussing the difference between English and Romanian medicine. Dr. Radko received his training in Bucharest, but he works here in London at St. Bartholomew's Hospital.

"And sometimes I take care of these boys," said Dr. Radko, smiling. He was a small man, balding, with a halo of dark hair and a goatee. "They get into all sorts of scrapes, don't they, Mr. Wiggins? I patch them up and try to make sure they get their cod liver oil. Nutritional deficiency is a problem in this great city, for all its wealth—particularly for children who do not get enough fresh air or sunlight. Forgive me if I do not shake your hands. We doctors have to be careful not to spread germs, you know—as Louis Pasteur taught us."

He picked up a black bag from a chair by Watson's bedside. "Now, if you will excuse me, I have to return to St. Bart's. Buster is asleep—I gave him laudanum for the pain. Mr. Wiggins, I have written out when he is to receive his next dose. Please do not give him any more, no matter how pitifully he asks. I do not wish him to become a lifelong addict to the narcotic. Charlie, you will be in bed for at least a week."

"Bloody hell!" said Charlie. "A week? I'll die of boredom in a week."

"I prescribe some instructive literature," said Dr. Radko. "I recently saw an advertisement for a book you might like—*The Mysteries of Astarte*. I'll see if I can find you a copy. And, Dr. Watson, although you described it as a flesh wound, that bullet went through muscle. You must not risk infection. You too are hereby confined to the sickroom for a week. I know you will not take too much laudanum—the problem in your case will be taking less than you need, because you think you can bear the pain. But this is no time to be a hero. You must rest and heal."

"Are the patients allowed—" Mary looked into the bag Mrs. Poole had given her. "Various kinds of biscuits, scones, tarts—I don't know what else is in here, it's packed too tightly."

"Absolutely, an unlimited dose!" said the doctor, smiling. "Now, if Dennys will get my hat and coat . . ."

When he had gone, Mary sat by Watson's bedside, recounting their adventures of the day before. She tried to ignore the peals of laughter from Charlie's bed, where he and Diana were telling jokes of some sort—she supposed they must be funny, to evoke so much merriment. She did not particularly think this was a time to joke, herself.

"I wish I could go with you to Cornwall," said Watson. "But alas, this leg—"

"You must not think of that," said Mary. "Here, I found a jam tart. Or would you rather have a cheese biscuit?"

Watson smiled. "I do not mind being condescended to, Miss Jekyll, when the nurse is so charming. However—"

"Yes, yes, I know, you would like to come with us. But you can't, Dr. Watson. Here, cheese first, then jam. Savory then sweet."

"And as for Miss Frankenstein, if her condition has not improved by this afternoon—"

"I shall call a doctor, I assure you. I might call Dr. Radko! He looks as though he would be understanding and sympathetic. I would, of course, have to explain to him Justine's peculiar condition—after all, he would be treating a woman who is almost a century old. Now, we have to go. We have business at the British Museum."

"And you'll keep me apprised of what's going on?" asked Watson anxiously. "I shall worry about you all."

"I promise." Mary gathered her purse. She would leave the bag of biscuits to be shared between Watson and Charlie—and Buster when he woke up. "Also"—she put her hand on his, giving it what she hoped was a reassuring squeeze—"we will rescue Mr. Holmes. I promise."

DIANA: Why wouldn't you let me have any of the biscuits?

MARY: Because they were for the invalids, not for
you! Have you no sense of sympathy for those who
are worse off than yourself?

DIANA: Not really. Anyway, Mrs. Poole could have
made more of them. It's not as though they were
the last biscuits on Earth.

The Trelawny Exhibit was closed. Mary could have kicked herself—of course it would be closed! Its central attraction had been stolen the night before. Outside the museum, the newsboys had been hawking the latest edition of the *Herald*, shouting, "Spectacular mummy robbery! Mummy stolen from British Museum! Read all about it!"

Mary had been hoping to take another look at the exhibit room. Would it look the way it had last night? Were there still small piles of ash beside the seven pillars, with their seven lamps— the remains of Moriarty, Godalming, Seward, Raymond, Morris, Harker, and Moran? Or had that strange energic wind blown them all away? But the doors to the exhibit room were shut, and there was a rope in front of it with a sign: CLOSED UNTIL FURTHER NOTICE.

"Well, that's it, I guess," she said. "I was hoping we would find more information somewhere in the room itself. But we can't get in."

"Can't, or won't?" said Diana. "I can pick that lock, easy peasy. And then we can just sneak in."

"Don't be ridiculous," said Mary. "There are guards walking around—there's one, and there's another one. We would get caught, and what good would we be to Alice and Mr. Holmes in prison?"

"I could get us out of prison, easy peasy."

Mary just shook her head.

"You never want to do anything fun," said Diana petulantly. "You are the most boring sister on the face of the Earth. If we can't do anything here, can we get something to eat? I'm hungry."

"There has to be somewhere else we can find information on the exhibit," said Mary. "Wait—the Reading Room! There must be a—I don't know, a pamphlet or something? Come on!"

She grabbed Diana's hand and walked out through the great front doors of the museum, then made her way across the courtyard to the circular Reading Room at its center. By the time she reached it, she could not stand Diana's complaints any longer. "Here," she said, giving her two shillings. "Go buy yourself something, and be back here in an hour. Do you have a watch on?"

"No," said Diana. "Ta, sister!" Then she skipped across the courtyard—heading where, Mary had no idea. Well, if anyone could take care of themselves in London, Diana could! Mary refused to worry about her. Anyway, not having her around would make Mary's task easier. She turned and entered the Reading Room.

At the circular central desk, one of the clerks, a supercilious young man with spectacles perched on his nose, said, "Do you have a ticket? You need a ticket, you know." He had sparse blond hair slicked back with too much macassar oil.

"Yes, in my purse," said Mary. "I'm so sorry, I should have had it ready for you." *Dear God, please forgive me for the lies I'm about to tell,* she thought. *I promise they're for a good purpose.* She rummaged around in her purse, then looked at the clerk, aghast. "Oh my goodness, I can't find it anywhere. I must have left it back at 221B Baker Street. You see, I work for Mr. Sherlock Holmes. I'm a sort of secretary—I do his filing and type up his cases. He specifically asked me to research the Trelawny Exhibit for him, and said he needed the information today. I believe he's interested in"—she leaned forward and lowered her voice, as though confiding in the clerk, whose eyes had been widening behind his spectacles ever since she had mentioned 221B—"the mysterious death of Professor Trelawny! I wrote ahead for an appointment and received my ticket by post. But I must have left it on the mantelpiece, right below the bullet holes Mr. Holmes makes during target practice. Oh, what ever will I do? Mr. Holmes will be *so angry*." She took a handkerchief out of her purse and dabbed her eyes.

"Do you really work for Mr. Holmes?" asked the clerk, with barely concealed excitement. All his superciliousness was gone. "What is he like? Does he really deduce things like it says in Dr. Watson's stories?"

"Oh yes!" said Mary. "He is exactly like that. And he looks at you with such steely gray eyes—it's as though he sees through to your soul. No one can fool Mr. Holmes. Why, he would know everything about you at once, if he saw you for only half a moment!"

"Really!" said the clerk, looking at her with undisguised pleasure. He reminded her of a little boy in a candy shop. "Do you think you could get me his autograph?"

"Of course!" said Mary. "That is, if he doesn't fire me. And he just might, if I don't get this information for him."

"Tell me what you want," said the clerk. "I'll find it for you myself."

Fifteen minutes later, Mary was sitting at one of the semicircular tables, reading *The Tomb of Queen Tera: A Guide to the Trelawny Excavation and Exhibition*, published by the British Archaeological Association. Half an hour later, she had what she needed. When she returned the pamphlet to the clerk, she said, "Thank you ever so much. If you could write down your name and address for me, I'll make sure to send you Mr. Holmes's autograph." Of course, she would have to rescue him from Mrs. Raymond and Queen Tera first! She very much hoped he was not already a pile of ash, blowing through the London streets.

Diana was waiting outside for her, eating a toffee apple on a stick. "See? I didn't need a watch. I had a cream tea at the Aerated Bread Company. Well, two cream teas, but I was especially hungry, on account of you not letting me have any biscuits earlier. And then I got this. Want a bite?" She held out the apple.

Mary stepped back to make sure she didn't get toffee on her dress. "Absolutely not. I don't know how you can eat such things without becoming sick!"

"All the more for me! Did you find out anything?" Diana took another bite of the apple. She had toffee all around her mouth.

"The Trelawny Exhibit only includes about a third of the artifacts from Queen Tera's tomb," said Mary.

"So?" Diana kicked at a pigeon that had walked up to her and was looking at her apple expectantly. "I don't have anything for you. This is mine. Go away!"

"So the rest of the artifacts are still at Professor Trelawny's house in Cornwall—Kyllion Keep, it's called. And it's near Marazion, just a short walk along the cliffs. That must be where Margaret Trelawny is taking Queen Tera. Don't you see, it all fits together now, like the pieces of a puzzle. They'll stay in Kyllion, preparing for Her Majesty's arrival, and sometime during her tour of St. Michael's Mount, they'll carry out their plan."

"Which is what?" asked Diana. She kicked at the pigeon again. "Shoo! I said shoo! Oh, all right, but only a little." She bit off a piece of the toffee apple and spit it at the pigeon, which fluttered up for a moment, then settled down next to it and began pecking at the toffee.

"I don't know exactly. But whatever they're going to do, we've got to stop them. Come on, we've done as much as we can. I need to check on Justine. If she still hasn't regained consciousness, I'm going to send for Dr. Radko."

But when they got back to 11 Park Terrace, there was no need to send for the doctor after all.

"Justine is awake!" said Mrs. Poole as soon as they entered the Athena Club. "And look who's home!"

Catherine poked her head out of the parlor. "Us, that's who. Or whom, I can never remember which. We arrived at Charing Cross an hour ago and took a cab home. Just in time to join the fun, it seems. So we're going to Cornwall? Before we leave, we have to telegraph Ayesha."

"Why in the world?" said Mary, taking off her hat. "Welcome home, and it's lovely to see you too! How is Justine? Is she doing all right?"

"What? Oh, politeness. Yes, it's very nice to see the both of you and all that. Because Queen Tera was the High Priestess of the temple of Isis where Ayesha was trained to use energic powers—if anyone knows how to defeat her, Ayesha will. We do need to defeat her, right? Mrs. Poole's account was a little garbled, but I understand that she reduced Dr. Seward and six other men to a sort of white powder. I wish I could have seen that! Come upstairs—Justine is awake. Beatrice pushed on her chest and then gave her something—some of her goop. I'll have to stop teasing her about it—after all, it did bring Justine back to consciousness."

BEATRICE: You tease me about that *goop* all the time.

CATHERINE: I'll stop. I mean, when I remember . . .

Justine was sitting up in bed, drinking some sort of green concoction, and Beatrice was sitting by her side, saying, "Just a little more. It will do you good, you'll see."

As they all scattered themselves around Justine's bedroom, Catherine and Diana on the bed, Mary in a desk chair she had pulled up, she thought of how nice it was to have all of them at 11

Park Terrace again. The Athena Club was once more together—except for its most recent member, of course. She hoped Lucinda Van Helsing was regaining her health and sanity in Styria. Thank goodness Lucinda was out of this particular fray!

But of course another member of their household was missing. When Mrs. Poole came up with a plate of sandwiches—cucumber and cress, egg salad, and potted ham—Mary thought of Alice, who would ordinarily have performed such a task.

"We have to get Alice back," said Catherine, as though she had divined Mary's thoughts. "Bea, I think we should telegraph Ayesha. You remember her story about Queen Tera, don't you?"

"Yes, we should certainly contact her," said Beatrice. "This Queen Tera sounds very powerful. What will my poison, or Justine's strength, or Catherine's teeth do against a woman who can wield lightning as her weapon? Justine, may I show them?"

Justine nodded and unbuttoned her shirt—Mrs. Poole had not tried to change her out of her male attire. It would have been difficult to put the unconscious Giantess in a nightgown! Beatrice pulled back the side with the buttonholes. There, on Justine's chest, was a red mark that resembled the burn marks Mary had seen on vampires killed by Ayesha.

"You see?" said Beatrice. "If Justine had been as other women are, I believe such a blow would have stopped her heart. Ayesha understands these powers. She will be able to tell us what to do. Perhaps we can build some sort of weapon that will replicate what Queen Tera is capable of doing—or at least some sort of defensive mechanism, a shield of some sort. If Ayesha can send us instructions on how to fight her . . ."

"Mrs. Poole, do you have a telegram form?" asked Catherine. "We'll have to send it to—the Hungarian Academy of Sciences? Where does Ayesha actually live? Do any of us know her address? Beatrice, do you?"

"Alas, I do not," said Beatrice. "But remember, Jimmy Bucket sent her a telegram once before. He will know how to contact her."

"That traitor?" said Diana, through a mouthful of potted ham. "If I ever see him again, I'll kick him so hard——"

"No, you won't," said Mary, "because we need his help. But does anyone know where to find him? Remember, he was court-martialed by the Baker Street Irregulars. I haven't seen him around since we returned."

"His mother lives in Camden Town," said Mrs. Poole. "She takes in washing and mending, including some of ours. I believe she has a basement flat on Hawley Street. Two rooms, for herself and three children, one of them sick with consumption. I don't know how she does it, truly I don't."

"I'll go," said Diana. "I know where that is."

"I'll go with you," said Catherine. "To prevent you from kicking the one person who knows where to send this telegram, among other things! 'Queen Tera risen from dead how do we defeat her please advise' should do it, I think. And after we send this telegram—then what?"

"First of all, I'm going to be the one who fills out that telegram form," said Mary. "For goodness' sake, could you be any more cryptic? And, Mrs. Poole, do you have two forms? Before we leave, I have to tell Mina what happened to Mr. Harker. She needs to know that her husband is dead. Second of all—well, second we go to Cornwall. Did you find out about the trains, Mrs. Poole?"

"There's a train direct to Marazion, but you won't catch it today if you still have to send a telegram and then pack your things," said Mrs. Poole. "You'll have to leave tomorrow morning from Paddington Station."

"Then let's start packing," said Mary. "There should be an inn or hotel of some sort in Marazion. After all, it's by the seaside. I'm sure it gets bathers on holiday, although probably not at this time of year. And I think Isaac Mandelbaum mentioned something of the sort. . . . Mrs. Poole, I'll send you the address where we are staying as soon as we get there. Whatever Ayesha replies, assuming she replies, send it straight on to us. I don't know if the high and mighty President of the Alchemical Society will have time to help the Athena Club—she was not particularly helpful the last time I spoke with her. In the meantime, we must do the best we can to save Alice, Mr. Holmes, and the Queen. Catherine, you'll come of course, and Beatrice?"

"And me," said Diana. "You are *not* leaving me behind. Not that it ever works, anyway."

"And me," said Justine. It was the first time she had spoken since Mary had entered the room. She sounded tired, but determined. "Do not tell me that I'm not well enough. I too shall fight Queen Tera, who has given me this scar." She put her hand on her chest. "Her plan, as I understand it, is not only to become Queen of England, but to re-create a Roman Empire in the modern world. We cannot allow that. It would be worse even than the British Empire. Forgive me, Mary, but I am Swiss—I do not believe in empires. They are always systems of tyranny over subject peoples. Tera would spread this tyranny over the Earth. She must be stopped."

Mary shook her head, but did not reply. She could not agree with Justine about the British Empire. Surely it had brought medicines, and education, and the benefits of religion to the colonies? Yes, there had been cruelties and oppression, but surely the Empire did some good as well? However, Justine was right—they must stop the Egyptian Queen. The question was—how?

# CHAPTER XII

## Morning in Marazion

There was a scratching at Alice's door. That would not be Mrs. Polgarth—housekeepers did not scratch at one's door. Although Mrs. Polgarth was not quite a housekeeper. For one thing, this was not quite a house. Alice had been startled to see it when they arrived, two days ago.

After the fire and fury at the British Museum, they had slipped out the back and returned to the house in Soho, with Mr. Holmes stumbling ahead of them. Helen had led Alice firmly by the hand, saying, "Come on, Lydia. Don't dawdle. We have a train to catch." Queen Tera had walked along behind them, beside Margaret, with Margaret's coat on. After all, one could not have a newly resurrected Egyptian Queen walking through Bloomsbury naked! Queen Tera was talking to Margaret in a strange language. "Is that Egyptian?" asked Alice.

Helen had answered, "It's Greek. Tera was a queen in Alexandria, the capital of Ptolemaic Egypt. She speaks Greek as well as Egyptian."

Alice had felt a sudden, ridiculous urge to say, *Well, it's all Greek to me!* But of course this was no joke. Seven men dead—if she closed her eyes, she could still see the flames curling around them, as though in an embrace. She could not forget the startled and then agonized looks on their faces, or the horror of flesh burning in an impossible fire. Then Justine had been wounded.

Could she have helped Justine in some way? She had tried to help Mr. Holmes, but to no avail. He was still too sick to help himself, or anyone else. And she had once again lost Mary. She had tried, as her mother pulled her out of the room, to look back and see whether Mary and Diana were all right, but the room had been filled with energic waves. She had never seen them like that, shimmering and sparking so they were visible to anyone, mesmerist or not. So this was Tera's power! She knew that she should be terrified, but she was just so tired. She had not slept all night.

As they had walked along the deserted streets, dawn was breaking over the tenements of London. When they arrived back at the house in Soho, Margaret had told her, "Lydia, dear, I need you to get packed. We are going to my house in Cornwall. I would ask Gitla to help you, but I can't find the Mandelbaums anywhere. I guess when the cat's away, the mice will play! I always thought of them as such reliable servants, but I suppose they saw our absence as an excuse to take a day off. At any rate, make sure you pack warmly. We will be by the ocean, and it can be cold at night." Alice had chosen three of the plainest dresses she could find in the wardrobe—no more of those silly fripperies for her!—as well as a warm shawl. Had Margaret noticed when she had tried to help Mr. Holmes? Had her mother noticed? Neither of them were treating her any differently. She was glad they still seemed to trust her. If she was to help Mr. Holmes and save the Queen, she must make them believe she was on their side.

An hour and a half later, they had been at Paddington Station, boarding a train to Penzance. Once they were seated in their first-class compartment, Queen Tera had looked at Mr. Holmes and said, "You are the detective, are you not?" When he nodded, looking particularly pale, she had continued, "You were sent by your Queen's government to stop Moriarty. But you will not stop us.

If you attempt to escape, I will electrocute you, as I did that man in the temple. Do you understand?" He had simply nodded again, then leaned his head back on the headboard, looking as though he were going to throw up. Alice wished she could have helped him in some way—at least wiped the sweat off his face. It was evident that he was very sick indeed.

From Penzance, they had taken a hired carriage to Kyllion Keep. The carriage had driven along a winding country road for a long time—too long for Alice, who had felt nauseous from the motion. The road had climbed steeply through a little town that Helen told her was Marazion. Then, they had drawn up to the ruins of a medieval fortress. Nothing of it now stood except a few stone walls, and one square tower that had formed its central fortification. That was the keep, about the size of a London house, built all of stone and looking almost impregnable. Around it was a moat with a little water at the bottom and a tangle of weeds growing out of it, chiefly stinging nettles, as Alice learned when she had accidentally brushed up against one.

Inside, the keep was equally forbidding. It lacked modern conveniences—there was no running water, only a well from which one could pump water in a small room off the kitchen, and the water closet was of the most primitive sort. The rooms that had been inhabited by Professor Trelawny himself were well furnished. His study, in particular, was fascinating, with Egyptian artifacts scattered on every surface. There were jars, both intact and in shards, as well as small statues, weapons of various sorts, a collection of papyrus scrolls . . . So many items that it would have taken Alice hours to look through them. But the other chambers were large, bare, and gloomy.

"Every penny my father could spare, he spent on his Egyptian excavations," Margaret had explained on that first afternoon. Her voice as she said it was expressionless, but Alice wondered if that

had made her angry. After all, those expeditions must have cost a
great deal of money. Perhaps Margaret would have preferred some
furniture for the other rooms, or paintings for the walls, or clothing
for herself? Now, of course, she could do whatever she liked with
his money and the keep itself. Evidently, she had chosen to spend
it on resurrecting Queen Tera and conquering the world, starting
with England.

This was the morning of the second day since they had arrived,
and someone—or something—was scratching at the door. "I'm
coming, Bast," said Alice. It must be Bast. Who else would be
scratching so persistently, and so close to the floor? She went to
the door and opened it. Yes, there was Queen Tera's cat, who
slipped right in and wove herself around Alice's ankle.

The first thing Queen Tera had done once they were settled
into the keep was go through the artifacts Professor Trelawny had
brought back from Egypt. Among them were a number of items
from her tomb, including the mummy cat Alice had seen in the
vision Helen had conjured up over breakfast in the headquarters of
the Order of the Golden Dawn, now defunct because its leaders
were piles of ash.

"Bast!" she had exclaimed when she saw it. "My Bastet. If
only . . . But perhaps your spirit hovers around you, as my spirit
hovered around me in my long sleep. Margaret, is any of the oil
left from the ceremony?"

"A little." Margaret had looked at Queen Tera dubiously. "But
I thought you might want to keep it for emergencies. You told me
it's difficult to make."

"Indeed." Queen Tera had placed the mummy cat on the stone
floor of the study. "It is pressed from the seeds of seven different
plants, only one of which grows in your country. Eventually, we
shall have more made, but what remains in that jar, we shall use
now. I have lost everything—Egypt, my temple, my priestesses.

But I can at least have my cat! To bring Bastet back to life, we need a sacrifice. What do you have that is expendable?"

"I'll find something," said Helen, turning and leaving the room. Alice had wondered where she was going.

Queen Tera had poured the last of the oil from a ceramic jar shaped like a cow's head into a brass bowl that Margaret had taken from one of the many glass-fronted cabinets. Then, kneeling by it, she had raised the energic waves—they sparkled and flashed, as they had at the British Museum the day before, around the corpse of the mummy cat.

By that time, Helen had returned, holding a young rabbit by the ears. It hung limp from her hand, as though stunned. Had she somehow mesmerized it? Alice could not help the prickle of tears that came to her eyes. Of course she had helped Mrs. Poole skin and butcher a hare before, for stews and pies. But this one was so young and vulnerable!

The white, heatless energic fire had consumed the mummy wrappings. Out of that flame had walked a beautiful black cat— the same cat she was currently scratching under the chin. Bastet meowed—clearly, she wanted something to eat. Cats were cats, even if they were two thousand years old! Bast was certainly older than Alpha and Omega, even if you did not count her millennia of sleep, but she reminded Alice of the Athena Club cats and Mrs. Poole's kitchen.

The second thing Queen Tera had done was look at Helen critically. "You have the power in you—you and your daughter. I felt it when you raised me from my sleep. How much of it can you use?"

"Only a little," said Helen, with more humility than Alice had seen her display thus far. "Illusions, mostly. And I can do this." She had put her hands close together, about an inch apart. Sparks had shot between her fingers, startling Alice. "But that is all. And even that, I have worked years to attain."

Tera had shaken her head. "I will teach you how to use your abilities so that you can draw upon the true energic powers of the Earth. Now you are using only the power of your own body, your own mind. That is why you can do so little. You must draw upon the great body, the great mind, of the Earth itself—of Geb who lies below us, and Nut who stretches above. There is power in the stones and soil, in the grass and trees, in the clouds above, even in the stars. Here, we can draw power from the ocean, with its restless waves. I have not seen such an ocean before—it fills me with longing for I know not what. First we will conquer this England of yours. That will not be difficult. And then we shall establish an empire such as the world has not known since Octavian. Margaret, what else did your father loot from my tomb? Show me the rest of the artifacts."

"How can she speak English so well?" Alice had whispered to her mother. "I thought you said she could speak Egyptian and Greek—but English didn't even exist, did it, when she was mummified?"

"Quiet, Lydia," Helen had replied in a low voice. "Tera might hear you and be insulted. Usually after death, individual consciousness returns to the energic power of the universe, which is like a great ocean. But not Tera's—somehow, and I have to confess that I don't understand all the details, her consciousness was bound to her tomb. The priestesses of Isis, at least those who were on her side, planned that if she died in the battle against Augustus, they would resurrect her later to fight the Roman occupation—that was why they left all the necessary implements and instructions for the ritual in her burial chamber. But they were never able to. She was betrayed by one of her own priestesses, who refused to fight when the Roman soldiers came. At least this is what Margaret told me. The Roman victory was too complete: The temple was requisitioned for barracks, the order was disbanded, and the priestesses were scattered to the corners of the known world. Tera's consciousness waited in her tomb for almost two thousand years. It sensed Margaret's presence even before she stumbled over the door in the sand. It summoned her—Margaret told me that it was like being called indoors by her nursemaid when she was a child after a day of playing on the rocks of Kyllion Cove. And when she put on the scarab necklace—well, it functions as a sort of conduit, like a telegraph wire. But a conduit of energic waves. Tera spoke to her through the necklace. She told her how to interpret the hieroglyphs correctly, how to enact the ritual—and what to leave out so that her father would not be able to enact it correctly. The conduit worked both ways. She has been inside Margaret's mind for months. It must be strange for Margaret now, not having that connection."

"But then . . ." Alice did not want to be quiet. She wanted to know what was going on. Anyway, Tera was not paying attention to them. She was sorting through the artifacts that had come from her tomb, looking for clothing, jewelry, small pots and jars of various sorts that seemed to contain cosmetics. "Was this your plan all along? Yours and Miss Trelawny's?" All that time her mother had obeyed Moriarty, was she planning his fiery death? And what about Margaret Trelawny's father and fiancé? "When Professor Trelawny died—"

"You don't think Margaret was going to allow her father to raise Tera from the dead, do you? That would not have done at all. She knew Moriarty through her father—once or twice, Moriarty had helped him smuggle valuable artifacts out of Egypt. Moriarty went to Professor Trelawny's funeral, and I accompanied him. That was where I met Margaret. Tera's consciousness in her sensed my mesmeric abilities. After the funeral, at a somber tea in the church refectory, she came up to me and whispered, "How would you like to rule the world?" That was the beginning of our collaboration.

Moriarty had already formed his Order of the Golden Dawn and begun infiltrating the government. And he was already familiar with mesmeric power from his friendship with my father. It was easy enough to lead him to the idea of the ritual. He was a fool—a useful fool for a while. We used him and his ridiculous order until he was no longer needed. That's all."

"But are we still kidnapping Queen Victoria?" Alice asked doubtfully.

"Of course. She's very old, much too old and frail to be queen. We want someone strong, someone who can build up the British Empire. Tera will rule for a while as Victoria, but once we have consolidated our power, Victoria will die in a convincing and innocuous way, and Tera will take her place as Queen and Empress. How she does that will depend on the specific circumstances. Will we need to assassinate the Crown Prince, or will he simply abdicate? That is still to be decided. As Moriarty discovered, Prince Edward has very little support in the government—I have no doubt the ministers and members of parliament would welcome a strong monarch. Moriarty had already started bringing them to his side, whether by persuasion, bribery, or blackmail—his efforts will be useful to us. What he began, we can continue by the judicious application of fear and mesmerism. Once Tera holds the reins of power, the world will see a ruler the likes of which it has never known. She will revitalize our empire in a way Moriarty would never have understood."

"And what will you do with Her Majesty?" Alice asked. She was afraid to hear the answer.

"Keep her here, in the dungeon," said Helen. "For a while, at least, until she is no longer needed. Of course we shall treat her well—no harm will come to her until absolutely necessary. We will, eventually, need a convincing corpse."

Alice had not known what to say. She has simply shuddered at the cold, precise way in which Helen had described this horrifying plan. She must try to stop it—but how?

"And you, Lydia." Tera had turned to look at Alice, who trembled just a little in her boots. The Egyptian queen was neither large nor imposing. In Soho, she had put on one of Margaret's dresses, which covered her from neck to toes in black crepe. Alice could not help thinking of her as a sort of ghost. The scarab necklace was still around her neck, over the bodice. Although there were wrinkles under her eyes and over her forehead, she certainly did not look two thousand years old. She moved with the ease and elasticity of a young woman. Nevertheless, Alice could not forget how she had blasted Justine with nothing but a pointed finger and the power of her mind.

"It is a beautiful name, Lydia. I always liked the Lydians. They were an ancient, gracious people, with beautiful art and an artistic approach to life. For you, I shall reestablish the temple of Isis here in this cold, remote island"—by which Alice assumed she meant England—"and gather young women from all over the world to study the ancient sciences we knew. You shall be the first among them. I see great power in you, as in your mother. Does this please you, Helen? Would you like this for your daughter, as for yourself?"

"Yes, Tera," her mother had replied. "It is what I have wanted all my life—to experience true power, rather than the shadow of it. I want Lydia to have that as well."

Queen Tera nodded. "Good. Now let us plan the conquest of this country. When it is in my power, as Egypt once was—although foolishly I gave that power to my husband and then my daughter, who destroyed my homeland—then we shall conquer the barbaric countries, this France and Germany of yours. After that, we shall bring the ancient civilizations around the Mediterranean and in Africa under our sway. And this new continent of America, it intrigues me. Eventually it too shall bow down to us."

"Won't a lot of people die, with all that conquering?" Alice had ventured to ask.

"People always die in war, child," Queen Tera had answered. "It is the way of the world. Now go and do whatever children do for amusement in this new era. We three must make our plans."

Bast meowed more urgently, bringing Alice out of her reverie. Yes, she would need to feed the cat, and not just the cat. But first, she must determine the whereabouts of Mrs. Polgarth—she did not want that woman to see what she was about to do.

What was Mrs. Polgarth, if not exactly a housekeeper? The keepkeeper? She came in every morning from Perranuthnoe on the milk and egg wagon to do the cleaning, and walked back to town after she was done for the day, so she was really more of a charwoman than a housekeeper—she did not have the dignity or authority of Mrs. Poole. Since they had arrived, she had been required to cook as well, which she grumbled about continually. Alice, with nothing else to do, had started helping her.

"You're a useful body," Mrs. Polgarth had said. "Unlike those fine ladies up there, working in the study all day. That Egyptian lady Miss Trelawny has visiting—she's so small, like a girl of fifteen although she's lost her hair so she can't be young. She's fifty if she's a day. But somehow, she frightens me. I think it's her eyes! They seem as old as time itself."

Alice walked out onto the landing while Bast wove around her ankles. She could hear Mrs. Polgarth in the hall below, singing something—probably a traditional Cornish ballad—while she swept the stairs.

> BEATRICE: Gilbert and Sullivan. Mrs. Polgarth has
> a passion for light opera and regularly goes to
> productions in Truro.

CATHERINE: How do you always know these trivial
things about people?

BEATRICE: They are not trivial, and because I ask.

"Come on," Alice said to the black cat. "You know where I'm going, don't you?" She picked up the blanket she had folded neatly that morning from the chair where she had placed it. That, a rather uncomfortable iron bed, and a washstand were the only furniture in her room.

Bast did indeed know, because the cat preceded her down the stone staircase to the ground floor. "Good morning, my dear," Mrs. Polgarth called out. "I'm doing sweeping and dusting. Do you need me to find you something to eat, or will you be all right by yourself?" She had a singsong accent, more pleasant to the ear than the harsh tones of London, although Alice sometimes found it hard to understand.

"No, thank you, Mrs. Polgarth," she said. "I know where everything is." It would be easier if the housekeeper was not there.

In the great stone kitchen, with its enormous fireplace and small iron stove, she found the bottle of milk and a small jug of cream that Mrs. Polgarth had brought that morning. She poured some of the cream into a bowl for Bast. Then she began to gather what she could—the end of a loaf of brown bread, some soft cheese, and an apple. When she was halfway through spreading the cheese on one slice, Mrs. Polgarth came in with the broom. Alice, startled to see her, almost dropped the knife.

"I'm almost done with the first floor, love. And the second floor won't take long. The hard part is the professor's study, and now that Miss Trelawny is in there all the time with your mum and that foreign lady, I can't do the room as it ought to be done anyway. I have time to make you a proper sandwich if you like.

Was breakfast not enough for you? I can make a bigger pot of porridge tomorrow, or perhaps you'd prefer something more substantial? I can fry up some eggs and pilchards. You're such a slip of a thing. Go on, take whatever you'd like, it will put some meat on your bones!"

"I thought I would make a picnic for myself," said Alice, with relief that Mrs. Polgarth had jumped to the wrong conclusion. "My mother and Miss Trelawny are so busy they don't have time for me. So I thought I would explore the castle. You know, the ruined part."

"That's a good idea—children should be outdoors until dusk, my gran always used to say. But bread and cheese is not enough of a meal for a growing girl. Here, take one of these buns—we make them special here in Cornwall. They're yellow from saffron, and stuffed with currants. You probably haven't seen anything like this, coming from the big city. I made a batch for tea later today— not that the ladies upstairs eat much. And Miss Tera, the Egyptian lady, eats least of all! Hardly anything touched on her plate . . . I'll put it all in a basket of some sort for you, shall I? Or here, take my marketing bag. That will be easier to carry. I do wish there was another child here for you to play with. It's a gloomy old place, ain't it?"

If Mrs. Polgarth had known the plot being hatched upstairs, how shocked she would have been! Could Alice ask Mrs. Polgarth to help her in some way? But how? If she told Mrs. Polgarth what was really going on, that Miss Trelawny and her houseguests were planning to kidnap the Queen and conquer England, the housekeeper would not believe her. Even if she did, what could Mrs. Polgarth do? Alice imagined her walking into the local police station and telling the constable on duty that the resurrected mummy of an ancient Egyptian queen was planning to kidnap Queen Victoria and take over the British Empire. It would never work. No, there was no one here who could help her. She would have to rely on herself.

She walked out the kitchen door, which led to what had probably once been a garden but was now overgrown with weeds. Turning right, she followed the stone wall of the keep. The ruins of the old castle were surrounded by the moat she had seen yesterday. Walking beside it, she could see the weeds growing in the mud at its bottom—nettles, small purple thistles, the white umbels of wild carrot. It was pretty but forbidding. At least if there had been a proper moat, Alice could have swum across it! But there was no way across that tangle of vegetation. She imagined there were probably snakes slithering around down there, and frogs hopping about on the damp bottom. She walked along the wall and turned a corner. On that side, hawthorns and blackberry bushes grew over the ruins and close to the wall of the keep. Yesterday, underneath a particularly prickly patch, she had discovered a small window. It was low down, close to the ground, and covered with bars.

She put the blanket around her shoulders so she would not get scratched. Yesterday, her neck and arms had gotten scratched quite badly when she had squeezed herself between the shrubbery and the wall. Now, she pushed herself carefully through the thorny branches until she could crouch by the window.

"Mr. Holmes!" she called. "Mr. Holmes, can you hear me?"

She heard a faint groan in response.

"Mr. Holmes, it's Alice! I've brought some more food for you."

The only light in the ancient dungeon came from that window. After they had arrived, Margaret had led Mr. Holmes away from her down a dark corridor, followed by Queen Tera. When she had asked her mother where they were taking him, Helen had said that was no concern of hers, that he would be someplace he could not get out of. Of course Alice had known that meant the dungeon. In the sorts of books she read, prisoners in ancient castles were always kept in dungeons. That was—well, simply how it was done. It was only in London that one had to resort to coal cellars.

By the time her mother had taken her to a small bedroom, it had been too dark to explore the keep. But the next morning, when she realized no one was going to watch over her, or even ask her where she was going, she went down that dark corridor. It led to the kitchen and Mrs. Polgarth. Clearly that was not where they were keeping Mr. Holmes, so there must be a secret door somewhere? She had gone back down the corridor, but been unable to find it. *If only Diana were here,* she thought. *She can tease me all she wants, if only she finds that secret corridor. Diana's good at doing things like that.*

> DIANA: Did you really think that? Did you really wish
> I was there?

> ALICE: I did. You would have gotten into that
> dungeon—easy peasy, right?

> DIANA: Of course I would have. I won't tease you
> anymore. I mean, not for a while, anyway. Not for
> the rest of the day, at least.

However, even a dungeon must have some sort of window, probably high up, covered with bars? That's how it worked in the books, as though every dungeon had been designed by the same firm of not very imaginative architects: stone walls dripping with moisture, small window high up to give the prisoner a glimpse of the outer world, and plenty of rats. Anyway, there had been nothing to do indoors, and no one to talk to other than Mrs. Polgarth. Margaret had barely talked to her at breakfast that morning, focusing instead on making sure that Queen Tera had all she needed—she was already a loyal subject of the future Empress of the World. And Helen had listened carefully to all they were saying, paying attention to Alice only to ask if she needed any-thing—more porridge? Another cup of tea? Incongruously for an English breakfast table, Queen Tera had been dressed in a linen robe that she must have found in one of the boxes from her tomb. No doubt it had once been white, but it was now the color of old parchment. The scarab necklace blazed around her neck. On her head she had placed a net of gold beads that hung down to little points, each of which had a bell on it. They tinkled when she moved her head. There were gold bracelets on her wrists and upper arms. Her eyes were heavily outlined with kohl. Alice kept stealing glances at her. She did, indeed, look like an Egyptian queen, both fascinating and frightening.

After breakfast, Alice had been more or less dismissed. Evidently, Queen Tera, Margaret, and her mother did not need her. That was good, of course, but she felt lost and alone. She missed her friends! She was only the kitchen maid, but she had felt, in some small way, as though she too were part of the Athena Club. After all, she had been present at the battle in the ware-house, and she had gone with Catherine to spy on the members of the Alchemical Society in Soho. Would Mary and the others think she had betrayed them? Or would they understand that she could have done nothing to help them, and accept her back as one of themselves—if and when they managed to stop Queen Tera? She hoped they were all right, particularly Justine, who had been hit by the strongest wave of energic force that Alice had ever wit-nessed. She was terribly worried about Justine. Could even the Giantess have survived such a blow?

But there was no time to worry, not when she needed to figure out how to help Mr. Holmes. Sure enough, walking slowly around the keep yesterday morning, she had spotted the window.

And there, in the dungeon, had been the detective, lying on a stone ledge that formed a sort of narrow bed, looking as wretched as she had ever seen him. She hoped he would look, and of course feel, better today.

"Alice, is that you?" Mr. Holmes staggered into the light coming through the small window. He did look a little better, but she could tell that he was pale and drawn, and that his face was damp with sweat.

"Yes, it's me. Here, I'm going to lower this bag of food."

She untied the sash of her dress from around her waist, then tied one end to the marketing bag and squeezed it between the bars on the window. She lowered it as far as she could. Dresses with sashes were for the likes of Lydia Raymond, not Alice the kitchen maid. Nevertheless, she was grateful for the frivolous thing. Even a frippery could be useful sometimes.

Below her, Mr. Holmes reached up—it was a bit of a stretch, even for him. He took out the contents of the bag. There was no furniture in the dungeon—he had evidently slept on the stone ledge, without a pillow or blanket. It reminded Alice of the coal cellar where she had been imprisoned, although she had at least been given a mattress. She remembered what it had felt like, being imprisoned there. Mr. Holmes must be feeling the same sense of despair, as though he might never get out of this place alive. Well, she would make sure he did—somehow.

"I'm afraid I don't have anything for you to drink," said Alice as he unloaded the bag onto the floor. Mrs. Polgarth had added thick slices of ham to the sandwich, then wrapped it in waxed paper. He spread the paper out and put the food on it, then began to eat, as politely as possible for a man who was ravenously hungry.

"I have enough water, thank you," he said, nodding toward a tin pitcher on the ledge. Both hands were holding the sandwich. "It's the one thing they seem to have given me. And if I were to run out, there is moisture on these walls. I believe it seeps in from the former moat you described. You have done—well, you have done a great deal, Alice. Henceforward, I shall never discount the ingenuity of kitchen maids."

"We know what's what, sir," she said. "Is there anything else I can get you? You still don't seem quite yourself, if you don't mind me saying so."

"No, thank you," he said. "I don't want you to endanger yourself any more than is necessary. And the symptoms will pass. Moriarty must have kept me drugged—two weeks? I lost track of the days. That was a clever trick of yours, Alice—substituting the salt. If it were not for that, I believe I would have been in an even worse state. I hoped, in the British Museum, that I might be able to fight against whatever fate Moriarty had in mind for me. Then when I saw Queen Tera rise from her tomb, I thought that I must still be under the influence of the drug, that it must be a hallucination. But I could tell you were seeing what I was seeing. Did Queen Tera truly kill all those men, Alice? These energic powers—are they real? I would not have believed in them if I had not seen them for myself. But when you eliminate the impossible, what remains, however improbable, must be the truth."

"Well, it depends," said Alice. "I could show you the parlor back in Baker Street—" She waved her hand. It was not necessary, of course—her mind did all the work. But Marvelous Martin had taught her to be theatrical, and she found that physical movements often helped her focus. At her gesture, the comfortable, shabby parlor, with its books and scientific instruments, rose around Holmes, replacing the gray dungeon walls. He looked about him, startled. "But it's just an illusion, you see." She waved her hand again, and it all seemed to melt—the bookshelves with their unsorted stacks, the comfortable armchairs, the table with its cigarette and pipe burns. The dungeon looked like its bleak self again. "I could not kill anyone, not for real. Only Queen Tera can do that. It was no illusion, Mr. Holmes. I saw them turn to dust, same as you did."

Holmes shook his head. "It's a fearsome power, Alice."

"It is, sir, and I'm afraid of it myself. I must go now. They haven't forbidden me from wandering about, but my mother does check on me once in a while. I don't want her to find me gone and ask where I was. She could tell in a wink if I was lying. Will you be all right?"

"I should, with time and nourishment, which you have brought me. Heroin is a terrible drug, Alice. I did not realize how terrible until now. I think, in future, that I will avoid . . . Well, no need to go into that. Its aftereffects should wear off soon enough, if I am left to myself. But will I be? I don't know why Tera did not kill me outright. It would have been simpler and more efficient, and I believe our resurrected Egyptian queen is a practical woman. It can only be because I may still be of some use to her, perhaps as hostage. Or perhaps she hopes to make me perform some action under her mesmeric spell? Well, it is useless to speculate on the basis of insufficient information. For now, at least, I am alive and capable of ratiocination, if not of action. How long do we have until the kidnapping attempt?"

"Today is Tuesday. The Queen is visiting St. Michael's Mount on Thursday. At least, that's what I overheard when I listened at the door. I know it's wrong to listen at doors, and Mrs. Poole would be shocked, but I thought under the circumstances . . ."

"You were quite justified in your actions, and I'm sure Mrs. Poole would agree with me."

MRS. POOLE: And so she would. You were very clever throughout, my dear.

ALICE: Thank you, Mrs. Poole. That means a great
     deal to me.

DIANA: How come you never tell me how clever I am?

"Well, then we shall have to try to escape tomorrow," said
Holmes. "I have no plan as yet, but as I have no other matter of
pressing concern, I shall be able to devote my entire attention to
developing one." He smiled up at her. It was a tired but somehow
charming smile. Alice could see why Mary felt a certain tenderness toward him. In the past, she had always found him daunting,
but it was hard to find a man daunting when he was in a dungeon, dependent on you for food and information! "You'll help me,
won't you, Alice?"

"Of course, sir. Mary would."

"Yes, she would. Mary is . . . well. I have a great deal of respect
for Miss Jekyll. A great deal. Let me rest and try to come up with
a plan of action. Meanwhile, if you hear any other news . . ."

"I will report it to you, sir. I'll be like one of your Baker Street
boys, since you don't have those here in Cornwall."

"You've certainly proven yourself as resourceful as Charlie or
Dennys! But try not to put yourself in any more danger. You are
already doing enough to make Queen Tera angry, and the anger of
that particular lady has deadly consequences." He had finished the
sandwich and bun, and was taking a final bite of the apple, which
he had eaten close to the core. He wrapped the core in the waxed
paper, put them both in the marketing bag, and reached up to tie
the bag to the ribbon. Alice could tell that it took an effort on
his part. Would he be strong enough to escape from the dungeon
tomorrow? She had no idea.

"Yes, sir," she replied. She was already in danger, and she
would put herself in more danger, because she needed to find out

as much about Queen Tera's plans as she could, and then figure
out how to rescue Mr. Holmes. She must search again for the
secret entrance. That was what Mary would have done. She was
not Mary—she could not be as cool and decisive in a crisis. But
she would do her best.

> MARY: I think you were quite as cool and decisive as I
> would have been. And thank you, Alice. You know,
> for taking care of him.

> ALICE: I only did what you would have done. I knew
> you would have been brave, no matter what the
> circumstances.

> DIANA: Are the two of you done praising each other
> yet? Because it's perfectly sickening.

It was afternoon by the time the members of the Athena Club
arrived in Marazion, after a train ride of seven hours during which
Diana had asked, over and over again, when they would arrive.
Mary had been worried about where they would stay, but the
proprietress of the inn at the center of town, called simply the
Marazion Inn, told her that a large party—seven gentlemen and
two ladies—who had reserved rooms had never arrived, so there
were plenty of rooms available. They only needed two: to save on
expenses, they had all dressed in feminine attire so they could
travel and lodge together. Mary shared one room with Catherine
and Diana, while Justine shared with Beatrice. Even in her weakened state, she was not affected by Beatrice's poison, and the
Poisonous Girl wanted to keep an eye on Justine's symptoms.

After they had finished unpacking, she, Catherine, and Diana
went down to the parlor of the inn, where tea was already set out.

Beatrice had told them that Justine needed to rest, and she herself was not hungry—if they could bring her up some mint tea afterward, cold, no sugar, she would have everything she needed.

The parlor was across the hall from a dining room, which was mostly empty at that hour—one elderly couple, who had brought their teacups to a table, sat in a corner, conversing in quiet tones.

"I'm sorry to lose the party of gentlemen, I won't lie to you," said the proprietress, when she brought them a plate of scones, with clotted cream and blackberry jam. "Autumn is always slow here. I think it's the best time of year myself—you can walk along the shore without running into bathers and their huts! I like to see the leaves turning, and the hips on the roses. I make a jam out of them, too—this is from my own blackberries, that grow by the lane out back. It's a beautiful time here, is autumn, but it's not as busy as summer, with all the families coming for their holidays, so a little extra money is always welcome. A party of gentlemen generally want large meals and plenty of them—ladies aren't so expensive in their habits. And gentlemen tip well. Don't misunderstand me, I'm glad to have you young ladies here! You liven up the place, and I can recover some of the loss. I'm Mrs. Davies. You just tell me if you need anything."

"Thank you, Mrs. Davies," said Mary. "We've heard so much about Cornwall, and we're eager to see the sights. St. Michael's Mount, for instance, and I hear there's an interesting old place called Kyllion Keep that was part of a fifteenth-century castle. We're only here for a few days, so we'd like to see as much as possible."

"Ah, St. Michael's Mount. You'll have to wait until low tide to walk over the causeway, unless you want to hire a boat. There's a low tide tonight, but I don't advise you to walk it in the dark—you'll miss your footing and end up in the ocean, like as not! Tomorrow morning, that's when you want to go, just after breakfast, which I serve from six to eight. It's a bit early for London folk, but we're early risers in the country. As for Kyllion Keep, it's not open to the public as a general matter, but the folks as live there are often away—Professor Trelawny died six months back, and his daughter, Miss Trelawny, has been in London since. You can ask Mrs. Polgarth, the daily woman who's been taking care of the house while Miss Trelawny is away, if she'll show you around. She comes by the inn whenever she's in Marazion, for tea and gossip— she and I were at school together. Hard to imagine now that we were once Nancy and Judy! Ah well, how time does fly. . . ."

"Where is Kyllion Keep?" asked Catherine. "Could we just walk there ourselves and look around the outside?"

"You could—it's about a mile and a half east of town, along the coast. If you keep following the coast path, you'll see it. But not today."

"Why not today?" asked Catherine. "There are a couple of hours of daylight left." She ignored the scones and jam, but placed a large scoop of clotted cream on her plate and started eating it with a tea- spoon. Diana took two scones, spread one thickly with jam, and bit into it. Mary sighed. It was always a trial to deal with the vari- ous nutritional peculiarities of the Athena Club. She assembled her scone properly, with jam and then a dab of clotted cream on top.

"Ah, you're not familiar with our Cornish weather!" Mrs. Davies shook her head. "The fog's rising. There, you see. . . ." She pointed toward the window, which looked out into the principle street of the town, called Turnpike Road. Sure enough, Mary could see a gray haze hanging in the air. When they had walked to the inn from the train station, the sun was still shining. Now it was hidden by clouds. "In another hour, you won't be able to tell the water from the land. I don't want you young ladies walking off a cliff by accident! Better wait until tomorrow and see if it clears up. I have to warn you, though: There's a storm coming—they do, this time of year. I hope you brought wellies!"

They had not, in fact, brought Wellington boots. They had not, Mary suddenly realized, brought most of the things they would need for rain in the country, which was so different from rain in the city, with its pavements. They had left so quickly that there had been almost no time to prepare. She was not even sure what Catherine, Beatrice, or Justine had packed. She had supervised Diana's packing to a certain extent—one had to. But she had not checked to see if her suitcase contained a mackintosh or umbrella.

By the time she and Catherine finished their tea, rain was coming down outside in a steady drizzle. Diana, who had devoured two scones spread thickly with jam and then asked to use the loo, had disappeared somewhere. Damn her! She never did tell anyone where she was going.

"We need to purchase the proper clothes for this weather," said Mary. "Mrs. Davies mentioned a general store on Turnpike Road. I don't think umbrellas are going to help us in a Cornish storm, but we need mackintoshes, waterproof boots, and waterproof hats if we can find them. Surely they sell them around here for fishermen?"

"Do we really have to go out in this?" asked Catherine. She looked out the window with obvious distaste.

"Only if we want to defeat Queen Tera and save the world," said Mary.

Catherine grimaced. "Can't we save the world in good weather?"

"The thing I've learned about adventures is they don't come when you want them to," said Mary. "They just sort of happen, like sneezing. Mrs. Davies is right—we could get lost in a fog like this, out on the cliffs. I hate to lose any time, but I think for the rest of the day we had better stay in Marazion and gather supplies. Not a single one of us has wellies—it's just not the sort of thing one needs in London—and Beatrice and Diana will probably need mackintoshes. Diana never remembers to bring hers anywhere, and Beatrice has gone out so little in London that she doesn't have one. I don't know about Justine—she lived in Cornwall for almost a century. She may have prepared for the weather."

"Well, I didn't bring waterproof anything," said Catherine. "What? Don't look at me like that. Pumas don't wear mackintoshes! They're smart enough to get under cover when it rains."

"I have money, but not a lot of money," said Mary. "And keeping five of us at this inn is expensive, so I hope you brought everything else you needed! Come on, let's tell Beatrice and Justine what we're doing, and then find Diana."

Beatrice and Justine were perfectly happy to let Mary and Catherine go shop for waterproof boots and coats, although Beatrice insisted she did not really need them. "What a lovely rain!" she said, looking out the window. "I will go out in a little while and stand in the courtyard. It looks so refreshing, and will revive me from our long journey."

"I think the plant girl has gone insane," Catherine whispered to Mary as they walked down the stairs again. Mary did not reply—each to their own, and she did not want to criticize Beatrice's personal habits. But she could not imagine deliberately standing out in the rain. It did not sound refreshing at all to her!

As they left the inn, Mary saw Diana in the yard in front of the stables, throwing a ball to a large black dog and talking to one of the ostlers, a boy not much older than she was.

"So this is where you've been," she said to her sister, feeling irritated, as she often did with Diana. "Next time, could you please let me know where you're going?"

"Nate says he'll let me ride the pony once the weather has cleared up," said Diana. "It's a real Dartmoor pony, caught wild in the hills when it was just a foal."

The ostler, who must be Nate, tugged at his cap in their general direction.

Mary surveyed her sister critically. "What *have* you been doing with yourself? You're absolutely covered in mud." And these were Diana's good clothes, not the ones she wore when she was pretending to be one of the Baker Street boys! How in the world would Mary get them clean again?

"Playing with Satan, of course," said Diana. "What's wrong with mud?"

"It's cold and wet and filthy," said Catherine. "How can you stand the squish of it? Mud is the main problem with England. Well, and the cold rain. And the snow. And the fact that it's surrounded by water."

"Do you mean the dog?" asked Mary. "You shouldn't call a dog that, no matter what he looks like—it's not kind."

"But it's his name," said Diana. "Isn't it, Nate?"

The ostler just nodded, apparently tongue-tied before all these women.

"Oh, for goodness' sake," said Mary. "We're going to the store without you. I assume you left your mackintosh back in London?"

"Of course," said Diana, throwing the ball again. "Go get it, boy! Go fetch! Who wants to go to a stupid old store anyway? Let me know when you're going someplace interesting."

"We'll see you later then. Come on, Cat. We have shopping to do. And no, you can't stay here—I can tell you want to crawl back into bed. But I need someone to help me carry parcels."

Mary could hear Catherine cursing under her breath as they walked out of the yard and past the King's Arms, the public house next to the inn, to find the general store Mrs. Davies had mentioned.

> MARY: I checked in the *Encyclopaedia Britannica*. It says
> pumas like to swim. Why are you such a coward
> about water?

CATHERINE: Pumas like to *swim*. In calm, clear, cool
  water, preferably in tropical jungles. Where does it
  say they like to walk around in chilly, intermittent
  rain that never seems to end? Also, as you may
  have noticed, pumas have fur—a thick, luxurious
  pelt of it. Moreau deprived me of that. I like water
  when it's not coming out of the sky, and when I
  know I'm not going to be shipwrecked in it.

MRS. POOLE: That must account for your endless baths.

By the time Mary and Catherine returned with the requisite
number of wellies and mackintoshes, in what Mary hoped were
approximately the right sizes, it was almost dark. The general
store was completely out of waterproof hats, having sold all its
stock in August. As they passed through the entry hall, Mary saw
Diana sitting in a corner of the dining room with the ostler they
had seen earlier and what seemed to be three of his friends, one of
whom Mary recognized as the boots boy. She was cutting a pack of
cards and dealing them to her companions. She must be gambling
again. Oh, for goodness' sake! Would she never learn to act like
a young lady?

DIANA: Why do you even continue to ask that
  question?

MARY: Because I haven't given up hope?

DIANA: Then the more fool you.

Should Mary try to stop her? Surely it was the duty of an older
sister. . . .

Just then, Mrs. Davies came up to her. "Miss Mulligan, I believe you wanted to see Kyllion Keep? Mrs. Polgarth, the daily woman, came in not half an hour ago. She's sitting by the window in the dining room having a cup of tea, if you'd like to speak to her."

Mary turned to follow Mrs. Davies' pointing finger. By the window sat an older woman, plump and comfortable-looking, in a knitted shawl and an old-fashioned straw bonnet.

"Shall I introduce you to her? She can tell you if it's possible to view the interior of the keep."

"Yes, please, Mrs. Davies." What could the daily woman tell them? Mary was not certain, but any information was better than none. She tugged at Catherine to follow her and gave her a look that she hoped conveyed the message *Let's see what this Mrs. Polgarth has to tell us.* Catherine gave her a look that seemed to reply, *I'm cold and wet and tired of carrying these damn parcels.*

MARY: How can a look possibly convey all that?

CATHERINE: Artistic license. Anyway, that's certainly what I was thinking at the time!

Mrs. Davies introduced them as two lady visitors eager to see the beauties of Cornwall. "Miss Mulligan and Miss Montgomery," she said. "All the way from London." Mrs. Polgarth nodded and said, "How do." She did not seem particularly impressed.

*You can catch more flies with honey than vinegar,* Mary reminded herself. How did Mrs. Poole do these things?

"It's such a pleasure to meet you, Mrs. Polgarth!" she said. "Do you really live in Kyllion Keep? The only remaining part of Kyllion Castle, built by Sir Allard Kyllion in the fifteenth century, and destroyed in the Civil War by Cromwell himself? I've read so much about it! About how Queen Elizabeth herself slept in the

Red Bedroom and saw the ghost of Sir Allard carrying his severed head, and how Lady Eselda fell in love with the pirate Black Jack Rackham and sailed away with him on his pirate ship. Is there anything left of the poisonous garden grown by Gryffin Kyllion, whom everyone thought practiced the Black Arts?" Thank goodness the book from the Reading Room had been so thorough. "My friends and I were very much hoping we could visit the keep—but perhaps it isn't open to visitors?"

"Well, miss," said Mrs. Polgarth, visibly thawing at this recitation of the glorious and bloody history of the keep, "it isn't open to visitors at the moment. You see, Miss Trelawny herself arrived home Sunday evening, with a friend from London and her daughter, as well as a distinguished foreign visitor, a lady from Egypt. She's still in mourning—Miss Trelawny I mean. Her father, Professor Trelawny, was a famous Egyptologist, digging up all them mummies we hear about in the newspapers nowadays. I think it was a curse myself—they do say all those old tombs have curses on them, and whoever opens them is doomed. The professor died in a fire six months ago, along with his assistant, a low sort of fellow that I never liked, and Miss Trelawny's fiancé. A handsome young lawyer, he was, and very much taken with her. Such a sad business. They say it was an accident, but that's how curses work, ain't it? So you see, I don't like to disturb her at such a delicate time."

"Oh, I had no idea," said Mary. "I'm so very sorry! What a terrible loss for Miss Trelawny—her father and fiancé gone, and at the same time. It's like a novel, isn't it?"

"Indeed it is!" said Mrs. Polgarth, nodding vigorously, as though she too had read those sorts of novels—as she probably had. "To be honest, I thought you might be one of those lady reporters who write for the penny press. We had quite a few of them after the accident. Well, I wish I could show you the keep, seeing as you know so much of its history, but you see I can't, not while Miss Trelawny and her guests are there. Though it would do the house good to have some young ladies in it! That little girl has no one to play with. I'm taking her a bag of sweeties—lemon and pear drops, peppermint sticks, anise humbugs, and something else. . . ." She looked into a small paper bag she had placed on the table, beside the teacup. "Oh yes, licorice. She'll like those, won't she? Children do like their sweeties. My Bert always did—he's grown now, of course, and in the navy. Last I heard he was somewhere near Minorca."

"How old is this child?" asked Mary. "It's a pity she can't meet my sister, who is just fourteen."

"Oh, that is a pity!" said Mrs. Polgarth. "This little girl must be twelve or thirteen, although she's a small 'un. Is your sister traveling with you?"

"She's upstairs, resting," said Catherine.

Mary looked at her gratefully. It would never do to have Mrs. Polgarth learn that her sister was in the other corner of the dining room, gambling with ostlers!

"Well, I'm sorry we can't visit the keep," said Mary. "But perhaps we can climb about on the ruins of the castle and look for evidence of Gryffin Kyllion's garden? It sounds like a wonderful place for a picnic."

"It is, indeed," said Mrs. Polgarth. "And you can climb about on the ruins, of course. Miss Trelawny owns the keep itself, but not the ruins or grounds."

"Could you show it to us on a map?" asked Catherine. "We bought a map of Penzance and environs, all the way from Mousehole to Porthleven. We thought it might come in handy." She looked about among the parcels and finally pulled out the map.

"Of course," said Mrs. Polgarth affably. Catherine placed the map on the table and leaned over it, her elbows on the wooden tabletop.

Was Catherine thinking what Mary was thinking? *Distract Mrs. Polgarth!* Well, whether she was thinking it or not, she was doing it very effectively. While Mrs. Polgarth pored over the map, pointing out the different landmarks, making comments such as "Here is the keep, and if you get to Perranuthnoe you've gone too far," Mary reached over to the paper bag of sweets. Hannah and Greta, the pickpockets who worked for Irene Norton in Vienna, would have done this so much more easily and elegantly! But it would take only a moment—yes, in a moment, it was done.

Ten minutes later, after they had bade Mrs. Polgarth good night and she had disappeared, her tea drunk, into the darkness, Catherine said, "So, what did you do? Send a message of some sort?"

"I dropped my Athena Club seal into the paper bag," said Mary. "I don't know what Alice will make of it—after all, she doesn't know Mina had the seals made for us. Beatrice was teaching her a little Latin, but I don't think she ever got to Greek. Will she understand the letters or symbols on the seal? The owl, the olive branch . . . I don't know. But there was no time to write a message, and I couldn't think of anything else."

"You did well, Miss Mulligan," said Catherine. "Come on, let's collect Diana before she gambles away our money. I want to check on Justine and make plans for tomorrow."

"From my experience," said Mary, "Diana rarely loses, at least for long. I sometimes wonder if she cheats."

> DIANA: I may lie and steal, but I never cheat at cards! That would not be honorable. Anyway, only idiots need to cheat.

Beatrice and Justine were doing well, although Justine admitted that she felt weaker than she had expected from the journey. They had evidently been discussing European politics. Mary could not imagine how they found such a topic interesting! Catherine said she would sit up with them for a while, so Mary left her fellow Athenians to it and prepared for bed. Tomorrow was going to be a long day.

She spent a sleepless night, tossing and turning, although the mattress was comfortable enough for a country inn. She was once again sharing a bed with Diana, who eventually came up from her card game and banged about the room without consideration for anyone else in it before collapsing into bed. Her feet were cold! And how could Mary have forgotten that Diana snored? Catherine, who came to bed even later, still retained some of her nocturnal habits and got up several times during the night to prowl around.

Sometime before dawn, Mary finally fell into a deep sleep in which she walked through the labyrinthine streets of London, trying to find Sherlock Holmes, who had somehow, inexplicably but with the compelling logic of dreams, turned into an orangutan. She searched for him through the streets and alleyways of Soho, knowing only that she had to find him before Big Ben struck the hour. She did not know which hour, or how long she had to find him, but she walked through that endless maze, calling and calling, while her voice echoed forlornly down the lamplit streets.

# CHAPTER XIII

# A Causeway Across the Sea

The next morning, Mary woke stiff and sore. It took her a moment to realize that Mrs. Poole would not be coming up to tell her it was time for breakfast or discuss the grocery bills. Where was she again? Not Vienna, not Budapest—no, a village in Cornwall. She had a terrible headache.

Catherine was already up and gone. Diana was still asleep, her head under the blanket, feet sticking out. At least she was not snoring.

Mary got up, put on her robe, and slipped out as quietly as she could—although, really, almost nothing woke Diana. She crossed the hall and knocked on the door of the room across from hers.

"Come in," called two voices—*Catherine and Beatrice,* she thought. When she opened the door, she was greeted by Catherine's "Oh good, you're up. We didn't want to start the confabulation without you."

"Good morning to you too," said Mary. "Bea, do you have anything for a headache? My head is throbbing." All of them already seemed to be dressed. This was not like her—usually, she was one of the first up.

"I have a willow bark powder," said Beatrice. "You can take it with water, and it should help in about half an hour. But really I think you need some breakfast. That will help you more than one of my medications. You are worried, and therefore you are clenching your jaw. That is giving you a headache. You need to chew on something, such as a piece of toast."

"We were just talking about what to do today," said Catherine. "The Queen makes her visit to St. Michael's Mount tomorrow. I say we all go to Kyllion Keep and try to stop them there, before they can attempt to abduct her. There are five of us and three of them—assuming Alice is still on our side and will stay out of the action."

"Based on what Justine has told me," said Beatrice, "I do not believe even the five of us are strong enough to prevail against Queen Tera. She is as powerful as Ayesha, perhaps more so—we did not see Ayesha use her power at such a distance, or turn seven men to ash. We cannot simply assault the keep. It would be foolish to do so. And Justine agrees with me."

"Justine?" said Mary. "Do you?" She wanted to hear, not just what Justine had to say, but how she sounded this morning. Had she recovered from Queen Tera's attack? She did at least look better this morning, although still very tired.

"Yes," said Justine. "I know too well that we cannot stand up against Queen Tera. And I do not think we can take the keep by force. If I understand correctly, a keep is—"

"The strongest part of a castle. The best fortified," said Catherine. "Yes, I know my English, thank you. It's Latin I have trouble with. All right, then—you're the planner, Mary. Plan something."

*Plan something! That's easy for her to say,* thought Mary, rubbing her temples. She wished her head did not hurt so badly. "We should at least go reconnoiter around the keep. Does it have any vulnerabilities? Justine's right, we can't simply walk in there demanding Alice and Mr. Holmes. Cat, you didn't see Queen Tera at the British Museum. She just pointed at those lamps, and the flames in them leaped up, engulfing seven men in some sort of fire. It didn't even look like normal fire—it moved like snakes, and it sparkled with all sorts of colors. And then you could just see them—Professor Moriarty and the others—burning up like pieces of paper, crumbling into ash. . . . It was the most frightening thing I have ever witnessed. And she blasted Justine from across the room. I assume she could do the same to us. Even if we got Alice and Mr. Holmes back, how would we stop her from kidnapping the Queen? We know, or at least we're pretty sure, that she's going to try to kidnap Her Majesty from St. Michael's Mount tomorrow. We can't let that happen."

Beatrice rummaged in a bag on the bedside table, took out a small packet wrapped in wax paper and a spoon that looked as though it were made of horn, measured some of the powder into a water glass, and added water from the matching bedside carafe. She handed the glass to Mary. "Drink this," she said. "It will taste a little bitter, but it will help your headache."

It tasted more than a little bitter, but Mary drank it down, then continued. "Can we perhaps get into the keep tonight and attack while they're asleep? A scouting expedition should let us know if there are ways to get in. But we have no way of knowing if an attack on the keep will work, so we also need to take a look at St. Michael's Mount. We need to be ready to protect the Queen tomorrow, no matter what. It's still early—damn, I've forgotten to put on my wristwatch." Of course she did not usually put it on until she got dressed and here she was, still in her nightgown. Her dream of the night before must have disturbed her a great deal. Ordinarily, she would have been dressed by now—and she would certainly not have said "damn"!

> DIANA: If you said it more often, you might not be
> such a bore.

"Almost seven," said Beatrice, looking at the watch pinned to her lapel. She wore it upside down, like a hospital nurse.

"Right. The tide should be down now—it rises again around ten o'clock, so we need to get across the causeway and back before then. Since we have two things to do today, I suggest we split up—some of us to the keep, some to St. Michael's Mount."

"I'll take the keep," said Catherine. "I still think attacking the keep today, or tonight if you insist, is the best idea. And I'll take Diana with me. She can pick any locks we need picked. All right, Diana?"

"Awww, how did you know I was here?"

Mary turned, startled. Sure enough, there was Diana standing by the door.

"I sneaked in so quietly, too! I thought I would take you all by surprise."

"You certainly took me by surprise," said Beatrice. "I did not even notice you had come in."

"Neither did I," said Justine. "That was clever of you, Diana."

Mary hated to admit that she had not noticed either. But she would not give Diana the satisfaction of saying so. The girl was already puffing herself up because Justine had called her clever!

"You can't outsneak how you smell," said Catherine. "You didn't take a bath last night, and you still smell like dog. Anyway, I heard your footstep outside the door, even before you turned the knob. Are you coming with me? We're not going to attack the keep by ourselves, or try to burn it down, or anything of that sort—so don't think you're going to do what you did at the mental hospital in Vienna!"

"You mean saving Lucinda all by myself?" said Diana.

"Cat, do you absolutely promise you won't do anything foolish, or let Diana do anything but reconnoiter? I don't want the two of you going off and getting yourselves electrocuted by Queen Tera. But we do need to split up, and I think I had better go to St. Michael's Mount." Mary stood up. Her head was, indeed, starting to feel better. "I'll try to find out Her Majesty's itinerary. That should give us a sense for when and how they might try to abduct her—and where we can defend her. I think this is a lot harder than what we faced in Budapest! I wish we had Mina here to help us."

"I shall go with you to St. Michael's Mount," said Justine.

"No, *cara mia*," said Beatrice. "You are my patient, and I say you shall do no such thing. Your heart is beating strong and steady today, but if we are to fight tomorrow, you must be as rested as possible. We cannot spend your strength on a scouting expedition. I shall go with Mary, and you must wait for what I hope will arrive—a telegram from Ayesha. I remain convinced that she is our best hope for defeating Queen Tera. She must know of some way to counteract or combat energic power."

"All right then, I'll get dressed," said Mary. "We had better grab a quick breakfast downstairs. We all need food—well, except for Beatrice. And then we'll try to figure out how to save the Queen!"

MARY: It's ironic, isn't it? There we were, calling on Ayesha, the President of the Alchemical Society and our enemy, to save us.

BEATRICE: Ayesha has never been our enemy. You simply do not understand her perspective.

CATHERINE: Life is filled with coincidences and strange reversals. If I made one of my Astarte books as complicated and unaccountable as real life, it would be criticized for being unrealistic. And I write about spider gods!

BEATRICE: Although they are quite realistic spider gods. I mean, it is obvious that you have done your research into the anatomy and mating behavior of arachnids.

MARY: I'm not sure what that adds to the books.

CATHERINE: Because you're not a writer.

As far as Catherine was concerned, autumn in England proved that if God did exist, He was an actively malevolent deity. Who else would have created all this rain? Although it was not raining today. Instead, water simply hung in the air as a curtain of gray mist, shifting so that sometimes she could see the landscape in front of her, and sometimes it was hidden from her eyes. Shrouded—yes, that was the word for it, the word she would use if she ever wrote a book about their experiences.

Although why should she? No one would ever believe it was a true account. Anyway, she was no Mary Shelley, merely a writer of stories for the popular press. *The Mysteries of Astarte* would be coming out soon. How would the public receive it? Would it be reviewed in *The Guardian* or *St. James's Gazette*? She did not think so. To the important journals, it would be merely an adventure story. But then, it would bring pleasure to readers like Alice, who had been the first to say, "You really should write down that story about Astarte and the spider god, miss. It's much better than the one I've been reading—see? *The Curse of the Loathsome Worm*. There's a girl in it, Miss Penelope Tulkinghorn, but the Loathsome Worm has already killed her, and now it's about how her fiancé and his best friend have to go down into the Worm's lair. And I'm only on the third chapter! I guess the other ten chapters are about them hunting the Worm or something. Why do the girls always get killed? Astarte never gets killed—she just kills people. You should write that story. I would read it—and pay a penny for it, or even tuppence! Really I would."

So Catherine had written it, and it had been serialized in *Lippincott's*, and soon it would be published as a real book. She was filled with trepidation at the thought. No, the idea of writing about their experiences—hers, Mary's, Diana's, Beatrice's, and Justine's, was silly. Who would read such an account? Anyway, the others would never allow her to write it. They would not want their lives, their thoughts, exposed to the public.

MARY: And we still don't. Really, Cat, you ought to
   listen to us when we tell you there are certain
   things we don't want the general public to know.
   After all, these are our *lives*.

CATHERINE: Who is this *we*? You're the only one who
   ever objects to anything. Diana says include more
   of her misadventures, Beatrice wants to make sure
   we address social issues, and Justine never objects
   to anything, no matter how personal.

JUSTINE: Forgive me, Mary, but I believe it is best
   for readers to understand the truth. Perhaps, in
   some way, they will see themselves in us and
   our experiences. That is what literature does, is
   it not?

MARY: If you call this literature! I mean, Catherine
   is a good writer—you're a good writer, Cat, I'm
   not saying otherwise. But this isn't Shakespeare or
   George Meredith!

CATHERINE: George Meredith is a bore. Anyway,
   since when have you been a literary critic? You're

just upset because I keep writing about things that you think are embarrassing.

MARY: Well, yes. There is that.

"I see a village," said Diana.

"Where?" Catherine walked up to where Diana was standing, on a stile in a stone wall. Yes, there to their left was a village that had not been visible through the hedge. She could see stone houses with flowers growing out of the rough walls that surrounded them, along a street that wound uphill toward a church steeple visible above their slanted roofs. It was a small place, much smaller than Marazion, with none of the seaside shops or tearooms. She looked down at the map she and Mary had bought yesterday, and that Mrs. Davies had marked with an *X* for the location of Kyllion Keep. "There isn't supposed to be a village between Marazion and the keep."

"Let me see." Diana almost snatched the map from her hands.

"Stop that! You'll tear it. Let's go into the village and ask where we are. Perhaps we got lost or turned around somehow?"

"How? We've been on this path the whole time." Diana pointed back behind them, at the path that followed the line of the cliffs. Almost all along its length, they had been able to look down to the sea below, crashing against the rocks. "Anyway, I never get lost."

The village turned out to be Perranuthnoe. When Catherine showed their map to the proprietor of the village pub, he said, "That's right, Kyllion Keep is almost a mile west of here, halfway to Marazion. I don't know how you could have missed it. It's surrounded by the ruins of the old castle—Kyllion Castle, it was called, once, until it was burned down by Cromwell. The cove is named Kyllion too, although no one goes there nowadays, on account of it's too rocky except at low tide. The Kyllion family

used to have a dock there. But none of the family lives there anymore, not since Lord Branok Kyllion was convicted of piracy in
the early part of the century and hanged at the assizes. Then it
stood empty until a Professor Trelawny bought it. But the keep
sticks out of the ground like a thumb above Kyllion Cove. I don't
know how you could have missed it, even in this weather."

MARY: Always ask at the pub. Sherlock taught me that.
The pub always knows.

CATHERINE: And there is always a pub. It's the one
thing you will always find in an English village.
Well, apart from the church.

They thanked the proprietor and walked back along the
coastal path, but saw nothing that looked remotely like a keep.
To their left, there were rocks and crashing waves. To their right
rose forests and fields. In one field, Diana chased a rabbit, and
Catherine waited impatiently. What was the point of chasing prey
if you weren't going to eat it? While she was waiting and pacing
around, she noticed a set of wooden steps going down the cliff
face. Below it, in the shelter of the cliff, where it would not immediately be seen from above, was a stone boathouse. She clambered
down the steep, narrow steps to take a closer look, but it was just
a boathouse, with a small sailboat stored inside. Around it the
rocks formed a cove that protected the boathouse from the ocean
winds, and there was just enough sand to pull the boat down to
the water without damaging the hull. She wondered whom it
could belong to—there did not seem to be anyone out here who
might want to sail a boat. And then she realized where they must
be. On the map, there was only one cove between Marazion and
Perranuthnoe. This must be it.

"I still don't see a keep," said Diana, who was waiting for her when she had climbed back up to the path again.

"I don't think you're going to." Catherine sat down on a rock. They had walked, what, two miles back and forth in this wretched weather? She felt thoroughly dispirited. "This has to be Kyllion Cove, which means the keep is here, somewhere. We just can't see it. Alice could make herself invisible, right? With her mesmerical powers. Well, from what we've heard, Mrs. Raymond has mesmerical powers as well, and so does Queen Tera—especially strong ones. How hard would it be for them to make a house invisible?"

"You mean it's just not there?" asked Diana.

"No, it's there all right. Or here, somewhere around us. Mesmerical powers don't actually make anything vanish. They just affect your brain so you think you're a pig, or the Prime Minister, or something. They're confusing our brains so we can't see the keep. Which means they probably know we're here. We'd better get back to Marazion and tell Mary."

"Can't we just walk around and see if we bump into it?" asked Diana. "Maybe we'll fall over a wall, and then we can feel our way. They can't confuse our sense of feel, right?"

"I don't know. Probably. They can probably make us believe just about anything they want, and we don't know the limit of their powers. Anyway, look at all this—" Catherine swept her arms around, indicating the cliff top and the crashing sea below. "Do you really want to walk around this area, hoping we'll bump into something? What if they make it look as though we're walking on solid land, and we're not? What if we walk over a cliff? Without knowing more about what they can make us see, or even feel, it's too dangerous. Let's go back—at least we can help the others."

"Fine," said Diana, kicking at the stone Catherine was sitting on. "I should have gone with them in the first place."

"But then you would have missed my scintillating conversation."

Catherine did not mean to sound quite so sarcastic, but she was seriously angry. This had been a complete waste of time, and evidently there was some water on that stone. It had soaked through her skirt, and now her bottom was wet!

Suddenly, Diana looked interested. "What does that mean? *Scintillating*." She tried out the word, as though tasting it. "I didn't learn half the things I should have at the bloody Society of St. Mary Magdalen. Tell me more words I don't know."

So they trudged back to Marazion through the mist, while Catherine searched her brain for rare and unusual words so Diana would, while she was trying out each one, leave her alone for just a moment. *Malaprop*, *sesquipedalian*, *tincture* . . . What else could she think of? It was exhausting being with someone who needed to be amused at every moment.

DIANA: You like teaching me words, and you know it.

CATHERINE: Yes, when I have a dictionary! Not when we're in the middle of trying to save Alice, and Mr. Holmes, and England!

This was exactly the sort of weather Beatrice liked. The sky was gray and overcast. Mist hung in the air—she could feel the moisture on her skin. For Mary's sake, for her sense of propriety, she was wearing this silly coat—but why would anyone not want to feel the atmosphere around them? Of course it was chillier than she liked, but that had been true since she had come to England.

"It looks slippery," said Mary, examining the causeway that connected St. Michael's Mount to the mainland.

The tide had gone out, but the stones of the causeway were still wet and covered with bright green algae. Here and there, Beatrice could see the slick shells of snails. On either side were sand, some of it covered with sea wrack, and weathered rocks. Behind them, low cliffs rose up to the town of Marazion.

"Perhaps it would be best if we held hands?" she said, holding hers out.

Mary stared at her, surprised.

"It's all right," she said, a little wounded by Mary's expression. "You see? I am wearing gloves."

"Well, of course you are. I mean, I expected you would be. We are paying a visit, after all. It's just that you don't often hold hands with anyone, gloved or otherwise." Mary took her hand. "Come on."

Beatrice was used to this sort of reaction—or at least, she should be used to it. It had, after all, been her life since she was a child. Her own father had avoided contact with her. When she was still too young to understand her own toxicity, she had found a stray kitten wandering in the garden. For one golden, never-to-be-forgotten hour, it had played with her, and then it had lain down on the garden path and slowly grown stiff and cold. Butterflies that landed on her shoulder would last a minute, or maybe two, before they ceased to move. The only one who did not avoid her touch, even now, was Clarence. And that was even more difficult, because she must avoid it for him, to make certain he did not burn his hand while holding hers. He was fearless, so she must be fearful. It was sweet to live in the consciousness of being loved—for he had told her that he loved her, as he had bidden her goodbye on the train platform in Budapest. But it also made life more complicated.

"Why in the world would anyone build a castle out here?" asked Mary.

Beatrice drew her mind back to the present. It was a relief to be on an adventure, to think of action and not emotion for a while. The problem of her own heart could wait. The immediate problem must take priority now.

"I'm certain they will tell us in the castle itself! Come." Beatrice held out her hand again. This time Mary took it, and she felt once more a pleasure she had not felt often in her life before joining the Athena Club—of being wanted and trusted.

They walked cautiously along the wet causeway, between water on either side, out to the island. Although the tide was low, there were still small waves on the water, crashing in white foam on the rocks. There was a storm coming—she could feel it.

The walk up the wooded hill to the castle, on a series of stone steps, was steep, and by the time they reached the front entrance, they were both breathing heavily. The castle itself was not as elegant as the French and German castles Beatrice had seen in her travels, which looked as though they had come out of fairy tales. But it was what a castle should be, when it was perched on an island in the Atlantic—gray and squat, as though hunkering down from wind and weather. It had peaked, small-paned windows high up on the stone walls, innumerable chimneys, and a turreted central tower that seemed to stand guard, looking out over the vast gray water. She rather liked its roughness, its gothic simplicity. Mr. Ruskin, who had written *The Stones of Venice*, would surely have admired it.

"Are you here for the tour?" A woman standing in the doorway was speaking to them in somewhat formidable tones. She was dressed in violet watered silk with a white collar and cuffs. A chatelaine hung at her waist. Was she the mistress of the castle? Mrs. Davies had told them it was owned by the St. Aubyn family. The head of the family had been made Lord St. Levan by the Queen herself.

"Yes, we are," said Mary. "Does it start soon? We are so looking forward to seeing the house, Mrs.—" Mary waited a moment.

"Russell," said the woman graciously. "In half an hour, miss. If you would like to tour the gardens yourself, I would be happy to provide you with a labeled map."

"Thank you, Mrs. Russell," said Mary. "We would like that very much."

When they were walking away from the front entrance, toward what looked like a series of terraces going down to the sea, Beatrice whispered to Mary, "How did you know she was a housekeeper? I thought she might be Lady St. Levan."

"I don't know, she just looked like a housekeeper," said Mary. "Lady St. Levan would never dress like that."

Dress like what? In what looked to Beatrice like a perfectly sensible, even fashionable, gown? It was so difficult, sometimes, to understand these English distinctions. Were they, after all, necessary? What mattered was the beauty and functionality of a gown, not what it announced about one's social position. Surely human beings were the same, underneath.

CATHERINE: You're such a socialist! Any day now, you're going to tell us that you've joined the Fabian Society.

BEATRICE: If you mean that I support food and shelter and medical care for everyone, then perhaps I should. And the Fabian Society does a great deal of good work in the East End.

MRS. POOLE: Godless radicals, that's what they are. Although, I have to admit, they do distribute food to the poor. "Whatever you do for one of the least of these," as the Bible says. Still, they're practically heathens!

The housekeeper had given them a map of the gardens. Beatrice was happy to wander around for half an hour, although she found the map sadly inadequate. It did not even include the Latin names of the plant species! It was fascinating to see such plants—quite tropical, some of them—growing in an English garden. There were stately palms, aloes whose sap could be used to soothe burns, agaves that could be applied topically for inflammation, and all manner of flowering plants that she would not have expected to see in this climate.

At one point she stopped and said, with suprise, "There is *Erythrina* growing here."

"So?" said Mary.

Beatrice looked at her, shocked. How could people know so little about plants? They stood upon grass, ate tomatoes and peppers and aubergines, purchased lilies for their tables, walked under beeches or oaks—and yet they knew nothing, absolutely nothing, about the plants with which they shared this magnificent Earth! Even Clarence had said to her, "Sweetheart, I don't know a radish from a rose," which was surely an exaggeration.

"It is more commonly grown in India and China," she explained. "It is a potent medicine, and also a poison if the seeds are ingested. One must handle it carefully, but I imagine the gardener knows what he is doing. My father experimented with it in his garden—"

"Really? That's interesting," said Mary, looking down at her wristwatch. "I think it's time for the tour. Come on."

Had Mary been listening to her at all? Sometimes Mary did not listen. She was a good friend, and had so far been a conscientious President of the Athena Club. But she did not always pay attention to the feelings of those around her. It was a sort of obliviousness, or perhaps obtuseness. Beatrice was not certain which word most clearly expressed her meaning in English. Of course, she could never say this to Mary. . . .

MARY: Well, now you have, in a sense. Am I really obtuse?

BEATRICE: Mary, I assure you that I was not thinking
of any such thing as we walked through the
gardens of St. Michael's Mount.

CATHERINE: Well, you were thinking of it last week
when Mary would not listen to you about the
foxgloves growing in the Vicar's garden, and it
took us two extra days to solve who had poisoned
those choir boys. I know you're trying to be like
Holmes, Mary, but it's not necessary to emulate
him to the point of ignoring everyone else.

MARY: Sherlock listens! Well, sometimes.

Beatrice looked around her one last time, admiring the
tropical lushness. Mary was already walking back toward the front
entrance of the castle. When Beatrice joined her a few minutes
later, the housekeeper said, "I think it will be just you two young
ladies this morning. I suppose the weather is keeping less energetic visitors away! The tour of the castle lasts half an hour, leaving
time for you to explore the chapel on your own later, so you can
make your way back across the causeway in plenty of time. If you
will follow me . . ."

In a cultured voice that seemed to speak to a larger crowd
than two—clearly, she was used to giving tours—Mrs. Russell
led them through the entrance hall, which had weapons on the
stone walls, as well as the St. Aubyn coat of arms over the mantel.
Mary and Beatrice followed her up a set of steep steps, through
the library with its impressive collection of volumes, then into a
large dining hall that must have been a refectory when the castle
was still a monastery inhabited by the monks of St. Michael. From
the dining room, they passed out onto the terrace, from which

Beatrice could see the harbor below and the causeway stretching back toward Marazion.

"If you'll follow me to the south terrace," said Mrs. Russell, leading them around the stone walls of the castle. "From there you can see the chapel, which as I said you may explore yourselves. But first I will show you the blue drawing room, used by the family for entertaining." She led them through a vestibule into a pleasant room painted the blue of a Wedgwood vase, furnished in a very pretty gothic style. It was not as artistic as Mr. William Morris's designs—there were no arching vines or medieval furnishings here—but Beatrice imagined that Mr. Ruskin would approve of it.

"This is a lovely room," said Mary, looking around at the paintings on the walls.

"That one is by Thomas Gainsborough," said Mrs. Russell. "And that one, by Sir Joshua Reynolds, shows Lord St. Levan when he was still Sir John St. Aubyn. It is a pleasant room, is it not? In the style of Horace Walpole's Strawberry Hill, I have been told. And that Chippendale sofa, upholstered in blue, is particularly important. Tomorrow, a very special visitor will be taking elevenses on it!"

"Do you mean Her Majesty?" asked Mary, clasping her hands together. "Right here, in this room? We read all about her visit in the *Daily Telegraph*."

"This very room," said Mrs. Russell in a satisfied tone. "I'll be serving her a variety of sandwiches—cucumber and cress, shrimp salad, Cook's special curried egg salad—as well as a Charlotte Russe. And the Lapsang souchong she likes."

"How wonderful!" said Mary. "I imagine Lord and Lady St. Levan will be thrilled. Will any guests be allowed on the island while Her Majesty is here? I'm sorry she won't be visiting Marazion. I should so like to see her again myself. My mother took me once, when I was a little girl."

"I'm afraid not," said Mrs. Russell. "The family are abroad in France, and Her Majesty particularly asked to make a private visit. She is coming here to commemorate a visit she made with Prince Albert in 1846, when Their Majesties arrived unannounced during a tour of Cornwall. Prince Albert played the organ in the chapel, and the Queen had tea with my predecessor, a Mrs. Thomasina Sims, who was housekeeper here at the time. She was a friend of my mother's and told me the story herself when I was a child. On this visit, Her Majesty will greet the servants who live in the village below, take refreshments in the blue drawing room, and then spend some time by herself in the chapel, praying. I understand that she is making a tour of places she visited when she was considerably younger. It is a sort of—well, I don't like to say it."

"I understand," said Mary. "She's seeing these places for the last time, isn't she?"

"Well, she is quite old now," said Mrs. Russell apologetically, as though she did not want to admit it. "As a young woman she climbed up the hill herself. This time we have arranged for her to be carried in a chair by the undergardeners. Of course, the island will be closed to visitors while she's here. The only boat allowed in the harbor will be the barge that rows out to fetch her from the Royal Yacht."

"Then I'm glad we're getting to see it today!" said Mary. "What about the tower? Is that still used for anything?"

"That is the chapel bell tower," said Mrs. Russell. "But at one time it was also used as a beacon. In the eighteenth century, there was a regular system of beacons on the cliff tops. If danger threatened—if Black Jack Rackham were sailing along the coast, for instance—each of the beacons would be lit, signaling the boats to return to the mainland. From St. Michael's Mount, you would be able to see the beacons light up along the coast, like a row of fireflies. We don't go up there anymore except to clean the bells—it's a cramped, narrow stair up to the top. But there's a sort of iron cauldron up there in which the beacon fire was lit. I suspect it's used as a bird's nest now! Let me show you the map room and the armory—then you can go into the chapel and make your way back down to the causeway before the tide turns."

An hour later, as Beatrice and Mary stood once again in the garden, Mary turned to her and said, "Bea, are you thinking what I'm thinking?"

Beatrice was not at all sure—she seldom thought the way Mary, or any of the other girls, did. But she might as well venture a guess. "That we should have warned Mrs. Russell? She was so kind, showing us all around the castle. Surely she should be warned that the Queen is in danger."

"No, I mean that I've thought of a way to warn the Queen. Or at least her ship, before the Queen gets into that barge. The captain, or whoever is responsible for that sort of thing on a ship, should be able to see a fire on the tower. I think we should light the beacon and warn her away from here."

Would that work? Beatrice was not certain. "But Mary, do you think the captain would understand it as a warning? After all, this is no longer the eighteenth century. And you must consider the weather—there will almost certainly be a storm. I can feel it. A strong wind or pouring rain would put out the fire."

"Well, that's the only thing I can think of at the moment," said Mary crossly, as though vexed. "The beacon was used to warn people—hopefully someone would understand that it's a warning? The problem will be getting some sort of fuel to the top of the tower. What would create a really fearsome fire? You're the one who seems to know all about chemistry and combustion. After all, you created the paprika spray we used on the vampires in Budapest. I was hoping you would be able to suggest something useful."

Beatrice thought for a moment. "There is of course kerosene, but I do not think it would burn well in a storm. Turpentine? We could soak rags in it. I believe you said the general store was well stocked. Turpentine would burn hot and bright."

"Isn't that what Justine uses to clean her paintbrushes? Can we find turpentine in a general store in Marazion?" asked Mary doubtfully.

"Of course. Turpentine is used by housewives to clean their floors, and by sailors to treat lice." How could Mary not be familiar with such a common chemical? But then, it was not she who did the marketing and cleaning at 11 Park Terrace. She could not be blamed for that—it was the social system that dictated that one person should clean, and another command. But it did leave those who did the commanding dreadfully ignorant about the facts of life.

Beatrice did not say any of this aloud, but there must have been something in her tone, because Mary turned back and said, "It's not my fault I don't know these things. I wasn't raised to, you know."

"You know other things," said Beatrice consolingly. After all, it was Mary who brought in the steadiest paycheck through her secretarial skills. It was she who did the accounts, she who organized them all. There was certainly value in that!

"Well, I don't know how to fight someone with Tera's power!" said Mary. "Even if we manage to warn the Queen, we still have to deal with Tera and Mrs. Raymond. Perhaps Justine will have a telegram from Ayesha with instructions for us. Come on, we have to hurry. I can see the tide starting to come in. I don't want to get stuck on this island."

Beatrice took Mary's hand again, and together the two of them hurried across the causeway toward the mainland. There was a storm coming—she could feel it. *Tonight,* she thought. *It will come tonight. I hope it will not prevent us from saving the Queen.*

BEATRICE: I truly do not understand why more people
do not pay attention to the vegetable creation.

Plants are fascinating, once you learn about them.
If you observe closely, you will see that they
think and feel, just as we do. They communicate
with one another. They even organize for mutual
defense against insect species.

CATHERINE: Maybe because plants are boring? They
just sit there.

BEATRICE: But they are not, Catherine, as I have just
been explaining! They are really not so different
from us. If you sat in a forest for an hour, I
promise that you would see wonders you have not
imagined. Leaves falling, the fronds of bracken
curling open, birds alighting on the branches and
bursting into song.

CATHERINE: Speak for yourself, plant girl. And I don't
sit in forests unless I'm waiting for a nice, juicy
meal to show up.

BEATRICE: I'm almost certain you're saying that
simply to upset me.

CATHERINE: If I succeed, will you leave me alone so
I can finish this chapter?

So this was the Athena Club! Lucinda looked up at 11 Park
Terrace. It was a tall brick building, three stories high, that
seemed no different from the buildings on either side, except
for the brass plaque over the bell, which was still ringing
through the house.

"Are you all right?" asked Laura. "You look pale—I mean, you always look pale, but you look paler than usual, and not very well. It's hard to tell with vampires, but I can always sense when Carmilla is sick somehow."

"I don't feel particularly well," Lucinda admitted. "Our journey was—long." Long and not particularly comfortable, although she had gotten used to the motion of the motorcar eventually. But it had been loud, and there had been the constant smell of the fuel Bertha Benz used. They were continually stopping so she could purchase another can along the road—evidently, it could be bought at pharmacies. A motorcar was certainly faster than a horse, and unlike a horse it never tired, but on the whole Lucinda thought she preferred slower means of transportation. Would motorcars become popular with the general public? Mrs. Benz was certain they would, but she herself had doubts.

"It's been a long trip, for both of us," said Laura sympathetically. "And that parade through London didn't help, did it? Although I think Bertha was thrilled at all the publicity. But here I'm sure we'll be able to rest. Here we will be among friends."

A moment after the bell stopped ringing, the door was opened by a boy with red hair and bony wrists who said, "Yes, miss?" to Laura in a strange, guttural voice. Was he a footman? He must be—he was certainly dressed like one, although the uniform seemed to hang on his frame, and both the arms of the jacket and the trouser legs were rolled up.

"I'm Laura Jennings, and this is Lucinda Van Helsing," said Laura, looking at him with surprise. Evidently, he was not quite what she had expected either. "Is Miss Jekyll at home? Or Miss Frankenstein? Or even Miss Hyde? We are friends of theirs from Austria. We arrived in London earlier today."

"If you will come this way, miss," said the boy, stepping back into the front hall to admit them. "I will tell Mrs. Poole."

He smelled strange, like a dog or some other small animal, not human. And yet he looked human enough? Lucinda wondered if her senses could have been affected by the long journey. After all, she had been smelling automobile fumes ever since they had left Styria. Perhaps it would take time for her nose to recover.

The footman, or whatever he was, left them to wait and scurried—really, he seemed to be scuttling—down the hallway. Lucinda looked around with curiosity. The front hall was elegant, with dark paneling and a gold-framed mirror over the side table, on which lay a card tray. The Athena Club had never seemed real to her before. Here she was at last, in the club headquarters. She was a member, she reminded herself—but she did not feel like one.

"Oh goodness," said a woman in the black dress of a house-keeper, who emerged from a door farther down the hall. The strange footman peeked out from the doorway behind her. "Miss Jennings, I am so pleased to see you, and Miss Van Helsing as well—Miss Jekyll has told me all about you. I'm Mrs. Poole. But I'm afraid none of the ladies are here right now. They're down in Cornwall trying to stop Mrs. Raymond and some Egyptian mummy she resurrected from kidnapping the Queen. I think you'd better come in. There's someone you should meet."

"Well, that's unexpected!" Laura whispered as they followed Mrs. Poole into what turned out to be a large, sparsely furnished but attractive parlor, with yellow walls and a frieze of flowers near the ceiling. "I thought England was going to be a nice, quiet holiday for us, but this is just like being in Budapest. Something always happening . . . Ayesha!"

For a moment, Lucinda thought Laura had sneezed. Then she saw the President of the Alchemical Society seated on the parlor sofa. Startled, she looked around her, doubting her own eyes. They were in England, weren't they? Yes, this house looked nothing at all like Count Dracula's house or the Hungarian Academy of Sciences.

"Miss Jennings," said Ayesha. She did not seem surprised, but then Ayesha never did.

"You remember me?" said Laura. Clearly, she had not expected Ayesha to. "We've only met twice, once after the battle and once—"

"Yes, I remember you perfectly well," said Ayesha, curtly. "Have you come to join in the fight against Queen Tera? I did not know the Athena Club had summoned you."

"No one summoned me," said Laura, clearly a little offended. "And I'm afraid I don't know what fight you mean, or who Queen Tera might be. Lucinda and I are here on holiday—or were supposed to be. We had no idea Mary and the others would be down in Cornwall fighting anyone. Who are they fighting this time, by the way? More mad alchemists?"

"Do sit down," said Mrs. Poole. "May I take your coats? Or, Archibald, why don't you do that, and I'll make another pot of tea. It sounds as though you ladies have a lot to talk about."

"Very well, but come back again and join us, Mrs. Poole," said Ayesha. "I would like you to describe the scene at the British Museum one more time, in as much detail as possible. Anything you remember may be important."

"Well, I wasn't there, of course," said Mrs. Poole doubtfully. "I can only tell you what Mary told me."

"Then that will have to do," said Ayesha, taking another sip of her tea. She looked completely at home in 11 Park Terrace—but then, she always looked both incongruous and completely at home wherever she was.

Laura took off her coat, which was still very dusty, although the maid at the hotel in Calais had brushed both their coats thoroughly the night before. She handed it to the doggy boy—or did he smell more like a monkey Lucinda had once seen at a fair, pulling coins out of children's ears? She was not sure. Her own outfit must be just as dusty from the road.

"All right," said Laura, sitting down in one of the armchairs. Following her example, Lucinda handed her coat to the footman, and sat down in the other. "It sounds as though we're in for more conflict and turmoil, or as Carmilla calls it, adventure. So tell us all about it."

By the time Mrs. Poole brought up a second pot of tea, Ayesha had told a tale so wild and unbelievable that Lucinda was half convinced she had made it up. An ancient Egyptian high priestess with seven fingers on her left hand? A ritual that bathed seven men in energic flames so that their skin shriveled off their bones and turned to ash? Could such things possibly happen? But Laura did not seem particularly surprised by these revelations.

"All right," she said at the end of Ayesha's story as Mrs. Poole was pouring her a cup of tea. "When do we leave for Cornwall?"

Mrs. Poole poured another cup of tea for Lucinda. "It's too late for the train to Marazion, although there's an overnight to Penzance," she said. "You might still be able to catch that. But Madam Ayesha said she would like to go to the British Museum."

Lucinda leaned over. She was so embarrassed—it would be terribly rude of her! And yet she had to do this. "Mrs. Poole," she whispered. "I'm afraid . . . that is, I am most grateful for your kind hospitality, but I cannot drink tea. I cannot drink anything but—"

"Of course!" said Mrs. Poole in a low voice, with a look of consternation. "I'm so sorry, miss; Mary did tell me all about you. A little later, I'll go out and—"

"I want to see the Trelawny Exhibit," said Ayesha, ignoring their whispered conversation. She put down her empty teacup, which Mrs. Poole immediately offered to refill. "No, thank you, Mrs. Poole. No more for me. I want to make it to the museum in time before it closes. There are things about this situation I do not understand. Why were all the ritual implements in the tomb? Clearly because Tera expected to be resurrected, and not two thousand years after her death. There was an inner circle of priest-esses—the most senior of them, all personally loyal to Tera herself. They must have planned to resurrect her in case she was killed, either by Cleopatra's henchmen if she prevailed against the Romans, or by the forces of Augustus. And then for some reason their plan went awry. Most of the senior priestesses were killed in the assault against the temple, and those who were not killed were forced to flee for their lives. When Heduana instructed us not to use our powers against the Roman soldiers—well, I do not know whether she was right or not. Perhaps if we had fought, we might have held the temple, at least for a while—but more of us would have died. At any rate, the ritual was not enacted when it was meant to be, and Tera had to wait two thousand years. I need to know more, to read what is written on the tomb artifacts. Mrs. Poole, I will accept your kind offer and spend the night here. I have no doubt it will be more comfortable than even the Savoy. I should be back in time for supper."

"Very good, madam," said Mrs. Poole. "But as for being more comfortable than the Savoy, well, I don't know about that!"

"I'll go with you," said Laura, drinking her tea a little more quickly than is usually advisable with hot beverages. "I want to see these artifacts for myself, and I can tell Bertha to send our bags over here. They're still in her trunk—*The Times* is putting her up at Claridge's in return for an exclusive. I can't read hieroglyphs, but I want to know more about this situation as well. However, Lucinda needs to rest. Don't you, my dear?"

Lucinda nodded. She was feeling light-headed and weak. She just wanted to lie down somewhere and sleep for a very long time.

"Then so you shall, miss," said Mrs. Poole. "I'll put Madam Ayesha in Miss Justine's room, since the bed is longer, and Miss Jennings in Miss Mary's. I think Miss Catherine's room would be just right for you. It was a bit of a mess when she left, and in general I do expect the young ladies to straighten their own rooms, seeing as it's just me

and Alice nowadays, although we used to have any number of servants when Mrs. Jekyll was still alive. But I picked up in there myself
this morning. I think you'll find it most comfortable, and I'll talk to
Mr. Byles myself about what he has that would be suitable for your
supper. I hope you don't mind sleeping in Miss Catherine's room for
tonight—as a member of the club, you should have your own room,
of course. The old governess's room, which Nurse Adams used for a
while, is empty except for Miss Catherine's typewriter, and she said
she could move that down to Mr. Jekyll's office whenever you decide
to join us. I'll have a room fixed up for you by the time you return
from Cornwall. I do hope the girls are all right. . . . I worry about
them so, when they're on one of these exploits of theirs!"

Lucinda was so tired that she just nodded. But when she was
lying in Catherine's bed, in the room that had once belonged to
Mrs. Jekyll, she thought, *This is the Athena Club, and I am a member. I
can come live here if I wish. There is, after all, a place for me in this world.*

DIANA: No, she didn't. Lucinda thinks in Dutch. I
asked her.

CATHERINE: If you want me to write that in Dutch,
you'll have to translate it yourself.

DIANA: Why don't you ask Lucinda?

CATHERINE: Because she's gone out hunting, and
honestly I wish I'd gone with her! At least you
wouldn't keep coming in here all the time and
interrupting. This is the problem with being in
the office—or the library, since we're calling it
that now. Some days, it's like trying to write in
Piccadilly Circus!

DIANA: But I'm bored. I want to play a game.

CATHERINE: Why don't you go into Beatrice's greenhouse and see how long you can stand her poison without fainting? I bet you won't last five minutes!

DIANA: Bet I will! You'll see. . . .

CATHERINE: Wait! Di, I didn't meant that. I was just joking. Come back here, you dratted child!

After her mother's death, Lucinda had assumed there would never be a place for her in the world again. And yet there was a place for her here in England, as well as in Styria. She would go back there—she still had a lot to learn about being a vampire from Carmilla and Magda. But eventually she would come back to London, to live with Mary and the others. She could already feel this house welcoming her, as though it knew she belonged. As she drifted off to sleep, she thought—in Dutch, Diana—*It is good to be a member of the Athena Club.*

# CHAPTER XIV

## Helen's Story

"Lydia, what is this?" asked Margaret Trelawny. She had the bag of candy in one hand and a pendant of some sort in the other.

"I don't know," said Alice, trying to keep a tremor from her voice. She must remain calm and collected. "I've never seen it before. I swear."

"How could the girl know, ma'am?" asked Mrs. Polgarth. They were all standing in Professor Trelawny's study, where Margaret had summoned them—Alice next to her mother, and Tera by the professor's desk, looking at them impassively. "I bought those sweets at Mrs. Turnbull's shop in Marazion. Someone must have dropped that—whatever it is—in the bag by mistake. It looks like an expensive piece—perhaps it fell off a chain or bracelet into the bag? And the lemon and pear drops, humbugs, licorice—those were supposed to be for Miss Lydia, not the Egyptian lady, if you'll pardon my saying so. While I understand that she might not have tasted English sweets before, it's impolite to open a bag not meant for you, and here in England, proper ladies don't usually go into the kitchen in search of food. They ring the bell and wait to be served. I don't know how it's done in Egypt, but that's how it's done in an English household."

"Lydia," said Margaret, ignoring Mrs. Polgarth, "Are you absolutely sure you don't recognize it? Look at this pendant—it's engraved, as though it were intended to function as a seal. An owl, an olive branch, the letters ΑΘΕ. What do those mean to you? I'm not accusing you of wrongdoing . . . yet. But you must be honest with me."

"She's told you that she doesn't know what it is," said Helen. "Why do you assume this was meant for Lydia? Who could have known that the bag of sweets was meant for her?"

"Everyone Mrs. Polgarth spoke with yesterday, I imagine," said Margaret. "Mrs. Polgarth, who did you encounter yesterday, after purchasing the bag of sweets? Who knows you were bringing them to Lydia?"

"Well, I didn't tell anyone direct-like," said Mrs. Polgarth. "I just said they were for the little girl staying at the keep. I mentioned it to Mrs. Turnbull, and old Widow Tremaine when I passed her in the street, and maybe, yes, I'm sure, Letitia Farquhar in the yarn shop, and Mr. Greengage the grocer when I put in your order, ma'am, and Mrs. Davies at the pub, and some nice young ladies who were staying at the inn, but they were visitors, and didn't know anybody in Marazion."

"What did the young ladies look like?" asked Margaret.

"Well, just ordinary young ladies," said Mrs. Polgarth. "One had light brown hair, and the other had dark brown hair, and a darker complexion. The first was fair and a little sallow. They were both nice young ladies, and meant no harm, I'm sure. In fact, they wanted to visit the keep, but I told them there were no visitors allowed, on account of you being home, ma'am."

Margaret turned to Helen. "Do those sound like the girls you captured? Mary Jekyll and—who were the others?"

"Diana Hyde and Justine Frankenstein. Not particularly. Mrs. Polgarth, was one of them very tall, taller than most men? Or very short, with wild red hair and a tendency to swear like a sailor?"

"No, ma'am. They were both perfectly ordinary, well-spoken young ladies. It must have been some sort of accident, that trinket getting into the sweets."

Margaret frowned. "I don't believe in accidents. Mrs. Polgarth, you may leave early today, and you need not come tomorrow either, although of course I'll pay you as usual. We expect to be out all day, so we will not need our meals cooked. We shall see you again on Friday."

"Very good, ma'am," said Mrs. Polgarth, looking at them doubtfully, as though not at all sure she approved of the situation. Then she curtseyed and left the room.

Margaret turned back to Alice. "Lydia, one more time, do you know what these markings mean?"

"No," said Alice. "I've never seen them before."

"She is lying," said Queen Tera, stepping forward. "I can see it in her energic field. There were two girls on the path this morning, searching for something. They passed one way, and then the other. I could sense their presence, so I altered the energic field around the house and hid it from their perceptions. When they passed a second time, I told Margaret and she observed them from the window of her father's room. Perhaps they were trying to find the child."

"Why didn't you tell me this?" asked Helen sharply. "I should have been told as well. What did they look like?"

"Just ordinary girls," said Margaret. "I didn't think anything of it at the time, or I would have found my father's binoculars and observed them more closely. I thought Tera was being too suspicious. Now, I'm not sure. And I have a vague recollection that one of them had red hair. They could have been two of those meddlesome girls you captured in Soho. Alice, do you know who they might have been? Is someone trying to contact you?"

Alice shook her head. What could she say that would not cause Tera to accuse her of lying again? She did not know what the pendant was, not really. And yet, if she remembered the little Greek she had learned from Beatrice . . .

Tera walked over to Alice. As she crossed the room, the bells on her beaded cap tinkled. "We have more important things to do than attend to such trifles. And this particular trifle has already taken too much time." She took Alice's chin in one small, bony, seven-fingered hand, and raised it until Alice was looking directly into her eyes. They were so dark that they were almost black. "You do know . . . something. Tell me, child, or I shall send a bolt of energy through you that will stop your heart."

"No!" said Helen. "You can't do such a thing to my daughter."

Tera looked at her calmly. "I can and will if she does not tell us what she knows." She turned back to Alice. "What do you say, Lydia?"

Tera's hand was so cold and hard! It held her chin with such strength that she could not turn her head, but had to stare into those dark eyes. "The letters are Alpha, Theta, and Epsilon," she said, her voice quavering. She tried to steady it. "They are the first three letters of Athena, the Greek goddess of wisdom. And the owl is the symbol of Athena." Beatrice had taught her that, when she was learning the Greek alphabet. She had not learned much Greek yet, but she recognized the letters. It must be a signal— members of the Athena Club must be in Marazion! Those girls Mrs. Polgarth described, and the girls passing by the house— perhaps the Athena Club was searching for her? Whatever she did, she could not betray them. "Other than that, I don't know." Tera let go of her chin—thank goodness, because it was beginning to hurt—and took the pendant from Margaret so she could examine it more closely.

"These symbols appeared on the Athenian drachma," said Tera. "I have not seen one in two thousand years. If someone is attempting to signal Lydia, then she cannot be trusted. It would be safest to dispose of her now."

"You can't do that!" said Helen.

Tera looked at her with raised eyebrows, the way she might have regarded a surprising new species of beetle. "I will not be told what I can and cannot do." Then she held out her hand, index finger pointed toward Helen, just as she had when she was about to blast Justine.

Without considering the possible consequences, Alice stepped between the two of them. "You leave my mother alone!" She was not at all sure how she felt about Helen, but she knew that she did not want her mother blasted by a resurrected Egyptian mummy.

"Oh, for goodness' sake, we don't have time for this," said Margaret. "Tera, if those girls were nosing around here today, they'll be back. I think we should take the boat to St. Michael's Mount tonight rather than tomorrow morning. We can spend the night in the harbor of St. Michael's Mount, and then implement our plan before the Queen's yacht arrives. I don't think they'll notice one more boat, but we'll simply have to take that chance. We have a busy day tomorrow. Once our plans have been carried out—once the Queen is here and Tera has taken her place—we can get to the bottom of this. In the meantime, I suggest we put Lydia in the dungeon with Mr. Holmes. Helen, it's only tempo-rary, until we can establish that she really is on our side. I can make sure she has decent bedding, and some food."

"The alternative I suggested is both easier and safer," said Tera. "Long ago, I was merciful, as you are. Because of it, I lost Egypt to my own daughter. I do not trust this girl. I think we should kill her now."

"No!" said Helen. "All right, I'll take her down myself, and see to her bedding. Lydia, let's go to your room and gather up your bedclothes. I'll find you a warm blanket—the dungeon will be cold tonight. And we'll stop in the kitchen to get some food. This is ridiculous, but it's just for one night. It will all be over tomorrow, and then things can get back to the way they were before."

MARY: I can't believe your own mother would put you in a dungeon!

ALICE: She was not a very good mother, but she was the only one I had.

MARY: Still, a dungeon! That's almost as bad as experimenting on your daughter, as Rappaccini and Van Helsing did.

ALICE: Remember that she was the product of an experiment as well. If things had turned out differently, she might have been a member of the Athena Club.

LUCINDA: And she did her best for you at the end. That is, after all, what matters.

In the kitchen, Helen looked around. "There must be food— where does Mrs. Polgarth keep the food?"

"It's in the pantry," said Alice.

"She always leaves dinner on the sideboard before she goes," said Helen apologetically. "I've never been down here before."

"I have," said Alice. "I'll pack something for myself."

"Yes, I think that would be best." Helen sat down on one of the chairs and looked at Alice. "You interposed yourself between me and Tera when she threatened to kill me. Why?"

"I don't know." Why had she done that? Perhaps because despite everything that had happened, this was her mother. "Why did you kill Moriarty? Why are you helping Queen Tera? I don't under-stand. . . ." There were so many things she did not understand.

Helen looked down at the table for a moment, as though lost in thought, then looked back up at Alice. "My father—Dr. Raymond. What he did to my mother drove her mad. But I was born possessing the power to perceive and manipulate energic waves, so he considered the experiment a success. I grew up in his household, cared for by servants. I saw my mother only when my nursemaid took me to visit her at the Purfleet Asylum, where she was confined on the third floor. He was one of the three asylum trustees. Lord Godalming—not Arthur Holmwood, but his father—and Professor Moriarty were the two others, at that time. Each time I came, she would be sitting on her bed, in one of those blue dresses they give the inmates—or patients, but as a child I thought the asylum was a prison because there were bars on the windows. She would look at the wall in front of her, or at the floor—never at me. I didn't understand why she would not look at me or speak to me. I would speak to her, call her mother, tell her that I was her daughter, that I missed her. Only once in all those years did she respond. I must have been eight years old. I sat next to her on the narrow white bed and asked, 'Mother, what do you see when you stare like that?'

"'The waves,' she said, in a voice harsh with disuse. 'I see the waves.' She turned to look at me. 'Daughter, you are drowning.' And then she screamed. She wrapped her arms around herself and screamed, turning her head from one side to the other. In her agitation, she fell on the floor and had what I believe to be an epileptic fit—there was foam on her lips. My nursemaid hurried me out of there—as we left, the attendants were running to her room with a straitjacket. The next day, my nursemaid told me that she was dead. She had died in the night, alone. After she died, my father sent me to live with a family on a farm in Wales, under the name Helen Vaughan. That was my mother's surname—he did not want me associated with him, in case there was a scandal of any sort. In those days, I could not yet control my powers. Two children died because of visions I had produced. One was my friend Rachel, the daughter of a prosperous farmer. At first she was entranced by what I could show her, and asked me daily to conjure scenes out of her book of fairy tales. But when the visions took a dark turn, she became convinced that my powers were of the Devil. She was a pious girl, and felt that by encouraging me, she had herself participated in witchcraft. She hanged herself in her father's barn. The other was a young boy, who claimed to have seen a satyr—half man, half goat—walking in the forest with me. He went mad with fear, and one night he ran out on the bog, where he was sucked into the mud and drowned. After that, the villagers feared and avoided me, so my father sent me to school in London. There, the other girls would not speak to me—they insisted that I had the evil eye. I did not know what to do with my life, so I did what most young women do when they wish for freedom—I married. Charles Herbert was not a bad man, but he was not a good one either. And he was a gambler who slowly, and then quickly, lost the fortune he had inherited. He discovered my abilities and made me use them to frighten men into giving him money. However, as you will discover, we cannot control how others respond to the illusions we create. Some of those men died, and the police began to investigate what they called the Paul Street Murders. I told Herbert I would not extort money for him again, that I was leaving him. He hit me—for the first time in our marriage, he used physical force instead of persuasion and the threat of abandonment. That was a stupid thing to do. Using my powers so often, I had come to understand how they worked. I had learned to control the waves. Now, I was stronger than he was. He died attempting to escape spiders that crawled up his body, spiders that stared at him with their multiple eyes, spiders walking all over him with their furred limbs. He had been terrified of arachnids all his life.

"Only after his death did I discover that I was with child—with

you, Lydia. By that time, I was suspected of his murder. But the
jury had no direct evidence on which to convict me: I had never
touched him. After I was acquitted, I went to a charity hospital,
for I had no money—Herbert had spent all I made for him. When
you were born, I did not know what to do with you. I did not
wish to be a mother, and had no means with which to care for an
infant. They allowed me to stay in that hospital for three months,
until you were weaned. Then I asked the sisters to take you to
an orphanage that was associated with the hospital. I told them
your name was Lydia Raymond—I did not wish to use Herbert's
name, for it was still notorious. After that—for a while, I lived
as I could, making my way in the great, pitiless labyrinth that is
London. Then, one night, Moriarty came to the small tenement
room in which I was living. He had been looking for me ever since
the trial. He was familiar with the work of the Alchemical Society,
for both my father and Lord Godalming were members, although
Moriarty never joined himself—he preferred organizations that
he could lead. Despite his great learning, he was not a scientist.
However, he had always been interested in my father's experiments,
and he said he could use my skills in his business. So I began to
work for him. For a while, I posed as a Mrs. Beaumont, contact-
ing wealthy gentlemen, making them tell me political secrets or
influence pieces of legislation in ways that were advantageous to
Moriarty. When I got in trouble with the police as Mrs. Beaumont,
he arranged for me to become the director of the Society of St.
Mary Magdalen. And there I stayed for many years, concealing
my activities for Moriarty under a respectable exterior. Until one
day Hyde showed up and asked me for suitable young women for a
series of experiments! He knew who I was, of course, and whom
I worked for. He and my father had been friends, colleagues, even
collaborators. Years before, as Dr. Jekyll, he had directed his
attorney, Mr. Utterson, to bring me his daughter Diana. Another

child created by experimentation! Another daughter of a member
of the Société des Alchimistes. She was a continual reminder of
you—my own child, whom I had given up. But of course she was
not you. How I loathed the little monster."

> DIANA: I always suspected there was a reason she
> disliked me so much. She would order me to be
> whipped, but never whip me herself.

> ALICE: Do you forgive her for how she treated you all
> those years ago?

> DIANA: Of course not. I may understand her better,
> but she's still a bloody bitch!

> ALICE: But in the end, as Lucinda said—

> CATHERINE: We haven't gotten to the end yet.

Helen was silent for a moment. Alice looked at her—this
woman who was, but had chosen not to be, her mother. How
did she feel about Helen Raymond, or Vaughan, or Herbert, or
Beaumont—whoever she was? A woman who had assumed so
many identities, and whose mesmerical abilities has resulted in so
many deaths? She had no idea.

"I look at you now, Lydia, and I wonder what it would have been
like if I had kept you with me all those years. Would you have been
different? Would I? We cannot know. When Margaret came to
me with her plan to resurrect Tera and said we would need seven
sacrifices, I thought of whom they should be—Moriarty, who had
helped me but also used me for his own purposes, and my father,
who had abandoned me. The rest I did not care about—I allowed

Moriarty to gather the members of the Order of the Golden Dawn. I was glad, however, that they included Godalming and Seward among them. They had not been responsible for my mother's death—they had become trustee and director of the Purfleet Asylum after her time. Nevertheless, it was satisfying to witness the destruction of two men associated with that place."

"So that was the plan all along?" said Alice. "But why?"

"For revenge," said Helen complacently. "The same reason Margaret gave her father an incomplete formula for the ritual, so that he and her fiancé both died. Did they not deserve it, these men who would not allow her to learn and study as she wished, who insisted that she be secondary to themselves? And for power, of course. Look." She held up her hands, palms almost a foot apart. She stared at them for a moment, with a frown creasing her brows, as though concentrating on them. Suddenly, lightning crackled between her palms. "There, you see? Tera is teaching me how to do it properly. Before, all I could do was cause superficial burns, like those on your servant boy, the hairy one who tried to stop us from rescuing you in the Jekyll residence. You just have to—well, intensify and direct the waves. It's a little like clenching your fist. Soon, I will be able to use the true energic powers of the Earth, just as she can. That is worth . . . everything. Lydia, I am truly sorry—I know you had nothing to do with that pendant. I promise this imprisonment will only be for one night. After that, we will be together, and I will teach you, just as Tera taught me. You will have that power as well. Now, gather up whatever food you want and bring it with you. I will try to make you as comfortable as possible. After all this is over, we will go somewhere—perhaps the Lake District?—and get to know each other properly. How does that sound?"

Alice did not know what to say. Rescuing her? Did her mother truly think she had rescued Alice from the Athena Club? It had been a violent abduction—but apparently Helen had forgotten that, or had chosen to remember the circumstances differently. She put the rest of the brown bread, a hunk of hard cheese, and two apples into Mrs. Polgarth's marketing bag, which the house-keeper had apparently forgotten after her unusual dismissal. In the pantry, she found another saffron bun and added that, as well as a pot of orange marmalade. At least she would be able to share all this food with Mr. Holmes! She would have liked the sweets as well, but Queen Tera had kept those. Apparently two-thousand-year-old Egyptian queens had a sweet tooth!

Then she followed Helen back to the hallway and the secret panel in the wall she had not been able to find. About halfway down the hall, Helen slid part of the paneling to one side to reveal a keyhole, with an ancient-looking key hanging beside it on a nail. She put the key into the keyhole and turned it, then pushed on the panel. It swung open to reveal a dark, twisting staircase. "Go on down," she said to Alice. "I'll come back for you tomorrow afternoon, once we've abducted the Queen and Tera has taken her place."

Alice carried her bedclothes and the bag of food down, down, twisting around as the steps turned. At the bottom, the passage opened into the underground chamber she had seen from under the hawthorns, outside the barred window.

And there was Sherlock Holmes, sitting on the stone ledge. "Well, Alice," he said. "So they've put you in here as well, have they? Tell me all about it. What is happening up there, in the world outside these dungeon walls? I'm sorry to see you down here, although your company is most welcome of course. You and I have gone from the frying pan into the fire, that's for certain. But at least we're in it together."

Alice walked over to the stone ledge and set down the things she had been carrying. She sat down beside Mr. Holmes, and stared ahead of her for a moment without seeing anything in particular. Then, she put her head in her hands and began to sob, terrible, racking sobs that echoed around the dungeon.

Sherlock Holmes put his arms around her. "There, there, my dear. I promise you that we'll get out of this situation and see our friends again. I don't know how, but somehow."

> ALICE: I don't know why I did that. Truly I don't.

> JUSTINE: Because you had just gained and lost a
> mother. She was your mother, but not, perhaps,
> the mother you hoped she would be. I know
> how that is—my mother sent me away at a
> young age to be a servant in the Frankenstein
> household. When I saw her again on my days
> off, she was not the same—the younger children
> took all her attention and time. I missed her even
> while I was with her. And then of course I lost
> her permanently when I died and Frankenstein
> transformed me. It is always difficult to lose one's
> mother. Lucinda knows that.

> LUCINDA: Yes—I cannot think of my mother's death
> without tears. She, too, gave her life for mine.

> ALICE: I wish things had turned out differently for
> both of us.

> MRS. POOLE: We all do, my dear.

"Kyllion Keep wasn't there," said Catherine. "All we could see was a boathouse by the water. We climbed down the cliff and looked through the window. There was nothing inside except what you'd expect to find in a boathouse. And there was no keep."

Mary looked at her skeptically. They were all sitting in the dining room of the inn, having an early dinner of fish stew. Catherine was only eating the fish, picking pieces out of the stew with her fork; Justine was eating everything but the fish; and Beatrice wasn't having any stew at all. Instead, she was eating a cup of Mrs. Davies' elderberry compote. It was the first time Mary had seen her eat anything with a spoon.

"You went all the way to Perranuthnoe, and didn't see the keep at all? How is that possible?" Mary turned and called to the proprietress, who was standing by the door, "Mrs. Davies, would you mind coming here a moment?"

"Yes, miss?" said Mrs. Davies. "Shall I ask Wenna to bring you more stew? It's real Cornish fish stew, my mother's recipe. The fish were caught this morning by one of our fishermen here in Marazion."

"No, thank you. Diana's already had two bowls. But we have a question about Kyllion Keep. Catherine says she and Diana walked all the way to Perranuthnoe, and all she saw was a boathouse."

"That's impossible," said Mrs. Davies. "I mean, begging your pardon, Miss Montgomery, but the keep's right there, sticking up out of the ground, as large as life and twice as solid, at the top of the cliff above the boathouse. You see, the boathouse belongs to the keep—Miss Trelawny uses it for a little sailboat she has. A mighty fine little boat, and she's a good sailor. When she was younger, she used to sail around the bay and pull it up on the sand below. Not that she had to do much pulling herself—there were always young men about, willing to help her. She was quite a favorite in the village, and at our dances. Any number of partners, she had! I was worried for a while that she might marry one of our fishing lads, which would have been below her station. Quite a wild young lady she was, but so lovely, with that long dark hair! I was glad when she got engaged to that solicitor from London. Such a handsome man, although handsome is as handsome does, my mother always says. But when they came here together, he was always genteel and wellspoken. So tragic, what happened—I don't wonder that she left for London after the accident. I imagine this area held terrible sad memories for her. Now, if you're not wanting any more stew, how about some pudding? I have a lovely quince fool to finish off your dinner."

"Yes, please," said Diana. "And I'll have Beatrice's fool as well, since she only eats goop."

"All right, then." Mrs. Davies nodded. "I'll have them out in a moment."

When she had gone, Catherine said, "We know Alice can make herself invisible." She put the remainder of her stew in front of Justine. "Look, I picked out all the fish. You can have the rest." She took the small plate on which Justine had put all her fish and started eating them as well. "Mrs. Raymond is stronger than Alice, and Queen Tera is even stronger. Could one of them have made the entire keep invisible? I mean, make us not see it. You know, by manipulating our perceptions of it. I swear, Diana and I walked along that path twice. We didn't see anything."

"That's true," said Diana. "I had to walk all the way to Perranwhatever and then all the way back. Does anyone else not want their fool? Because I'm hungry."

"I don't think Mrs. Raymond could," said Mary. "If she could make an entire house invisible herself, she wouldn't have needed to summon Queen Tera. But Tera? Who knows what she can do. See, this was the problem with confronting them at the keep in the first place. They're behind stone walls, so they have physical defenses. They can anticipate our moments and prepare for us. And they can see us coming—keeps have windows, remember? I told you it wouldn't work. We need to surprise them in some way. I guess we'll have to go with the plan Beatrice and I came up with on the island."

"All right then, since you're such a genius planner," said Catherine, "tell us your plan."

Mary put her soup plate in the middle of the table. "Imagine this is the island. And this spoon is the causeway. This butter knife—Justine, give me yours as well. These butter knives are the harbor. It's shallow, so to get Her Majesty to the island, they will send a barge out to her yacht, to bring her in. Our first line of defense is the beacon—I don't have anything to represent that, so you'll just have to imagine it. Or wait, I'll put this piece of bread on top of the fish bones. All right, that's the tower, except it really should be taller—you all saw it across the water when we were coming up from the train depot. St. Michael's Mount has a beacon at the top of the tower that was once used to warn the inhabitants of Marazion when there were pirates in the cove. We're going to light the beacon and warn the Queen's yacht away from the island."

"How are we going to get into the castle?" asked Catherine.

"I'm going to pick the lock," said Diana. "That should be obvious. Mary doesn't even need to say it."

"Right," said Mary, annoyed at Diana, although she was of course correct. "There are three doors: the castle, the chapel, and the tower. All the locks look as though they date from the medieval era."

"Easy peasy," said Diana.

"We will climb up the tower," said Beatrice. "The housekeeper, Mrs. Russell, described a narrow staircase leading to the top. There, we will light a fire with rags soaked in turpentine. Perhaps some of you can come with me to the general store? I will need help carrying all the things we must purchase. I estimate that we will need a gallon of turpentine—it will be difficult to keep a fire burning in the storm that is coming tonight."

"There is one additional complication," said Mary. "No one will be allowed to cross the causeway tomorrow, so we have to cross at the next low tide, which is at eight o'clock tonight."

"Mary, I told you it is dangerous," said Beatrice. "How can we cross the causeway in the dark? We could miss our footing and be swept out to sea!"

"We'll have to carry lanterns," said Catherine.

"No lanterns," said Mary. "Someone might see us. But it's a full moon tonight—we should be able to see our way. At least, I hope we'll be able to. Anyway, we don't have much of a choice. We don't have a boat, do we? We could hire one, but none of us knows how to sail. And I don't think any of the local fishermen would be willing to carry five women over to St. Michael's Mount after dark! Anyway, we'll need to be there before low tide tomorrow morning to implement the second part of our plan. Our second line of defense is the spoon—I mean the causeway. Queen Tera and whoever is with her—I assume Margaret Trelawny and Mrs. Raymond, although they may have Alice with them as well—will need to cross the causeway at low tide, which begins at eight thirty a.m. They will probably make themselves invisible so they won't be seen crossing. On the island, there is a stone wall that separates the village from the castle grounds. Cat, give me your butter knife. That's the stone wall although it's more curved. In order to get to the castle, you have to pass through that wall. Just where the causeway touches the land, where the spoon touches the soup bowl, there is an arched gateway in the wall that leads to the path up the hillside. I'll use more bread for that. They'll have to pass under that arch unless they want to go to the other side of the village, where there is another opening—but that one leads up through forest. I think they'll choose the easier route. Before they can cross to the island, we'll put fishing line across the gateway, with a bell attached. When they walk into the fishing line, the bell will ring. We'll be hiding behind the wall, and we'll know they're there, even if we can't see them. Then, we can spring out and spray Beatrice's pepper solution into the air above the fishing line. We don't have paprika, but she says she can make it with ordinary pepper, although it won't be as strong. Hopefully, it will disrupt their concentration long enough for the illusion to dissipate, and we'll be able to see them. If we can see them, we can wound Tera in some way before she fires off any of her lightning bolts, which will at least give us a chance. I wish we knew of some way to disrupt the mesmerical waves, but we still have not heard from Ayesha. No telegram again today—I asked Mrs. Davies and she even checked at the telegraph office for me. Nothing."

"That sounds awfully complicated," said Catherine. "Are you sure this is a good plan, rather than simply a plan? It sounds like the sort of convoluted plan that could work in theory, but is unlikely to in practice."

"Catherine," said Beatrice suddenly, "When you said the boathouse contained what you would expect to find—did you mean a boat? Was there a boat in the boathouse?"

"Of course there was a boat," said Catherine. "What else would you expect to find?"

"And was it in good repair? Did it seem seaworthy? After all, Mrs. Polgarth said Miss Trelawny had not used it in a while."

"How should I know?" said Catherine. "We didn't go in, just looked through the window. Anyway, I don't know anything about boats. I would have no idea if it was seaworthy or not."

"Don't look at me," said Diana. "I don't know anything about boats either. Here are the fools!"

Wenna, the waitress, took the empty plates. Another waitress, older and stouter, set the quince fools, in their individual cups, before each of them. Diana immediately appropriated Beatrice's.

After Mary had thanked the waitresses and Beatrice had asked for another cup of tea, Mary said, "I think I know what Beatrice is getting at. If they have a boat, they don't need to go over the causeway. They can sail to the island anytime they wish. Well, so much for stopping them at the causeway, then! We'll have to retreat to our third line of defense in the chapel."

"What chapel?" asked Catherine. She spooned all the quince out of her fool and into one of Diana's, then started eating the custard.

"There is a chapel attached to the castle," said Beatrice. "It's a place for contemplation and prayer. The Queen will have a meal with the housekeeper, Mrs. Russell. Then, she will retire to the chapel to pray. It is the one time during her visit that she will be entirely alone. We believe they will be waiting for her there."

"It would be the logical place to abduct her," said Mary. "But I wish there was a way we could fight them before they could get so close to the castle itself, and to the Queen! I don't want to wait that long."

"Could we destroy Miss Trelawny's boat?" asked Justine. "We still have an hour until sunset. I could go into the boathouse and break it apart with my hands. If they are planning on sailing to the island tomorrow, they will find the boat in fragments."

"Oh," said Mary. "That's an excellent idea." Why had she not thought of it herself? She should have thought of it. She was the planner, wasn't she? "All right, Catherine can show you where the boathouse is located. You'd better start soon, though. You don't want to get lost on the cliffs in the dark. If they can't use the boat, they'll have to go over the causeway, and we'll be waiting for them. Cat, I'm sorry it's not a better plan, but it's all I could come up with. Look, it's already six o'clock. I think you'd better get to the boathouse with Justine, and we'd better go shopping for the material we need.

"Wait," said Catherine. "What is our third line of defense? You said there was a third line. What are we supposed to do in the chapel?"

"Well, to be honest, we hadn't quite worked that out," said Mary. "Some of us will have to hide in the chapel, of course. And then——we protect the Queen anyway we can? You and I will have our pistols, Diana will have her knife, and of course Beatrice and Justine have their own defenses. But if the Queen is there, fighting in the chapel could put Her Majesty in danger."

"I have an idea," said Beatrice. "I was thinking of the myth of Perseus. When he went to fight Medusa, the goddess Athena gave him a certain weapon. . . . I do not know if my idea will work, but perhaps it's worth trying."

"What is it?" asked Diana. Her mouth was full of quince fool. Why couldn't she close her mouth when she chewed?

"Let me think about it a little more before I describe it to you," said Beatrice. "It may be a foolish idea after all."

"Anything is worth trying at this point, foolish or not," said Mary. "All right, let's reconvene in, what, an hour? Cat and Justine, you're going to destroy the boat. Beatrice, Diana, and I will go shopping for equipment and supplies. We'll meet again at seven o'clock in Justine and Beatrice's room, which doesn't have Diana's clothes scattered all over it. Then, we'll have an hour to get to the causeway."

> DIANA: It had Catherine's clothes all over it as well. She's as messy as I am, so I don't know why you're always complaining about me.
>
> CATHERINE: Pumas don't fold their clothes.
>
> DIANA: Pumas this, pumas that! I think you're using being a puma to avoid all the rules the rest of us have to follow. Anyway, I bet you're making half of this puma stuff up.

CATHERINE: What do you know about pumas, monkey girl?

JUSTINE: Catherine, I must admit, Diana does have a point. You mention being a puma when you wish to avoid some sort of obligation or responsibility.

CATHERINE: You realize that to a puma, you're all just meat?

"What do you mean the boat wasn't there?" said Mary an hour later, when they were all sitting in Justine and Beatrice's room.

"I mean it wasn't in the boathouse," said Catherine. "They knew we were there today, searching for the keep. They must have anticipated that we would come back to stop them somehow. The keep was there, by the way—a large, square tower. Diana and I couldn't possibly have missed it this morning if Queen Tera hadn't been messing with our heads. Justine broke the lock on the front door of the keep—since they already know about us, I thought we might as well. We went inside, but we couldn't find anything. We looked all over for Alice and Mr. Holmes, but everyone was gone. Once I thought we heard a cry of some sort, but it was just a big black cat. It was creepy in there, with all those Egyptian artifacts!"

"If they know we're trying to stop them, the logical thing for them to do is sail to the island tonight and stay hidden somewhere until daybreak," said Mary. "Well, there goes our second line of defense! I guess there's no reason for us to guard the causeway. We should focus on the beacon and chapel. Beatrice found everything she needed."

"Rags," said Beatrice, holding up a large bundle. "A gallon of camphine, which will burn hotter and brighter than turpentine.

Pepper, alcohol, and two atomizers, just like the ones we used in Budapest. And look . . ." She held up a silver hand mirror. "We purchased it from a shop of old furniture and bibelots on Turnpike Road. I'm afraid Mary had to pay a rather high price since it's an antique. I cannot guarantee it will work, but Tera's weapon is light—therefore, we will attempt to deflect it, or reflect it back at her. Like Perseus with his shield. And we bought five rucksacks, such as scouts use for hiking and camping, to carry it all."

Catherine looked at the pile of equipment on the floor dubiously. "These aren't particularly powerful weapons to use against Queen Tera and Mrs. Raymond. Even with our pistols, we're inadequately armed."

"Well, they're what we have," said Mary, frustrated. She agreed with Catherine, but did not want to say so. It would not help to carp and criticize. "We will simply have to do the best we can. Do you want to save the Queen or not?"

Catherine did not look particularly satisfied with that answer. "Of course, but I would rather not be electrocuted by a two-thousand-year-old mummy in the process! All right, how do we carry all this stuff? Will it fit in the rucksacks? Also, we need different clothes. I don't know about you, but I'm not fighting Tera in an afternoon frock."

Half an hour later, the five of them stood on the rocky shore below Marazion, dressed in clothes borrowed from Diana's friends the ostlers, with rucksacks on their backs. Luckily, some of the boys were rather big, although Justine's ankles showed beneath too-short trousers. Mary stared at the causeway. In the light of the full moon, it shone like a silver ribbon across the black water. "Come on," she said. "Let's do what we have to do."

As she stepped on the wet, moonlit stones, she offered up a small prayer: *Dear Lord, let me not drown tonight. If I have to die, let it be tomorrow, on dry land. Amen.*

# CHAPTER XV

# *Abduction at St. Michael's Mount*

B y the time the sky began to lighten, Mary was stiff and cold
and very, very cross. They had crossed the causeway without mishap the night before, although Justine had twisted
her ankle as they had climbed from the village to the bottom of
the path that led up the hill. Even here, the way was treacherous,
filled with stones that could trip you and send you tumbling. Mary
wondered once again how the Queen would make it all the way up
to the castle, even if she was carried. Well, hopefully she would
never set foot on St. Michael's Mount!

Justine had insisted that she would be fine, and Beatrice had
felt her ankle in the darkness to make sure it was not broken. The
logical place for them to wait out the night had been a stone dairy
at the bottom of the path. Luckily, all the cows were out on the
hillside—they would not come in until morning for milking.
There was enough room in it for the five of them to sleep on a
pile of fresh hay, although only four were in the dairy at present.
Diana was asleep, leaning against Justine. Catherine was curled up
in one corner, exactly like a cat. Only Beatrice was not there. She
was out in the garden, sitting somewhere among the plants. She
did not want to poison the air inside the building.

Mary had slept only fitfully, leaning against her rucksack,
which contained her pistol, a bottle of pepper spray, the silver
mirror, and a bunch of rags. She simply could not make herself

sleep anymore. She was too cold and, she had to admit, too worried about what that day would bring. Would they be able to save the Queen? Would they be alive at the end of it, or small white piles of ash? She did not want to think of that possibility. Neither did she want to stay here, staring into the darkness with nothing to do! Quietly, so as not to wake the others, she got up and went out into the cold morning. The sun would be rising soon, although the sky was so cloudy you could only tell because it was a lighter shade of gray. Rosy-fingered dawn indeed! This dawn was wearing gray gloves. It was just light enough for Mary to find her way around without stumbling over anything. She did not want to twist her ankle as well.

She found Beatrice sitting in a flower bed beneath one of the rocky cliffs, where she could be seen from the castle only by someone looking down directly from the south terrace. When she saw Mary, the Poisonous Girl smiled. She looked more content than she had for a long time.

"Good morning," she said as Mary walked up to her.

"Is it?" said Mary. "I mean, I suppose it is. I suppose all mornings are good, in a sense. The world wakes up again, and no matter what else is happening, the birds are singing, the trees are growing. . . . This castle has been here for hundreds of years, this island for thousands. Or do I mean hundreds of thousands? Anyway, I suppose in that long history, our actions mean very little."

"You are philosophical this morning," said Beatrice. "What has caused this mood?"

"I don't know," said Mary. "Perhaps the thought that we might die today? We've always had help before—from Mr. Holmes and Dr. Watson, from Irene Norton and Mina Murray and Count Dracula. We've never been on our own, just the five of us. And we've never been up against anyone as strong as Queen Tera."

"That is true," said Beatrice.

"Do you believe our souls go to Heaven after we die?"

"I am a good Catholic," said Beatrice. "But somehow, I have always though that my soul would return to the Earth and come up as some sort of plant—a flower, a tree. Perhaps I do not have a soul as others do. I would like to sink down into the dark soil and come up again each spring. That would be Heaven enough for me."

Mary looked at her doubtfully. "If you say so. Personally, I would rather not die, at least not yet. But if I had to die, I would like to go someplace where I could see all the people I care about."

"Are you thinking of Mr. Holmes?" asked Beatrice.

"What? No—I mean, I don't know. I was thinking of you and Cat and Justine, and, yes, Diana. Mrs. Poole, of course. Alice, Mina, Irene . . . so many people. And of course Mr. Holmes and Dr. Watson."

"Mary, it is sometimes permissible to lie to others, but it is never wise to lie to oneself." Beatrice plucked a leaf of some sort and began to chew on it. That was probably her idea of breakfast!

"What do you mean? I'm not lying to myself! Anyway, what about you and Clarence?"

Beatrice looked up at her, startled. "But I'm not lying to myself about the fact that I am poisonous. Do I feel love for him? Yes, I cannot deny it. Perhaps if I loved him less, I would try to give him what he wants—my companionship. What you would call a relationship. Then he would become poisonous, as I am. Would I want to place on him a burden I have borne all my life? Could I do that to a man I love? And imagine, Mary, if we had children. They would be poisonous as well. I could not birth more creatures such as myself. I am not my father—I will not create a race of monsters."

"You've really thought this through," said Mary, feeling a pang in her chest—pity for both Beatrice and herself. The Poisonous Girl looked so sad! Mary wanted to put her arms around Beatrice and comfort her. But that was the whole problem, wasn't it? No ordinary human being would ever be able to comfort Beatrice in that way. Justine could breathe her poison, Count Dracula could heal from her burns . . . but the man she loved was denied to her. Was that Mary's situation as well? Of course, what she felt for Mr. Holmes was different—compounded of regard for his intellect, respect for the work he did. . . . No. Beatrice was right, she needed to stop lying to herself. Regard and respect were the wrong words altogether.

"I've had to think it through, since he will not. Clarence believes we shall be together someday, and I cannot convince him otherwise. Sometimes, I do not even wish to try. Look, dew on the acanthus leaves." Beatrice rubbed the dew on her hands and then rubbed her hands against her face. "It is good for the complexion."

"I'll stick with cold cream and Pear's soap, thank you very much," said Mary. "We should probably get back to the others."

Beatrice stood up and drew on her gloves, then offered Mary a hand. Mary took it and pulled herself up. The bottom of her trousers, where she had been sitting, was damp.

"Forgive me, Mary, I do not mean to pry into your affairs, but you should tell Mr. Holmes how you feel—that you care for him."

"What if I'm not sure how I feel about him?"

"I think you are sure—you simply do not want to admit it to yourself. Listen! I hear a lark, high up in the heavens. Is its song not beautiful? I wonder what it is doing here. They usually stay inland and do not venture over water."

"Yes, very nice," said Mary. A lark was some sort of bird, wasn't it? Someone had written a poem about a lark—something something blithe spirit, bird thou never wert, except that a lark was in fact a bird, as far as she could remember. She herself was more familiar with pigeons and sparrows. She felt a raindrop on her face, and then another. The lark continued making lark noises.

When they reached the dairy, Catherine and Justine were awake.
Diana was still asleep, with her head on Mary's rucksack.

"Let sleeping Dianas lie!" said Mary and Catherine in unison.
Mary smiled. Well, if she was going to die today, at least it would
be among friends.

They ate a breakfast of hard ginger biscuits called fairings that
they had bought at the general store. Mary wished very much for
some tea, or even a little milk, to wash the biscuits down with,
but this morning, at least, they must do without.

"Let's go over the plans again," said Catherine. "When we get
to the chapel, Beatrice and Diana will climb up the tower. The
rest of us will hide in the family pews. And then we wait. As soon
as Beatrice sees the Queen's yacht approach the harbor and the
barge set out to meet it, she will light the beacon. Hopefully someone in the yacht will understand that it's a warning and start to
withdraw. If it does not and the Queen steps onto the barge, Diana
will run down and tell us. At that point, it will be our task to
capture Miss Trelawny, Mrs. Raymond, and Queen Tera as soon
as they enter the chapel, before they can get to the Queen." She
turned to Mary. "Why can't we just capture them now and avoid
all this fuss? I know what their boat looks like. I can probably spot
it in the harbor."

"First of all, I doubt that," said Mary. "You couldn't even
describe it when I asked. And second of all, they're probably
no longer on it. They're probably hidden in one of the village
houses or up at the castle. Remember they can make themselves
invisible—there's no reason for them to stay out all night in this
weather when they can find more comfortable accommodations.
I bet they're somewhere much nicer than a cow house! They are
on this island, and we have no idea where. Our best opportunity
will be right here in the chapel. They will need to come here to
capture the Queen, so as soon as we see them, we'll do our best to

capture them instead! And after we've saved Her Majesty, we will make them tell us where they've hidden Alice and Mr. Holmes. They weren't in the keep, so where are they?"

"I hope they're still alive!" said Catherine. "And that Alice is still on our side. She could be helping them, you know."

"Of course they are still alive!" said Justine, as sharply as Justine ever said anything. "And I do not believe for one moment that Alice would betray us."

Mary had been about to say the same thing, in the same tone. Why exactly did Catherine need to bring up such things just now? This was not a time to be pessimistic. Of course Alice and Mr. Holmes were still alive. They had to be. And she had complete— well, almost complete—faith in Alice.

ALICE: Almost complete?

MARY: After all, she was your mother.

Through the dairy window, Mary could see that it was beginning to rain more heavily. She looked at her wristwatch. "It's half past seven—the sun should just be rising soon. We have to leave— the cows will come to be milked, and we want to be hidden in the chapel by the time the household is awake. I'm sure the kitchen staff is awake already, but I don't want to run into any footmen or, worse, Mrs. Russell. Come on, help me shake Diana! For all we talk about letting her lie, she's almost impossible to wake up in the mornings."

DIANA: So you really do say that about letting me
lie—and sometimes you do it! I thought it was
some sort of joke. It's a way of keeping me out
of things, isn't it? If I'm asleep, you can leave me
behind whenever you want to. How convenient

for you! Why do you even keep me around, if you
don't want me to participate? From now on you
can open all the locked doors, and climb all the
brick walls, and save all the Lucindas yourselves!

CATHERINE: Well, it sort of is a joke. Diana—Di,
come back here. I think she's genuinely hurt. Di,
I'm sorry. Oh, for goodness' sake, I didn't mean to
hurt your feelings. . . .

Getting into the castle was not difficult. Diana was able to pick
the lock of the forbidding front door, made of dark wood bound
with iron, and a second door that led to a terrace surrounded by a
crenellated stone wall, "easy peasy." From there, Beatrice looked
back toward the mainland. The sky was growing brighter—she
could see the small white houses of Marazion and whitecaps on
the sea where they had crossed over the causeway last night. Now,
it was underwater.

"Come on," said Mary. "The chapel is over there. We need to
hide before anyone sees us."

As far as Beatrice knew, no one had seen them. Once, Catherine
told them to hide in the trees beside the path. A minute later two men
had passed, bringing a large chair down from the castle. Presumably
the chair that the Queen would be carried up in? But Catherine listened carefully before they had opened any doors, to make certain
there was no one about. *So far, so good,* Beatrice thought. It was a
useful English phrase that Mary had taught her.

Once they were in the chapel, Diana picked the lock of the
small door that led up to the bell tower. Beatrice had to stoop to
pass through the doorway. Evidently, the monks that had built
it had been shorter than her. Then she turned and said to Mary,
"Good luck, and I hope we will be able to tell you that our mission

succeeded." The stairs inside the tower were narrow, and the ceiling was so low that she had to keep stooping all the way up. Lugging a metal container of camphine and two rucksacks filled with rags to the top of the tower was more difficult than she had anticipated. She had to keep stopping and resting on the steps.

"Why do we need this again?" asked Diana.

"To light the beacon fire," said Beatrice. "You are so very good with fires. Remember how you rescued Lucinda from the Krankenhaus all by yourself?"

"Of course I do." For a moment, Diana looked like a hen that had laid an egg and was very proud of itself indeed. "All right, I'll carry this metal thing for a while. Why did they have to make it out of metal, anyway?"

"Because camphine is highly flammable," said Beatrice. "It will make bright, strong flames." At least, she hoped it would. Even within the stone walls of the tower, she could hear the wind rising. She wondered how hard the rain was coming down.

They passed a wooden platform and the chapel bells. She hoped no one would try to ring them while she and Diana were in the tower—the noise would be deafening. Ah, there it was, the trapdoor that must lead to the turreted top of the tower. Finally! She raised the trapdoor and looked about her.

Yes, the wind was rising, and darker gray clouds were rolling in from the east. Rain fell fitfully. She closed the trapdoor again.

"We must wait here on the platform, beside the bells," she said. "It is too wet outside—we do not want our rags to become damp. We must keep them as dry as possible before we attempt to light the fire." She looked at her lapel watch. Several more hours until the Queen's yacht would arrive in the harbor. At least the slats that let out the ringing of the bells let in plenty of air. There was no danger of her poison building up.

"I hate waiting," said Diana.

"But Mary told me that you had invented a most interesting game. I am thinking of something. I bet you cannot guess what I am thinking about." She sat on the platform—it was ancient, but seemed sound enough to hold her weight.

Diana sat down on one of the steps and looked at Beatrice, eyes narrowed, as though trying to guess what she was thinking simply from the expression on her face. "Is it bigger than an elephant?"

CATHERINE: Diana, I'll play that game with you, the one where you guess what I'm thinking. I'll play it as long as you want. Are you seriously not talking to me?

DIANA: Go to hell. And I mean all of you.

If you have to hide in an ancient stone chapel for several hours, waiting to see if you will need to rescue the Queen of England, there are no better companions to wait with than Justine Frankenstein and Catherine Moreau. At least that was what Mary thought as they crouched in one of the pews, the one farthest from the door. It was high enough to hide them completely from anyone coming into the chapel. Justine had found a Bible that someone had left on one of the cushions and was silently reading something devotional. When they had first hidden, Catherine had taken out a piece of string and tied the ends together. Then she had proceeded to teach Mary a particularly complicated version of Cat's Cradle. "I figured we would need something to do while we were waiting," she said. "I learned this from Doris and Edith, the Twisting Jellicoe Twins, who made it up when they were children. We have at least two hours to wait. Let's see if we can make up new variations."

Every once in a while Justine would read from the Bible to them, quietly so it would not echo around the chapel. " 'To every thing there is a season,'" she read, "'and a time to every purpose under the heaven. A time to be born, a time to die; a time to plant, and a time to pluck up that which is planted; a time to kill, and a time to heal; a time to break down, and a time to build up; a time to weep, and a time to laugh; a time to mourn, and a time to dance; a time to cast away stones, and a time to gather stones together'. . . . I think that is the most beautiful verse in Ecclesiastes."

"Also, a time to fight evil Egyptian queens," said Mary. "Which should be in about"—she looked at her wristwatch—"an hour."

Just then she heard a grating sound. It was the chapel door opening—not the large one they had come through, but the smaller door close to the altar. Queen Victoria's yacht would not arrive for another hour. Had it possibly arrived early? Could the Queen already be here? Unlikely. As far as she knew, queens operated according to regular schedules that were published in the *Royal Court Circular* and reprinted in the *Daily Telegraph* as well as other papers of general interest. It must be one of the castle staff coming into the chapel to pray. That seemed the most likely explanation. They were well hidden, and none of the staff members would use the family pews. As long as they were quiet, they should remain undiscovered.

But it was not just one person. She heard several sets of footsteps. She looked at Catherine and Justine—it was clear that they had heard the same thing as well. Justine looked alarmed, Catherine looked resolute

As though in a dance to which they all knew the steps, Justine put down her Bible, Catherine put down her string, and all three of them crouched farther down in the pew. Catherine drew her pistol out of the rucksack on the bench. Taking that as a cue, Mary drew her pistol as well.

The footsteps continued down the nave. There was another sound, as of something being dragged over the stone floor.

Catherine held up three fingers. Whoever they were, there

were three of them. Mary's revolver was a reassuring weight in her hand. With it, she had shot Beast Men and vampires. She hoped it would serve her as well today. Justine looked at them both, alert but calm. Thank goodness for Catherine and Justine! She could not have asked for better companions.

MARY: And I still can't.

The footsteps continued all the way down the nave, toward the back of the chapel. There were some sounds that Mary could not make out, then a door opening. Mary heard what sounded like speech, but it was so muffled and distant that she could not distinguish any words.

Catherine held up a hand, as though to signal *Wait*. Whatever was happening, it was not over yet. A door closed. The footsteps retreated back up the nave, to the chapel door through which they had entered. Then the chapel door clanged shut.

The three of them looked at one another. "Come on," said Mary. "Let's go see what that was all about."

She crept out of the pew first, pistol in hand. The dragging noises had gone down the aisle toward the back of the chapel. The only thing there, as far as she knew, was the organ, behind an ornate wooden wall that separated the organ from the rest of the chapel. There was a door in the wall, but Mrs. Russell had said it was only used by the organ player to access the instrument, and provided just enough room to play. Why would anyone want to drag something to the organ? "Catherine," she said. "What did you hear? Your ears are better than mine."

Catherine was standing at the other end of the wooden wall. "I heard this door open and close," she said. Ah, there was another door, hidden in the ornamental woodwork! Mrs. Russell had not mentioned that one on the tour. Carefully, holding her pistol in her right hand, Catherine opened the door with her left. When she saw what was beyond, she opened it farther to show Mary and Justine. It was a long, narrow hall, obviously a passageway that led to the service areas of the castle. On the floor, close to the doorway, lay the bodies of three women. Two were in maids' uniforms, one in the black dress with white collar and cuffs of a housekeeper in her most formal attire.

"Mrs. Russell!" said Mary. "That's the housekeeper Beatrice and I met yesterday, the one who is supposed to serve elevenses to Her Majesty. The others must be parlor maids. Are they . . ."

Justine knelt down and put her hand on their throats. "They are breathing, but not deeply. I believe they are in some sort of mesmeric trance. Shall I attempt—"

"Yes," said Mary. "We must try to wake them up."

However, as much as they shook the parlor maids and housekeeper, none of the three would awaken. Mary even slapped Mrs. Russell on the cheeks, and Mrs. Russell, if you ever read this, she apologizes for having taken such a liberty. But to no avail. The three remained unconscious.

"Well, at least now we know how to identify Queen Tera and the others," said Mary. "I'm guessing they brought the housekeeper and parlor maids here so they could impersonate them. Which means they will try to abduct the Queen not in the chapel, but in the blue drawing room, where Mrs. Russell is supposed to serve tea to Her Majesty."

"Then we must confront them there," said Justine. "Mary, you must lead the way, since Catherine and I do not know where it is. Should we tell Beatrice what has happened and where we are going? But she is at the top of the tower, on the battlements. I do not think she would hear us from below."

"There's no time for one of us to climb up there," said Mary. "And it would not change what she and Diana have to do—either way, they have to warn off the Queen's yacht. I think we need to confront Queen Tera and her—what, henchwomen? Whatever we want to call them, we need to find and confront them *now*."

"And I suggest we change into their uniforms," said Catherine. "We would immediately be conspicuous in the castle dressed as we are. But if we're dressed as maids, there's at least a chance no one will look at our faces. No one looks at maids, not really. If we go into the castle, we should look as though we belong there."

As quickly as they could, they took the uniforms off the two maids, leaving them in their shifts. And then, while Mary felt a horrible sense of guilt—imagine if someone had done such a thing to Mrs. Poole!—they took off Mrs. Russell's black dress. Mary and Catherine attired themselves as the two maids, and Justine put on the housekeeper's dress, which was the longest. On her, it was both too large and not long enough. Again, Mrs. Russell, if there's any way we can recompense you, as well as Phyllis and Nora, for this indignity, we shall endeavor to do so.

> MRS. POOLE: I should hope so! While I know what
> you did was necessary under the circumstances, I
> cannot approve treating a woman like Mrs. Russell
> in such a fashion.

"Well," said Mary to Justine, "hopefully no one will look at your ankles!"

Using the silver mirror they had brought to fight Queen Tera, Mary and Catherine put on the parlor maids' caps, which took some tucking-up of hair. Luckily their aprons had functional rather than purely ornamental pockets. Mary put her .22 in one and the silver mirror in the other, with its handle sticking out. She saw Catherine putting her .32 in one of her apron pockets as well.

Justine pulled down her bodice, which was, like the rest of the dress, both too large and too short. When she raised her arms, there was a gap between her bodice and skirt. "I shall take the bottles of pepper spray," she said. "Mrs. Russell's dress has pockets hidden in the lining. How practical." She put a bottle of pepper spray in each.

Mary looked at all of them critically. "I think we'll do. Justine, your collar is sticking up. Here, let me smooth it down. Now you look perfectly respectable, except for your short hair. But there's nothing we can do about that."

"Why do maids' uniforms have to look so ridiculous?" asked Catherine. "Look at all these starched ruffles. Why can't maids wear whatever they want to?"

"You sound like Beatrice," said Mary. She looked at her wristwatch again. "Whatever you think of maids' uniforms, we don't have time to overthrow the social order today. The Queen's yacht will be drawing into the harbor in a quarter of an hour. Of course, the timing won't be exact, particularly if there's a storm. Beatrice should be lighting the beacon right about now. Come on! We need to get to the blue drawing room."

She led the way out of the chapel, through the door that Miss Trelawny, Mrs. Raymond, and Queen Tera had used. To their right across the terrace was the entrance to the vestibule that led to the blue drawing room. It was a good thing they had dressed in servants' clothing, because the servants were already starting to assemble on the terrace. The Queen would likely be brought up the way they had come that morning, through the front doors of the castle and directly to the north terrace, then into the blue drawing room—the St. Michael's Mount staff would try to make it as easy for her as possible. That was good—it meant the blue drawing room was the only place Queen Tera could abduct her now. Well, Mary was going to prevent that from happening!

A man who looked like a butler was bustling around the terrace, directing a small army of footmen. But as Catherine predicted, no one paid attention to them as they passed. The convenient thing about a uniform was that if you were wearing one, no one noticed the woman inside.

As Mary walked through the vestibule, she pulled her pistol out of her apron pocket. She saw Catherine do the same. Thank goodness all the servants seemed to be gathering outside on the terrace! Someone would surely have remarked on two maids carrying pistols.

She stepped through the arched doorway into the blue drawing room, pistol drawn, ready for whatever might happen—for a lightning bolt, even. The room was empty. Well, not empty—there were the Chippendale sofa on which the Queen would be sitting, the rest of the furnishings, the paintings and bibelots. But no one was there.

Where were Queen Tera, Mrs. Raymond, and Miss Trelawny? Had they made themselves invisible? But why? Surely the whole point was for them to look like the housekeeper and two housemaids so they could fool the household—and Her Majesty.

"What about that other room?" asked Catherine in a low voice, pointing at the door to the right of the fireplace.

Through that doorway was another small room, but Mrs. Russell had indicated that it was used primarily to store extra chairs for larger receptions. As quietly as she could, Mary crossed the blue drawing room, waving for Catherine and Justine to follow her. The door to the storage room was closed. Carefully, she turned the handle and opened it, entering the room pistol-first. It, too, was unoccupied, and filled only with chairs and a few small tables. It was painted the same delicate shade of Wedgwood blue as the drawing room.

"I have no idea," she said to Catherine and Justine. "I assumed they would be here. Why else would they have taken the housekeeper's and maids' uniforms? Could I have misunderstood their plans?" If only Sherlock were with them! He would be able to figure out this mystery, as he had figured out so many others. But he was not, so she would need to figure it out for herself. Somewhere in her chain of deduction, she must have made a mistake. . . .

Catherine put a hand on Mary's arm. Startled, she looked at the Puma Woman. Catherine did not often touch anyone. Now, she had a finger to her lips. *Be quiet,* she seemed to be saying. Then she put that finger to her ear, and then her nose. Finally, she pointed back toward the blue drawing room. Justine was listening intently. Could she hear something that Mary could not? No, now she heard it too—someone was in the blue drawing room.

Catherine walked quietly back to the doorway into the drawing room and stood listening. Mary waited for a moment, but the only sound was of footsteps. If Queen Tera was in there, she wanted to act, and quickly. She stepped past Catherine and stood in the doorway with her pistol in front of her, finger on the trigger.

There, in the middle of the blue drawing room, stood Mrs. Russell, supervising two parlor maids. They must have entered while Mary and the others were in the storage room. One of the parlor maids was dusting the ornaments on the mantel in a way that no competent parlor maid had ever dusted, without picking them up, simply moving the feather duster over them. In a moment, Mary was sure, one of the marble busts would crash to the floor. The other was plumping a pillow on the blue sofa, although it was not the sort of pillow that needed plumping, being filled, most likely, with horsehair. They looked like actresses playing at being parlor maids in a theatrical performance. But of course it was not Mrs. Russell, because she was lying unconscious in the hall, and they were not parlor maids. Which of them was Queen Tera? Which were Mrs. Raymond and Margaret Trelawny? And who was producing this illusion? Mary had no idea. Which of them should she shoot? She had to choose one, but she hesitated. At that moment, Mrs. Russell noticed her standing in the doorway.

She snarled and raised her left hand. It had seven fingers. Mary pulled the trigger and shot the housekeeper in the shoulder.

In the quiet drawing room, the sound of the shot was almost deafening. Mrs. Russell screamed and collapsed. But what hit the floor was not Mrs. Russell—it was the small figure of Queen Tera, dressed not in the housekeeper's black dress but in a white linen gown, on which a red stain was rapidly spreading. It matched the ruby scarab at her throat. And the two parlor maids were no longer maids, but Mrs. Raymond and Margaret Trelawny. Mrs. Raymond looked at Mary with astonishment and dismay. Miss Trelawny cried out and knelt beside the fallen figure of Tera, putting her hands on the Egyptian queen's shoulder to staunch the blood.

"Good shot," said Catherine. She and Justine had come through the doorway and were standing just behind Mary, to either side. "Now let's get those two."

From where she was kneeling on the floor, Miss Trelawny raised one hand, pointed at Mary, and said to Mrs. Raymond, "Kill her."

CATHERINE: That was an excellent shot, Mary.

MARY: It was a lucky shot. If I had shot Margaret
    Trelawny instead, Queen Tera would quickly have
    electrocuted us, and that would have been the end of
    the Athena Club. Or at least three of its members!

Beatrice checked her lapel watch. It was time. "Come," she said to Diana. "We must light the beacon fire."

"Were you thinking of Big Ben?" asked Diana.

"Yes," said Beatrice. It had in fact been Mary's wristwatch, but there was no more time to play Diana's game.

"Then why did you say it was smaller than an elephant?" asked Diana.

"Is Big Ben larger than an elephant? I meant only the clock face. You can carry the rags, and I shall carry the container. *Vieni, cara mia.*" Beatrice opened the trapdoor. The wind had picked up, and rain was coming down in a steady drizzle. Would they be able to light the fire? From the top of the tower, she was able to see the horizon on three sides. On the other, she could see the coast, with the houses of Marazion white against the gray hills. The ocean was gray, with white foam on the tops of the waves where they rushed in and crashed against the shore. And there—she could see the Queen's yacht, white against the gray water, getting closer to St. Michael's Mount. But it was still farther out than she had expected. The weather must have put it behind schedule. She should wait a little longer to light the beacon fire. Ten minutes should do it. She took off the silly waterproof coat that Mary had insisted she wear and laid it over the rucksacks filled with rags. They must be kept dry, at least. Then she pulled off her gloves and put them into her trouser pockets. She would need bare hands for what was to come.

"Are we just going to stand out here in the rain?" asked Diana.

"Yes," she replied, checking to make sure the matchbox was still in the pocket of her coat—what the English called a mackintosh, which she found difficult to pronounce.

"Oh. All right. Look, there's the keep. I can see it all the way from here. And there's the inn. I wonder what Mrs. Davies will make for dinner tonight? I told her Beef Wellington was my favorite, and she said she would try to make it just for me."

The yacht sailed closer, closer. . . .

Beatrice checked her watch again. It had a few water drops on it. Now was the time.

"Or sausages. She said she had some sausages from a pig that was killed in August, from a farm near Perranuthnoe."

Beatrice was about to tell Diana to be quiet and pull out the rags when she noticed that Diana *was* pulling out the rags, even as she was describing some sort of special Cornish sausage called, improbably, Hog's Pudding. Apparently, her obsession with their dinner menu did not preclude her from getting things done.

And then she heard, above the wind and rain and Diana's chatter, a grating noise. It was the trapdoor opening. She watched it rise an inch, two inches.

Someone had followed them—presumably, someone who was going to try and stop them from signaling the Queen. Unlike Mary and Catherine, she had no pistol, only her poison. Quickly, she moved to the trapdoor and stood with her hands outstretched, her fingers curved, ready to burn the face of whomever came through it.

"I'll slit his throat with my knife." Diana was standing next to her, knife out, also ready. Annoying as she could be, you could always count on her in a pinch.

The trapdoor continued to rise, revealing a man's head with dark eyes, two days' worth of beard, and dark, tousled hair under a checked cap.

"Oh, it's you," said Diana, lowering her knife. "It's only Isaac Mandelbaum," she said to Beatrice, apparently disgusted at not being able to stick her knife into anyone. "He was pretending to work for Moriarty, but really he's on our side."

Beatrice stepped back and lowered her hands. "Mary said you work for Mycroft Holmes."

Cautiously, as though afraid they might still attack him, Isaac climbed up the remaining steps and closed the trapdoor behind him. He had a leather satchel slung over one shoulder. When he saw the rags in the metal basin, he grinned. "I see that we had the same idea, more or less. I'm here to warn the Queen as well. It's a pleasure to meet you, Miss—"

"Rappaccini," she said. "We're going to light a beacon fire. What is your plan?"

"Signal flags," he said, pulling two sticks with pieces of cloth wrapped around their ends out of his satchel. "But I'm afraid the captain won't see them in this rain. I have two compatriots down by the dock who will attempt to warn the Queen if she comes ashore. We tried to warn her through more direct channels, but Moriarty's co-conspirators are still in positions of power around her. They do not yet know he is dead, and are continuing to implement his plans. We need to stop them as well, but the first step is making sure the Queen does not set foot on St. Michael's Mount. Perhaps we could work together? It would be a pleasure to work with such a charming collaborator."

"Are you going to flirt with Beatrice or light the fire?" asked Diana. She crossed her arms and glared at them.

"Hello, Miss Hyde," he said, grinning. "It's a pleasure to see you again, although we keep meeting under such inauspicious circumstances."

"I'll inauspicious you!" said Diana. "Who sent you? Was it that that big slug who stays in his fancy club instead of actually helping anybody? At least his brother gets out and does things!"

"All right, Mr. Mandelbaum," said Beatrice. *Per carità!* Could they not concentrate on the task at hand? "Take that container and douse the rags with the liquid inside. Be careful—it's camphine, and highly flammable. Don't get any on yourself. You would not want to go up in flames."

Isaac nodded, picked up the container, and unscrewed the cap. He poured the contents carefully but thoroughly over the rags. Beatrice put her hands up to her nose—the camphine smelled foul. The rags were wet—not soaked, but certainly not dry. Would they catch fire? She worried that she had waited too long.

Isaac stepped back and put the container down on the stones.

"You, too, Diana," said Beatrice. "Step back, and give me my mack—" The word stuck in her mouth. "My coat. You should have folded it neatly instead of tossing it down in that untidy fashion."

Diana made a rude gesture, but handed her the mackintosh. Beatrice took her matchbox out of the pocket, struck a match, and tossed it on the camphine-soaked rags. She need not have worried after all. The rags blazed up—the fire rose higher and higher, white and hot. Hastily, she stepped back, all the way to the battlements.

On the other side of the tower, Isaac had unfurled his flags. She was startled to see him step closer to the fire and wave his flags through the flames. In a moment, the ends of both flags were on fire! Then he turned and walked to a corner of the tower facing the shore—and the Queen's yacht. He raised both flags and began moving them from one position to another, sending a message: *Danger? Retreat?* She had no idea what he was signaling.

What would it look like, from the yacht below? The sky had grown darker. Against it, the beacon would flame brightly, and beside it, the fiery flags would dance the message that there was danger here: *retreat, retreat, retreat* they seemed to say.

After repeating the same motions several times, Isaac turned and threw the flags into the fire—they were almost completely burned to the sticks. In another moment, the sticks themselves would have been consumed.

He looked at her, firelight dancing over his face, which was covered with sweat from the heat of the flags, despite the drizzling rain. "We've done what we can do." He was not grinning now. His dark eyes were serious, and the set of his jaws was grim. Beatrice joined him at the battlements that faced the shore. She could feel the heat of the fire on her back.

Had they done enough? They stood together at the top of the tower, looking down at the yacht, which continued its steady movement toward the harbor. In one corner of the tower, Diana paced back and forth. "It didn't work," she said.

For an agonizing minute, and then another, nothing happened. Then, the yacht began to turn. Slowly, it turned away from the entrance to the harbor, away from St. Michael's Mount, away from danger—toward the safety of the great gray sea.

"*Grazie a Dio,*" said Beatrice.

"I'll go tell them," said Diana. "At least they won't have to fight Queen Tera in the chapel!" She opened the trapdoor and disappeared down it. Beatrice could hear her clattering down the stairs.

"We did it, Mr. Mandelbaum," she said.

"We did indeed, Miss Rappaccini," he replied, grinning and wiping sweat from his forehead with a damp handkerchief. "I understand Miss Jekyll is down below. Shall we go help her?"

Beatrice nodded. This day was not over yet, but at least they had done one thing right—they had saved the Queen.

> CATHERINE: You were heroic in the tower, Diana. It was you and Beatrice who saved Queen Victoria.
> Oh, come on, I said I was sorry. . . .

Mrs. Raymond pointed one finger at Mary. Lightning crackled from it, but reached only halfway across the distance between them before it sputtered and went out. She pointed her finger again, but with the speed of a puma, Catherine pulled the silver mirror out of Mary's left pocket, leaped forward, and held it in front of her. This time the lightning bolt was stronger. It hit the mirror squarely in the center. The mirror shattered, but the bolt ricocheted off and struck an elaborately gilded eighteenth-century clock on a marble side table. Mary cried out. There was blood on her hands—some pieces of the mirror had hit her.

"Use your gun, Helen!" shouted Margaret Trelawny. "I can't reach mine." She was still kneeling by Tera, who appeared to be unconscious, with both hands on the wounded shoulder of the Egyptian queen.

Justine pulled the bottles of pepper spray out of her pockets.

She held them in front of her and advanced toward Mrs. Raymond. Catherine pulled out her pistol. If she could shoot Mrs. Raymond, this fight would be over, more easily than they had anticipated. Unlike Mary, she would not bother trying for the shoulder. If she killed Mrs. Raymond, so be it.

For a moment, Mrs. Raymond simply looked at them— Catherine advancing with the mirror in one hand and a pistol in the other, Justine with the bottles of pepper spray. Then she raised both her arms. Suddenly, a gray fog rose from the floor. It roiled around their legs, then waist high, then at the height of Catherine's chest. In a moment, she could not see anything.

"Justine!" she called. "Where are you?"

"I am here." That was Justine's voice. And Catherine could smell her—she smelled like lavender, probably from Mrs. Russell's dress. She reached out—her hands found long, slender ones. Yes, this was Justine, although Catherine could barely see her face in the fog.

"Where is Mary?" she asked.

"I do not know." Justine looked frantically around, but there was no around to look at—only fog.

Gray fog everywhere. Catherine took an experimental step to see if she could feel anything in her immediate vicinity and stumbled over a Chippendale side chair with blue upholstery. So at least they were still in the blue drawing room!

"What now?" she asked Justine.

"I think it's starting to dissipate," said the Giantess from her vantage point. Yes, the fog around Catherine's head looked lighter, although her body was still lost in it. But in a few moments, that too started to blow off, until the room was at it had been. The fog was gone. So were Queen Tera, Margaret Trelawny, Mrs. Raymond, and Mary Jekyll.

DIANA: I can't believe you let them take my sister.

CATHERINE: Well, we certainly didn't mean to! It just happened.

DIANA: I was talking to Justine, not you. I'm never talking to you again.

Alice put her finger up to the keyhole. She concentrated as hard as she could. A small bolt of lightning leaped out of her finger and into the lock. She pulled at the door. It did not open.

"I'm not strong enough," she said.

"But you're getting stronger," said Sherlock Holmes, who was sitting on the steps just below her. "Look at how far you've come since last night. Apparently, those electrical impulses are a physical phenomenon controlled by your brain. The more you practice creating them, the easier it will become. There's no reason you cannot do what Tera can, with enough time and practice.

"But there isn't enough time." Discouraged, she sat down on the step beside him. "They're kidnapping the Queen *today*, and we're stuck in here. We're never going to get out of here or see our friends again."

"We most certainly will," he said. "Don't you trust me, Alice?"

She looked at him doubtfully. "Well, you are Sherlock Holmes."

He threw back his head and laughed. He must be feeling better—this was the strongest she had seen him since she had found him drugged at the house in Soho. "Yes, you're right. I am, aren't I? Mr. Sherlock Holmes, the great detective, immortalized by Dr. Watson in *The Strand*, a shilling an issue, promises you that we will get out of here. And I promise as well. Come, let's have something to eat, and then get some rest. You need to build up your strength. I believe in you, and I know that you or I, or the both of us, will find a way out of this dungeon."

Alice nodded and squeezed his hand. Ever since she had first met him, she had been afraid of Mr. Holmes. Now, she wondered why. Once you got to know him, he was not so very fearsome after all.

ALICE: Well, he is still a little fearsome.

DIANA: Bollocks.

It was almost dark by the time Catherine, Beatrice, Justine, and Diana stepped off the small fishing boat piloted by Isaac Mandelbaum and his two compatriots, who had not given their names. They were both ordinary-looking young men who could have passed for bank clerks, but Catherine suspected that they belonged to an organization more secretive than even the Old Lady of Threadneedle Street, as the Bank of England was called by those who worked in her mysterious halls.

"We shouldn't have left the island without Mary," said Diana. She punched Catherine on the arm, but in such a dejected way that it barely hurt.

"Diana, Mary is not on the island," said Justine. "We searched everywhere."

Once they realized that Mary was gone, Catherine and Justine had made their way as quickly as possible out of the blue drawing room, hoping not to be noticed. Luckily, the terrace had been filled with scurrying maids and footmen, while the butler shouted orders. Everyone had been staring up at the tower and the flames that danced at its top. So Beatrice had lit the beacon! Had it worked? Had it driven the royal yacht safely away from St. Michael's Mount?

As soon as they entered the chapel again, Diana had greeted them with "Where have you been? We saved the Queen. What in the world have you been doing, and where is Mary?" Beatrice and Isaac Mandelbaum had appeared a moment later to explain the situation. Catherine had breathed a sigh of relief. They were still in trouble, a great deal of trouble, but at least they had done one thing right—they had indeed saved the Queen.

In the hallway behind the wooden wall that held the organ, Catherine and Justine had changed once again into their ostler's clothes, leaving Mrs. Russell's dress and the maid's uniform Catherine had been wearing folded neatly on the floor beside the sleeping servants. Even then, the parlor maids were starting to stir. They would awaken soon, and hopefully they would wake up Mrs. Russell. She was snoring slightly—Catherine thought that was a good sign.

Then, they had searched every inch of the island. Mary was not on it. Neither were Miss Trelawny, Mrs. Raymond, and Queen Tera.

"How do you *know* Mary's not on the island?" Diana asked now. Isaac Mandelbaum's boat was carrying them closer and closer to shore. "Maybe they made her invisible. Maybe they're all invisible and hiding out for a while."

"I think it is unlikely," said Beatrice. "From what Catherine told us, it sounds as though Queen Tera is seriously wounded. They will want to take her somewhere she can rest and heal. That is probably where they have taken Mary as well."

"Their most likely destination is the keep," said Justine. "That is where they are strongest and safest. If I were planning a defense, it is certainly where I would choose."

"Then we'll attack the keep," said Catherine. "Four of us against Margaret Trelawny, Mrs. Raymond, and a wounded Queen Tera, in a fortress designed to keep out invaders. Easy peasy, as Diana always says."

"Are you being ironic?" asked Justine.

"Of course I'm being ironic. We caught them by surprise today.

We're not going to catch them by surprise tomorrow. It looks as though Mrs. Raymond has been practicing throwing lightning bolts, although she's nowhere near as good as Queen Tera. How are we going to fight them? I have no idea." She sounded angry, which didn't help anything, she knew that. But she was deeply worried. If Mrs. Raymond or Margaret Trelawny hurt Mary, she would tear them limb from limb.

As they disembarked at one of the small natural harbors that appeared around Marazion at high tide, they all shook hands with Isaac except Diana, who was already halfway up the stone steps carved out of the cliff. He leaned down to kiss Beatrice's gloved hand. Catherine wondered what Clarence would think of that!

"I am only sorry that we cannot help you further," he said. "But our instructions were very clear—save the Queen, and then return immediately to London. There is still a great deal of work to do there—Moriarty's allies remain in positions of power. They must be our immediate priority until they no longer threaten to topple the government. But I shall let Mr. Holmes know of this situation and the continuing threat Queen Tera poses. She did not succeed today, but I am certain she will try again."

"That's all right," said Catherine. "We'll save Mary, and Alice, and Sherlock Holmes. Somehow." Even to herself, she did not sound confident.

They followed Diana up the steps to the top of the cliff and then down Turnpike Road to the inn. When Catherine stepped through the inn door and followed the smell of supper being served in the dining room, she saw Diana standing at one of the tables, with an enormous grin on her face.

"Look who I found," she said.

Seated at the table were Ayesha, Laura Jennings, and Lucinda Van Helsing.

# CHAPTER XVI

## The Battle of Kyllion Keep

Mary opened her eyes and immediately closed them again. Her head was throbbing

"Mary. Miss Jekyll."

She turned toward the voice instinctively—the voice in the world she most wanted to hear, which meant that it couldn't be real. It must be a hallucination.

"Mary, look at me. I need to determine whether you have a concussion."

She opened her eyes. There, above her, was the solemn, concerned, and, if she had to admit it, beloved face of Sherlock Holmes.

"Miss Mary." It was Alice, hovering anxiously at the periphery of her vision. Oh, thank goodness! She held out one hand toward Alice, who took it in both of hers.

"Alice!" she said. "Are you—I mean, can you talk to me now? Talk freely?"

"Yes, miss." Alice looked down at her anxiously. "You do know I was just pretending to be with Helen—with my mother, so I could help Mr. Holmes? I would never betray you or the Athena Club."

"Of course," said Mary. "But that doesn't matter now. Where are we? My head feels as though it's a bowling ball and someone has been using it to knock down pins."

She tried to sit up, but the room was spinning around her and she had to lie back down again.

"Don't try to get up, not yet," said Sherlock Holmes. "How many fingers am I holding up?" He held up three fingers on his other hand.

"Eight, like an octopus," she said.

He smiled. "I think you'll be fine. I'm going to get you some water. In a little while, you may be recovered enough to eat something."

"Where am I?" she asked. It was embarrassing talking to him while lying on the floor like this, but she did not have much choice.

"In the dungeon of Kyllion Keep," said Alice. "My mother and Margaret brought you last night. I don't know what happened, but Margaret is very angry. Did they kidnap Queen Victoria?"

"I don't think so," said Mary. She tried to remember what had happened. She had shot Queen Tera in the shoulder—she recalled that distinctly. Then a gray fog had filled the room so she could no longer see Tera or any of the others. The next thing she could recall was lying, tied up, on the bottom of a boat. It was obviously moving on the water, because she could hear the lapping of waves and its motion made her ill.

"I told you to kill her," Margaret Trelawny had been saying.

"I fully intend to," Mrs. Raymond had replied. "As soon as we find out who she's working for and what we're up against. At first I thought she and her friends were just a group of meddling girls, come to steal my daughter back to be their servant again. But they're obviously more than that. Who arranged to light the beacon fire? It was obviously lit to warn the Queen away from the island. Have allies of Moriarty's discovered what we've done? Are they trying to thwart us for reasons of their own? Or has someone in the government discovered our plans? There's more going on here than we thought. We have enemies, and I want to find out who they are. Once she tells us, I will gladly dispatch her myself."

So their plan had worked! From where she was lying on the

bottom of the boat, Mary could not see anything but the gray clouds overhead, so she raised herself up on one elbow. Yes, there was the tower of St. Michael's Mount, with the beacon fire on top, still flickering against the dark sky.

"I don't think so, missy," Mrs. Raymond had said in her nastiest voice. "I'll deal with you when I have the time. Until then, I want you to sleep. Close your eyes, like a good girl." The last thing Mary remembered was the sensation of her body slumping and hitting the wooden hull.

"I think we saved the Queen," she said to Alice. "That, at least, we got right. And Queen Tera is wounded, but I don't know how long that will last. I suspect she has the power to heal herself."

"If they had succeeded in kidnapping Her Majesty," said Holmes, "they would already have left for London. Instead, they are still here. We heard them this morning, moving about, through the door. We do not know what they will do now, or why they continue to keep us here. But I think we must try, once again, to get out."

"How?" asked Mary. "If we're in a dungeon, that is. I mean, if Diana were here, she would be able to do it. But I can't open locks the way she can."

"I don't suppose you happen to have a hairpin or anything else sharp about you?" asked Holmes. "I studied with one of the most notorious lockpicks in London. If I had the proper instruments . . . Here, drink this." He handed her water in a tin cup.

Did she? Last night her hair had been braided and pinned up. Today—Mary sat up, fighting the sense of nausea that swept over her, and drank a few sips of the water, then the whole cup. She had not realized how thirsty she was! Her braid swung down her back—no pins. She was still dressed in a parlor maid's outfit, but her cap and apron were gone. Of course, so was her pistol. Someone, probably Mrs. Raymond, had taken anything she could have used to attempt an escape. There were scratches over her hands and wrists. She remembered—a mirror had shattered, and she had held up her hands to ward off the pieces of flying glass.

"I washed your hands with some of our water," said Holmes. "I'm afraid we don't have any soap, but none of the wounds are serious. When you've recovered some of your strength, can you tell me what happened? It seems I have missed a great deal."

"Yes, of course." She nodded. "Could I have some more water? And perhaps something to eat." That might help settle her stomach.

"Why don't we all have breakfast?" he said. "Then you can tell us what has been going on in the world outside these stone walls. And then we can try once again to open the lock."

Open the lock how? Hadn't they already established that none of them had the proper tools? But Mary was too tired to inquire further. She merely nodded and took whatever Alice handed her. She began eating it mechanically. It was a piece of brown bread, spread with orange marmalade. The bread was dry and not particularly appetizing, but she devoured it nonetheless.

> MARY: Cat, I wish you would leave out the parts about me and Sherlock. They're—well, they're private.

> CATHERINE: But that's what our readers want to know most of all—did Mary and Sherlock Holmes, you know. I mean, I've had letters from American readers in particular asking about the two of you. Readers are curious.

> MARY: Well, that's just rude!

"Do not assume that yesterday's wound will seriously weaken Queen Tera," said Ayesha. "The priestesses of Isis were healers before they were anything else. She will not be able to heal herself completely overnight, unless she has more of the oil she used to kill Moriarty and the others—and good riddance to them, particularly Raymond and Seward! It was one of our most secret recipes, and has the ability to concentrate energic power. In that case, I cannot predict her strength. But even if she cannot fully heal, she will be stronger than you expect."

They were once again sitting in the dining room of the inn, but this time morning light streamed through the window. They had just finished breakfast, according to their various dietary requirements—and thank you, Mrs. Davies, for putting up with the idiosyncrasies of the Athena Club! Catherine looked with amusement at the President of the Alchemical Society. She was probably the most unusual sight the Marazion Inn had ever seen, with her ageless beauty, her hundred long, dark braids, and her eyes outlined with kohl. Even though she was sitting, you could tell that she was taller than most men.

"What do you think she intends to do?" asked Justine. Illogically, Catherine was pleased that Ayesha was not, at least, taller than Justine, although how that was relevant to anything she had no idea.

Ayesha frowned. "I believe that with Margaret Trelawny and Helen Raymond, she is attempting to re-create what she had at the temple of Isis—an inner circle of priestesses who were absolutely loyal to her. It was they who would have broken our vows and fought the soldiers of Octavian, they who prepared her body for interment and resurrection. Their first plan may have failed, but Tera will not stop attempting to create an empire to rival that of Rome."

"But why?" asked Justine. "Why does she wish to establish an empire in the modern world? Are the current empires, cruel and venal as they are, not enough?"

"Tera is two thousand years old," said Ayesha, "but she has not lived two thousand years. She remembers only a world of great empires. She was once queen of all Egypt, and I believe she longs for that power again. Before we engage her in battle, I shall attempt to reason with her. I shall explain to her the folly of this plan. But I fear that she will not listen. If she does not, you must be prepared to fight her as well as Margaret and Helen. You should expect them to fight fiercely on her behalf, with every weapon at their disposal, as her priestesses did at Philae."

"We can fight anything they have, except mesmerism," said Catherine. "How do we fight Tera's and Mrs. Raymond's illusions?"

"I shall try to take care of that," said Ayesha. "I want all of you to concentrate on Margaret Trelawny and Helen Raymond. Also, on finding Mary, Lydia Raymond, and Sherlock Holmes. Catherine, Justine, Beatrice, and Lucinda: you shall find and fight the two women. You each have powers that will help you defeat them. Laura and Diana: I want you to search the keep from top to bottom. Find Mary, Lydia, and Holmes, and get them out of there as quickly as possible."

"Why don't I get to fight?" asked Diana. "I have powers too!"

"Because your power is finding and opening," said Ayesha. "You always say you can find anything, do you not? And you can open all the doors, or so you have insisted. Laura has a pistol and will protect you."

"Oh. Right, then." Diana looked especially aware of her own importance.

"Should we try to conceal ourselves in some way?" asked Justine. "Perhaps circle and approach the keep from the back?"

Ayesha shook her head. "There is no point in concealment. They will know we are coming. Tera will be able to sense our presence—especially mine."

"Let's go," said Catherine. "The sun is up, it's not raining or fogging or whatever else the weather does here. . . . What are we waiting for?"

Ayesha smiled. "Very well, then. Let us go defeat Queen Tera—or convince her to surrender, if we can. I hope this will end peacefully, so there is no need to fight after all. But you should be prepared to do so."

MARY: Why do you think Ayesha helped us? I mean, I don't think she even particularly likes us, except for Beatrice.

BEATRICE: That is not true! She has said several times that she respects the Athena Club and its members.

MARY: Respect is not the same as like—it just means she doesn't blast us to bits when she sees us. But she didn't have to come all that way to help fight Queen Tera.

CATHERINE: She didn't come for us. She came for Tera. She came to see her old High Priestess, who was threatening to destroy the world. I wouldn't say that Ayesha is on our side, but she's not on the other side either. She's not our enemy.

MARY: Maybe. I haven't made up my mind about that yet. I think the evidence is inconclusive.

An hour later, Catherine and the others were standing in front of Kyllion Keep, which towered against the sky. The storm had passed. The sky was no longer a gray expanse. It was filled with clouds in long white furrows, and sunlight fell fitfully over the stones of the keep. The morning air was cold. Catherine, who was always cold in England except on the hottest summer days, shivered.

She looked at Ayesha, standing in the middle of the crescent they made: herself and Justine on one side, Beatrice and Lucinda on the other. Catherine was the only one with a pistol, but she was also prepared to fight with tooth and claw if necessary.

> DIANA: You don't have claws anymore. Moreau made
> sure of that.

> MARY: Now that was entirely uncalled for. You may
> be mad at Catherine, but there's no reason to be
> cruel.

> DIANA: Well, maybe we're even now.

Diana and Laura were somewhere on the other side of the keep. "Even a fortress has more than one door," Laura had said. "Let's go look for a back way in. I'm sure we'll find one if we look carefully."

Ayesha presented a formidable figure. Today, she was dressed in a long black coat over what appeared to be black bloomers. Her outfit had gold stars on it. It had taken a while for Catherine to realize they represented the constellations. Her black braids hung down her back, past her waist.

They had been standing there for several minutes. During those minutes, Ayesha had not said or done anything. She was just standing there. What was she waiting for?

A figure appeared at the window above the front entrance of the keep. It was Queen Tera, in a white robe like the one she had been wearing yesterday. There was no blood on her shoulder, and she did not appear to be wounded or weakened in any way.

She looked down at them and said something in a language Catherine did not understand.

"Yes, High Priestess," said Ayesha. "I too have survived into this new era. Let us speak the language of this country so the others may understand."

"It is an ugly language," said Tera. Her voice was harsh, her accent strange to Catherine's ears. "But it is good to see you, my daughter in Isis. I have been lonely among these infants, who have never seen Memphis, or Alexandria, or Rome. They imagine their empire is magnificent—this edifice of a day, this moth that flutters for an hour. It was built only a hundred years ago, but already it begins to crumble and crack. Have you come to join me in remaking the world? I will allow you to be my second in command, as Heduana was before she betrayed me. But you shall not betray me, will you, Princess of Meroë? You see, I remember you well, Ayesha. When I felt your presence outside these walls, I was pleased. And these others, no doubt they are your servants in this new world. How is it you have lived so long? You must have discovered some secret that even the priestesses of Isis did not know. You will share it with me, and I shall give you a portion of this world to rule for your own, as Alexander gave Egypt to Ptolemy. Would you like this wretched island of England? Or perhaps you would prefer a land with better weather?"

"Forgive me, mother in Isis," said Ayesha, "but I have not come to help you conquer an empire. I want no more empires. In my long life, I have seen for myself the misery they cause. After your death, Rome destroyed Egypt, as this British Empire destroyed my adopted homeland around the Zambesi. Already, as you say, the empires of this world are breaking apart. I look forward to a new day of science, when man may be ruled by rationality rather than fear and brute force. Will you not join me in creating such a world? As Queen, you were the one effective ruler of Egypt for a generation. As High Priestess, you taught us to heal, to harness the energic powers of the Earth. In this new world, you could become a teacher, a scientist, a voice for reason and order. Why do you now want to create an empire?"

Tera looked down at them. Her ruby scarab glowed in the

morning light. "Daughter, for two thousand years I lay entombed. All that time, I dreamed, and what I dreamed was that someday, I would create a great empire, greater than that of Octavian, which would accomplish all you desire—under my rule. In that empire, all men would be forced to lay down their arms, to take up productive employment rather than exploiting one another, to become better than themselves. War, poverty, hunger would be at an end. All would be equal—prejudice would be eradicated. Any who oppressed or used violence against another would be struck down by the power of Isis. It would be a world made perfect and peaceful, ruled by the priestesses of Isis—calmly, rationally, and for the greatest good of the greatest number."

"And what of those who did not wish to obey you?" asked Ayesha.

"They would be persuaded by the use of mesmeric power," said Tera, as though stating the obvious. "If that proved ineffective, they would of course be eliminated. Why should those who oppose peace, prosperity, and rational rule be allowed to create disorder for others? I shall create a world of order, in which all men will be content and productive."

"Then they will not be free," said Ayesha. "Freedom includes the ability to disobey."

"What is freedom? A breath of air when you say the word. You say the syllables, and like that it is gone. Better than freedom are peace and prosperity. That is what I would bring the world."

"I cannot allow you to do that," said Ayesha. "I have seen such *peace and prosperity* in Africa, have heard of it in India and Asia. It is neither peaceful nor prosperous. Mankind must be taught to be rational, to cast aside centuries of tribalism and even nationalism. I believe such a thing is possible, that with education and time—"

"Beware, daughter. This world is already on the path to war. Your choice will lead to death and destruction. In Margaret's mind, I have seen the embers of what will become a conflagration among the Germanic tribes and in the lands of Gaul. I would save this world from despair such as you have never known."

For a moment, Ayesha hesitated. She seemed undecided.

Catherine grabbed her by the arm. Fiercely, she whispered, "Moreau used to say things like that—order, humanity, civilization. It was always supposed to be for the benefit of mankind. But he ended up making monsters."

Ayesha looked at her, nodded, and turned back to the Egyptian queen.

"No empire ever rules justly," she said to Tera, head thrown back, looking up at the small woman standing high above her in the window. "I learned that when the British came to Kôr. Your intentions may be good, but you too would rule the world as a tyrant."

"You have spoken, my daughter," said Tera. She raised her hands. A wind rose and howled around them. It brought a white smoke that glittered like opals. The last thing Catherine saw before the smoke hid the keep from her sight was the front door opening, and Mrs. Raymond and Margaret Trelawny stepping out. Mrs. Raymond had her hands raised, like a witch casting a spell. Margaret was holding a pistol in one hand, with her other hand under the butt to steady it. The pistol was pointed directly at them.

> JUSTINE: I sometimes wonder if Queen Tera was right. Irene Norton says if things continue as they are, within a generation there will be such a war in Europe as we have never seen.

> MARY: Well, then we must try to prevent it. The Athena Club must try to prevent it. War is never inevitable.

CATHERINE: The way you primates behave? I would
    not be so sure about that.

"You can do it, Alice," said Mary. "I have faith in you."

"As do I," said Sherlock Holmes, standing behind and a little below them on the steps.

Once again, Alice pointed at the lock. But today, the spark that came from her finger was even weaker than it had been the day before.

"I can't," she said, shaking her head. She felt her eyes prickle. She was about to cry with frustration.

Suddenly, she heard a meowing outside the door.

"That sounds like a cat," said Mary.

"It's Bast! Poor Bast. Mrs. Polgarth isn't coming today, and I think they've forgotten to feed her. Why resurrect a mummy cat if you're not even going to take care of it?"

The thought of poor Bast without her breakfast made Alice so angry. She pointed at the door. A crackling beam of light sprang from her finger. Suddenly, the lock shattered and the door sprang open. They were free!

"Come on," she said. "I'm going to feed Bast, and then we're going to fight Queen Tera, somehow or other."

MARY: You couldn't open the door for us, but you
    could for a cat?

ALICE: Poor Bast. We would never treat Alpha or
    Omega like that, no matter how much Mrs. Poole
    insists they're supposed to hunt mice for their living.

DIANA: Mrs. Poole puts out food for them every day!
    I've seen her.

ALICE: Anyway, I'm so glad Ayesha allowed us to keep Bast. She's a good kitty, isn't she? Come here, Bastet. You're a very good kitty, you know that?

MRS. POOLE: And a spry one, for being two thousand years old! I think she catches more mice than those two scalawags put together. There's a little extra liver left over from breakfast, which I'm not saying she can have, because animals should not eat food meant for humans, but it's on the kitchen counter, is all.

The world was filled with white smoke. Beatrice turned around and around, confused. Where was she? She could see shapes here and there. For a moment, she saw Mrs. Raymond—but no, it was her father, Dr. Rappaccini! He looked at her with mournful eyes. And there beside him was her lover. Giovanni, who had died drinking the antidote to her poison. He too was looking at her—sadly, accusingly. How was that possible? In the rational part of her mind, she thought, *Memories too must be formed of energic waves. Mrs. Raymond is making me see things.* But somehow, that did not prevent her from seeing them as though they were real.

Justine stared at herself, at Justine Moritz, the maid of the Frankensteins, surrounded by glinting lights in the white smoke that swirled around her. How pretty that Justine was! What blue eyes she had, what golden hair, what a joyful smile. She herself—what was she? A corpse? A shadow? She fell to her knees and wept in shame at what she had become. This facsimile of a life—would it not be best to end it? To go to the grave Frankenstein had denied her?

Catherine was surrounded by Beast Men. They grunted and pawed at her. She was not like them! She was not! "Recite the Law," said the Hyena-Swine. "Are we not men?"

"Not to go on all fours," said the Bear Man.

"Not to suck up drink," said the Boar Man.

"Not to claw bark of trees," said the Leopard Man. "His is the House of Pain. His is the deep salt sea. His are the stars in the sky."

And there was Moreau, walking toward her through swirls of white smoke. "You are my greatest creation," he said. But he had a goat's horns on his forehead. How had she not noticed before that he was a Beast Man as well?

Lucinda smelled a rabbit. It was the sweetest, tastiest rabbit she had ever smelled. She wanted nothing in the world so much as to drink its blood. She crouched, low to the ground, so she could smell it better. "Where are you, little rabbit?" she said. "Come, I wish to bite you through the throat and lap up your warm, sweet life. Come to me, little rabbit!" There—she could see it leaping ahead of her, as white as the smoke that surrounded her, mocking her with its sprightly movements. She followed it, almost crawling over the ground in her haste. Somehow, it seemed quicker to go on all fours, like one of Carmilla's wolfdogs. She threw back her head and howled.

Alice opened the kitchen door. "What in the world?" she said. There was a sort of white smoke everywhere, all around the keep. It was thickest close to the front entrance, but was spreading rapidly around the entire building. She stood just at the edge of the swirling vapors. It seemed to glint with a thousand lights, and she could see shadows in it, moving around. Above it, at the level of the second-floor windows, floated a black shape, flapping its wings like a crow. No, it was a woman in a black coat, with her black hair spread out around her like snakes. At the window above the front entrance to the keep stood Tera. She spread out her hands, and they crackled with electricity.

"I see Catherine," said Mary. "Come on! We have to help her!" She ran toward the white smoke.

"No, Mary—you'll be blinded, just as they are!" shouted Holmes.

But it would not much matter whether or not they ran into the smoke, because it was spreading all around the keep. Alice saw it swirl about her ankles. This was energic power, Tera's power. Her mother alone could never have been this powerful, although Alice suspected she was in there somewhere, in the smoke, augmenting Tera's power in some way. She could feel, faintly, her mother's energic signature.

Mary entered the white billows and looked around her. There was Catherine, but what was she doing crawling on the ground? And where were the others? They must also be lost somewhere in that confusing white smoke. "Justine!" she called. "Beatrice! Diana! Where are you?"

Alice turned to Mr. Holmes. "I don't know what to do!" she cried in anguish.

"I'm going to get Mary," he said with a grim determination she had never yet seen on his face.

"No!" she cried as he leaped forward and sprinted toward the white smoke. He would be lost in it just like Mary. She had to follow him. This was all her fault. If she had not been Lydia Raymond, she would never have been kidnapped, and the Athena Club would never have been involved in such a dangerous adventure. Somehow, she had to save them all.

Catherine crouched low and bared her fangs, then turned toward the Beast Men. There was Mary, running toward her through the smoke. "Mary, help me!" she cried. "They're going to tear me apart with their teeth!"

Yes, Mary could see them now—the grinning, slobbering Beast Men! Where was her pistol? She must have left it at home, back at 11 Park Terrace. But she could see Catherine's .32 lying there on the ground. She picked it up.

"Mary, no!"

Who had said that? It was a man's voice, but which man? Moreau? Hyde? Van Helsing? She turned toward the sound. It was Adam Frankenstein! Had he risen again from the dead? She would make certain that he would never rise again, that he would stay dead forever. She pointed Catherine's pistol at him and pulled the trigger. The shot went straight and true, through the monster's heart.

Alice wandered in the glittering smoke, alone. She would be alone forever. No one would ever love her or care for her, because she was not worthy of love. Had not her own mother abandoned her? Her very own mother—but there she was, looking younger than Alice had ever seen her, with long black hair that tumbled down her back in thick curls. "My Lydia," she said, holding out her arms. "We shall never be separated again."

Alice walked into them. To be held as she had never been held before. To be comforted as she had never been. That was everything.

"My beloved daughter," said young, beautiful, kind Helen. She kissed Alice on both cheeks. "Now we shall be together always."

"Traitor!" It was Margaret Trelawny, standing in the swirling smoke, looking at Alice with fury in her eyes. "This is all your fault. How did you betray us? How did you reveal our plans to our enemies? I don't know how you did it, but you did it somehow." She pointed her pistol at Alice.

"No!" shouted Helen Raymond. She threw her arms around Alice and turned, so that she stood between Alice and the pistol.

A shot rang out. Helen's body slumped in Alice's arms. Incredulously, Alice stared down at her mother. It was no longer the beautiful young Helen that she held in her arms, nor was it the grim Mrs. Raymond she had encountered in the society of St. Mary Magdalen. It was a middle-aged woman, still beautiful, with signs of suffering and sorrow on her face, and strands of gray in her long black hair. "Lydia," said Helen softly. She reached up to touch Alice's cheek—then her hand fell, and her eyes closed, and Helen Raymond lay dead in Alice's arms.

On the second floor of the keep, Diana followed Laura down a long hallway. Where was Mary? They had looked in every room, but seen no one. The first floor seemed to be filled with a strange white smoke. Even up here, it was creeping along the floor. Laura had a pistol in her hand. Diana had her knife. She was looking forward to using it. No one stole *her* sister! Mary was annoying, Mary was a bore, but Mary was *her* annoying bore. They had not found her on the first floor, so she must be up here.

Laura threw open the last door on the hall. It opened to a large room filled with shelves on which were placed Egyptian artifacts. There were urns and statues and broken objects that looked distinctly Egyptian, or at least ancient and foreign, which in Diana's mind amounted to the same thing. This must be Professor Trelawny's study.

At the far end of the room, in front of a large window, stood Queen Tera. She had her back to them. Out the window, Diana could see lightning crackling across the sky. In the air floated— could that possibly be Ayesha? Queen Tera held out her hand, and lightning surged through the President of the Alchemical Society, lifting her black braids until they all stood on end. Her body arched backward and she screamed in pain.

Diana clutched at Laura's arm. "I think Queen Tera's winning."

Laura looked at her with a grim, determined smile. "Diana, would you like to see how we hunt vampires in Styria? I will shoot her, but that will only startle her and slow her down. Then you must cut off her head. Remember that it must be completely severed. She must not be allowed to regenerate. Understand?"

Diana nodded. Diana Hyde, vampire hunter! This was even better than rescuing Lucinda Van Helsing.

Laura aimed her pistol, pulled the trigger, and emptied all six bullets into Tera's back. The Egyptian queen's body jumped as each bullet entered her back. Then, she fell to the ground.

"Quick, the knife!" said Laura.

Diana looked at her knife. It was sharp, but there, on the wall of Professor Trelawny's study, was a knife that looked even sharper. It was twice as long, with a curved blade on which were etched letters of some sort. She grabbed the hilt and pulled the knife off its hook on the wall. Then, she ran to the fallen queen.

Tera was staring up at the ceiling. Wounded and bleeding, with her blood spreading over the floor, she pulled back her lips and snarled like an animal. For a moment, Diana quailed. Yes, you did, Diana, don't deny it. Any of us would have under the circumstances. Not even Diana could remain unaffected by the look of baffled anger on the Egyptian queen's face. Quickly, she knelt down by Tera's side and sliced through her slender throat. The knife entered easily until it hit bone. Then, it was gross, really really gross, to saw at that neck, with blood all over the floor, tendons snapping, bones breaking, and Tera twisting her head back and forth, making that terrible snarling sound. Almost too gross even for Diana. Finally, Laura had to kneel and help her. At last, at long last, Tera's head lay completely severed on the floor of the study. Only then did the light go out of her eyes. She stared up at the ceiling, eyes still open but now sightless.

Diana looked at Laura, breathing heavily. Both of them were covered with blood—Diana's trousers and Laura's skirt were soaked in it, and there was blood spattered all over their shirts and hands.

"Like that?" said Diana. "Did I do it right?"

Laura nodded. "You did very well. I couldn't have done it better myself."

Down below, around the base of the keep, the smoke started

to dissipate. Beatrice was sitting on a stone wall that had once been part of the castle, crying bitterly into a handkerchief. She looked up, startled. Where was she, and why had she been weeping as though her heart would break? Justine stared at her hands. The fingernails were bloody, and there were scratches up and down her arms. Had she really tried to take herself apart? That made no sense. Yet it had seemed a logical idea just a moment ago. Catherine was crawling on the ground, growling. She sat back on her haunches. What in the world had she been doing? There were no Beast Men, not anymore. Moreau's creations had all been destroyed—she was the only one left of her kind. For a moment, the thought made her feel lonely. Lucinda sat on the grass by another stone wall, chewing what seemed to be weeds. She spit them out. How disgusting! She would have to rinse out her mouth with water, or preferably blood. Mary stood over the fallen body of Sherlock Holmes, who was groaning and clutching his side. She dropped Catherine's pistol. "Oh my God," she said. "I think I've shot him." Alice sat holding the body of Helen Raymond, which would never rise again. She leaned down and kissed her mother on the forehead while blood soaked through the dress she had brought from the house in Soho, the dress her mother had chosen for her. Ayesha knelt on the ground, her head in her hands, clearly in pain. There were still bits of lightning playing around her, as though she had been electrified. Margaret Trelawny stood in the midst of them, turning and pointing her pistol about. "You won't get away with this, any of you!" she cried. "When Tera becomes queen, she will kill you all!"

Suddenly, something sprang toward Margaret. It was Lucinda—how quickly she moved! In a moment, Margaret lay on the ground, the pistol knocked from her hand and lying on the grass. Lucinda crouched over her, growling. Then, realizing who and where she was, she looked around as though ashamed of herself. "I'm sorry," she said. "I don't know why I did that."

> CATHERINE: You see, there are some useful things
> about being a vampire. Your instincts and reflexes
> are almost as good as mine.

> DIANA: Then why didn't you disarm Margaret
> Trelawny, I'd like to know? But no, it was Lucinda.
> Nohow.

Ayesha stood up, although she staggered a little, and glared at Margaret lying on the ground. "That's quite enough from you," she said. "Thank you, Lucinda. I think"—she looked around at them all, considering the situation—"that our work here is done."

> ALICE: I think that sometimes, just for official
> purposes, I would like to go by Lydia. You can
> still call me Alice, of course. But I was born
> Lydia Raymond, and I would like to use that
> name, sometimes. On legal documents and the
> like. If nobody minds, that is.

> MARY: Of course we don't.

# CHAPTER XVII

## Rescue in Southwark

I've never been south of the Thames," said Alice. "Truth to tell, it doesn't look that different from Soho."

"But you have been many new places recently," said Beatrice. "Cornwall, for instance. That is quite different from London, whether north or south of the Thames."

"Yes," said Alice. She paused for a moment, then said, "These adventures—they don't really stop, do they?"

"No, they do not," said Beatrice, looking at her thoughtfully. "Would you like them to? You did not need to come with me. There are other ways we could have planned to rescue Martin and the other mesmerists."

"No," said Alice. "I should be here. At least, I think I should. But after this, I think I would like to go back to being kitchen maid for a while."

They were standing across the street from a tenement. It looked very much like one of the tenements of the East End, and very different from the elegant house by Lincoln's Inn Fields where Beatrice had last seen Professor Petronius, when he had exhibited her at the Royal College of Surgeons as the Poisonous Girl.

"I hope the Baker Street boys were right and this is the house." Beatrice looked at it appraisingly. "Are you quite certain, Alice? We could ask Mr. Wiggins and his followers to rush in and effect a rescue, as they did at the British Museum."

"And a lot of good that did!" said Alice. "If the Baker Street boys did that, I'm sure someone would get hurt. I don't want anyone to get hurt, especially not Martin—he's such a gentle soul. All right, I think I'm ready, miss."

But was Beatrice ready? She wished she did not have to face Professor Petronius again. She would much rather have forgotten that particular episode in her life. Instead of standing here, she wished she could be back in her conservatory of poisonous plants, surrounded by their silent companionship. That was where she was happiest nowadays—and with Clarence of course, but her plants provided her with an uncomplicated joy, whereas her happiness at being with Clarence was always complicated by the care she had to take not to hurt him. Inwardly, she sighed. If only things were different! But they were not, and no amount of wishing would make them so. She might love Clarence, but she was a scientist. She believed there were implacable realities of life that could not be changed, and her poisonous nature was one of them.

Here, again, there was no use wishing the situation could be different. What had to be done might as well be done now. "All right," she said to Alice. "Set fire to the house."

Alice waved her hands. Suddenly, Beatrice could see flames through the upstairs windows of the tenement. Smoke poured through them, black and acrid. It all looked so real! The rising flames, the dark smoke—she could even feel the heat of it. Then, she heard a scream.

The door of the building opened with a bang. First, out rushed an elderly woman. Ah yes, that was Professor Petronius's housekeeper—a Mrs. Thorpe, if Beatrice remembered correctly. She had been kind enough to Beatrice in her own way, but completely under the control of the man she had always referred to, reverently, as the Professor. She was followed out by a tall man in a black frock coat, with a top hat in one hand and a pistol in the other. As soon as he stepped out the door, he automatically put the top hat on his head. He still had the thick black mustache that Beatrice remembered—a bit too black to be convincing. She suspected him of using hair dye.

"Come on, come on," he shouted. "Come out here at once!" Behind him came a line of three men and two women, the men in shirtsleeves. One of them was tall and lean, with long, dark hair. That must be Martin—he fit Catherine's description perfectly.

"Over here, and don't any of you dare make a run for it." Professor Petronius waved his pistol at them. "Even if you manage to get away from me, Mrs. Raymond will hunt you down personally! You don't want to face her wrath again, do you now? So just stand here like good boys and girls, in a straight line as though doing recitation at school, until the fire brigade comes and puts out that blaze."

"There won't be much left by that time," said Mrs. Thorpe. "I don't know how it could have started. I banked the stove so carefully, and there was no fire burning in any of the upstairs rooms."

"Which means one of you set it deliberately!" said Professor Petronius, waving his pistol around in a way that Mary would have found completely irresponsible. "Which of you did it? When Mrs. Raymond finds out—"

This was the part Beatrice had been worried about. Would Alice be able to do it?

"Petronius!" It was the voice of Mrs. Raymond, and it emanated from the effigy of Mrs. Raymond that stood at Beatrice's side. Good for Alice! It was a perfect imitation.

Professor Petronius noticed them for the first time. He stepped back, startled. Mrs. Raymond strode toward him. "This is your responsibility. I told you to keep guard over these mesmerists, and see what has happened?" She pointed to the blazing house and looked at him coldly. "However, I have no more need of them, so you are to let them go. As for your pistol, lower it immediately or I will turn it into a poisonous snake."

Looking at her with an expression of incredulity, Professor Petronius lowered his pistol. "But you said I was to guard them, to make sure they didn't escape. You said you might still have use for them." He sounded upset, as though he had been ill-used.

"The situation has changed," said Mrs. Raymond haughtily. "They are useless to me now." She turned to the group of mesmerists, who were huddled together and staring at her with fear—it was clear that Mrs. Raymond had made an impression on them. "All of you, go! I do not need you anymore. Except you, Marvelous Martin. You must stay. And as for you, Professor, I would like you to leave London and never return again, on pain of my wrath, as you called it."

"But I haven't been paid!" he protested. "You promised me twenty pounds for my services!"

"Why don't I pay you instead?" said Beatrice sweetly. "You remember me, don't you, professor? I'm working with Mrs. Raymond now. Let me show you how I repay those who help me as you have."

Professor Petronius was so startled to see her that he simply stood, mouth agape, while she approached, stood up on her tiptoe, and kissed him on the cheek. It was a longer kiss than any she had given Clarence.

"Bloody hell!" shouted Professor Petronius, jumping back and clapping his hand to his cheek. "You bitch!"

"That was to thank you for all the help you gave me when I first came to England," said Beatrice, in her usual sweet tones. When he lowered his hand, she could see the shape of her lips seared into his cheek. That mark would never come off, not as long as he lived. "Go, Professor—although in truth you are no professor, but a charlatan. Leave London, as Mrs. Raymond has ordered, or I will come find you and leave a similar mark on the other cheek!"

He glowered at her, then turned and, without a word, ran up the street toward the Thames. Mrs. Thorpe ran after him, shouting, "Professor! Professor, wait for me!

Beatrice turned to Mrs. Raymond. "I always knew he was a coward," she said with satisfaction.

"But I'm not," said Martin, in his deep, sad voice. The other mesmerists were still behind him, huddled together. Evidently, despite their fear, they had not wanted to desert their friend. "I won't tell you any more about Alice. I'm sorry I told you what I did, and I hope you never find her."

"And we're not going without Martin," said a woman standing behind him. "We're circus people, and we stick together. If you want to keep him captive, you'll have to keep us as well."

Beatrice turned to Mrs. Raymond, to see how she would respond. The director of the Magdalen Society waved her hand. The flames in the house died down, then disappeared as though they had never been. And there, beside her, stood Alice once more.

"My dear girl," said Martin, evidently astonished. "What in the world—"

"I've learned a few new tricks," said Alice, smiling. Then, she threw her arms around Martin in a way Beatrice could not help envying. "I'm so glad you're safe—that you're all safe," she said, looking at the other mesmerists, who were also looking at her—most of them respectfully, some a little doubtfully, as though expecting her to turn back into Mrs. Raymond at any moment.

"That was an impressive demonstration," said the woman who had stood up for Martin. "Thank you for getting rid of Professor Petronius, Miss—"

"I'm not a miss, I'm just Alice," said Alice. Now that she was back to herself, she spoke with her usual shyness.

"You're not *just* anything," said Beatrice. "Come, let us all return to Park Terrace. Mrs. Poole will have luncheon waiting, and you're all welcome to join us."

MRS. POOLE: Well, you could have told me we'd have a troupe of mesmerists coming to lunch! Five extra mouths to feed is no laughing matter!

BEATRICE: I am truly sorry, Mrs. Poole. Luckily Mary, Diana, Catherine, and Justine were out that day, although I remember Lucinda kept asking the mesmerists to make things appear and disappear.

ALICE: That's what gave Martin the idea for our show. There had never been a show of mesmerists working together before—it was always one mesmerist giving a demonstration. A show of all the best mesmerists in London—well, other than Merton the Magnificent, who had gone home instead of coming to lunch. You can't blame him, with Mrs. Merton having a new baby and all. The show's been quite successful, with all five of us working together.

BEATRICE: Especially you, Alice. You are becoming the star attraction.

ALICE: Oh, I very much doubt that! Martin is still so much better than me at talking to people. I'm good at manipulating the waves, but I can't do the patter the way he can.

LUCINDA: I'm so glad I gave you the idea! It's

a wonderful show, especially the part in the
mummy's tomb when the sarcophagus rises and
the mummy appears—I scream every time I see it.

Catherine looked around at the headquarters of the Baker
Street Irregulars. She was not particularly impressed.

"You're going to come with me," Diana had said earlier that
morning. "You're the one who got Jimmy court-martialed in the
first place, and I want you there to protect him in case any of the
Baker Street boys decide they don't like our suggestion. Not that
I can't protect him myself with my little knife, but you have *teeth*.
Sometimes I wish I had sharp teeth. It would be useful to carry
your weapons around in your mouth all the time."

Jimmy Bucket had looked at them, frightened. He was a small
boy, with brown hair that seemed to have been cut with nail scissors. It stuck out every which way. "I don't know if I should go
back to headquarters," he had said. "Wiggins was powerful angry
with me. He might court-martial me all over again."

"First of all, he can't do that—you can't court-martial someone
twice. And second of all, we're not going to let him," Catherine
had said. "Don't you want to be a Baker Street boy again?"

"Ye-es," he had responded, sounding as though he were not
entirely sure.

But he was standing steadily enough beside her now.

"Why should we reinstate him?" asked Wiggins. His arms
were crossed and he was leaning back against his desk. His mouth
was set in an obdurate line. Behind him were Buster and Dennys.
Evidently, Buster was well enough to start taking up his old duties
again, although he was seated in a chair rather than standing up,
and gauze bandages were visible where his shirt collar was unbuttoned. He was looking fixedly at the floor.

"Because I asked you to," said Diana.

"Because the Athena Club is asking you to," said Catherine. This was not all about Diana! Not everything was about Diana.

"And why should I do what the Athena Club asks?" Wiggins looked at them skeptically.

"Because we rescued Mr. Holmes," said Catherine. "We were there when you couldn't be, and we will be again in the future. And you will be there when we can't. Would you rather fight us or have our assistance? Would you rather be our friend or foe?"

"Why do you care so much about Jimmy Bucket anyway?" asked Wiggins.

"I don't," said Diana scornfully. "If it were up to me, he would stay court-martialed."

"It's Beatrice and Justine who care," said Catherine. "Beatrice says he's just a little boy who didn't know better, and Justine says you can't blame a man for stealing bread when his family is hungry."

"Whatever that means!" said Diana. "Sometimes I think everyone else in the Athena Club is barmy."

Dennys rolled his eyes. Evidently, he agreed with her.

Wiggins looked again at the scrawny boy standing before him and hanging his head in penitence, or shame, or perhaps both. "Well? What do you have to say for yourself, Jimmy?"

Jimmy looked up at him with watery blue eyes. "I'm sorry, Mr. Wiggins. I didn't mean no harm. Lady Crowe said she could help with my sister's treatments if I told her about the ladies—Miss Moreau and the others. What they were doing, when they went out, that kind of thing. And she did—Jenny is doing ever so much better now. I wouldn't have done it for any other reason, but she's my only sister, and I don't know what Mum would do without her. My little brother can't do anything to help—he's only four years old. I'm the man of the house since Da died. So I had to do something, you see."

"That doesn't justify breaking your oath to me and the Baker Street Irregulars," said Wiggins severely. "If I let you join again, do you promise not to do such a thing ever again so long as you're a member? You'll be on probation. And you won't be reinstated a second time, you know."

"Yes, sir," said Jimmy, sniffing and wiping his nose with his sleeve. "But will the boys accept me back? They wouldn't look at me as I came upstairs. Buster won't look at me even now."

Buster looked up and stared at him, eyes narrowed. Jimmy shook a little in front of that glare.

"They'd better, or they'll feel the prick of my little knife," said Diana, drawing that knife out of wherever she kept it—she must have some sort of sheath in her waistband. She glared back at Buster. "And the bite of Catherine's teeth!"

Not likely! Catherine had no intention of biting any Baker Street boys. For one thing, she was not sure how often they washed. Dennys looked clean enough, but Buster had dirt around his collar.

"Well, Buster, Dennys?" asked Wiggins. "Shall we give Mr. Bucket another chance?"

"No," said Buster decisively, in his deep voice.

"Are you pulling our leg?" said Dennys. "We don't want traitors here."

"Oh, so it's no from the two of you, is it?" Wiggins turned his head as though to look at them, although he could only have seen Buster at that angle. "I'm inclined to let him back in, myself. So that's two against one. And whose vote counts around here?"

"Yours, Bill," said Dennys, immediately. "If you say he's in, he's in, and the boys won't gainsay it. They won't be happy, but they'll accept it if you say so."

Wiggins nodded. "Well, I do say so. Buster, make sure all the boys know that Jimmy's under my personal protection. And Diana's, of course." Diana had been about to protest, hadn't she? Now, Catherine noticed that she was looking at Wiggins with smug satisfaction. "All right, Jimmy," Wiggins continued. "You'll get one more chance, on account of your age and family circumstances. But it's your last one!"

"Thank you, sir," said Jimmy, looking down again and shuffling his feet. Catherine hoped he was properly grateful for what they had done that morning. She could think of many things she would rather have been doing than pleading Jimmy's case in front of the Baker Street Irregulars. But at least Beatrice and Justine would be pleased.

She was startled when Wiggins turned to her and said, "Miss Moreau, are you really a puma? Charlie says you showed him your teeth."

Oh, for goodness' sake, as Mary often said! "Yes, I'm a puma," she replied impatiently. In a moment he would ask to see her teeth as well, and then she would have to be the Puma Woman, just like in the circus, for an audience of Baker Street Irregulars! Ah well, perhaps it was good for Mr. Holmes's boys to learn about the abilities of the Athena Club. They would no doubt have to work together again in the future.

> MARY: They were very helpful when we had to
> recover the naval treaty Colonel Protheroe so
> stupidly left on the table in his study while he went
> out on the balcony for a smoke. Although I think
> Wiggins and Charlie are going to have to decide
> which of them is Diana's admirer. They almost
> came to blows about who was going to rescue her
> from the Russian Embassy.

> DIANA: As though I needed rescuing! And if they're
> going to be such idiots, I don't want anything to
> do with either of them. I don't need an *admirer*,
> thank you very much.

LUCINDA: I admire you, Diana, for your courage and
cleverness. If it were not for you, I would probably
have died in that madhouse in Vienna.

DIANA: Well, that's different. You can admire me
without being *stupid* about it.

Mary looked down at the face of Sherlock Holmes. It was
softer in sleep than when he was awake. The alert, inquisitive
look that always characterized it was gone. It was still lean, angular, with a certain elegance to it that lay deep in the bone. But it
seemed younger, less lined with cares. She pulled up the blanket
to cover his bare shoulder, with the white linen bandage wrapped
around it and down his side. He shifted and turned. For a moment,
she though he might wake up, but his eyes did not open.

"How is he? Dr. Watson asked me to check on him and send
word as soon as he wakes." Bill Wiggins was standing in the door
of the infirmary. Behind him were Catherine and Diana.

While she was glad to see them, she was grateful to have had
the infirmary to herself that morning. Buster was ambulatory,
Charlie was hopping about despite doctor's order, and Dr. Watson,
who was still recovering, had been moved to 221B Baker Street so
he could be nursed by Mrs. Hudson. Watson had not wanted to
leave Holmes, but Dr. Radko had insisted. "His wounds are much
worse than yours," Dr. Radko had said. "He needs absolute quiet,
while you are ready for company and amusement. He will recover
better if you are not here. However, you may visit as soon as you
are well enough."

In the meantime, Mary had been the one at his side. She had
barely left it for the last few days. "Sleeping well," she said. "He
does not have a fever. But he has not woken yet."

"Right, then," said Wiggins. "I'll come back later to check on him, and Dr. Radko is coming this afternoon. He says it's a miracle Mr. Holmes survived."

"Mary, you should get out yourself," said Catherine. "You've been here three days now. Have you slept at all? You don't want to make yourself sick, either. Mrs. Poole says unless you come home for a bath and change of clothes, she's going to come fetch you herself."

"I lay down on one of the other beds for a while," she said. "Dennys showed me a place to wash, and Alice brought new underclothes this morning. I'm all right, Cat. I just want to be here when he wakes up. I was the one who shot him, you know."

"That was an accident," said Wiggins. "You can't blame yourself for that, Miss Jekyll. You didn't mean to shoot him."

"Thank you. I'll try not to." But she did blame herself, didn't she? It was completely her fault. Whether or not she had meant to shoot Sherlock, she had pulled the trigger that had sent the bullet into his shoulder. He had almost died from loss of blood because of her.

"Remember we have a meeting with Ayesha this afternoon," said Catherine. "You'll be there, right? We need to discuss Athena Club business before she leaves for Budapest."

"Yes, I'll be there," said Mary, scarcely listening. If only he would wake up! She felt something around her shoulders and looked up, startled. Had Diana actually hugged her?

"We'll see you back home, Sis," said Diana. "Remember, if he dies, you've still got us!"

"He's not going to die!" said Catherine. "Dr. Radko said so, and so did Ayesha. Mary, he's not going to die. Mr. Wiggins, could you show us out? I think I'd better take Diana home before she tries to say anything else helpful."

"What?" said Diana. "What did I say this time?"

When they were gone, Mary looked back down at the sleeping face of Sherlock Holmes. She remembered how she had knelt by him in the field beneath the keep, pressing her hands to the place where the blood was bubbling up, bright red. Ayesha had come up beside her and said, "Move aside, Mary." Then, as Mary stood watching, the President of the Alchemical Society had put her hands on the wound. A bright light had spread from them, a light that glimmered like opals. She had stayed like that for five minutes, ten, fifteen. The other girls had been doing things—carrying the body of Mrs. Raymond inside, for she had died almost instantly of Margaret Trelawny's pistol shot, and locking Margaret herself in the dungeon. She had heard about all that later. At the time, she had noticed only the ghastly face of Sherlock Holmes as Ayesha fought for his life.

Finally, she had risen. "He will live," she said. "I have done what I can. Time must do the rest. He will be ill for a long time, but he will not die."

Mary had knelt beside him in the grass and cried, as she had never cried before in her life, because our Mary never cries—but she cried that day, ugly racking sobs, and her tears fell like the rain in Marazion.

"Mary." The voice was familiar, although oh so tired!

Startled, she looked up. Sherlock Holmes was awake! He was looking at her with kind gray eyes.

"I shot you. I almost killed you." She wanted to make sure he knew that—her culpability.

"I know. I remember."

"I don't expect you to forgive me. You could have died."

He reached up and touched her cheek. "Mary."

"If you wish me to hand in my letter of resignation, I will of course do so. I can't imagine that you would want to work with me after—"

"Mary, come here." He pulled her down toward him, and suddenly it seemed so natural, so inevitable, that she should lean down and kiss him with all the longing of the last few days, the last few months. His lips were soft and firm, his hand on her cheek both strong and tender. It was everything she had scarcely known she wanted in one moment of perfect, intensely felt life.

"Mary," he said when she had pulled away again, afraid of hurting him, "I've never seen tears in your eyes." He brushed them away with one finger.

She took his hand in hers. "They're tears of gratitude, I think. But you should sleep now."

"Yes, nurse," he said, smiling, but his eyes were already half closed. She sat with him, holding his hand, until he fell into a deep, healing sleep.

> MARY: Cat, is it absolutely necessary for you to
> include that scene?

> CATHERINE: Yes.

Justine hesitated. Should she be here, standing in front of Dorian Gray's elegant town house in Grosvenor Square? She still did not know what to think of Mr. Gray. And yet, somehow, she had felt that she should see him again, perhaps only to make up her mind about him.

Not certain whether she should or not, she rang the bell. Before it had stopped ringing, the door opened. She was startled to see Mr. Gray himself standing there, holding the door.

"I am short of domestic staff at the moment, Mr. Frank," he said. "My English servants have left me, and I have sent my French staff ahead to my house in Antibes, where I intend to spend the winter. Do you wish to step over the threshold? You are most welcome, but you should be aware that you are entering the house of the most scandalous man in London. Or so my aunt Agatha calls me."

Beatrice had mentioned a scandal of some sort, involving the playwright Mr. Wilde. But Justine never paid attention to such gossip.

"Mr. Gray," she said, "I have come to correct a misapprehension. You see, when we met in the opium den where Mary and I were looking for Mr. Holmes, I was in disguise. I am, even now, in a disguise of sorts." She looked down at her masculine clothes. "I am not Justin Frank, but Justine Frankenstein. Because of my height, it is easier for me to go about London dressed as a man. I apologize for the deception. I did not want our acquaintanceship to continue under false pretenses."

"But you wanted it to continue?" he said with a smile. It was the innocent, angelic smile of a choir boy. "Come in, please come in—that is, if you wish."

Justine stepped over the threshold and followed Dorian Gray down the hall into a parlor that made her gasp with astonishment. What would Beatrice think of this, if she could see it? The art on the walls, the furnishings, the bibelots, reminded her, more than anything else, of Irene Norton's parlor in Vienna.

"Do you like it?" asked Mr. Gray. "I'm a collector, of sorts." He looked as pleased as a child when you admire his new toy.

> BEATRICE: I have seen his parlor since. It is magnificent, but might be more elegant if there were fewer *objets d'art* in it. He cannot seem to help his acquisitive instinct.

> CATHERINE: And he collects people the way he collects those knick-knacks of his. I think he's collected Justine as yet another curiosity.

> JUSTINE: He most certainly has not. I know the rest of you do not like him, but Mr. Gray is my friend.

BEATRICE: We did not mean to criticize your friend,
Justine.

DIANA: Of course you did.

Justine was less susceptible to physical beauty than most women.
She could feel the beauty of a sunset or a flower, but in men and
women, she had always admired intellect, probity, evidence of inner
worth. And yet there was something about Dorian Gray—something delicate that reminded her of a porcelain figurine or a musical
instrument. He was short for a man, half a head shorter than she
was—quite the opposite of Atlas or Adam Frankenstein! His golden
hair shone in the late morning light like a halo around his head. If
she painted him, and it occurred to her that she would like to, it
would be as a seraph, with wings rising from his shoulders. And
yet Beatrice had warned her that he was reputed to be extravagant,
profligate, immoral. "The charge of immorality is nonsense," said
Beatrice. "It is leveled by a prudish society against one who chooses
not to live by its strictures. However, he is not a good man. Remember
that he has abandoned Mr. Wilde, who is languishing in prison. And
I have heard that both young men and women have been led into
trouble, attempting to imitate his aesthetic lifestyle." Justine had no
idea what to make of all this.

"Come," said Mr. Gray. "Let me show you my Tanagra
figurine—or better yet, since you have told me that you are
interested in art, come see this painting. It is by Mr. Whistler,
in quite a new style."

Justine walked over to the painting. Yes, it was indeed new—
a visual nocturne, the coming of twilight over the Thames. "I am
myself a painter," she said. "But I have never attempted anything like
this. Perhaps I should try. After all, this is a new era, as Catherine
keeps pointing out. Perhaps I should try to be more modern."

"Mr. Frank—Miss Frankenstein," said Mr. Gray. "Please understand that it makes no difference to me what you call yourself, or what clothes you wear. Whether you are Justin or Justine is immaterial. It is you, yourself, that I wish to know better. Although the name Frankenstein—I have heard it before."

"Yes," said Justine, startled that he had recognized it. But of course he must be very well read. "It was a book by Mrs. Shelley—"

"About Victor Frankenstein. Yes, I have read it. Many believe it to be a work of fiction, but alas, I know it to be fact!"

Justine looked at him with alarm. "Why alas, Mr. Gray?"

"Because I learned it through a misadventure that happened to me in my youth—it is what started me down the road I now travel. An association with an older man, a Lord Henry Wotton, a member of the Société des Alchimistes. You will not have heard of it, I'm sure—it is a very select society of men interested in the sciences, biology above all. Lord Henry told me that Victor Frankenstein had belonged to the same society, a century before, and that Mrs. Shelley's tale was true, at least in most particulars. Are you, then, related to the Frankenstein family? You mentioned that you were Swiss."

"In a sense," said Justine, warily. So Mr. Gray knew about the Société des Alchimistes! What sort of association had he formed with this Lord Henry Wotton, and how had it set him on his current path, as he so enigmatically claimed? She would very much like to hear more of his story. But there was no time this morning. She was due back at 11 Park Terrace.

"If you could stay for luncheon—I have some cold tongue, caviar, and champagne," said Mr. Gray.

She would have liked to, although she would have had to explain to him that she did not eat flesh food. But she did not want to be late for the meeting with Ayesha.

"Thank you very much, Mr. Gray," she said, "but my friends are waiting for me."

"Of course," he said. "I envy you—friendship is the one luxury that money cannot buy. *Au revoir,* Mademoiselle Frankenstein."

When she held out her hand, he leaned over it, turned it over, and kissed the palm. As she walked home from Mayfair to Marylebone, she could feel the imprint of that kiss inside her glove.

> BEATRICE: Are you quite sure you want to go to Antibes with Mr. Gray for two weeks? Would you rather not stay with me and Catherine in Paris? There will be museums, and restaurants, and a painting from the Louvre to recover from whoever has stolen it. . . .
>
> JUSTINE: Yes, I'm sure. I'm going to paint in the south of France. He has expressly invited me.
>
> BEATRICE: I think it is a mistake. . . .
>
> CATHERINE: But we all get to make our own mistakes. After all, Bea, you and I have made plenty of our own.
>
> BEATRICE: Alas.

Lucinda was sitting on the window seat in the parlor. It had been lovely to spend a quiet morning all by herself, while everyone else was out on their respective errands. For the first time, she had been able to talk to Mrs. Poole, who reminded her of the Van Helsing housekeeper, Frau Müller. While she was growing up, Frau Müller had always been there, to bandage a scraped knee or provide a ginger biscuit. What would the world be like without women such as Frau Müller in it?

Just before lunch, Alice and Beatrice had brought back a group of mesmerists, who had eaten in the dining room with its large mahogany table. What an entertaining meal it had been! They had made water glasses and napkins disappear, turned apples into golden balls and slices of toast into butterflies that flew about the room. Magpies had flown out of a meat pie. Of course Lucinda knew it was an illusion, that with the passes of their hands and their patter they were merely manipulating her perception of reality. Still, she had not laughed so much since her mother had taken her to the fair, years ago, and she had seen the jugglers with their sharp swords, the little dogs with ruffs around their necks jumping through hoops, the Harlequin and Columbine of the *Commedia*.

And no one had commented on the fact that her lunch had consisted of a bowl of blood. Sheep's blood, specifically, which was not her favorite, but Mrs. Poole had gone to get it from the butcher, Mr. Byles, especially for her. Of course, Beatrice had been drinking a bowl of something green that smelled foul to her sensitive nose, so she had not been the only one with unusual culinary needs. How comfortable she felt in this house, where no one bothered her and everyone accepted what she was! When she had agreed to become a member of the Athena Club, she had not truly understood what she was agreeing to. But now she knew. It meant becoming part of a new family in which she would always be welcome.

"Lucinda!" She turned from looking out at the street without seeing it, lost in thought, toward the door. There stood Laura in a walking suit. "Oh, my dear, I wish you'd come with me," she said. She had already taken off her hat and gloves, and was holding a letter in her left hand. "Piccadilly Circus, lunch at Harrod's Department Store, and then a walk through Hyde Park . . . It was all so perfectly *English*, even more so than I'd imagined. It's heavenly here! I mean, I do miss Styria, and Carmilla, and Magda, and everyone at home, and the dear old schloss itself. In Styria I used to think I was very English, and now I realize how Styrian I am, even in my nostalgia. Still, it's glorious to see all the places my father used to talk about with such longing. How I wish he could be with me now! Although I do think the cakes are better back in Austria, but don't tell Mrs. Poole I said that."

"Miss Jennings," said Mrs. Poole, appearing suddenly behind her at the doorway. Lucinda wondered if she'd heard that remark about the cakes. "I see you found the letter that came for you today. There was also a telegram. I didn't want to leave it on the hall table with the regular mail, in case it might be something private."

"Thank you, Mrs. Poole," said Laura. She glanced quickly at the telegram. The housekeeper had already disappeared again down the hall. "Now isn't that just like Carmilla! 'Vampire nest destroyed coming to England how would you like to tour the Lake District darling all my love C.' I think she feels a little guilty for abandoning us. What do you think, Lucinda? Would you like to tour the Lake District?"

Lucinda shook her head. Really all she wanted was to sit here and feel the life of this house flow through her, to feel herself surrounded by friends.

"And this is a letter from my cousin, the Reverend Mr. Jennings. I wrote to him almost as soon as we arrived. He is my last living relative in England." Neatly, she tore open the letter and glanced down the page. "He regrets to say that he is ill and under the care of a mental specialist named—I can't read it, his writing is so spidery. Dr. Hesselius, I think. Therefore, he cannot come to London, but would be happy to receive me at his home in Warwickshire. I'm not entirely sure where that is, but he says there's a day train from London. I suppose there is just enough time to see him before Carmilla arrives. Goodness, what a busy visit this is proving to be! We saved the Queen, and I had lunch at Harrods, and now I'm going to see where Wordsworth wrote his 'Tintern Abbey' and that daffodil poem."

"It is not time for our meeting?" asked Beatrice, coming in with a mug of tea in her hand. Why must Beatrice always be drinking things that smelled so foul? But they probably did not smell foul to her. Lucinda reminded herself that not all the world shared her vampire senses. "Lucinda, if you don't mind, I will share the window seat with you." Beatrice sat on the window seat, as elegantly as always. Well, Lucinda would simply have to learn to bear certain smells. As her mother had once told her, a lady may feel disgust, but she must never show it.

"Of course. Please." She slid over and made more room.

"The Athena Club's meeting with Ayesha? Then I shall be off," said Laura.

"You are most welcome to attend," said Beatrice. "I do not think Mary would mind."

"Attending a meeting with the Princess of Meroë, Queen of Kôr, and President of the Alchemical Society, as Count Dracula calls her, is not my idea of fun," said Laura. "Whereas shopping is. I barely brought any clothes with me, and I'll need more if I'm going to tour the lakes! Ta now."

"Wait for me!" Just as Laura was leaving it, Diana burst into the room. "Don't start without me! Oh. No one's here yet."

"Apparently, we do not count as someone," said Beatrice to Lucinda with a smile.

"You know that's not what I meant," said Diana, glaring at her. "Where are the others? I thought Catherine was right behind me."

"Look what came in the mail!" said Catherine, striding into the room like a puma that has caught its prey and is dragging its bloody carcass across the forest floor. In her hands she held a book.

"Is that it?" asked Beatrice, rising and going over to see. "Has it come? Is that—"

"Yes," said Catherine triumphantly. "*The Mysteries of Astarte* by Miss Catherine Moreau. It's going on sale today all over England. Now I just hope people buy it!"

"They will," said Justine, standing in the doorway. She had apparently just come in, because she still had her cap and gloves on. "It's an excellent book, Catherine. Congratulations."

"Oh, you know, it's just my first one," said the author, with false modesty. "I'm sure the next one will be better. And easier, now that I've written one book and know how!"

> CATHERINE: Which, for any of my readers who may
> be wondering, is not the way it works. Every book
> is as hard to write as every other book. They are
> never easy.

> MARY: But I would think the process gets easier, over
> time?

> CATHERINE: You would think. But no, it doesn't. I've
> had just as hard a time writing this book as I had
> with the first one. Which is available for sale—

> MARY: Please. Just stop.

"Aren't we supposed to be meeting with Ayesha?" said Catherine, looking around the room. "We're all here—well, except Mary, and I don't know if she's going to make it. She's still waiting for Holmes to wake up."

"My poor Miss Mary," said Mrs. Poole, coming in again, this time with the tea tray. "I should send some sandwiches over there. Who knows what sort of food the Baker Street boys have."

"Speaking of which, I didn't get any lunch," said Diana. "How about some sandwiches for me? And jam pockets. I saw some in the kitchen."

"Patience, impossible child," said Mrs. Poole. "I'm bringing up a proper tea for Madam Ayesha. This is her last meal before she leaves for Budapest, and I want to make sure she sees the best of our English traditions."

"I'll help you bring it up," said Laura. "No, I insist, Mrs. Poole. You have too much to do already. Think of it as the Styrian way."

Lucinda watched these exchanges with amusement. They were all affectionate in tone, even when the words themselves were not. This was what families should be—their members might not always agree, but they always loved one another. Alas that her own family had not been like that! Throughout her childhood, her father had been a cold, repressive presence. She and her mother had both been frightened of him, and had found solace in each other's company. Her mother . . . she would remember the good days, when they were together, rather than the sight of her mother lying dead on the ground like Mrs. Raymond. She had not spoken to Alice about her mother's death. Perhaps she ought to?

The front doorbell rang.

"Who's going to get that?" asked Diana. But Catherine was still showing her book to Beatrice and paying no attention to such trivial matters as who was at the door.

"Would you like me to——" said Lucinda, half rising from the window seat.

"No, I'll go," said Diana, in a tone of disgust for a world in which she would need to answer the front door. "Do I have to do everything around here?"

But someone had preceded her, because a moment later, in came Alice, followed by Ayesha. "If you'll give me your coat, ma'am," said Alice. She was no longer the Alice who had fought Margaret

Trelawny or held her dying mother in her arms. She was once more the perfect maid.

Ayesha looked at her with surprise, then gave her the dramatic black coat she had been wearing. Today, the President of the Alchemical Society was attired in a dress the color of paprika, with black embroidery on the sleeves and hem. Her braids were twisted up into a high chignon.

"Hello, Beatrice," she said, "and greetings to the Athena Club. Where is your president? Is she not here with you?"

"She's still with Mr. Holmes," said Beatrice. "I don't think she is going to make our meeting."

"Well, then we shall have to carry on without her." Ayesha sat in one of the armchairs by the fireplace. As though in response to a command, the others also took their places—Catherine and Diana on the sofa, and Beatrice once more on the window seat next to Lucinda. Alice looked undecided, as though not sure whether to stay or go back to the kitchen, but just at that moment Mrs. Poole came in with a tray of sandwiches, followed by Laura and Archibald, also bearing trays.

"Madam Ayesha," said Mrs. Poole, "Would you care for refreshments? There are sandwiches, and Victoria sponge, and two kinds of tart, apple and lemon, and a German chocolate cake, or at least that's what it's called in Mrs. Beeton's book, for those who prefer something more continental. I've never baked such a cake before, so I hope it tastes all right!"

Finally, Bast herself came in like a black shadow. She rubbed against Ayesha's skirt until Madam President picked her up. Then, she curled into a circle on Ayesha's lap.

"If you will all sit," said Ayesha. "Yes, all of you, including you, Mrs. Poole. I know how necessary you are to the Athena Club, and have no intention of excluding you from these proceedings. And Archibald as well."

"And me?" came a voice from the doorway. It was Mary, bare-headed but still taking off her gloves. "I see you were about to start without me. No, that's perfectly all right—I know I'm late. I'm happy to tell you, though, that Mr. Holmes is awake. I sent Jimmy to tell Dr. Watson, who insisted on coming over in a cab even though Dr. Radko had told him to stay in bed and rest. So he's with Mr. Holmes now. I'll go back after our meeting. Don't mind me, I'm just going to get myself a cup of tea. I don't remember the last time I slept, not really. Madam President, if you would continue?" She pulled off her gloves, poured herself a cup of tea, and settled into the other armchair.

"Welcome to the meeting, Madam President," said Ayesha, smiling in a way that was no doubt meant to be welcoming but did not make her any less formidable. "Let us get directly to business. Yesterday, I visited the headquarters of the English branch of the Société des Alchimistes. That building has been put to inappropriate uses more than once—Seward used it for his meetings with Van Helsing, Moriarty used it for his Order of the Golden Dawn, and I imagine Tera would have made it her London headquarters. Walking through its empty rooms, I was faced with a decision. I could sell the building, in which case it would be put to other uses—or I could reopen the English branch."

"Reopen it!" said Mary, leaning forward. She seemed astonished. "That's a terrible idea, after all the trouble it's caused."

"You did not allow me to finish," said Ayesha mildly. "I could reopen the English branch, with Beatrice as chairwoman."

"Oh. Well, that's different." Mary leaned back. "If Beatrice were in charge—still, I don't know. Do we want alchemists in London?"

"There are already alchemists in London, or at least in England," said Beatrice. "This way we would know who they are. They could be monitored and regulated. I would make certain they adhered to ethical standards. But, Madam President, I wish you had discussed this matter with me beforehand." Her voice was calm, but Lucinda could tell that she was upset at not having been consulted.

Ayesha waved her hand, as though Beatrice's statement was of no concern. "You would have accepted the responsibility in any case. I did not have time to spare, and telling you together with your fellow members of the Athena Club is more efficient. This morning I made financial arrangements for Jenny Bucket to be treated at a sanatorium in Switzerland. Lady Crowe has helped her a great deal, but even I cannot cure tuberculosis. There she will receive the best treatment available. Then, I stopped in Scotland Yard to discuss the case of Margaret Trelawny with your friend Inspector Lestrade."

"He's not my friend," Diana muttered so quietly that only Lucinda could have heard it.

"She is still in prison in Penzance. Based on your testimony and the evidence of the pistol shot, she will be charged with the murder of Helen Raymond. Some of you will likely be called to testify in court. However, I do not know if she will be convicted— according to Lestrade, passersby saw a fog around the keep that morning, and she claims that she shot at a shadow in the fog, thinking it was an intruder and not her friend Helen. She is well known in those parts as a respectable woman, and the jury will likely be on her side. I do not think we have seen the last of her."

"And I don't think she's going to stop trying to conquer the world," said Mary. "From what I overheard while I was her prisoner, she struck me as a ruthless, ambitious woman."

"Those are not necessarily bad qualities," said Catherine.

Alice shook her head. "You didn't know her the way I did. She's a bad'un, as Mrs. Poole would say. I hope she's going to stay behind bars, even if she doesn't hang for my mother's murder."

"Lydia," continued Ayesha, "the gravestone I ordered for your mother's grave in the churchyard in Perranuthnoe should be arriving this week."

"Thank you, ma'am," said Alice.

"Our final order of business concerns Archibald." The Orangutan Man turned to look at Ayesha. "He cannot stay in London."

"But this is where he lives," said Catherine. "You can't just take him away from us."

"Nevertheless, he cannot stay—you know this to be true. You have already exposed him to Lestrade, who made some pointed remarks about the 'queer creature,' as he said, that you kept as a footman. If he should start questioning what Archibald is or where he comes from, it could expose the Société des Alchimistes once more."

"Is that your primary concern?" asked Beatrice. "The welfare of the Société des Alchimistes?"

"What about Archibald and what he wants?" asked Catherine heatedly. "He is not a beast anymore. He can't simply be sent away somewhere, or put back in a cage."

"Then we shall ask him," said Ayesha. "Archibald, would you like to come with me? I will take you back to Borneo, where I shall find a tribe that will accept you, perhaps not in the forest where you were captured, but close by. Or would you prefer to remain here?"

Archibald looked at her with large, dark eyes. "I want to go home," he said. Lucinda could hear the longing in his voice.

"Well then," said Ayesha. "I think the matter is settled. If someone could pack his bags?"

"I'll do it," said Alice. "He doesn't have much. I wish he were staying—but if he wants to go home, then he should. We'll miss you, Archibald." She stroked his hand for a moment before standing up.

"Thank you, Lydia. And do you feel that you will receive adequate training here in using your energic powers?"

"Yes, ma'am," said Alice. "Martin is teaching me. He's a very good teacher. And I don't want to throw lightning bolts or anything like that. I don't want to be like Queen Tera."

"Or like me?" said Ayesha, with another of her cold smiles. "You will quickly surpass any mere mesmerist. When you feel ready to learn more than he can teach—and you will, in time— come to me and I will undertake your education myself."

"Yes, ma'am," said Alice, in a voice that clearly conveyed *I never shall*. "May I go now?"

Just then, the doorbell rang. "That must be Mr. Vincey," said Mrs. Poole. "You mentioned that you were expecting him, ma'am. You go pack for Archibald, Alice dear. I'll get the door."

Ayesha rose, picking the black cat up in her arms. "As for Bast—"

"Oh no, you don't!" said Catherine. "You may take Archibald, since he wants to go, but you're not taking Bast away from us!"

Ayesha looked at the Puma Woman with amusement. "You wish to keep a two-thousand-year-old resurrected mummy cat here at the Athena Club?"

"She's a cat," said Diana. "Just like any other cat. She ate half a slice of ham that Catherine gave her this morning, and tried to steal Omega's ham too!"

"Ham!" said Mrs. Poole from the doorway. Behind her stood Leo Vincey, looking as handsome and discontented as ever. The scars that Lucinda had left on his cheek were almost completely gone. She still felt ashamed of herself for having inflicted them.

"When did those rascals get ham, and who gave it to them? No wonder they never eat the mice they catch, but leave them underfoot for me to step on!" She strode into the room as though to scold one of them—whichever one of them was responsible for such an outrage.

"Well, to be honest, most of us did," said Catherine. "It was at breakfast. I gave them a bit, and so did Diana, and even Justine—yes, you did, I saw you," she said, although Justine was shaking her head. "Lucinda and Beatrice just sat there quietly drinking their noxious liquids, but they certainly didn't stop us. Only Mary is completely absolved of responsibility."

"And I brought the ham," said Alice. "I mean, it was part of breakfast, but I did bring up a bit more than usual, knowing the cats might want some." She ducked out through the doorway, no doubt to pack the few possessions Archibald had acquired during his stay at the Athena Club.

Mrs. Poole shook her head. "You are all quite impossible."

"Are you ready, my love?" asked Leo, maneuvering his way around Mrs. Poole. "The train to Dover leaves in an hour."

Ayesha looked around at the assorted members of the Athena Club. "I am. Try, if you can, all of you, to stay out of mischief for a while. And if you need me—well, try not to. I do, after all, have a scientific society to run. The Société des Alchimistes does not manage itself, you know. Among other things, we have the next issue of the journal to get out!"

"We don't get into mischief," said Mary indignantly. "It sort of happens to us, or around us, or in our general vicinity."

Ayesha looked at her with an expression of amusement before turning and walking out the door. A moment later, she was standing in the hallway with Leo Vincey's arm around her waist, holding Archibald's hand and waiting for Alice to bring his possessions. Then they had climbed into a cab, and they were gone. Lucinda saw their cab driving away down Park Terrace toward Marylebone Road.

When Alice was once again seated on the carpet next to the fireplace, drinking a cup of tea, Mary said, "Well. It's always an adventure having her around, isn't it?"

No one had a response to that, although Catherine rolled her eyes.

"I have an order of business myself," said Mary. "Mrs. Poole, please sit. You can move Bast out of Ayesha's chair—I mean, it's not her chair, obviously. Unless you want to put Bast on your lap?"

"Not likely," said Mrs. Poole, brushing Bast off the chair and sitting where the President of the Alchemical Society had sat. Bast protested with a loud meow, then went over and jumped up on the sofa between Diana and Catherine.

"We all discussed it last night—I mean, the members of the Athena Club discussed it. Alice, we would like you to become a member."

Alice, who had just taken a sip of her tea, spit it up, mostly into her cup but partly on the carpet. "Oh no!" she cried, looking at the drops of tea soaking into the carpet in front of her. Frantically, she soaked them up with her napkin. "I'll get this clean, Mrs. Poole, I promise."

"Never mind that," said the housekeeper. "I'll do it later. Just answer Miss Mary's question. It would be a great honor for our Alice, miss," she said to Mary.

"I think Alice has to be the judge of that," said Justine. She had not spoken for so long—the Giantess was often quiet for long periods of time—that Lucinda was startled to hear her voice. "Alice may not consider it such an honor. After all, we are members of this club because we are, as Catherine calls us, monsters."

Alice stood up. "It's not that. It's just—I don't think I'm very good at adventures. Mary is so clever, and Catherine is so brave, and Justine is so strong. I don't feel as though I'm any of those things. I don't want to be kidnapped and put in dungeons again, or see my friends in danger. I was glad that I could help Miss Beatrice free Martin and the other mesmerists, but I just want to be a kitchen maid. At least for now."

"For now," said Mary. "So that means someday—"

"Don't be daft," said Diana. "You were as clever as any of us!

And you can break locks with a lightning bolt. I wish I could do that, although my way is quicker and more reliable."

"And as brave," said Catherine. "You stayed to help Holmes when you could have gotten away."

"And you *are* one of us," said Beatrice. "You may not have been experimented on directly, but your powers are the result of experiments in biological transmutation by Dr. Raymond, passed on to you from your grandmother, through your mother. You are as much a monster, if Catherine wishes to use that word, as any of us."

"Please excuse me," said Alice. Tears were welling up in her eyes. She put her tea-spattered napkin up to them and ran out of the room."

"Oh goodness," said Mary. "What did we say?"

Lucinda rose from the window seat. "You see, her mother died not a week ago. When my mother died——" She did not know how to explain it to the other members of the Athena Club. After all, none of the others had experienced what she and Alice had——their mothers dying in their arms. For a moment, a memory came back to her of her mother reaching up and touching her cheek one last time with love and tenderness before the light went out of her eyes. "I will go to Alice. I think eventually she will decide to join us, as I decided to join the Athena Club. But you must give her time."

She found Alice sitting at the kitchen table with her head in her hands, sobbing. She sat beside the kitchen maid and put one arm around her.

"It's just that I'm not ready," said Alice through her sobs, in a voice muffled by her hands. "I don't know if I'll ever be ready."

"You will," said Lucinda. "Transformation is difficult, is it not? It is the most difficult thing of all. You have been clever and brave and strong, but now you must rest for a while. It is out of adversity that one grows and becomes what one is meant to be——but there must be periods of peace and happiness as well. Plants must have sunshine as well as storms."

Alice leaned her head on Lucinda's shoulder. "Are all vampires so philosophical?"

Lucinda laughed. "Alice, I think you and I will become good friends. Come, dry your tears. I cannot eat cake, but you can, and I believe you need a slice of *gateau au chocolat*. Let us go upstairs and rejoin our friends, who are concerned for us. Friendship and chocolate cake—they do not heal all ills, but they certainly help."

MARY: Alice, I'm glad that you decided to join us after all.

ALICE: It just took me a little while, miss. I mean Mary. I needed time to realize that I wasn't just a kitchen maid any longer—that I had changed and grown.

JUSTINE: It is not so bad to have been a kitchen maid. I learned many valuable lessons working in the kitchen of the Frankenstein family as Justine Moritz.

ALICE: Oh, I'm grateful for all that, I assure you. If Nurse Adams, I mean Frau Gottleib, hadn't arranged for me to be sent here from the orphanage and Mrs. Poole hadn't decided to hire me, I don't know where I would be right now. Still in that orphanage, like as not. Or out on the streets, as Kate and Doris were.

MARY: Instead, you're where you belong—home.

# CHAPTER XVIII

# A Meeting of the Athena Club

T he Athena Club was meeting, with all members present. Mary was sitting in an armchair under the portrait of her mother. Ernestine Jekyll looked down with cornflower-blue eyes, which was appropriate, since it was spring. A warm spring at that! The roses were already starting to bloom in Regent's Park. Miraculously for London, it was not even raining.

Catherine was sitting on the sofa. Alice and Diana were sharing the sofa with her, both cross-legged, both with cats on their laps: Diana had Alpha while Alice had Omega. Bast was curled up next to Catherine, whom she had adopted as her particular human. She looked like a small puma next to the Puma Woman. Beatrice and Lucinda were perched next to each other on the window seat. Beatrice was drinking a cup of green goo. Lucinda was drinking a cup of something red. The rest of us were drinking tea, like ordinary women who are not monsters. And yet we were monstrous, each in our own way. Justine sat on the floor with her knees drawn up and her long, slender hand wrapped around a mug.

It had been six months since we had defeated Queen Tera, Margaret Trelawny, and Mrs. Raymond. Those six months had been relatively calm, all things considered. There had been the affair of Prince Rupert and the Oldenburg jewels, which had necessitated a short trip to Schleswig-Holstein; Countess

Olenska's haunted castle (not haunted at all, except by her drunken brother, who had escaped from an Australian penal colony); the naval treaty stolen from Colonel Protheroe's study, which we had intercepted before it could be sold to the Russian Ambassador; and Miss Lettie Pruitt's missing King Charles Spaniel, Ivanhoe, who had been found in one of the lowest dens in Bethnal Green, with a bitch of the most disreputable sort. But life at 11 Park Terrace had been quiet, which was a relief to most of us and agony to Diana, who complained of being *so bored*.

However, such adventures did not pay the bills, particularly when certain princes paid in diamonds that turned out to be paste.

"Weekly accounts," said Mary. "Five pounds from my work with Mr. Holmes now that I'm a partner of sorts, plus a one-pound bonus for solving 'The Case of the Pentonville Vampire,' who of course was nothing of the sort. Dr. Watson says he's going to include me in that one, when he writes it up for *The Strand*."

"Nothing," said Diana. "Why won't you let me go up for the part of Hebe, cupbearer to the gods? It's a respectable play—based on Greek mythology and all that."

"Because I've seen the costume and she's barely dressed. Be grateful that I'm letting you work in the theater at all!" said Mary in an *end of conversation* tone.

"One pound even from the show I helped Marvelous Martin put on," said Alice. "He has a new show at the Tivoli, and he wants to make me his regular assistant!"

"Nothing this week," said Justine. "But *Sunset over the Matterhorn* and *A Field of Swiss Wildflowers* are both hanging in the Grosvenor, and I hope one of them will find a buyer. Mr. Gray has been very helpful in introducing me to art patrons from the continent."

"Eight pounds, ten shillings," said Beatrice. "St. Bartholomew's has become one of my regular customers, but I've decided to give charity hospitals a discount on my medicines. That is the correct word, is it not—discount?"

"One pound two shillings from my first week of piano lessons," said Lucinda. "And I wish to thank all of you for purchasing the piano," which now stood against the far wall of the parlor. "I know it was a significant expense."

Catherine just looked smug.

"Well?" said Mary. "Out with it. I know you want to tell us."

"Sixty pounds!" she said, as though she could not believe it herself. "For *three* more books. I'm going to call them *Rick Chambers and Astarte*, *Something Something on Venus* (I'm not sure about that one yet), and *Invasion of the Cat Women*. Also, Longman, Green, and Co. says the first two novels have sold well enough that there will be authorized American editions, although they pirate books terribly there."

"Sixty pounds!" said Mary. "Well, I think this calls for a celebration."

"It's too early in the day for spirits," said Mrs. Poole from the doorway. She had a tray in her hand. "How about treacle tart? Catherine told me the good news earlier this afternoon. Alice, Diana, if you could put those dratted cats down and move the table . . ." The tray contained the aforementioned tart, as well as an assortment of small plates and dessert forks.

"And you sit too, Mrs. Poole," said Mary. "Let's all celebrate together."

Just then, we heard what none of us had expected on a quiet Saturday afternoon: the doorbell.

"Perhaps it's Mr. Holmes and Dr. Watson coming to join us," said Justine.

"More likely the rag-and-bones man," said Mrs. Poole. "I'll go send him packing."

After she had gone to answer the bell, Beatrice said, "Mary, there's a carriage out in the street, with a coachman, two footmen, and four horses. Who would drive such an elaborate equipage in this part of London?"

"Maybe some sort of dowager Duchess coming to hire us, to find her long-lost heir or Pekingese," said Catherine. "Does the carriage have a device on it?"

Beatrice looked out the window again. "No, it's—well, it's just black."

"Mary," said Mrs. Poole from the doorway. "Girls. Please stand up."

Her voice was so sharp and commanding that we all immediately stood up, as though at school.

Mrs. Poole stepped into the room and moved to one side. "We have a distinguished visitor, who wishes to remain incognito."

The woman who walked into the room after her was small, plump, and altogether ordinary looking. She was dressed in black crepe, with a black bonnet on her head. Her black veil was folded back over it. She could have been any widow driving around London, perhaps to stop for some shopping on Tottenham Court Road or a walk in Hyde Park, except that in profile, she resembled the image on a gold sovereign.

"Holy—" said Diana, but luckily did not finish the exclamation.

Mary immediately curtseyed, and saw to her relief that the other members of the Athena Club were following her example.

"Miss Mary Jekyll," said the woman. Even after all these years, she still had a slight German accent. "It has come to our attention that you and your fellow members of a certain club were instrumental in warning us of danger this past autumn. If we had been apprised of this sooner, we would have come to visit you at an earlier date. However, we would like to thank you now, in person, for services to ourselves as well as to our Commonwealth. To that end, we would like to present you with these—Rochester?"

A dour-looking woman in an afternoon dress of brown and

green tartan stepped into the room—a lady-in-waiting of some sort? She was carrying a large wooden box. She opened it and tilted the box so they could all see what lay inside on the black velvet: seven gold medals on seven crimson ribbons.

"The Order of St. Hilda is given for personal and confidential service to the monarch. Come forward, each of you."

Of course, Diana was first in line. One by one, we each came forward, while the woman in black presented each of us with one of the medals from the box. Mary was last.

"Thank you, ma'am," she said, curtseying again.

"We are grateful for your brave and loyal service," said the woman. "Now, Mrs. Poole, I see a treacle tart. Could you cut us a slice, and one for Rochester as well? We have developed a sweet tooth in old age."

After they heard the front door shut again, the "Gee-up!" of the coachman, and the rumble of carriage wheels driving away along Park Terrace, Mary said, "Well. That was—" But she did not finish her sentence.

"Does anyone else want the last slice of treacle tart?" asked Diana. "Because I do."

"Diana just asked if anyone else wants the last slice before taking it," said Catherine. "This is a day of miracles indeed."

There was a moment of silence, and then Justine burst out laughing. We were all startled—Justine so seldom laughed! Then Mary started laughing, and the rest of us joined in, until Mrs. Poole, who had just come in with another pot of tea, said, "What in the world has gotten into you girls?" Which prompted a fresh round of laughter.

*Nothing,* thought Mary, looking around the room. *Nothing in particular has gotten into us. This is just another ordinary evening with monsters.*

Nowadays, if you came to 11 Park Terrace from wherever

you are, whether Bethnal Green or Brazil or Abyssinia, and rang the bell below a brass plaque on which is engraved THE ATHENA CLUB, you could ask to see the leather-bound record book of the club, which is kept in what was once Dr. Jekyll's office and is now the library as well as Catherine's writing room. If Mrs. Poole invited you in and showed you the first page, you would see the following signatures in varying states of legibility, with ink spatters beside Diana's:

MEMBERS:
Miss Mary Jekyll
Miss Diana Hyde
Miss Beatrice Rappaccini
Miss Catherine Moreau
Miss Justine Frankenstein
Miss Lucinda Van Helsing
Miss Lydia Raymond

SUPPORTERS:
Mrs. Irene Norton
Miss Laura Jennings
Carmilla, Countess Karnstein
Wilhelmina, Countess Dracula
Victoria Regina

Dear Reader:

I hope you have enjoyed this history of how we came together, we monsters. If you have begun with this book, I advise you to purchase volumes I and II of the Extraordinary Adventures of the Athena Club—only thus can you learn how Mary, Diana, Beatrice, Catherine, Justine, Lucinda, and Alice came to live together as a family of sorts. And if you have read all these volumes, you may also wish to purchase one of my other books published by Longmans, Green, and Co., only two shillings each, available at all reputable booksellers and also in train stations throughout England:

*The Mysteries of Astarte*
*The Adventures of Rick Chambers*
*Rick Chambers and Astarte*
*Rick Chambers on Venus*
*Invasion of the Cat Women*
*The Death of Astarte*
*The Resurrection of Astarte*
*Rick Chambers, Jr. in the Caverns of Doom*

My latest novel, *Astarte and the Idol of Gold*, will be available this spring for the same very reasonable price. American readers are urged to purchase authorized copies from Scribner's Sons.

Respectfully,
Catherine Moreau

# ACKNOWLEDGMENTS

One of the great pleasures of following the members of the Athena Club on their adventures has been visiting all sorts of magical places, such as St. Michael's Mount off the coast of Cornwall. I would like to thank all the guides who work on the island and in the castle for so patiently answering my questions when I went on the tour three times in a row and wandered around plotting fight scenes in those elegant rooms. A general thanks to everyone who helped me in London, Cornwall, and Budapest, whether they knew they were helping or not, and a special thanks to Bernhard Stäber and Aleksandra Kasztalska for helping with German and Polish translations, respectively. Any mistakes in translations or historical details are of course my own. Thank you once again to everyone at Barry Goldblatt Literary, especially my agent Barry Goldblatt, who encouraged me to write this series in the first place, and Patricia Ready, who always answers my panicked questions with humor and patience. An enormous thanks goes to my editor, Navah Wolfe, who believed in this group of unusual young women and guided me with endless patience and insight as I tried to write their stories to the best of my ability. Thanks also to the whole crew at Saga Press, including Bridget Madsen, Krista Vossen, Elizabeth Blake-Linn, Alysha Bullock, Caroline Pallotta, Mike Kwan, and Madison Penico without whom this book would not be one, and LJ Jackson, who coordinated publicity, bringing it to the attention of readers like you. Artist Lisa Perrin captured the spirit of the Athena Club so perfectly on its cover, and I'm most grateful. My biggest thanks goes, as always, to my daughter, Ophelia, who read the books first. Her laughter and attention were the best compliment I could receive. And finally, thank you, yes *you*, who have made it this far. I hope you enjoyed spending time with Mary, Diana, Beatrice, Catherine, Justine, Lucinda, and little Alice—who learned, in the end, that even a kitchen maid can be a heroine. I know they all enjoyed spending time with you and would love to have you over for tea at 11 Park Terrace the next time you're in the vicinity. Mrs. Poole is already baking a treacle tart . . .

# THE SINISTER MYSTERY

## —— *of the* ——

# MESMERIZING

# GIRL

## *Theodora Goss*

*This reading group guide for* The Sinister Mystery of the Mesmerizing
Girl *includes an introduction, discussion questions, and ideas for enhancing
your book club. The suggested questions are intended to help your reading group
find new and interesting angles and topics for your discussion. We hope that
these ideas will enrich your conversation and increase your enjoyment of
the book.*

# INTRODUCTION

The members of the Athena Club are familiar with Ayesha and know the story of how she gained her awesome powers as a young woman in ancient Egypt. But as Mary, Justine, and Diana rush home to England to rescue Alice, who has disappeared from 11 Park Terrace, they have no idea that their foe is inextricably linked to Ayesha and her past. For, unbeknownst to Mary and the others, Alice has been taken by her mother, Helen Raymond, as part of a dastardly plot to raise Ayesha's former high priestess from the dead. And that's only the first step of the plan, as a mysterious group of villains calling themselves the Order of the Golden Dawn intends to take over Great Britain with the help of mesmeric powers, a kidnapped queen, and the unbelievable powers of the revived high priestess, Queen Tera.

To complicate matters further, Sherlock Holmes is missing, having fallen prey to his archnemesis, Moriarty. So as Mary attempts to find both Alice and Holmes, she must do so without the assistance of the one man who could be most useful. As the entire Athena Club—including Lucinda—converge on London, it becomes obvious that they must travel to the shore and risk their lives to save their friends, the Queen of England, and their very country. But are their combined powers enough to defeat the might of Queen Tera? And will they be forced to sacrifice something they love in order to save the world from an awful fate?

1.  Why do you think the book is dedicated to Mary Shelley? Were mothers important to the members of the Athena Club? What did their mothers have to do with their monstrosity?

2.  As Justine returns to London, she contemplates Adam's death and her life with the Athena Club with a sense of peace and a seeming air of contentment. Is it wrong of her to feel this release at Adam's death? Could she have found the same feeling if he were still alive? Do all the other members of the Athena Club feel this same contentment? If not, what prevents them from feeling it?

3.  Beatrice feels that "it would be good for Clarence to fall in love with someone else . . . only not Ayesha. One could not compete with someone like Ayesha." [p.21] What does she mean by this statement? Why would she be in competition with any other woman that Clarence loved? Why does she feel that she needs to push Clarence away? Is she committed to doing this?

4.  Why must Lucinda learn to hunt, instead of just having blood brought to her? Does the understanding that she must kill to survive help her during the course of the story? Does her vampirism make her more monstrous than the other members of the Athena Club?

5.  Upon returning to London, Mary muses that she "had come home, but she was not the same Mary who had left—not

quite." [p. 31] Is it simply the act of traveling that has changed Mary, or are there other influences that contributed to this change? Is this the only change that Mary—or any of her friends—have gone through in the course of this trilogy?

6. According to Diana, what makes a person dull? Does Mary fall into this category? Why is Diana so hard on the other members of the Athena Club? Do their responses represent their true feelings toward her?

7. When Alice meets Dr. Seward for the first time, she thinks "Strange, that evil should look so bland." [p.87] Is this true of all the evil people that they encounter? How does this blandness help evil men accomplish their dastardly deeds? Do our heroines look bland? Knowing the morals of each group, which one would you expect to look more distinctive?

8. What is the ultimate goal of the Order of the Golden Dawn? Why do they feel so strongly that they are right in pursuing this goal? Do Miss Trelawny, Mrs. Raymond, and Queen Tera have a different purpose in attempting to take over the government?

9. Why does Miss Trelawny warn the Order about risking their lives for the "power and wisdom of ancient Egypt?" [p. 115] Is she truly concerned about their safety? Does her warning in any way release her from responsibility for what happens during the ritual?

10. Mary has found that all the prostitutes she has met are "simply ordinary women trying to get by without family to support them, or friends to offer them help, or the training required for more respectable employment." [p.123] Was Mary, or

any of the members of the Athena Club, ever in danger of having to become a prostitute? What other opportunities were available to women at the time? Has that changed in our day and age?

11. Moriarty reminds Alice of a preacher who had visited the orphanage while she was there. In what ways is this an apt comparison? Is there anyone else in the story for whom this comparison is apt?

12. What aspects of Ayesha's experience make her stand in opposition to Queen Tera? Would a younger Ayesha have made this same decision? Does her experience make her a good leader, or does it, as Beatrice says, make her so she "no longer understands human morality" and needs to be reminded of "the need for empathy and compassion?" [p.163]

13. After hearing Ayesha's story, Catherine thinks that it must be terrible to never grow old or die. Why does Catherine think this? Would Ayesha agree with her? There are other immortal characters in the book, or at least characters who will live far longer than normal humans . . . would they agree with Catherine?

14. As she tries to get into the Diogenes Club, Mary thinks that "she wanted to be just a little more like Irene—smarter, bolder, more courageous." [p.187] She is not the only character who tries to emulate another—Alice tries to act more like Mary, and Laura travels across Europe in a motorcar in an attempt to be more like Carmilla. Why do each of these characters want to take on the traits of others? Do they already exhibit any of the characteristics they seek to emulate? How do you think Irene, Mary, and Carmilla would

feel to know that the others were trying to be more like them?

15. Why does Mary hesitate to hold Beatrice's hand while they walk along the causeway? Where does Beatrice think the hesitation comes from? What does it mean to Beatrice when Mary takes her hand without hesitation? Does the friendship of the Athena Club mean different things to the different members?

16. What is Alice's relationship to her mother? In what ways is it similar to, and in what ways is it different from Helen's relationship to her father? How did Helen's death change Alice's feelings toward her? Can Justine and Lucinda truly understand Alice's feelings about losing her mother?

17. What is Sherlock Holmes' role in this story? How does it differ from the part he usually plays, either in this trilogy, or in other stories about him? What does his change in agency mean for the other characters?

# ENHANCE YOUR
# BOOK CLUB

1. Egyptology and the archeological fever of the period play an important role in the story. Research one aspect of these subjects that interests you, and report your findings back to the group. Mummification, important archeological finds, the history of women in archeology, Egyptian burial rituals, or legendary curses are just some of the topics you could choose.

2. Beatrice finds it difficult to believe how little the general public knows about the plants that surround them, particularly when it comes to medicinal and poisonous plants. Take a walk through a local park or wooded area, foraging for edible or medicinal plants that you can use in your everyday life. Be sure to consult a detailed botany book or a local expert to ensure that you don't confuse an edible plant with a poisonous one! Alternatively, you could plant some useful, medicinal plants in your yard or garden and begin using them in a purposeful way.

3. The Order of the Golden Dawn takes a very strong anti-immigration stance, even going so far as to champion eugenics. We are currently facing a very strong anti-immigration sentiment, not just in the United States, but in many other countries as well. Divide into two groups and stage a debate between pro- and anti-immigration factions. It could be interesting to join the side that does not share your beliefs, and see if you can reach a better understanding of their position.

4. Alice sometimes has trouble viewing the other members of the Athena Club as her peers, since she was (well) trained by Mrs. Poole to be a servant in Mary's household. Find one of the many books, movies, or television shows that deal with the division between the upper class and their servants (*Downton Abbey; The Remains of the Day; Upstairs, Downstairs;* etc.), and compare the attitudes you find there to the situation at 11 Park Terrace.

# ABOUT THE AUTHOR

Theodora Goss is the World Fantasy and Locus Award—winning author of the short story and poetry collections *In the Forest of Forgetting, Songs for Ophelia,* and *Snow White Learns Witchcraft,* as well as the novella *The Thorn and the Blossom* and the novels *The Strange Case of the Alchemist's Daughter* and *European Travel for the Monstrous Gentlewoman.* She has been a finalist for the Nebula, Crawford, Seiun, and Mythopoeic Awards, as well as on the Tiptree Award Honor List. Her work has been translated into twelve languages. She teaches literature and writing at Boston University and in the Stonecraft MFA Program. Visit her at TheodoraGoss.com